About the auth

Strap yourselves in.

C.M.Vassie's acclaimed earlier work *Scravir - While Whitby Sleeps* was either total fiction or a dry but well-researched account of how it was that a group of skeletally-thin cadavers appeared in the town during Whitby Goth Weekend in the autumn of 2016. Take your pick.

This book is a continuation of that grim episode. An attention-seeking *what happened next,* as it were, running from place to place before perhaps settling back in Whitby's old town where it all started. Or did not start.

The bodies continue to pile up, as bodies do in these grim tales. Have our heroes learned anything? Can you keep a bad man down? What is a bad man? Will the author answer these questions or continue toying with us?

Of the author, we know fractionally more than previously. They hang around in Whitby from time to time and, since Scravir was first published in 2021, they have produced another novel *The Whitby Trap,* and *The Whale Bone Archers,* a collection of frankly improbable short stories, also set in Whitby.

Not much to go on but it is a start. Of sorts.

Finally, if you are in Whitby and, having read this book, foolishly decide to undertake a midnight walk in the old town's lacklit streets and yards, don't - just don't - pretend you weren't warned.

Readers' reviews of SCRAVIR - While Whitby Sleeps

"A terrific and thought-provking read"
P Ralph

*"Fascinating to see events unfolding in some familiar places.
The characters were well described and the story was told from
different perspectives, which I liked. Gripping from beginning to
end."*
J Tranmer

"I loved reading Scravir. Well done C M Vassie, more please!"
C Mcnamara

"Exciting and intelligent dark blend of gothic and contemporary"
M Kendall

*"Just finished reading this and thought it was absolutely brilliant.
Can't wait for the sequel ☺ "*
R Carroll

*"A fast-paced modern gothic thriller. When you start this novel
you are immediately transported to Whitby, you can almost smell
the fish and chips. Its exciting twists and turns will have you totally
hooked."*
T Paylor

*"Difficult to put down. It's an unusual storyline with more than one
thing going on. Set in my home town I can relate to all the places
mentioned in this book, it's written to make you feel like you are
actually there when all the events take place making it scarier.
Looking forward to the next book."*
M Czapla

*"Just as gripping as advertised and really well written. From the
perfect descriptions of the town to the complex characters it's a
book I was hooked on from start to finish and then found myself
panting for a sequel to continue the story."*
J Dunning

C.M. VASSIE

SCRAVIR II
Lacklight

injini press

First published in Great Britain in 2023 by injini press

C.M.Vassie has asserted the right to be identified as the author of this work in accordance with the Copyright, Design and Patents Act 1988

Cover illustration: D.K.Vassie
Map of Whitby: C.M.Vassie

A catalogue record for this book is available from the British Library

ISBN: 978-1-7391132-2-3

10 9 8 7 6 5 4 3 2 1

www.injinipress.co.uk

Beware the lacklit yards in old Whitby...

C. M. Vassie

WHITBY

Lighthouse

West Pier

East Pier

Whitby Pavilion

Whalebone Arch
X

Royal Crescent

Khyber Pass

Pier Road

Henrietta Street

Church of St Mary

199 Steps

Clif Street

X Dracula Experience

The Yards

Sandgate

Church Street

Swing Bridge

Endeavor Wharf

Church Street

The Ropery

Railway Station

North Sea

X Daniel's tent

Campsite Field

The Yard

The Barn

Farview Farm

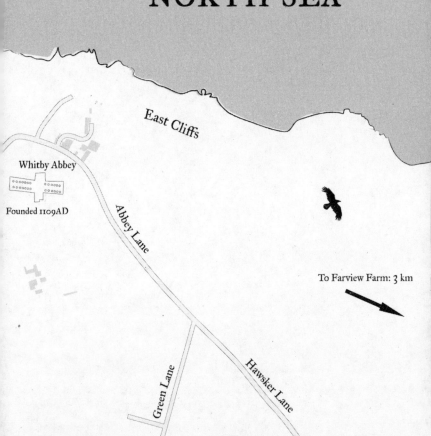

NORTH SEA

East Cliffs

Whitby Abbey

Founded 1109AD

Abbey Lane

To Farview Farm: 3 km

Green Lane

Hawsker Lane

We're all just one dodgy bungee jump from eternity

CHAPTER 1

Europol, Rotterdam

9th January 2017

Gert is wearing a visitor's pass.

A year ago he didn't need one.

'Have you been scuba diving recently, Gert?' Antoine asks. 'God knows you've earned it. I know a great spot in …'

'It's not over.'

'It is over!' Antoine insists.

It is late evening. Across the open-plan empty office on the third floor, sixty-three sleeping computer screens stare blindly at nothing. Gert is pacing up and down in the kitchen area.

'Can we sit down?' Antoine adopts a calmer tone. 'You're making me feel dizzy. I am only saying it's time to move on. You did good. You saved lives and helped bring matters to a close. You're a hero. You're limping by the way, are you receiving physio?'

'Has anyone checked the castle in Romania?'

'I've told you. Local police are satisfied that ...'

'So the answer is no. You don't get it. Thor Lupei survives by corrupting people. He buys silence. Doesn't it strike you as odd that …'

'STOP!' Antoine smashes his fist on the work surface in frustration. 'Daniel Murray told police that he saw Lupei's body burning in the caves beneath the castle, and Romanian police corroborated that a month ago.'

'And what about the scravir?'

'You saw the fire on the farm in Whitby, and the burned-out

bus. The scravir, whatever they were, are all dead. The British police have confirmed that. Trust me.'

'And you say *I* lack objectivity. This isn't like popping a zit, Antoine. It runs deep, goes back centuries, and people have always looked the other way or blamed the victims. Like they always do. Like when my brother was killed years ago. How do you know that Lupei isn't controlling what goes on here in Rotterdam? In this building? Right now?'

'HE'S DEAD!' For a second it looks like Antoine is about to punch Gert. Instead, he takes a deep breath. 'Lupei was a human being who did some bad shit and now he's dead. Listen to me, Gert, if you carry on down this path you'll end up on the streets, hungry and alone. You've already lost your job. Twice. Your paranoia is …'

'OK, heard the podcast, bought the t-shirt,' Gert shouts back. 'Maverick cop goes apeshit, ends up in asylum. Always kept himself to himself, said a colleague. Sad obsessive blah blah.'

'What do you think of the coffee?' Antoine offers a top-up.

'Classic distraction. Very good. Almost worked. So what else did the interviews with Daniel Murray reveal? Local police said he was implicated in a murder in a lay-by on the road down from the castle.'

'That was a mistake. The mobile phone was incorrectly logged as being at the crime scene when in fact it was …'

'Hello! Does that sound like crap to you? And can we agree that theft of human organs is not just bad shit?'

Behind Gert, a cleaner steps out of the lift pushing his trolley.

'Alleged theft. And are you claiming that mistakes never happen and demanding that police are banned from ever correcting the record?'

'WAKE UP, ANTOINE!' Gert shouts, his hands cupped around his mouth to make a megaphone.

The cleaner retreats into the lift.

Antoine walks away between the empty workstations then turns, arms outstretched. 'Three-quarters of this entire floor is busy with cybercrime and terrorism. There's limited time available for monsters and vampires so ... sorry but ...' Antoine searches for the right words. 'Look, Hervé will sack me as easily as he sacked you if I don't ...'

'Hervé is fixated on promotion to a cushy job in the justice department in Brussels; I get it. But what if it's *not* over? How many more deaths? Give me the resources and I'll prove that Lupei is alive.'

'Give you resources? You don't even work here anymore.' Antoine throws up his hands in defeat. 'OK. In the morning I'll ask Romanian police to send photos of the body of Thor Lupei and of the damage in the castle. But for now please take a sodding break and stay away; I take enough shit on your behalf as it is.'

'Yeah, I know,' Gert says in a softer tone. 'You're a good mate. You will tell me if anything new comes up?'

'I won't have to, because nothing new will come up. In the meantime promise me that you will drop this monster vampire conspiracy theory and get a life. Find a new hobby, have wild sex in a yurt, go bungee jumping, take up knitting, whatever, I don't care. I just don't want to read your name on the cover of an autopsy report. OK?'

CHAPTER 2

Mikăbrukóczi Castle, Romania

5th December 2016

The fresh fir fragrance of conifer resin comforts and envelops Maria as she crouches in her father's old overcoat on a mountain that, not long after midday, is already deep in shadow. The temperature is falling. In a few weeks masked carollers will climb the steep road from the village in multi-coloured animal costumes, singing and laughing and rattling their bells, and Christmas will have arrived.

For now the road carries only a large black Mercedes. From her vantage point up on the hill, hidden behind a thicket of dead brambles and snow, Maria watches the car turn into the yard and pull up in front of her family's farm.

Already at the front door, her mother stands arms akimbo, grey hair tucked under her red headscarf. The driver climbs out, opens the rear door and the familiar bloated figure of the town's mayor steps out into the cold air of the farmyard, his jowled face smeared in weak winter sun.

Maria is too far away to make out what they are saying. The mayor stabs his finger angrily in her mother's direction. The driver lights a cigarette and turns away to stare at crows fighting on the barn roof. Her mother throws up her hands in exasperation. The mayor follows her into the house.

With her brother and father down in the village there is no one else at the farm. Maria chooses the path that keeps her hidden from view. Snow squeaks under boot. Emerging by the road behind the hedge, she crosses briskly to the back of the house, praying the shutters are closed and that she won't be seen. She grips the door handle with one hand and turns with the other to stop the spring from squealing, as she did during the long honeysuckle evenings last summer when escaping to spend time at the river with Dumitru, the first boy she has ever loved.

Raised voices from the kitchen. On tiptoes she grabs a poker from the fireplace in the backroom.

'They say there was a fire beneath the castle. Did your good-for-nothing daughter see anything?' The mayor's voice.

'Thank you so much for worrying about her.' Her mother's tone is scrupulously polite, but Maria recognises the familiar lace of sarcasm. 'I will pass on your best wishes.'

'If Lupei is dead I need the proof. It is more than two weeks since …'

'Yes, yes, you explained.'

'I can have you arrested.'

'Why are you afraid? Is there no one in the town hall with the balls to cross the castle threshold?'

'You are in league with him!' the mayor shouts. 'Bringing death to the region. Destroying our culture. Do as I ask, or I will …'

'You will what?' her mother speaks softly. 'If we are in league with Lupei, how will you attack us and hope to get away with it?'

'Bitch. Rot in hell. All of you.'

The front door slams. Seconds later the Mercedes starts up and drives away.

'How long have you been standing there?' her mother asks as Maria opens the kitchen door.

Maria says nothing but understands that she must return to the castle.

It is a thirty-minute walk along the steep narrow path beneath the trees up the mountain.

For nearly a month Maria has done as she has been told. After all, she is not yet seventeen and has only worked at the castle since the summer; the other staff members are three times her age. The day after Maria bumped into that foreign boy, Daniel, at midnight in the Great Hall, Soreana, a sour-faced old pumpkin who scrubs floors and polishes door handles until she sees her wizened face staring back, came to the farm and told Maria to stay away until she hears differently.

It isn't the money, she is still being paid; it's about what happened that last night at the castle. The Maestru, Thor Lupei, requested a feast for two. He was so happy, showing off, showering Daniel with the best food and fine wines, playing that blues music he loves, and showering Maria and the other servants with compliments. Then, the following morning, she arrived for work only to be turned away at the gate by Radu Felini. Since then only rumours and now the mayor saying if Lupei is dead …

On the path ahead a red squirrel pauses in a shard of sunlight, then vanishes behind a tree. Maria carries on up the path.

Someone told her Lupei fixes people; that he is a healer as well as a music star. Is that why Daniel was there? When she first saw him, Daniel was in a wheelchair then, later that night in the Great Hall he was walking, if a little unsteadily, and asking directions to Lupei's office.

Had Lupei fixed him?

Others say that Lupei destroys people. A murderer, sorcerer, thief. Those who fear Lupei avoid paths like the one she is climbing, claiming that an army of monsters prowl the lacklight beneath the trees, killing villagers who travel alone. They call these monsters scravir and blame every misfortune in the region upon the scravir and Thor Lupei.

Maria crosses a small glade where the snow reaches her knees. Tiny mounds of snow perch like hats on the top of the fence posts. Overhead a brief splash of blue, pale as mallard eggs, is swept away by the low clouds sweeping the treetops.

A ping on her phone reminds her she is meeting Dumitru by the stream later.

Back beneath the conifers, where the snow has not reached, the path climbs steeply. She is only minutes from the castle. Maria fears neither the path nor the scravir. Not because she thinks they are folklore fantasy, she knows they are real. She has seen them, but she knows they are not like the wolves that venture down from the high mountains on the harshest days of winter. The scravir are slaves; they obey their master, Thor Lupei. That is why, instead of hiding away at home, exchanging silly stories about a catastrophe, Ovidiu, Soreana and the other older servants should be at the castle checking that all is well and offering help if help is needed.

The master has always been fair to her and the other villagers he employs. He sees through the corruption and the self-interest of those families who have run the town and the valley for generations, he has talent and receives important visitors; that is why the mayor and all the others are jealous of him.

Maria emerges from the forest and joins the single-track road for the last fifty metres to Mikăbrukóczi castle. Hidden from view, a crow sounds the alarm. The snow is thicker here than down the mountain, soft muffling every hard surface. There are no tyre tracks or footprints.

Set into the ramparts is a gatehouse. Beside the massive wooden gate hangs an iron chain that she pulls, feeling the cold on her fingers. Bells rattle on the other side of a wall over a metre thick. Her breath blooms and feathers as she stamps her boots. Here above the clouds the air is clear and she can see across the valley to her uncle's barn tucked in below the huge rock they call Old Man's Nose.

Bolts are drawn back and the small door set within the gate

opens to reveal a familiar face.

He isn't pretty with his patchy thinning hair and his missing nostril. The staff call him Pepene, Romanian for watermelon, because of a gaping grin that reveals too many teeth and too much gum.

Pepene is scravir. The most powerful in the castle.

He stoops to look out, his huge emaciated frame towering above her, his grey pockmarked skin stretched tightly over his skull. Rough brown peasant clothes. Like all scravir, he is mute. When she first set eyes on him, Maria found him frightening; the numbtrance eyes, feral mouth, hands clenched as if on the cusp of a violent act. But he is a slave, instincts dulled and under the control of his master.

'I have come to see Maestru,' Maria announces.

Pepene steps back and ushers her across the threshold with a deferential sweep of his hand.

They cross the ground that in summer is a broad green of grass and alpine flowers but now, in December, is featureless snow broken only by the single huge tree, its leaves long since flown, its branches an empty cage in which sits an owl. A shriek echoes as the bird takes flight and disappears over the castle walls on silent wings.

It is a bad omen to see an owl in daylight and Maria mutters *Doamne Fereste* three times under her breath to cancel the bad luck before it festers. *God forbid, God forbid, God forbid.* She strides towards the main building, overtaking the scravir.

The dark oak door is unlocked. As always. She pushes it open, steps inside and stamps the snow from her boots, with Pepene in her wake. Everything looks in order. Flanking the walls of the entrance hall are the three suits of armour, gleaming brightly beneath the recessed spotlights, each holding a different weapon: a long sword, a metal-headed mace, and a battle axe. Hanging on the walls are animal heads: two wolves, a stag and a chamois. Beyond them, in the stairwell, faded tapestries are interspersed with a dozen vintage electric guitars. She recalls Lupei's amused expression as she open-jawed while he was listing the famous musicians who had previously owned them.

Maria enters the Great Hall and immediately feels uncomfortable standing in that glorious space with her auburn hair hanging loose instead of tucked inside her maid's cap. Logs crackle and hiss aromatically in the fireplace. Cherry and oak, Thor Lupei is very particular about the wood.

There is another odour. Whispering. Masked by the smell of the fire. Maria wrinkles her nose.

'Where is Maestru?' she asks the scravir.

Pepene heads out into the entrance hall. She follows him round one corner and then another and stops. Where previously she has only ever seen dark oak panelled walls she is face to face with the open doors of a lift. The scravir steps in and waits for her to join him.

She hesitates.

One of the old servants, Ovidiu, told her of this lift but she did not believe him. Why would you take seriously the words of a man who has reached sixty years of age without doing anything more challenging than chopping wood, clearing snow and peeling vegetables? A fool who claims that wolves lay eggs and all Italians are afraid of pine cones.

And yet here it is.

A lift.

She studies Pepene's face but cannot read it. What is he thinking? Is he thinking? Down in the town you would not find a single soul who would put him- or herself alone in a lift with a scravir, though it is also true that none of them has ever met one.

Maria knows that some parts of the castle are out of bounds but she cannot shake off a growing fear that something is not right, that something has happened to Thor Lupei. As the lift doors start to close, she steps forward and sticks a foot in the way. The doors spring back to the open position.

The others are all fools and cowards: Marius, the chef; Ovidiu and Paul, the two half-wits employed to cut vegetables, chop wood, and clear snow; Soreana and Cecilia, the two bossy old women from the village who scrub floors and polish door handles; and Radu Felini the manager. She is not being nosy. If the Maestru is unwell who will call the doctor and prepare his food and medicines? And if Lupei has gone away on a foreign trip then he will never know that she went looking for him. After all Pepene won't say anything; he is mute.

Satisfied with her reasoning, Maria steps into the lift. The doors close and she feels herself descending, which is strange, she isn't aware of there being a *beneath* to the castle.

The lift doors open onto a corridor whose walls are lined with photos showing Thor Lupei standing tall, his long white hair flowing over his shoulders, beside strangers she has never seen at the castle, couples, individuals, groups. Different places: cities, beside rivers and seas, in town squares, in front of fireplaces and in gardens. Almost everyone in the photos is smiling. They must be fans of his music. She knows he has a band though she has never seen them play live. Dumitru had shown her a shaky video of a concert he found online: Thor Lupei and the Hounds of Hellbane. There are no official videos. Maria asked Lupei why not and he replied that mystery is more alluring than self-promotion.

Half a dozen photos appear to have been snatched from the wall, their broken frames scattered across the floor. Shards of glass crunch underfoot. The unexpected mess upsets Maria; who is responsible and why hasn't the mess been tidied up?

At the end of the corridor is a second lift. She enters and Pepene presses a button. When the doors reopen they step out into a bright modern space with Scandi-minimalist furniture in pastel shades and potted plants. Who cleans this part of the castle? Surely not the two old women; their tongues wag up and down like leaves in the breeze, the whole village would have heard by now.

Behind her, the lift doors hiss and click shut.

As interesting as is the area she stands in, it is nothing compared to the area beyond the vast floor-to-ceiling window that divides the large space in two. Open-mouthed, Maria takes it all in, while snatching a short sweeping clip of the scene discretely on her phone to show Dumitru later. In front of her is what must be an operating theatre, packed with machines and computer screens connected by a forest of cables. Trolleys covered in gleaming metal instruments she cannot name.

Set against this ordered neatness is a scene of chaos. At the far end of the operating theatre equipment is strewn across the floor. A cabinet overturned, files and papers. Broken bottles, scalpels. An operating table on its side. And beyond that an open doorway through which are strobing lights and what appears to be a person lying half in vision. Trousered legs and brown leather shoes. Maria films another short clip on her phone. Feeling guilty, she glances over her shoulder at Pepene; he is looking in the other direction.

Maria is intensely aware of the whispering odour. Stronger here than in the great hall. Sweet, metallic, savoury … as if a barbecue has caught fire, burning everything in sight, including the grill. She shivers involuntarily.

Pepene stands beside a closed door, his hand resting on the handle, like a marionette awaiting a pull on his strings.

'Where is he, Pepene?' There is a strident tone to her voice, she is trying to sound more in control than she really feels. 'How can I help him if you cannot even tell me where he is?'

The scravir blinks slowly. The familiar ugly grin divides his face, like a slowing tearing sheet of paper. He pulls open the door.

Maria has seen enough. She will return tomorrow with

reinforcements, dragging the other servants up the mountain herself if she has to. Turning tail, she crosses back to the lift and presses the call button. She sees Pepene reflected in the stainless steel doors of the lift, his head tilted to one side, as if in thought. Maria wants out. She wants fresh air.

Where is the bloody lift?

The lift pings and the doors open and she hurries in. She spins round to find the lift control panel and is surprised to find she has 4 options: 1, 0, -1 and -2. This must be minus two. Why wasn't she paying more attention earlier? As she pushes the button she notices that the scravir has started walking, in her direction.

'It's OK,' she says out loud. Though she is speaking to herself the scravir appears confused. 'I'll find my own way out, don't worry,' she hopes she sounds calm.

Why aren't the doors closing?

She presses the button again and feels her eyelid twitching the way it does sometimes when she is stressed. The doors start to close.

'See you later.' As if she is simply popping out to collect the post.

The scravir's smile is fading. The doors meet and the lift mechanism engages. There is a tapping sound from the other side of the door.

The gentle vibration of the lift tells Maria she is moving and she breathes a sigh of relief. She will text Dumitru as soon as she is outside to let him know where she is. Still a good hour of daylight left.

The lift stops with a tiny shudder. Maria brushes a strand of auburn hair away from her face and waits for the doors to open.

Suddenly everything is spiralling out of control.

Where is the connecting corridor with the photos and the broken glass? Instead the doors have opened onto a narrow passageway cut into bare rock. Smoke hangs fat in the air along with that odour, not a whisper now but an ugly shout that screams of danger. A monotonous bleeping like a car alarm. Pulsating light.

Where is she? Which button did she press? Has the lift made a mistake and taken her to the wrong floor?

'You cannot leave.' A slow voice, dry as raked stones.

Has it come from the passageway or down the lift shaft?

'Vă rog. Salveaza-ma!' Maria mutters, please, save me.

It's the owl. You knew it was bad luck, why didn't you just turn away?

'Doamne fereste, Doamne fereste, Doamne fereste.'

Before she can reach out to push a lift button the doors start to close and the display panel above them flashes **Level 0**.

Pepene has called the lift! He is dragging her back!

Or has she miscalculated? Is the operating theatre below ground?

'You cannot leave.' The same voice, muffled through the walls of the lift. How can it be? The scravir are mute.

Losing her cool, Maria pushes the -1 button over and over. Then the -2 button. The doors lock shut and the lift snaps into gear. The lift begins to vibrate. She is moving but she cannot decide in which direction.

How can you be so headstrong and stupid?

Doamne fereste, Doamne fereste, Doamne fereste.

God forbid.

She bangs the buttons again, vainly attempting to control the destination of the lift. The illuminated display above her flickers a couple of times then dies.

But the lift is still moving.

Doamne fereste, Doamne fereste, Doamne fereste.

She imagines Pepene's face pressed up against the lift doors, waiting for them to open. His big ugly grin and his missing nostril. The slightly fetid potting shed aroma that exudes from him. How can he be talking? He is more than forty centimetres taller than she is. What was she thinking?

The lift stops.

Her heart is thumping in her throat. She is hyperventilating. The doors begin to move. She closes her eyes, bracing herself for whatever fate has in store.

Then opens them.

Thank you, thank you.

The corridor with the photos. Maria rushes out before the doors can change their minds, whips off her scarf and places it between the doors, and races across to the other lift, the broken glass crunching under her feet. Behind her, the doors of the lift she has just vacated are closing and opening, closing and opening as the mechanism comes into contact with the scarf. Pepene cannot reach her.

Jumping up and down impatiently, she awaits the second lift. She is in it before the doors are half open, pressing the 0 button and willing the doors to close.

Moments later she steps out of the lift into the entrance hall. Her feet want to take her outside, to run across the snow past the tree, all the way to the gatehouse and out into the safety of the forest. But Maria has something else she must do. She heads into the Great Hall and out again through a different exit along a corridor she knows well; she took the British boy this way. She says boy but he isn't a boy. A student perhaps? Anyway, Daniel wanted to reach Maestru's office; he told her Lupei had sent him to collect papers.

Maria is curious. She cannot help herself; she has to know what happened. Homo Narratus, the storytellers. The heavy door opens in a rush of cold air onto a small courtyard, its shadows swathed in snow like cobwebs cluttering an attic. A flash of blue sky high overhead as she pauses to text Dumitru a message then hurries across the courtyard and pushes the next door, that creaks and sighs, and she is back undercover and in the oldest part of the castle.

The air is chill, no heating here. She can see her breath. The stone staircase, with the worn uneven steps she climbs two at a time, releases her onto a wide corridor thick with passing time and lined with suits of armour and medieval weapons. Not weapons that kill precisely with a single small hole, a lethal shot fired cleanly, but metal surfaces that rip rough-ragged to dismantle fraying flesh from bone in barbaric chaos.

Maria wonders if such weapons would kill a scravir; Pepene is safely locked away though, it won't come to that.

She stops in front of a large ornate carving made of solid oak. A feral forest is chiselled into its wooden surface: jackals and jays, wildflowers and wolves. From just above her head, a carved crow stares down, its eye hard and cold. At ground level a wild boar glowers up at her. Even the robin perched beside the keyhole is malevolent.

The door to Thor Lupei's office.

It is here that she brought Daniel Murray. She clicks the stone beside the door. Has the hidden key has been replaced?

The hole is empty.

She warned Daniel that his heart must be pure or he would never re-emerge from the room beyond the door; parroting what she herself has been told.

All those who entered this room without his permission have died. Very dark magic. You will be safe because he has asked you to go in but I cannot enter.

Now she fears the worst. Had he lied? Had he come to steal from the Maestru? Should she push the door to see if it is unlocked? Is her heart pure?

She is ripped from her reveries by the door itself.

The wooden crow has blinked and is turning its head to look past her and down the corridor. Behind her a faint rattle of rusty links on a chain heralds the arrival of a metal ball, the size of an orange and studded with spikes.

CHAPTER 3

West London

Wednesday, 4th January 2017

He is running. Always running. To keep warm. To clear his head. To get fit. To erase the memory of his empty legs.

He is haunted by flashbacks. Dragging his body hand over hand across a cold castle floor, thighs thin as broom handles, calves as slack as the leathered sag-skin corpses they drag from ancient peat bogs. Broken as Brexit.

But that was six weeks ago. Ancient history. Before he stepped beyond the lacklight lip that loiters at the dark edge of his being.

Now he runs. On healthy legs.

One step ahead of his demons.

Daniel Murray thinks of Tiffany often, standing at her front door in the murky winter light. He feels her blue eyes upon his back, watching him walk away, wet footsteps ringing in the alleys that wind down towards the harbour. The freckle on her left cheek, her broad Yorkshire voice. The salt of the North Sea hanging thick and chill in the Whitby air. The yellow-eyed gulls squabbling among the chimney pots.

'Where are you staying, love?' she shouts after him.

No one else has ever called him love. But instead of racing back to fall into her arms he grits his teeth and keeps walking because …

… because what?

Because I feared what might happen.

Tonight there is no sea air, only the sour smoke of terraced streets that squat beneath an orange West London sky.

He jogs past the Happy Valley Chinese takeaway on Lateward Road, nearly tumbling over the bin outside the front door as he dodges some git speeding round the corner on roller blades. Daniel has spent hours standing at the counter of the Happy Valley over the past week, his bike propped up against the shop window, waiting to collect online orders. Fried rice and fortune cookies promising money and happiness to the occupants of seedy flats in Ealing Broadway. And the same for the posh houses that flank the River Thames at Strand on the Green, where the herons stand as still as folded umbrellas stuck in the low tide mud.

All to earn a few poxy quid; his regular job having sacked him. Bloody gig economy.

Turned out being banged up in a Romanian castle was classed as 'unauthorised holiday'. And, to be fair, compared to the soul-destroying tedium of his low-grade junior logistics assistant job in a west London estate agents, being in a dungeon was a bloody holiday.

He runs up Brook Road South. A new route; never be too predictable. Past the Griffin pub tonight. Brentford lost against Newcastle. It's heaving in the boozer; a sea of sorrows rinsed in pale ale. And plenty of drown-faced fans milling about outside. He heads north, the football ground on his right. There's noise festering at the Royal Oak on New Road. Half a dozen morose supporters are gathered round an outside table clutching plastic glasses and hurling abuse at anything that moves.

'Hey! You with the hat. Oi, pal.'

He ignores them and runs on to Brook Lane North where the road narrows before the footbridge. A small business park on the right; its blue-sky gates intended to communicate the soaring prospects awaiting all those bold enough to rent a dreary two-storey garage in west London. Beyond the gates there squats a tree and in the tree there squats a man and on his head there squats a red and white striped bobble hat. The man is perched owl-like on one of the lateral branches, singing drunkenly. Spotting Daniel, the man points an accusing finger, loses his balance and tumbles backwards, landing heavily in the undergrowth.

Daniel slows and stops. The instinct to help. He looks up and down the street. Empty. If he leaves quickly no one will know he was here. A groan emanates from the bushes beside the gate. Daniel imagines the beery breath, slurred insults, self-pity. But they are not the reason for his rising unease. What worries Daniel is the possibility of human physical contact.

He starts to walk on.

'Help! Hey, pal! Wait. I think I've broken my …'

Daniel glances across the street. There are houses. He'll push a few doorbells. Someone will answer. They'll hear the noise and cross the road to explore or call the police.

Loud groaning over the wall. Daniel slaps his forehead in frustration. Against his better judgement he clambers over the blue gates. A pair of white trainers bright in the leaf litter beneath the tree.

'You OK, mate?' he asks.

More muffled groaning. Daniel drops down beside the slumped figure. The bobble hat has fallen over the man's eyes. Blind drunk.

'Can't stay out here all night, guvnor. Someone you can call?'

No answer. Grabbing a stick, Daniel pokes a leg.

'Come on, mate. Get up and we'll call you a cab. You live in Brentford?'

More groaning. Nothing intelligible.

Don't touch him. Just leave.

Have to touch him, he needs help.

Not from me, he doesn't.

Overcoming his anxiety, Daniel grabs the man's coat sleeve and attempts to lift him into a sitting position. Dead weight. Even with both hands it's like trying to turn over a double mattress single-handedly.

A subtle shift.

One moment Daniel is worrying about going to get help, the next his body is acting autonomously. No longer interested in seeking help but sensing an opportunity. Following a path Daniel barely understands and can barely control.

We eat and after that you will practice awakening the creierul anticilor that lies within you.

The words in his head are as clear as if his teacher were beside him, whispering in his ear.

Before he killed his teacher.

Daniel glances left and right, his nerves fuzzy as shortwave static. A tube train rattles past close by. Across the street in a puddle of lamppost light a dead leaf rocks in a gust of air. The drunks outside the Royal Oak are shouting and laughing.

Daniel's fingers have reached for and found the man's hand. Cool and rough. The fingers flinch and relax.

Daniel has feared this moment. It is why he walked away from Tiffany and why he avoids human contact. Deep in the primal centre of his brain - medulla oblongata, midbrain and pons - an ember glows as if caught in a whisper of wind. Daniel wants it to stop, simultaneously repelled and fascinated. But he cannot. His mind has a mind of its own.

Big mind little mind.

The man groans, attempts to withdraw his hand. Daniel's fingers tighten their grip. The man tries to sit up, muttering incoherently. Every muscle in Daniel's body shakes as he wrestles the ganglion spark that glows, grows and growls.

His primal being is a tiger that has been pacing behind the bars of its cage waiting for this; the moment when a keeper leaves a door open. As if from a great height, Daniel witnesses the coalescing of forces that will destroy his victim in a mayhem moment.

'Get off me!' the man shouts, pushing Daniel away. 'Wanker!'

Daniel falls back and in a second the drunkard is on top of him, pummelling him with clumsy fists. Daniel lifts his feet and pushes his attacker back into the bushes. Branches crack and snap. Leaping to his feet, Daniel scrambles to the gate and is almost over it when the man grabs the tail of his jacket. Daniel lashes out, fist connecting with the side of the man's face. The man is still howling as Daniel races north up the lane.

The silver roof of a Piccadilly line train snake-rattles beneath him as he races over the footbridge.

Daniel doesn't stop running until some twenty minutes later. The sensor light in the alley at the side of the house is dead. Twist the keys, push open the door, step inside. Close. Listen. Squeeze past the bike. Listen. Two flights of stairs. Unlock. The bedsit door swing opens silently on well-oiled hinges. Scan the room. Switch bathroom light on from his phone. Nothing. Step inside. Disable the alarm. Two deadlocks and throw the bolts. Check the locks on the sash windows.

With a deep breath Daniel kicks off his trainers, chooses one of his favourite blues tracks, *Lookin' Good* by Magic Sam, cranks up the volume, grabs a glass of cold water, throws up in the sink, and crashes down on the tatty sofa, still shaking from his run.

The guitar riff screams raw energy, spinning and tumbling, its rough sonic sandpaper muffling Daniel's dark mood.

His phone rings. He rolls over, kills the music and prises the mobile from his trouser pocket, hoping it isn't the neighbour complaining about the noise.

It isn't. It's worse.

'Where have you been?'

'Out.'

'Where out?'

'What do you want, Dad?'

'They tell me you lost your job.'

'Oh, sweet. You're ringing to offer me some cash to tide me over.'

'I know someone looking for a van driver. But I can tell you this for nothing, nobody wants a shirker.'

'Is that what Mum said before she left us?'

'You can't talk to me like that.'

'Oh? I just did.'

A brief pause.

'They're telling me you're responsible for Alex's disappearance. You and that black boy you used to hang around with. What was his name? George? Jezzer? Are you there? Anyway they come sniffing round my gaff. Two big buggers. Told them you moved out.'

Daniel climbs off the sofa and crosses to the window. 'Who? Who were they? You didn't give them my address?'

'Why wouldn't I? None of my business. Not my fault my son's a loser.'

Daniel snaps. 'You know nothing about me, you dumb old twat.' He cuts the call, hurls his phone on the bed and stares out into the empty street. How long does he have?

He thinks about Jordan. His friend has been round twice, leaned on the doorbell, called through the letterbox and left a dozen messages. All of which Daniel has ignored. Too late to call now. Daniel drags the large sports bag out from under the bed and starts to fill it; he'll find a shed or a doorway somewhere. For a few days, until things blow over. To be on the safe side.

Two hundred quid under the mattress; it'll have to do. There are delivery jobs everywhere. Collecting his phone, he looks around him at the place he has called home for the past year. Aside from the new locks on the door, the alarm, a PlayStation, a couple of posters - blues legend Buddy Guy and an aerial photo of a random tropical island somewhere in the Pacific Ocean - and his acoustic guitar loitering in the corner by the bed, there is almost nothing to show he was ever here.

Just passing through.

He shoulders his bag, pulls open his front door and switches off the light then, on the threshold, he stops. He curses under his breath. Light spilling in from the hall is picking out a sealed and addressed envelope propped up against the microwave. A letter that has been sitting there for over a week.

Outside a couple of cats are screeching the absent moon. Daniel steps back into the room, grabs the envelope and leaves, pulling the door to behind him.

The empty room darkly sits, as empty rooms do, with only the orange glow of a streetlight shining across the ceiling and the slow tip tap of water dripping into the dented steel sink.

Seconds later Daniel is on the street in front of a red pillar box. Indecision throbs between his ears then, at last, the dam bursts. He thrusts his hand into his pocket, pulls out the envelope, shoves it into the post box's open mouth and disappears down the street.

He walks, too weary to run. Did he overreact? Should he go back for his bike? A couple of guys talked to his Dad about Alex, so what? Could have been anyone.

And that is what worries him. He has been meaning to visit Alex's parents but has yet to work out what he could possibly tell them.

Hi Mrs Westernra, just popping round to tell you I saw your son's broken body among a pile of corpses in a castle dungeon in Romania. So you can stop worrying about his disappearance. Is your husband in?

Daniel turns up his collar and heads west; maybe he can knock on Jordan's door.

Except that Jordan lives with his mum.

Maybe she's on shift at the hospital.

Maybe she isn't.

Without really thinking where his feet have taken him, Daniel is stepping out of the rain and into a small familiar space tucked out of sight. A childhood hideaway where he has always felt safe. The closing door judders on rusty hinges. At least he won't die of cold. Not tonight.

He fumbles his way in the gloom to where three chairs must still be gathered in a circle around an old biscuit tin. The food will be inedible but the ...

'Don't move a muscle, Blood.'

A hoarse whisper in the darkness, inches from his ear.

'You feel that tiny sharpness just below your left scapula? Like someone is prodding a pencil between your ribs? Yes, you do, don't you?'

Daniel's senses jangle.

'That's my friend, Mr Slicer,' the voice continues. 'Nine inches of cold hard steel. Don't make him angry.'

Behind Daniel a boot takes a step, scraping the rough concrete floor and kicking what might be a couple of nails that spin across the floor like stones skimmed across a lake. The sweet smell of ganja hangs in the air. And something else, greasy takeaway food.

'When the Good Lord gave me this place to rest my weary head he did not have in mind for you to barge in and disturb me.'

'It's OK, I'm leaving,' Daniel says quietly.

'No, you're not leaving. It's too late for that, Blood. You are going to sit down and explain everything about the world to me. And Jonah is going to listen and learn and then decide what to do with you. Understood? UNDERSTOOD?'

'Yeah, OK. Sure.'

'Put that bag down very carefully so Mr Slicer stays calm

and put your hands behind your back.'

A muffled light clicks on and hints the room, as if from a torch hidden in a carrier bag. The inside of a lockup garage, cardboard boxes full of junk piled high against a wall. It isn't string being wound round his wrists, Daniel decides. Smooth, more like plastic. Electrical cabling perhaps. He keeps his hands as far apart as he can. A hand on his shoulder pushes him to the ground and finally his captor steps forward to look at him. The torch is now resting on a dusty tabletop. The man is wearing three coats and fingerless gloves. A wispy beard clings to his face like sea-lettuce to a rock. The dark skin of his face is gaunt as greaseproof paper, his eyes sunken. Fat dreadlocks burst out from under a large crochet beanie hat.

'So, Blood, what bring you skulking at the dead of night?'

'Same as you. I'm cold and wet.' Daniel can see his breath.

'And that gives you the right to break into my home?'

'I've been coming here since I was a kid.'

It is the truth.

'Wrong answer,' the man explains, kicking Daniel violently in the shins. 'Didn't your mum teach you manners?'

'I wish I could remember my mum,' Daniel answers truthfully.

The man cocks his head to one side thoughtfully. 'So much suffering ina Babylon,' he observes.

'Look, I have enough shit to deal with, and so do you,' Daniel starts. 'So why don't I just go? I can keep a secret. … Hey, that's my bag, OK?'

The man drags Daniel's bag across the floor and unzips it.

'No secrets in here, mate. Not in Jonah Tallman yard.'

'Just my clothes and some crap, Jonah,' Daniel says, hoping that using the other man's name might be seen as respectful.

Jonah rummages about, pulling out clothes, a pair of trainers, a removable hard drive, two paperback books, a wash bag.

'What's this? These old papers?'

Larceny's whispers. The memory of souls saved and lives lost. A retroglyph of time taken, gifts given.

'That's private,' is all Daniel says.

'I said no secrets, Blood.' Jonah is leafing through what looks like the unbound yellow pages of a large and ancient book. It is covered in a dense scrawl of tiny letters arranged in columns. 'So?'

Daniel says nothing. He is trying to decide whether, if he moves quickly, he might kick his captor hard enough to throw him off balance.

'Don't even think about it,' Jonah growls. He takes his torch from the table and shines it on the book, turning the pages slowly as he tries to make sense of what he reads. 'You write this?'

Daniel shakes his head. 'Something they give us at college. On our language course.'

'Read that for me then.' Jonah pushes one of the pages under Daniel's nose.

The letters are as unintelligible as they have been on every other occasion Daniel has looked at them.

ϛΛhΘΛhψsΘϵhΛnsιΛϵΛn
nϝιΛnΛsnnsΛhΛιΛΛΛιϛΛ
hϙhτϵΛnnΛΛΛϙsψιnΛϙs
ψϙshιsnnϛΛnϵnnιsϛΛs
ΛτΛhΛnsΛϝιsιnΛnϝϙnΛι
ΖϵΛhhΛhΛϛΛhnϝhnψϵΛ
nnψΛτϵιϝhΛmshhΛψιhn
nsΛhΛmmΛΘΛhψnsϝιΛΛι

On the floor with his arms tied behind his back, Daniel is forced to confabulate. 'They only just give it us. They said some of it is in Latin, and some in German or Italian. Don't know what that bit is written in. That's all I know. I think they give us a dictionary to …'

Jonah stares hard into Daniel's eyes. 'What your name, Blood?'

'Daniel.'

'And Daniel in the lion's den, they thought they would never see him again,' Jonah sings an old reggae song softly in his deep bass voice. 'Oh no, what a la la bam bam bam.' Jonah's teeth are smiling but there isn't the slightest flicker of mirth in his tired eyes. 'You a thief, Blood?'

'I told you; it's the homework they gave us. It just looks old. They photocopied it or something.'

'I'm stupid because I'm black, right? That look like Latin or German to you?'

'What?'

Jonah puts the torch back on the table, reaches into one of the pockets of his coats and produces a lighter. He squats on his haunches in front of Daniel, clicks the lighter and a small flame begins to dance.

'Guess I'm going to burn your homework, Blood. They'll print another one off for you, won't they?'

The flame licks the chill air like a hunting dog straining on its leash. Russian roulette. Daniel hopes his face isn't betraying panic. If he tells his captor what the pages represent he loses all control of the situation … and the journal. If he says nothing then …

The decision is taken from him as Jonah lights a corner of a page. A cool whisper of blue narrow flame creeps along the edge of the paper like poison gas drifting along a trench.

'Stop,' Daniel shouts.

Jonah arches an eyebrow.

'Just stop. Put it out!'

Jonah smothers the page in the folds of his coats. The two men stare at each other.

'Well?' Jonah says eventually.

'I stole it,' Daniel confesses.

'And?'

Daniel looks confused momentarily.

Jonah clicks the lighter and the flame reappears. He holds all the cards.

'OK. It's old. I stole it from this guy's house along with some other stuff. I wanted to find out what it was before trying to sell it. In case it's worth a few bob, you know? I swear. That's all I got.'

Jonah shakes his head sadly. 'Going to be a long night, Blood.' He puts the unbound pages on the floor beside him, reaches into one of his many pockets and produces a small pouch from which he extracts what looks like a dark green packing peanut. This he crumbles between his fingers, catching the falling material in the palm of his other hand.

'Time for lickle spliff,' he says and, before Daniel can react, Jonah tries to rip a strip from the top page of the journal, but the page doesn't rip. 'This isn't even paper. Some kind of animal skin, is it?'

Jonah grabs a sheet of paper from one of the boxes on the floor and tears a strip. He pours the contents of his palm onto the strip of paper then rolls it deftly into a neatly tapered joint. A second later the spliff is alight, the air is thick with the sweet pungent scent of marijuana and Jonah is lost in thought. He climbs to his feet and walks to the other end of the room leaving the book on the floor in front of Daniel.

'Three books,' Jonah says quietly, his back to Daniel. 'You notice that?' Two large smoke rings rise and grow over his head. 'The Book of Jonah, the Book of Daniel, and the Book of Secrets. Which one of those is not in the Bible? You're hiding some pretty shit from me, bwoy. Mr Slicer isn't happy. He wants to cut you up bad.'

Daniel refuses to panic, fortune favours the focused.

Jonah takes another toke on his spliff then presses it against the brick wall of the garage to extinguish it. He places what is left of the spliff carefully in a coat pocket and turns to drag a large cardboard box to the centre of the room. In the box nestles a sleeping bag. Ignoring Daniel, Jonah collects the journal and tucks it inside the sleeping bag. He steps past Daniel. A heavy object is dragged across the concrete floor behind him.

Suddenly Daniel's arms are yanked back and secured to something.

'I'm going to have forty thinks now,' Jonah announces as he grabs the torch from the table and climbs into his sleeping bag, 'while you can chew over what you need to tell me.'

The torch is switched off. For a second the darkness is silent then Jonah is singing softly.

'Time is on my side, I and I know it. Time is on my side …'

Daniel is numb with cold. It paws him in the damp air and seeps up from the concrete floor. To generate some body heat he bounces his ankles and weaves his shoulders about. His fingers fumble behind his back to feel the cords that bind him. Eventually he gets lucky, a fingertip brushes against a smooth flattened cord that he guesses is electrical cable. It is strong, copper wrapped in plastic sheath, but its strength is also its weakness. While Daniel cannot break the cable he can bend it against itself. He rocks his wrists back and forth, using the little play that exists as a result of his keeping his hands apart while they were being bound. Turn and twist. Push and pull. Turn and twist.

Time flies …

… as fast as lichen spreading across a rock.

In what feels like barely a couple of hours Daniel's fingertips touch the end of a wire. Forearm muscles aching from exertion, he works this wire back and forth back and forth, tiring the copper wire, tempting its atoms into a different alignment. Gradually it weakens until he can ease it back through its knot.

He works methodically, pausing every now and then to check that his captor is still asleep, and to rock his body and bounce his knees up and down and generate some heat.

When the moment comes he almost misses it; the slightest shift in tension on the wires and his left hand can wriggle free. His eyes have long ago adjusted to the lacklight, the faintest slither of photons creeping through the crack above a door hinge and the vaguest brown pool at the bottom of the far wall are enough to see by. His right hand also free, Daniel is now seconds away from escaping.

But he cannot leave without the journal.

The secrets contained within the discoloured ancient pages are Daniel's passport to a new life. Though he doesn't yet understand more than a fraction of the words scrawled across the paper, he does know what they represent and his body bears the scars of how hard he fought to obtain them. Daniel creeps across the floor and collects his other belongings, shoving them back into his sports bag that he places near the exit door. Having checked that the door is not locked, he stretches quietly to bring the life back to his muscles then, when he is ready, he gets down on his knees. He doesn't want revenge; he just wants the journal and a head start to the door.

The man is sleeping with his back to him, snoring gently.

Where is the book? The thought of rummaging about in the sleeping bag worries him. The other man, Daniel does not wish to refer to him by his name any more - it's too much information - is armed.

Daniel rehearses the movement. How long will he have? Four or five seconds. If that.

Maybe if he goes back north and apologises, tells Tiffany he was an idiot. She said she didn't need a hero so he'll tell her he made everything up. There wasn't a castle and he didn't see Alex's broken body. The police never found anything ...

Cut the crap. Get the book and leave.

He takes a deep breath and leans towards the sleeping man. He can smell the marijuana and the acrid smell of sweaty clothes and bad breath. How long has he lived here like this in poverty in this shithole?

None of your business. Take the book.

Another slow breath, as if he's about to dive from high on a cliff top down into a pool. His mind clears and he is ready. He slides his left hand beneath the cardboard and in between the sleeping bag and the back of the outermost coat. Nothing. He reaches round quickly, confidently. Unless his captor is lying on the journal he will find it in the next couple of seconds. He guesses right. Vellum beneath his fingertips. The rough pages he knows so well. He grabs them and starts to withdraw his hand. Almost done.

The fierce grip on his arm comes suddenly. The voice is barely above a hoarse whisper.

'What's up, Daniel? Forget you still in the lion's den?'

Daniel is off balance, pulled down towards the malodorous savoury acrid smoky mouth. He acts on instinct. His right hand lunges and his fingers find and wrap themselves around the man's neck. He uses his grip to push back, to stop himself from falling.

Simultaneously he feels the energy surge in the primal centre of his brain. Creierul anticilor. The brain of the ancients. In his mind's ear his erstwhile mentor, Thor Lupei, is telling him to focus his thoughts and send them flying along his synapses and out through his body.

This time he releases the flow without hesitation.

The man is muttering about Mr Slicer when Daniel's energy leaps like the flux from an arc welder's electrode, across his fingertips and into the man's neck. The muttering morphs mid-sentence into a chaotic jumble of gasps and choking as layers of living cells in Jonah's neck are siphoned away like sand from a windswept beach. The fingers that have gripped

Daniel's left hand release their hold.

Daniel's right hand is tingling. Still clutching the precious pages, he is withdrawing his left hand from the damp sleeping bag when a sharp point stabs the flesh between forefinger and thumb. A searing line slices effortlessly across the top of his fingers. He howls aloud. The pain is intense, but still Daniel refuses to relinquish his grip on the papers. Mr Slicer is constrained by the sleeping bag itself, the blade cannot swing freely.

The man is trying to speak now but can only emit a strangulated rasping noise.

Daniel's left arm and the ancient pages emerge from the sleeping bag as his whole body trembles with adrenalin and the energy he has awakened. He wants to run but is as yet uncertain that he has weakened the other man sufficiently to make his escape. Encased in his sleeping bag the other man's body is also shaking. And twitching. The feet kick frantically, the head rocks back and forth. But Daniel holds his grip, his right forearm growing, stronger not weaker.

Finally, as the thrashing body beneath him starts to tire, Daniel lets go of the man's throat. For a few seconds he lingers on his knees, catching his breath, until he hears a gurgling gasp and then silence.

As if snapped out of a dream, Daniel is back in the real world. He hears the ghostly woosh of a freight train passing on midnight rails. The distant pulse of a police siren. He smells mouldy bedding.

Daniel staggers to his feet, clutching the pages of the ancient book, reaches to retrieve his sports bag, and pulls open the door. Silhouetted against the orange night sky he looks down to the floor. He is alone. He has killed a man. A man with a name.

'Sorry, Jonah. Wrong place, wrong time.'

And with that, Daniel steps outside. He weighs a half a kilo more than when he entered the garage.

Fifty meters on, a thin glistening trail of blood drops leading back towards his crime, Daniel stops again in front of the red pillar box and kicks it with all his strength. He wants to take back the letter but it is too late. The die is cast. The cuts to his hand are throbbing. His right arm is tingling. Using his teeth, he ties a tourniquet around his left wrist to stem the blood flow then leans against the pillar box, bends over double, and vomits onto the pavement until his sternum aches and his throat is raw. When he is done he glances up towards his bedsit. The lights are on. A silhouette in the window.

Daniel hurries away.

CHAPTER 4

Whitby

Saturday, 14th January 2017

Tiffany glances at her watch, two hours to the end of her shift. Usually the hours fly through. Pensioners meandering into the restaurant for early lunches, squeezing mushy peas into their toothless jaws, like mortar pressed between two bricks. The regulars and a few tourists, not many this time of year. Then the takeaways, couples who hum and ha over whether to have cod or haddock, asking her which is best. Tiffany always picks whatever they've got most of out back. No one has ever complained. She watches them head off up the street towards the pier, leaning into the wind, breathing in the fresh air off the sea, enjoying their day out.

Places feel different when you're visiting. Not that Tiffany hates Whitby. Far from it. There is something magical about her home town, the aching cries of the gulls, the boats rocking in the harbour, the sea mists that hug the muffled streets of winter, and those long long summer days when the sky barely breathes black before daybreak dawns orange pink above a velvet sea and the …

'You sleeping rough, Tiff?'

She turns from the counter to find the top of the Dave's head visible on the other side of the fish fryer.

'What?'

The boss is clutching an envelope in his hand. She grabs it.

'Why's that been sent here?' Dave says. 'Been thrown out of your flat?'

Tiffany looks at the front of the envelope. The letter has a London postmark.

'This were franked ten days ago,' she says, her heart missing a beat.

'Point being?'

'Where's it been?' she asks. 'In your bloody office?'

'No need for that.'

'You hid it deliberately?' Tiffany says, tearing the envelope open. Something falls to the floor. She drops down to pick it up; a memory card smaller than her thumbnail, like the one in her phone. She gets up and drops the card in her trouser pocket.

'I did not deliberately hide it. It disappeared under all the other marketing crap. That's all. And I've just noticed, when did you decide to go blond?'

'Bastard.' She pulls out the letter and unfolds it. It is from Daniel.

'Hey, hey! Wash your mouth out and give me that back, you can have it when you finish your shift.'

Tiffany folds the letter and stuffs it in her pocket. Dave's hand is still waving over the hot boxes.

'No way, it's mine,' Tiffany says turning back towards the counter where an old man is waiting patiently. One of her regulars. His fleece jacket is torn and the stuffing is hanging out. She wonders how he makes end meet. 'Sorry. What can I get you?'

'Just chips. And scraps. You in trouble, Love?'

Tiffany shakes her head. 'He's all bark.'

Dave shouts over the fryer. 'You're lucky. I were about to throw it away.'

Tiffany looks at the old man as she wraps his order. She rolls her eyes in the direction of her boss and mouths the word bastard.

'You'll be all right,' the old man winks. 'Temper on you is

like me mam's, bless her soul.'

Two hours later Tiffany strides out of the front of the shop, removes her green hat and shudders at the feel of her greasy hair. It's four o'clock. The amusement arcades are empty. She passes the bandstand and strides along the pier, chooses a bench beneath a streetlight, facing the harbour. She pulls Daniel's letter from her trouser pocket. For a couple of minutes she sits there, letter on her lap, staring at three gulls fighting over a limp chip.

She knows what her mum would say. *Forget him, love. They're not worth it.* But her mum has never done adventure. Furthest her parents have ever travelled on planet Earth is a day trip to Calais on their honeymoon. Came back with three hundred cheap fags, two bottles of whisky and a terror of foreign places on account of a sandwich that had a "funny vegetable" in it. All of which is ironic since Tiffany was regularly subjected to abuse at school on account of her surname being Harrek. Not English enough for some.

It has been over two months since she last saw Daniel. And two months since the Dutch policeman, Gert Muyskens, told her that the phone call Daniel had made after his escape in Romania had been made on a phone stolen from a dead man. Tiffany had insisted that she trusted Daniel one hundred percent and Muyskens agreed. Sort of.

They were both lying.

She turns the letter over. How light it feels. A couple of sheets of paper and a milligram of ink.

A fishing boat churns the chill waters below her and Tiffany imagines herself dropping the letter over the railing, watching the sheets glide and spin like autumn leaves to touch the sea, soft as kisses while she walks away to get on with the rest of her life.

Instead she clutches the letter and stares across the harbour towards the cottages on Henrietta Street where Katie, Alex and the others stayed over the Whitby Goth weekend in November. She looks towards the one spot on Earth where Daniel Murray kissed her, and hugged her so hard she almost passed out.

She opens the pages and stares abstractly at the scrawled marks as if she were a drone studying a carpet of irregular buildings and roads from a great height, all arcs, scratches and lines. Distant voices call up from far below and she lets herself tumble down towards the hungry words.

Dear Tiffany,

Hope everything is good in Whitby. Here in London it's been really cold and …

Too small-talk. Daniel tears the letter up and starts again.

Hi Tiffany,

Sorry I walked away. I wish I could undo …

Too needy. Daniel crunches the letter up and drops it on the floor where it lands beside half a dozen other balls of crumpled paper. He is in his bedsit, on a stool by the kitchen work surface. It is night. Three takeaway pizza boxes are stacked by the sink.

Hi Tiffany,

OK, this is weird. I've never written a letter before. Except to Father Christmas and a couple of times to my Nan. My mum always took me to a friend's house where they had a proper fire, and the letters would curl up as they burst into flames then float away up the chimney. Dad couldn't be arsed. He wouldn't even put the letter in an envelope. He'd check the letter for spelling mistakes then put it in an ashtray and light it with his cigarette lighter.

There's a load of stuff I have to give someone and you are literally the only person I trust. Except Jordan, but I can't face talking to him yet. Can you apologise to him for me? He must think I am a total jerk.

The micro memory card contains files I need you to look after. Thor Lupei was bad, but he wasn't all bad. Power is like a knife; you can use it to kill someone or to cut a slice of bread. At the start Lupei used his power for good, to help the poor and the sick. He showed me stuff I cannot unsee and he taught me things that turn everything I ever knew on its head.

It's not going to be easy, I know that. Whatever anyone says, I am not a bad person. There's loads I didn't tell the police because they would have locked me up. I would never lie to you, Tiffany. You are the best thing that ever happened to me, I can't explain it but that's how I feel. No one wants to go out with a loser, I get that, but I swear I'm different.

I totally respect you and I know I have no right to ask anything from you so if you go to the police I will understand. The only thing I ask is that you wait a few weeks, to give me a chance to get away. I want to understand more about Lupei and prove it is possible to use his powers for good things. If I am right I hope that you will want to be with me. If I am wrong then I promise I will kill myself rather than become like him.

I love you,

Daniel

PS. That compass I gave you detects the presence of the scravir I think. You press the black spot on the base. No idea how or why it works. Hope you never see it working.

Tiffany sits quietly beneath the darkening sky. The iron railings between her and the waters of the harbour look tough but really they aren't. Every year they fix them, sand them down, weld them, paint them. And every year they corrode and sag. Waste of time. Nothing lasts forever.

Three little words. Eight letters.

Beside Tiffany on the stone spit that reaches towards the lighthouse is an old wooden capstan. She imagines men singing as they turned, heaved and wound ropes as thick as her arms to secure the whaling ships that once moored there.

I love you.

Now, like her, the capstan remains alone on the pier, a bruised stump, echo of epic adventures past. She is a ropeless rusting kelp-smothered anchor buried in the seabed securing a phantom ship that long since sailed.

Among the tombstones up on the cliff top a scruffy figure is shuffling. Only the head is visible from the pier, like a peppercorn rolling along the edge of a tabletop. The horizon is thick with rain. In impulse Tiffany leaps to her feet and tosses the top sheet of the letter over the railing. In the next second, as if waking from a dream, she regrets the act and shouts "NO". Shoving the remaining sheet in her pocket, she lunges forwards. The airborne paper is already below the lip of the harbour wall then, as if to taunt her, a gust of air catches it and it floats back up, hovering at eye level just beyond reach. Tiffany scrambles up onto the first rung of the railing and leans out over the black waters, stretching and straining. The railing cracks. She loses her footing and tumbles forwards. The sheet of paper is now moving away from her at speed, like a seagull shearing away. Her feet rising in an arc behind her are now almost as high as the top railing as her hips slide across the hard iron. Tiffany thinks about impermanence, about her parents, about her dead brother and the promise she made to live her life for both of them. Someone somewhere is shouting. A smacking sound. The water laps the wall, covering jagged rocks that lie just beneath the surface.

Arms around her waist force a scream to belch from her open mouth. Her arms slap the railing and she is no longer falling. Strong hands hold her and pull her back.

Her feet back on solid ground, gasping for air, she turns. A tall and thickset guy in a blue ski jacket releases her gently. Behind him three men are racing past the bandstand towards them.

'Bloody hell,' the man says in a Scouse accent. 'Yer mam tell you you were a seagull?' He smiles.

'Leave her alone you sick bastard,' shouts one of the men drawing near.

'Don't be stupid,' Tiffany shouts back. 'He just saved my life.'

The three men stop a few feet away, fists twitching. Two are short, skinheads in denim. The third, in a parka, is a head taller. Tiffany recognises this third man as an occasional customer at the chip shop.

'Let her go,' snarls parka boy, squaring up.

Tiffany's rescuer stands his ground, doesn't even turn towards the three local men. 'Like the lady told you, I just stopped her from falling so let's all calm down.'

'Don't tell me what to do, Paki.'

One of the skinheads side-glances towards parka boy, as if the word Paki sounds as weird to him as it does to Tiffany. Parka boy takes a step forwards. Tiffany steps round her rescuer to stand between them.

'Typical small town,' she tells parka boy. 'Half-headed haters with seagull shit for brains.' She turns to the two skinheads. 'It were good of you to check I were all right. I am, thanks, and there's nowt to worry about so you can all bugger off. Take him with you and ask his mum to put him to bed with a cup of tea and a biscuit. OK?'

The wind taken out of their sails, the two skinheads grab parka boy by the sleeves and spin him round. He is still muttering as they frogmarch him away.

'Yer boss with the verbals, know what I mean?'

'They're just big puppies, lads round here,' Tiffany explains.

'So what's with the paper? Or is leaning over railings what tatty heads do for fun on an evening in Whitby?'

Tiffany's hand flies to her trouser pocket. Empty. The second sheet has also gone.

'It were a letter.' Her words hang hollow. 'I made a mistake and now I've lost it.'

The guy bends down and carefully picks up something from under his right boot. 'Caught it just as it started to move. That's why I couldn't turn round when Fun Boy Three turned up.' He offers her a crumpled sheet of paper.

Tiffany pulls the paper open. Beneath the muddy footprint the words are still there, nestled within the folds. ... *prove it is possible to use his powers for good things ... you will still want to be with me ... I love you.*

She looks up at the stranger.

'Don't lose it, kiddo,' he smiles. 'I'd hang around but I've a train ...'

CHAPTER 5

**Message from Gert Muyskens
to Miss Tiffany Harrek**
Sunday, 15th January 2017
Hoi Tiffany! Gelukkig Nieuwjaar.
Happy New Year. I know, a little late :-)
How is the fishes and chips
business? You probably hoped you
would never hear from me again but,
hey, life is a field of cabbages ... I
need to meet you urgently. (Any
excuse to revisit to your lovely
Whitby!) How about tomorrow
night? 20.40 in Arguments Yard?
Is that good?
Gert.

CHAPTER 6

Golden Lion Pub, Whitby

Monday, 16th January 2017

'Did I ever tell you about Antoine Hoek, my friend at Europol?' Gert Muyksens stirs his coffee.

'Sorry?'

Tiffany glances up from her smartphone. Beneath his mop of greying blond hair the Dutch policeman has lost a little weight; his dark grey suit hangs a little loosely, which is probably a good thing. Between them, unspoken, is a bond as deep as the sea, the bond that comes to those who have faced death together and survived. She puts her phone on the table.

'It's my mum, she's worrying a lot since …'

'If I am your mum I will worry a lot.' His pale blue eyes smile.

At the far side of the room, by the bar, people are watching the football and talking loudly, but Tiffany and Gert have the dining area to themselves.

'Antoine would kill me if he sees me drinking this shit,' Gert laughs. 'He is a black belt in coffee making. He sees an individual coffee bean and he tells you the exact hillside it grew on, down to the square metre, and the date it was picked. Antoine loves detail and he's one of the good guys. We don't always agree but I trust him. One hundred percent.'

Tiffany smiles. She likes the soft strangeness of Gert's accent, calming and soothing, but it is getting late and she is sleepy.

Gert appeared exactly on time, eight-forty outside the sweet shop beside the entrance to Arguments Yard. She took him back across the bridge to the Golden Lion and since then have talked about everything and nothing. Or rather he has talked and she has been content to listen; cheese, politics, Brexit, football, music …

Out of nowhere a memory appears, she is arriving back at the cottage on Henrietta Street with Daniel after taking Hannah to Scarborough Hospital. Tiffany feels herself standing on tiptoes to reach Daniel's cheek, rough with two-day stubble.

The Dutch policeman senses her flagging attention.

'I'm sorry. You want me to get to the point,' he says.

She brushes a strand of hair from her face and nods.

'When he's not making coffee, Antoine creates algorithms,' Gert begins. 'He sets them loose like an army of street children rifling through a city dump, hunting for treasure. One of the best data sifters I have ever met. Without him we might never have tracked Lupei or found Daniel. Did you know that?'

He pauses.

Tiffany is unprepared for what comes next. What has she been imagining? That Gert crossed the sea to Whitby just to reminisce about old times? That the policeman's presence might enable her to feel closer to the tall geeky guy who strode out of the pouring rain and into the chip shop, asking for directions to Farview Farm? She is suddenly afraid. What if this meeting on this day changes all her other days? What if he brings news she doesn't want to hear?

Tiffany is staring blankly at the window.

Gert reads her indecision; it's his job.

'I was asking if you have spoken with Jordan recently,' he says.

'Has something happened?'

'Nothing like that,' he reassures her. 'Did you visit Daniel, in London?'

'Oh my God. Something has happened!'

Gert reaches into the breast pocket of his jacket and extracts a piece of paper that he unfolds and hands to Tiffany. 'Antoine spotted this,' he explains. 'And there have been two other cases. One in Paris and another in Italy, a village in Abruzzo.'

What he doesn't tell her is that the email containing the press cutting hasn't come from Antoine directly but from an anonymous Dark Web account. He assumes it is from Antoine, who does use similar dark web accounts on occasion. However, since Antoine made Gert promise to drop his obsession with Daniel, Lupei and the scravir, and since Gert swore to do just that …

But who else could the email be from? Anyway, Tiffany doesn't need to know the details.

'It's good to be on holiday,' Gert says randomly.

The paper is a printout of a story from the online version of the Ealing & Acton Gazette.

Mystery death

Police have made a grisly discovery in a South Ealing garage. The body of a Rastafarian man thought to have been in his fifties was found on Monday night in one of a row of lockup garages following complaints from residents about a foul smell.

Speaking on condition of anonymity a source told the Gazette that the man, who has not yet been identified, appeared "partially emaciated". When asked what this meant the source declined to …

'SCRAVIR!' Tiffany grabs the policeman's arm. Heads

turn at the bar. 'You have to stop them!' she hisses, lowering her voice. 'They've come to kill Daniel and Jordan, haven't they? We have to …'

Gert raises a hand to silence her. The drinkers at the bar return to the television screen and the football. Only villagers from a mountainous region of central Europe where eagles soar and wolves and bears roam at night would understand the word *scravir* and, if such a villager were in the snug of the Golden Lion, they would already have left and be busy barricading their doors and windows.

'So you haven't spoken with either of them?' Gert asks calmly.

'Jordan called about a month ago. He'd said Daniel weren't answering his door and asked if I knew where he were.'

'And *do* you?'

Tiffany shakes her head. Gert strokes his chin thoughtfully.

'You see, Tiffany, there are people who think the problem isn't scravir; it's Daniel.'

'That's rubbish.'

The Dutch policeman grimaces and rubs his eyes. 'It's not just London. There have been attacks in Abruzzo and Paris and …'

'Well, that can't be Daniel, can it? He's here in the UK.'

'So you *have* spoken with him?'

Tiffany sighs. 'No. I'm just saying that …'

'Let me give you a little scenario and you can explain to me where I am wrong. OK? When Daniel was found by the police in Romania he refused to say what had passed between him and Thor Lupei.'

Tiffany fidgets, unsure of where this is leading.

'Local police found the body of an emaciated villager in a car parked in the forest less than three kilometres from Lupei's castle. It turned out that Daniel had used the victim's mobile phone to call the police for help.'

Gert doesn't tell her that Romanian police have now changed their tune or that Europol have accepted the new explanation.

'What are you saying?'

'What if Daniel lied about everything? What if he is ill? What if Lupei infected Daniel? What if Lupei and Alex and Daniel are working together?'

'It were stupid when you first said it in December, and it still is. Why would you even *think* that? Do you want to arrest him? Didn't the Romanian police check out what had happened at the castle?'

'Tiffany. We're on the same side. This is personal for me too. Lupei killed my brother.'

They sit in awkward silence.

'Have you heard from him?' he says eventually.

She doesn't look at him. Her shoulders contract fractionally.

'No.'

A pause.

She looks up at Gert. 'I trust him. OK? When he's ready he'll contact me. He needed to get away. To clear his head. Said everyone were blaming him and it weren't his fault.'

Gert nods and stares her out.

'Before he left,' she adds defensively. 'He said that *before* he left Whitby.'

She is hiding something but he knows he will get no more from her tonight.

'I need sleep,' he says, stretching. 'Forgive me. It's OK, don't get up. Finish your drink. I'm up the hill in a bed & breakfast. We'll speak tomorrow.'

Muyskens climbs to his feet and collects his coat from the back of his chair. As he pulls it on he pats the pockets.

'I almost forgot. A present. No, two presents from the Netherlands.' He pulls a round cheese from each pocket; one red, the other yellow. 'There is also a green one but I left it in my bag. The red cheese is for when you have eaten too much and need to stop.'

Tiffany is confused.

'Traffic lights, you see. The red cheese is …'

She shakes her head pityingly; it must be a Dutch thing. 'Thanks, Gert. I'll get you some Wensleydale. Or kippers? Orange ones. And some spinach. Do you have those in Rotterdam?'

'A Yorkshire streetlight theme,' he laughs. 'Sounds good.'

As he reaches the door, Muyskens stops and turns. 'Oh. Did Daniel tell you anything about his mother?'

Tiffany thinks. 'Middlesbrough. He said she were from Middlesbrough. Walked out on him when he were just six, she told him he and his dad were too boring.'

Gert Muyskens shakes his head as if something doesn't add up.

'Why? What is it?'

Gert puffs his cheeks 'Nothing. I'll call you tomorrow. Goodnight.'

The door swings shut. Tiffany sits there staring at a stain on the table top, trying to organise her thoughts. Clarity arrives in a rush. She leaps to her feet.

'Wait! Wait!' she shouts.

Heads turn at the bar. Let them stare. She throws open the pub door races out into the night. Running up Golden Lion Bank to the foot of Flowergate.

The street is empty.

One of the yards perhaps? But which one? Maybe he meant on the other side of the harbour. She about turns and runs back towards the swing bridge. A sea fret has rolled in off the sea, chilling the air; she can barely see the waters of the Esk. Rigging taps against the masts of the boats moored along the harbour wall like Morse code in the fog. A dog barks.

Tiffany hurries past Sandgate towards Church Street.

There's not a soul about.

'You can't do this, Gert! It's not fair.'

'Are you OK, Tiff?'

'What?'

Tiffany turns to see her flatmate Tina in the doorway, all glammed up to go clubbing in Middlesbrough. Stilettos, four coats of face paint, eyelashes longer than draught excluder bristles and enough hair lacquer to beehive a backcombed yak.

'You've washed that same bloody mug three times, pet.'

Tiffany looks down at her hands. She is standing at the kitchen sink. Since she arrived back at her flat on Cliff Street she has gone from one displacement activity to the next; moving a pile of laundry here, changing the toilet roll there, taking a dustpan and brush round the bathroom floor. And pretending to do the washing up.

'Taxi's here in five minutes,' Tina reminds her. 'Are you ready?'

Tiffany shakes her head.

'Oh, great. Thanks a million.' Tina turns heel and storms off. 'You're sad, you know that?' she shouts from the corridor. 'Wasting your life over what? Some skinny loser you knew for ten minutes.'

The front door slams shut. Tiffany has no appetite for dancing. On autopilot, box of chocolates in hand, she parks herself in front of the television. A vacuous American sitcom where every line of dialogue requires a slug of canned laughter. Crunching the mute button she drops the chocolates. Leaves them scattered, brown lumps across the hairy green rug.

Her mind is swimming in the shallows of a dark pool full of monsters, the sort that slide slick talons from under parked vans to slash and slice the ankles of the unwary.

She goes to her bedroom and returns with the compass Daniel gave her and sits in front of the television, turning the compass round and round between her fingers. The tiny black crow that is the needle keeps pointing north. She presses the black spot on the base. Now the crow starts to spin this way and that over the points of the compass, as if searching for something. When she pulls her finger away the crow needle swings back to point north.

See? There are no scravir. They are all dead. That's why the needle doesn't settle. Gert is just an obsessive. Nothing can hurt me. It's over.

Cocooned in dull routine behind a fish and chip shop counter, Tiffany has slowly persuaded herself that life can return to normal. She has taken the silence of friends as proof that they too have reclaimed their lives and moved on.

But evil does not vanish; it shapeshifts and regroups.

Or maybe it's just a dodgy compass. She drops it to the carpet. Should she text Jordan? No point trying Daniel. He hasn't replied to any of her previous attempts to contact him. Don't want to look like Desperate Deborah, as her gran would say.

Gert perhaps? Trouble is once you've told a lie you can't go back. She could have told him about the letter. But it is hers. She isn't ready to pass it over. And Daniel has asked her to keep it to herself.

She buries her head beneath one of Tina's unicorn cushions and sighs in frustration.

CHAPTER 7

North Yorkshire Moors

Wednesday, 17th January 2017

Half-buried in last summer's spent fern fronds, the twisted brown skeletons of brambles and two wind-stunted hawthorn trees, squats a stone shed. It lies in a dimple on the landscape, surrounded by heather, the bright purple flowers long since bleached to grey. Drab drizzle mist haunches the shed roof.

Emerging from the moss that clings to the grey slates, raindrops coalesce, wriggle like tadpoles to the roof's lip then tumble to the pebble-strewn puddle below.

Within the shed the air hangs chill. Puny light seeps through the single small dust-shuttered window and, in the driest darkest corner, a bed of straw flinches, rustles and whispers.

There being so little flesh on her bones, she unwinds slowly and deliberately like a chameleon thawing on a branch. It is an age since she last ate. Abandoned. Alone.

A second bleat. Close by. Harsh blunt, plaintive.

Curiosity aroused, she climbs unsteadily to her feet, senses sharpening.

Beneath a fading sky the sheep grazes. It fails to notice the creak of the wooden door; a sound so sporadic slow that it passes for the shifting wind-shaken notes of the trembling heather. Nor does the animal sense the incremental creep, the infinite patience, the advancing feet placed so carefully that even the cold hard earth beneath them fails to register their passing. The moment of rush release, when it comes, is decisive and brutal, overwhelming the prey in a frenzy of grasping violence. The last cry the animal will ever make is stifled half-formed.

Dragging the carcass back to the barn is hard work. Wool and disorderly legs snag repeatedly in the vegetation, but eventually the job is done. A blade found hanging rusty on the wall is put to use and soon her hands and arms are red with blood. Pausing from time to time to check she is alone, she eats.

Then sleeps beneath the straw, then eats again.

Even here in the dank depths of winter shuttered in a shepherd's shed on the North Yorkshire Moors, mouthful by mouthful she will get stronger. She will survive.

She is scravir.

CHAPTER 8

Mikăbrukóczi Castle, Romania

14th December 2016

Police Constables Zamfir and Nistor park their grey Dacia Logan outside the castle gate. The last stretch has been treacherous; without snow chains the squad car would almost certainly have slipped off the road at several points. On the way up the mountain, they have had their usual bickering about tidiness, Zamfir complaining about pastry and biscuit wrappers, Nistor complaining about the smell of cigarettes.

They have arranged to meet Radu Felini, the staff manager at the castle, and are pleased to see that he is waiting for them on the road. All three men are of medium height and sporting moustaches, but only Felini's moustache is grey and only he has the build of a street fighter.

'Domnilor, I am pleased to meet you,' Felini calls all police *gentlemen* though he has yet to meet one who fulfils the requirements of the honorific.

'We are sorry about the circumstances,' Nistor says as he and Felini shake hands. 'So close to Christmas. You know that her mother found the body? In the forest. It doesn't bear thinking about.'

'Maria was a lovely girl. It is very sad,' Felini says.

'The staff and Mr Lupei must all be very upset. The boss is here, isn't he?'

'Everyone is in shock.' Felini replies, not answering the question.

'Maria was at school with my own children,' Nistor says.

'I have just been shopping to buy their presents. How can we celebrate Christmas after everything that …'

'Do all that another time.' Zamfir dislikes small talk. He turns to Felini 'You can let us in, right?'

From the folds of his coat Felini produces an iron ring thick with keys and jangles them ostentatiously.

'And the castle is currently empty?' Zamfir continues.

Nistor notices a fractional moment's hesitation. 'We have all been on leave these past few weeks.' Felini thrusts a huge iron key into the lock at top of the door that is set into the gate, then squats to repeat the act at ground level.

'Paid leave?'

'Of course. Maestru Lupei is a generous employer. We generally return to prepare for his arrival a week before he comes.'

The door groans open.

'Must oil hinges,' Felini says to himself. 'Please,' he beckons the policemen forwards. 'What makes you think Maria visited the castle before the tragedy?'

The policemen step through the doorway and wait for Felini to slide the bolts shut behind them. They follow him across a pristine expanse of snow towards the main building.

'We will come to that. So these stories of monsters …' Nistor starts. 'You must have heard what is being said.'

'Old wives' tales. People are jealous. Maestru is an outsider so they peddle stories,' Felini retorts.

'And yet, we have a series of deaths that all start when your employer moves into this castle,' Zamfir says.

Like a pike poised in a stream beneath the shadow of a sagging willow tree, Felini spots the hook concealed in the bait. He says nothing.

The men stamp the snow from their feet and enter the main building. Felini ushers them past the suits of armour and into the Great Hall. Nistor is interested in everything.

'The original owners had class,' Zamfir mutters. 'They would never have littered a historic monument with a cheap display of electric guitars.'

'I've seen photos,' Nistor says, 'It was an empty ruin. No roof. Plants growing everywhere. And now...'

'Restoring the castle has been a pleasure,' Felini says. 'I will show you ...'

'Forget the guided tour,' Zamfir interrupts. 'Show us the operating theatre and explain why a private castle needs such a thing.'

'The operating theatre?'

'Don't make me repeat myself.'

Felini studies the two policemen. He nods curtly. 'This way, gentlemen.'

He takes them back into the entrance hall.

'On the second suit of armour,' Felini sweeps his hand to steer their eyes, 'you will notice the hole where an assailant successfully pierced the cuirass with his sword and killed the wearer. A DNA test showed that traces of the blood remain centuries after the incident.'

Felini is a master of misdirection. The policemen cannot help but look where he has directed them and, in doing so, fail to notice the scravir Pepene standing at the top of the stairs, clearly visible, reflected in the high gloss finish of the black Gibson J-160 E Acoustic guitar hanging in the stairwell.

'Is he a collector? The guitars? And the armour?' Nestor asks.

'They are souvenirs, I understand,' Felini replies.

Beyond the entrance hall the wood panelling slides back smoothly to reveal the lift doors. The three men step inside and make their descent.

The broken photo frames have been swept away in the corridor between the lifts. An unsubtle scent of synthetic flowers masks other odours.

'I expected his music to appeal mostly to young people,' Nistor says, observing the photos of Lupei with various couples. 'How old is he by the way?'

Stepping into the second lift, Felini shrugs. 'I just work here.'

Felini watches the policemen take in their surroundings when the lift doors open and the motion sensor switches on the lights. He imagines them both as children opening their Christmas presents: one with eyes wide in wonder, his face bright with anticipation; the other consumed with jealousy as to what his siblings have received and smouldering anger at his parents for their poverty and lack of ambition. Why has the police station sent these two and not other more compliant and understanding officers?

'Wow! You could not imagine this,' says Nistor.

'Who would want to?' retorts Zamfir. 'How do we get to the other side of the glass?'

The operating theatre has been tidied up. The upturned furniture is now upright and in its place, the air a fake cacophony of lavender, rose and sandalwood.

Nistor has his phone out of his pocket. He takes a few photos, uploads them and his bits of video to the cloud while there's a good signal, then scrolls through his files.

'Someone has been busy. It was quite a mess when Maria saw it.' He shows Maria's film footage to Felini. 'The door is over there.'

Felini does his best to hide his agitation at the footage. Why had he not considered that the girl might have made use of her smart phone? Who else has seen the film?

'What's behind the door?' Zamfir asks.

'Offices and er …' Felini hesitates, '… bedrooms, I believe. For when the Maestru welcomes guests. No photos please.'

'He welcomes guests to an operating theatre?' Zamfir sneers. 'OK. Open up.'

'You have a warrant?'

'Don't mess with me.' Zamfir's façade of politeness, such as it is, collapses. 'Open. That. Fucking. Door.'

Felini stands his ground.

Zamfir lurches forwards grabbing the older man by the throat, throwing him back and pinning against the wall. 'A child died just days ago, having sent her boyfriend a film clip of this room and a story of being chased by …' He hesitates, not wishing to say the word out loud.

'Does the Chief Inspector know what you boys are up to?' Felini looks from one man to the other. 'You're not local, are you?'

Zamfir takes a breath and steps back, releasing Felini's throat. Felini guesses the men are acting on their own.

'That's better.' Felini steps past the two policemen towards the operating table. 'So you have seen what you came for. Shall we …'

The metal of the pistol pressing Felini's ear is still cold from the outside air.

'I've asked you nicely,' Zamfir says softly, releasing the safety catch.

'OK.' Felini walks away from the gun to the far side of the room, clicks the button on the wall and a door swings open to reveal a passageway. 'This way, gentlemen.'

Nistor notes that there is no body over the threshold as there was in the film that Maria sent her boyfriend.

Neither policemen can see Felini's finger pressing the pager in his pocket.

The walls are rough-hewn stone blocks. The passage curves away to the right, dropping gently into the mountain. After ten metres the stone blocks end to leave a tunnel gouged out of the solid rock. It is impossible to walk three abreast. Felini leads the way with the two policemen in his wake. In silence. There is a cloying smell: sweet, fetid, burnt. The air is dead, no echo, no sense of space.

Nistor feels trapped.

The passage turns to the left, the lighting hidden behind overhangs. Felini ignores the side passages, and heads round and down into the entrails of the mountain.

'Wait! Are these the *bedrooms*?' Zamfir sneers beside a closed door.

'Storerooms. I'll take you to the bottom and then you can check everything on our way back up,' Felini says over his shoulder.

Their shoes scuff the dry grit beneath their feet like sandpaper scraping a sarcophagus. Nistor has the curious sensation that each step is taking him backwards through the centuries. Zamfir's knuckles grip his gun.

'Does Mr Lupei use this part of the castle?' Nistor asks.

'Maestru Lupei uses all the castle,' Felini replies.

'Can we talk with him?'

'That is not possible at this time.'

'When did you last see him?'

Felini does not answer. Nistor wonders if he heard the question but does not repeat it. After what feels like an eternity, the passage ends at the mouth of a large cave, at least that is what Nistor decides must be ahead of him. While the overhead lights do not reach the end of the passageway, the sounds of Felini's footsteps changed as he entered the lacklit velvet void. Echoes are ricocheting off distant surfaces unseen.

Both Nistor and Zamfir have been policemen long enough and have visited enough crime scenes to recognise the smell. Something or someone has died here.

A laser-thin whisper of light comes on ahead of them, qualifying the darkness. The two policemen look at each other. The focused beam originates in the ceiling and terminates in a disc just two centimetres wide on a table positioned in the centre of the cave that must sixteen metres across. There are five tall holes set into the rock walls of the cave, black against blacker. Presumably the exits to other passageways.

Nistor spins on his heel. Felini is nowhere to be seen.

Zamfir takes a step forwards.

'Wait,' Nistor says, his eyes adjusting to the light. 'Just ahead of you. What's that?'

Something sticking up out of the floor.

'Where's the bastard gone? Hey! HEY!'

The two men inch forwards, testing the floor before transferring their weight. The thing sticking up is at once familiar and unfamiliar. Is it a chair? Nistor drops to his knees and shuffles forwards until he is in touching distance. He wishes he had brought the torch from the squad car.

Either a chair set into a spherical black base or … a hole through which is the top of a ladder. If it is a ladder then it is a decorative piece because it would appear to have two ornate handles at the top.

Yes, there is a hole in the floor and it is a ladder, dark, its surface blistered, the side rails not straight but more organic in shape. Like the branches of a tree. And the handles look less like handles close up and more like …

Nistor leans forwards. The rungs are crude and clumsily welded to the rails. At the top of the ladder each handle is splayed and undulating in form, at right angles away from the side rails. And each ends in five nodules, resembling … Nistor reaches out to touch the ladder … and recoils in horror.

'What is it?' Zamfir asks.

Nistor is so absorbed that he has forgotten Zamfir. He jumps visibly, shakes his head. 'Legs. Human legs.'

'No. It's a ladder.'

'I know it's a fucking LADDER!' Nistor shouts, struggling to control his rising panic. 'It's made of flesh and bone.'

Zamfir walks forwards, his grit-scraping footsteps masking the sound of other quieter feet making their way down the winding passage that leads from the castle.

Nistor has his phone out. 'We need reinforcements. This is a crime scene.'

'Good luck with a signal,' Zamfir snorts. 'We're buried in a million tons of rock.'

Zamfir grabs the ladder and pushes it. The surface, burnt and fragile, tears away in his hands to reveal a harder surface beneath.

Bone.

In his hand are skin and muscle. Like the crackling on roast suckling pig. He grabs the second rung. Same thing.

Nistor has given up on calling for help but he has activated the torch on his phone. He leans forward and peers over the edge and into the abyss.

'Oh God!' He throws himself backwards, away from the hole, his phone slipping from his hand and down into the void. He lies on his back, gasping for air, a look of terror in his eyes.

'WHAT? What is it?' Zamfir demands.

Nistor cannot answer. He rolls onto his side and throws up.

The hole is now a feeble pool of light, lit from below. Unable to get any sense from Nistor, Zamfir edges closer to the hole, crouches and peers down.

The phone has landed at the foot of the ladder and is resting among a jumble of limbs and bones, partially burned bodies. A twisted wheelchair lies on its side, its rubber tyres melted and hanging like the clocks in Salvador Dali's surrealist paintings.

But the most frightening, unspeakable thing is the ladder itself.

Zamfir does not want to believe his eyes. At the foot of the ladder is a human body, its legs pointing upwards. The ladder is the extension of the man's limbs, as if someone has stretched human legs, or grown them, until they were some four metres long. The trousers are ripped to shreds and the legs appear to have rungs of flesh and bone running between them.

It makes no sense.

The body that has been treated so abominably belongs to a human being. The victim is partially burned but enough remains to see the howl of anguish on his face, and the strange construction of his right arm, a metal frame like a sheath around his bones.

Zamfir films the scene on his phone. He places his phone on the floor beside him and is turning away when he hears Nistor groan and at almost the same instant he feels a hand on his back, unbalancing him, pushing him over the void. Frantically he throws his arms out to catch the floor beyond the hole, to brace himself, but a foot stamps down hard on his back, popping his arms out of their sockets. Howling, he tumbles forward, bouncing against the human ladder and down into the castle's oubliette.

The fall breaks his neck and he is dead.

Pepene, wearing his rip-faced smile like a festive decoration, draws himself up and turns towards the other policeman but Nistor is already on his feet, scrambling away. Zamfir must be dead, there is nothing to be gained from staying in the cave. He must get out. He must survive.

Being young and fit, Nistor easily outpaces Pepene as he races towards the light of the passageway. Thankfully, there are no tricky junctions to remember, he simply has to follow the rough curving walls of the main tunnel all the way to the top. The side passages disappear behind him one after the other until finally the walls are made of carved stone blocks. Seconds later he throws open the doors and emerges into the operating theatre, where he is promptly smashed across the back by a heavy object, sending him staggering across the room. Losing his balance, Nistor crashes to the floor.

In a second Felini is all over him, kicking him and showering him with punches. Nistor rolls away from the blows, spots the steel trolley and grabs at it. It tips over, an assortment of tools, scalpels, pincers, and steel bowls clattering to the floor around him.

Felini grabs the policeman's leg and drags him away across the floor but not before Nistor has caught hold of a scalpel. With all his strength Nistor twists his body and plunges the blade into Felini's calf. Felini cries out, releasing his grip, allowing Nistor to scramble to his feet. Before Felini can gather himself together, Nistor takes hold of the trolley and swings it in a wide arc, smashing Felini's head, knocking him out instantly.

Nistor is close to the lift when he sees Pepene emerge from the cave passage and into the operating theatre, on the other side of the glass. The horror stories he has heard from terrified residents are correct. The lift doors are opening. Nistor jumps in and selects -2. The policeman paid more attention than Maria. The lift descends and opens onto the corridor with the photos of Thor Lupei with his fans. Into the second lift then up and out into the entrance hall and beyond that the outside world.

The bright snow squeaks beneath his boots as Nistor sprints to the main gate where he pulls back the bolts, yanks open the door within the gate and steps out of the castle. The car is where they left it. He flings open the door and jumps in.

Wait, didn't he lock the car?

The electronics have been ripped out around the steering wheel.

'Damn, damn, damn!'

Nistor slams his fists on the dashboard. Leaping out of the car he runs towards the trees. He has to call for help but his phone is in the oubliette beneath the castle.

It's OK, I have another!

He had grabbed Zamfir's phone as he'd scrambled to his feet in the cave. If he finds a path down off the mountain he should be safe. Some twenty metres into the gloom of the forest he stops to catch his breath and pulls Zamfir's phone from his pocket.

What's his bloody code?

Nistor has his back to a tree as he tries to remember the movement Zamfir's finger makes when he is unlocking his phone. It all happens so quickly. A sharp excruciating pain above his right ankle as if something is biting him. He howls and yanks his leg away.

Or tries to.

His leg doesn't move an inch. Has he trodden on a mantrap? Looking down he does not see the metal jaws of an iron snare.

He sees a hand and fingernails digging into his flesh. A shivering flow like electricity. His leg is struggling to support him. As he falls Nistor catches sight of a thin face with deep eye sockets, smiling dirty teeth, and flaking scalp. A parody of a human being is squatting beside the tree, gripping his ankle, draining the muscle from his leg.

Nistor screams for help at the top of his voice but, besides the castle, there isn't a building for well over a kilometre.

In his left hand Nistor is still holding Zamfir's phone. Almost without thinking he presses the phone into the ground, burying it beneath the thick carpet of leaf litter, all the while kicking out at the scravir with his good leg.

It is an unfair contest. Nistor's right leg now reduced to little more than skin and bone, the scravir turns its attention to the policeman's left leg, grabbing it as it kicks him and sucking the muscle from it as effortlessly as a lab technician uses a pipette to remove liquid from a vial. His victim immobilised, the scravir clambers to its feet, a medieval mace in his hand. Nistor stops shouting as the spike-encrusted iron sphere swings out in an arc and strikes him with full force on the side of his head.

CHAPTER 9

West London

Wednesday, 18th January 2017

End of the line. The doors hiss open and a hundred people rush away down the platform. Tiffany steps out as a scrawny pigeon hops onto the tube train and wanders down the compartment in search of food.

For Tiffany, a Whitby girl who has only visited once before on a school trip, London is sensory overload; the smell of passengers crammed together in a tube train fifty metres below the streets, tall buildings peering down at her, the hive hustle rush that never slows. People of every race and culture, all glued to their phones. Up the steps and out into Ealing Broadway. She spots him almost immediately, standing outside the coffee shop, wearing a camouflage parka over his suit.

'Hey, Tiffany! This used to be a Polish delicatessen. Great sausages,' he says, smiling broadly. 'Nice coat, by the way. Suits you. So does blond hair, should have told you in Whitby.'

'Why didn't you tell me you were leaving Whitby yesterday morning?' she ignores the compliments.

Gert's grin vanishes. 'You OK?'

'You come all the way up North, wind me up with a load of bollocks about Daniel being evil then bugger off. Now I'm worried sick about him.' The anger she has bottled up for over twenty-four hours comes pouring out of her. 'I didn't even dare tell my mum I were coming; I know what she'd say. So, no, I'm *not* OK.'

'I'm sorry, Tiffany. Maybe I should have …'

'Don't bother. I'm here to help Daniel.'

Gert flags down a black taxi and they climb inside. Tiffany gazes out at the passing crowds. Everyone busy. Life against the clock. Makes Whitby look like a sleepy village. She glances at Gert checking his phone. The traffic is gridlocked.

'Who are we seeing?' she asks. 'You said that …'

'His father. He lives near here.'

'Daniel's dad?' she says incredulously.

Gert nods.

'Daniel said his dad were a prat,' she says.

Gert grunts noncommittally.

Tiffany stares at the driver's shaved head. Hair is climbing out of his shirt; a man who has to decide where to stop shaving. The dashboard meter is ticking faster than a hospital heart monitor. Five pounds already and they are still only thirty metres from the station.

Shops give way to a plantation of tower blocks then shops again. The taxi turns south, leaving the main road, skirting an unkempt park then a large pub. Street after street of terraced Victorian houses. A light industrial estate. A bridge.

The further they go the less cared-for the houses look. A pile of broken plastic toys strewn in front of an entrance. A barricade of cardboard boxes. A rusting motorbike. Someone has sprayed the words 'sod off Mark' in red on the petrol tank. Gert taps the driver's shoulder and the taxi pulls up outside the last house in the row. Flaking paint hangs from the front door like a bankruptcy notice on a boarded-up shop. Bloated black plastic waste bags slouch on the path.

As the taxi disappears round the corner Gert knocks three times. Then knocks again. Tiffany stands uncomfortably.

'He's on holiday.'

They turn to find middle-aged man in a green shell suit, overweight, goatee beard, large gold medallion, crossing the road towards them.

'Ibiza,' he adds as he produces a key. 'I'm collecting the mail and feeding the cat while he parties! You friends?'

'Daniel's friends,' Tiffany explains.

'Ah, the prodigal son. Well he's not here either. Pops in regular like but chalk and cheese those two. Got his own gaff.'

'I've come from Yorkshire,' Tiffany adds.

'Long way to come and see a locked door.'

'Does Daniel live close by?' Gert asks.

'Down South Ealing. Ten-minute walk, maybe fifteen.'

'Do you have the address?' Tiffany says.

'You're keen! *Must be love, love, love,*' he sings. 'I'm Mark,' he sticks his hand out. 'Tell you what. I don't 'ave his address but wait here, I'll check if it's on the old boardarooney in the kitchen. Alright?' Mark turns towards Gert. 'You the proud father then? Eh?' He winks. 'Only kidding! No harm meant. Give us a minute.'

'Who is your fan?' Gert points towards the graffiti on the motorbike petrol tank three doors down.

'Some smart alec little shit.' Mark steps between Gert and Tiffany to reach the front door. 'And I'll skin the bugger alive if I catch him.' He shoves the key in the lock and disappears into Daniel's family home, scooping junk mail off the floor as he goes.

Tiffany steps forward and peers through the front window. It is piled high with junk; clothes, cardboard boxes, old toys, a bicycle, an ancient PlayStation, a tatty sofa and chairs.

'So your big police machine finds an address for Daniel's dad but not for Daniel,' Tiffany mutters. 'How does that work?'

Gert wonders if it is worth barging in and having a look round.

'You're in luck!' Mark emerges waving a piece of paper. 'There you go. Like I said, look. Fifteen minute walk … Nice kid really, Daniel. I'll tell Wayne you popped by. What were your names again?'

'Tiffany.'

'… and Paul,' Gert adds.

Tiffany glances at Gert, why the false name? Should she have done the same?

'Must have been tough when Daniel's mother went back to Romania,' Gert says.

'What?' Mark pulls the front door shut.

'They must have struggled.'

Mark looks Gert up and down, reappraising his assessment of him. 'Before my time, mate,' he says breezily. 'Only been here six years. Anyway, have a good one.' He spins on his heels, crosses the road and enters a house on the other side.

'That was a waste of time,' Tiffany says.

'Maybe not. What next? Bedsit or garage?'

'Which is closer?'

They walk in silence, Tiffany is still not ready to chat with Gert. The house bricks are sandy yellow colour, not the red colour you see in Whitby. Tiffany knows from checking her phone on the train that it goes on and on like this for miles, houses, shops, a small park, more houses.

A flock of green birds fly overhead, shouting as they go. She stares up in amazement.

'Parakeets, tropical birds. We have them now also in Netherlands,' Gert tells her. 'Tough. Survivors. Like you. You'll have them in Whitby one day.'

'Yeah, OK!' Tiffany snorts. 'Have you seen size of gulls in Whitby? They'd eat these for breakfast.'

'Here we are.' Gert points at the street sign.

The houses on this street are larger but unloved, all divided up into flats and bedsits.

Tiffany is fretting about what she will do if Daniel answers the door. Will he be annoyed at her turning up unannounced? Will he want her to stay? Will Gert give her and Daniel some time alone? What about her train? What about work?

It's the red post box that sets her off. It comes in a rush like a tube train bursting from a tunnel. The parakeets, parked cars, dirty air, rattling footsteps, distant police sirens, all disappear for an instant and Tiffany stops, overwhelmed by the certainty that Daniel posted his letter to her from this very spot and that he really does love her and that she loves him and that nothing on Earth will undo that from now until the end of time.

No matter what. Now and forever, Amen

'Come on. Nearly there,' Gert says gently, his hand briefly on her shoulder.

Behind his back she wipes a tear, hoping he won't turn round and notice.

The large Victorian house is divided into nine small flats and bedsits, with a side entrance opening into a narrow corridor. Squeezing past a bike they reach a musty stairwell where decades of dirt have trudged the threadbare carpet. At the top of the stairs are three doors. The door to number 6 is ajar, the door frame splintered. It's been kicked open. Tiffany's heart sinks.

The room is a mess. Kitchen drawers, cutlery and papers are strewn across the floor. The mattress and bedding have been hauled off the bed, the bed frame is up on its side, clothes hauled out of the wardrobe and dumped.

Tiffany stares dumbly at the back of the door. Four bolts and chains. A deadbolt the same type as the one fitted on the back door at the fish and chip shop in Whitby to prevent break-ins.

He knew they would come. Who would? Lupei? No, he's dead. One of his helpers maybe. Someone like Eric, that doorman at the Pavilion.

The recent visceral memory of a skeletal figure grabbing her ankle and trying to drag her under a van on the Rotterdam ferry. She shivers involuntarily and takes a deep breath to steady her nerves.

On further inspection, the door frame is only damaged in one place. He wasn't inside; the bolts and chains weren't set.

Daniel is smart, he was one step ahead of them.

'He's OK, isn't he?' she says.

No answer. Gert is on his knees rifling through the clothes. 'We're looking for letters, receipts. Travel tickets. Tiffany, are you listening?'

'Sorry Granddad, waste of time. My generation doesn't have that junk,' Tiffany is still staring at the door. 'It's all on our phones.'

'Touché. But we still have to …' Gert's voice drifts to nothing; she is right. He climbs to his feet.

A tap drips a metallic tattoo in the sink. A poster of a black guitarist hangs on the wall behind the sofa, the cushions of which have been ripped open and hurled across the room. A broken acoustic guitar is slumped against a wall like a defeated boxer.

Gert moves to the kitchen area, rummages through the crap on the floor by the sink. Stuff thrown out of the drawers. Buttons, rubber bands, coins, pizza menus, scraps of paper.

Tiffany imagines Daniel playing his guitar.

'Why Romania?' she asks, remembering the conversation from earlier. 'You told that man that Daniel's mum went back to Romania. Why would …'

'Where was Thor Lupei from?' Gert climbs to his feet. 'Where did he take Daniel and Alex when he abducted them? Romania.'

'What's that got to do with Daniel's mum?'

'She's from Romania. I checked.'

'And?'

'What if Daniel meeting Lupei wasn't an accident?'

'WHAT! Daniel didn't decide he were going to Whitby until the day before. But you think Lupei, a man Daniel had never met, somehow planned the whole thing? That's insane!'

'Yeah, maybe you're right,' Gert says cryptically. 'Let's go.'

Gert picks through the mail by the door: catalogues, a letter from the letting agent, leaflets and junk mail. Nothing of value.

They pull the bedsit door shut and head back downstairs. Tiffany is increasingly uneasy. Is Gert trying to protect Daniel, to rescue him, or to catch him?

She is glad to get back out on the street.

'You OK?' Gert has stopped and turned.

'Yes. Is that it? Are we done?'

'No.'

Two minutes later they are behind a row of shops and walking towards a line of lockup garages. A man is waiting for them.

'Don't worry, this is all arranged,' Gert tells Tiffany.

He strides towards the other man, extending a hand. 'Luke, isn't it?'

Luke has the sullen face of a man who keeps getting served food he doesn't like, and the large belly of a man who eats it anyway. He ignores Gert's offer of a handshake. 'Over here.'

Gert and Tiffany follow. Tearing aside the black and yellow crime scene tape that criss-crosses the door of the last garage, Luke produces a key from his jacket pocket and unlocks the two heavy duty and very new padlocks securing the door. The door grinds and shrieks, metal on metal, as he hauls it upwards. Gert and Tiffany step forwards.

'Just you,' the man points at Gert. 'Who's she?'

'My assistant,' Gert replies smoothly.

The man shakes his head. 'She stays outside.'

Gert looks at Tiffany. 'I won't be long,' he reassures her. 'It's OK, Luke is one of the Metropolitan Police's finest.'

Gert steps into the shadows of the lockup. Luke stands at the entrance, arms folded, blocking Tiffany's path. Tiffany stares past him. A powerful torch beam is sweeping about in the lockup. Sounds of stuff being dragged across the concrete floor.

'Hey. Hey!' Luke calls out. 'Don't touch anything.'

'Understood,' Gert's voice echoes. 'Just making a path through to the back.'

Tiffany doesn't like the way the man is leering at her. She thinks about the newspaper clipping Gert showed her in the pub back in Whitby. A 'partially emaciated' man was found in a garage. This garage? She peers into the lockup; it is too bright outside for her eyes to make out what Gert is looking at.

'So the victim, the Rasta, were found here?' she asks, making herself useful. 'You found him?'

Luke ignores her.

'Can you ask him about the Rasta, Gert?' she calls out.

'You ask him.'

'I did.'

'Tell us about the Rasta,' Gert says from within the lockup.

'You've seen the report,' Luke answers, his gaze fixed on Tiffany. His mouth breaks into a smile; it isn't pretty and his eyes aren't joining in.

'Was he known locally?' Gert asks.

The London policeman steps towards the lockup and watches Gert.

Angry at being ignored, Tiffany wanders off round the side of the garage.

'We had a guy in Rotterdam, he lived for six months in a skip before anyone noticed.' Gert continues. 'Except it turned out that a couple of police officers knew all about him. They were blackmailing him. He died and they got fifteen years each for organising his murder. Europol took just …'

'Piss off,' the man snarls. 'Finished in there?'

Gert nods. 'It's so clean in here you might think someone was covering something up.'

Luke steps forward and grabs the garage door. 'OK, pal,

that's it. You've seen enough. You can tell your mates at Europol we're quits.'

Gert makes his way out of the garage and watches the London policeman snap the padlocks back in place and reposition the scene of crime tape.

'And if you're still here in ten minutes I'll arrest you. And your *assistant*.' Luke sneers as he turns towards the girl. 'Shit, where the bloody hell has she gone? Oi! OI!'

No sign of her. A pigeon lurches up into the sky, the pink noise of its wing beats audible for a second. A blackbird shrieks as it shoots out from behind the last garage.

In its wake, Tiffany steps out onto the concrete.

Luke hesitates, wonders briefly if the girl really is a police officer. He decides not: too young, too wet behind the ears. 'I'd go home if I were you,' he advises. 'Getting pally with foreigners doesn't go down well round here.'

'Don't you have to cooperate with other police forces?' Tiffany challenges him.

'That what he's told you? That he's police?' Luke sneers.

Gert stuffs his hands deep in his pockets as he watches the other man swagger off. 'Sorry, Tiffany, I'd convinced myself that they were cooperating. They usually do. I was hoping we might find some evidence but the whole place has been disinfected. They're covering something up.'

Tiffany shrugs and the pair of them head back towards the street.

'What was he saying about you not being a policeman?'

'He didn't say that.'

'He implied it.'

Gert doesn't answer straight away. Has he lost his job? Do the people in Rotterdam not know he is here? Is he working undercover for Europol instead of the harbour police? Tiffany knows he is hiding something from her.

But then she is hiding something from him.

In the narrow space between the garage and the garden wall of a neighbouring property, having pushed through a clump of buddleia branches and waist high nettles, she saw something on the garage wall.

Pulling her hands inside her sleeves to protect them she hauled brambles and ivy away to get a better look.

Beside the side door to the garage, covered in scene of crime tape like the main door, the bricks are covered in graffiti.

She hasn't decided what to make of it and has no intention of telling Gert what she has seen. She can't tell him until she has thought it all through and understood everything, but she knows they were there. All three of them. Daniel, Jordan and Alex. The knowledge that there really is a link between the Rasta's murder and Daniel is scaring her more than she can admit even to herself.

'They're employing me freelance,' Gert says finally. 'To avoid complications.'

None of it is adding up. Tiffany is no longer sure what to believe or who to trust. Can she even trust Daniel?

CHAPTER 10

Messages from Tina
to Miss Tiffany Harrek
Wednesday, 18th January 2017

12:04 Message from Tina
Yer mam's called three times.
Says where are you?
GIF: What can I even say?

13:23 Message from Tina
Dave's rung. Can you do shift
tomorrow? What do I tell him?
GIF: Step your game up, Sir

13:41 Message from Tina
Your bloody uncle now. Says
your mum's upset. Blah blah …
What is it with your family?
GIF: Just make the call, Honey.

14:07 Message from Tina
Just checked. Last train from
London to get back is @ 4.
Doesn't reach Whitby while
10:16 Don't miss it!
GIF: Please NO

CHAPTER 11

West London

Wednesday, 18th January 2017

'One last stop.'

Tiffany looks up from her messages. 'I can't. I'll miss my train.'

'I promise. After this we go to the station. Not the underground. I'll take you to straight to King's Cross. OK?' Gert puts on a winning smile.

Tiffany sighs. 'The train leaves at four.'

'Got it.' Gert turns to the taxi driver. 'Can we do that?'

'Hangar Lane by 3pm and we're OK,' the driver advises.

'Gives us twenty-five minutes. Good. Thanks, Tiff.'

Tiffany texts Tina:

> Yes to Dave. Yes I know last
> train is @ 4pm. Tell me mam
> I'm shopping in Leeds.
> GIF: Sponge Bob Square Pants:
> Don't worry, my friends!

Tiffany is no longer looking where the taxi is going. She is stressed out and has had enough. She wants to be on the train heading back up north. Until this week she has felt safe with Gert. They have a bond, the kind you have when you have faced a traumatic event together and survived. They have saved each other's lives. But now she is conflicted. Gert is abusing her loyalty to him. She cannot and will not betray

Daniel. However bad it looks.

The taxi has stopped.

'Wait here please,' Gert handing the driver a twenty pound note. 'We won't be long.'

Gert has pushed the front doorbell before Tiffany is even out of the car. The door opens straight away to reveal a middle-aged black woman in a blue matron's uniform beneath her coat.

'Mrs Barcelle?' Gert asks.

'He isn't here.'

'Hello, I am Gert Muyskens and this is Tiffany Harrek. We would like to speak with Jordan.'

'I've told you, he's not here.'

'But you know where he is?'

'Far away where no one can reach. Safe.'

'May we come in? It will only take a minute,' Gert smiles.

Janice Barcelle looks from the tall man, who has something of the policeman about him, to the confused-looking young woman with the wavy hair.

'No.'

'I'm a friend of Jordan's,' Tiffany says, finding her stride.

Mrs Barcelle's face says *where would my son meet a northern girl let alone befriend one*?

'We met in Whitby,' Tiffany explains.

The small terraced house is only a few streets along from Wayne Murray's but, unlike Daniel's childhood home, this house is tidy and looked after.

'I knew I shouldn't have opened the door.' She makes a show of checking the time on the silver fob watch pinned to her chest.

'Sorry. I have to get to work.' Her voice is brisk.

'Jordan's friends, Daniel and Alex, have both vanished, Mrs Barcelle, and we're worried that your son might also be in danger,' Gert says.

'And who the hell are you?'

'I'm with Europol,' Gert looks at Tiffany as he says this, warning her with his eyes not to interfere.

'Five minutes.' Jordan's mum opens the front door wide and beckons them inside.

Tiffany and Gert follow her into the front room.

'They've been friends a long time, haven't they?' Gert says.

'Since primary school. Against my better judgement.'

'Do you know if Jordan and Daniel have been in contact?' Gert asks. 'Since Whitby?'

'Told him to stay well away. After what happened to Alex and thing.'

'They don't always do what we ask, do they?' Gert smiles sympathetically. 'Are you aware of the recent murder in a lockup garage round the corner?'

'I'm a relative of the deceased because I'm black. Is that it, Mr Policeman?'

'Not at all,' Gert protests. 'It is simply that the circumstances of his death,' he pauses to pick his words carefully, 'bear some resemblance to the deaths that occurred the weekend that your son, Alex and Daniel were in Whitby.'

'And what is that supposed to mean?'

'The media said that victim found in the garage was an unidentified Rastafarian. Was he known in the black community?'

'Of course he was known but the police, them never ask us. A proud man. Went by the name of Jonah Tallman. Just a small child when he come to England with his parents during Windrush. Nineteen fifties. Then suddenly, two years back, he had a whole heap of trouble. Them tell him he didn't belong in UK. No passport you see. They were going to throw him on a plane back to Jamaica. So he went underground.'

'I'm sorry,' Gert says.

'Not your fault. Where you from?'

'The Netherlands.'

'Like I say, not your fault. And none of it has anything to do with my son, before you ask.'

'Is Jordan all right?' Tiffany asks his mother. 'He saved my life, Mrs Barcelle and I really want to …'

'He's not here, I told you already.'

'I've left messages and tried his mobile but …' Tiffany continues.

'His phone is sitting in that drawer,' Janice points towards the minimalist TV bench across the room. 'And switched off. Ring it all you want, he'll not answer.'

Maybe it is something in Tiffany's eyes; Janice Barcelle sighs softly. 'I'll tell Jordan you called by. If and when. I'll not promise anything. And now I must get to work.'

Jordan's mum stands in the doorway as the taxi drives away. It might look to a neighbour as if she is waving them off but Gert knows she is simply making sure they leave. And she will stand there for five minutes or more, oblivious of the passing traffic, even though she is late for work, wondering why this nightmare has been visited on her son.

Tiffany is as silent as salt in the taxi on the Hangar Lane Gyratory system, inching towards central London. Gert understands. He has been hoping she will open up, but so far nothing.

'You know I have to ask,' he says.

Tiffany turns away from the window briefly and sighs. Her expression tells him he is being unfair.

'It's my job,' he explains.

'Except that it isn't, is it?' she counters. 'No one is paying you to be here.'

He nods slightly, acknowledging that she is correct. 'OK, it isn't work, it's personal. Did Daniel give you any …'

Tiffany looks him in the eye and shakes her head.

She cannot help thinking fleetingly of the letter and the tiny memory card that is sitting unexplored in the little box with her earrings, but she blanks it out and hopes the nosy policeman doesn't notice. She thinks of the graffiti on the lockup garage wall then blocks that out too.

A short smile of resignation, as he raises his hands. 'OK,' he mumbles.

A cyclist is racing along the pavement, overtaking the slowly moving traffic. Gert wonders who occupies the rooms behind the soot-spattered windows of the houses that press against the road. Would anyone choose to breathe this roar rowdy fume-stenched sprawl?

Tiffany is checking the news on her smart phone. In fifty minutes they will have reached King's Cross.

'Tell you what,' Gert says. 'Let's play a game. I suggest things that may or may not be true and all you have to do is indicate when I say something mad. However you like. You don't tell me anything. I do the talking. No promises broken, no confidences …'

Tiffany shakes her head pityingly; her eyes say you never give up do you? Gert senses her resistance softening.

'Your parents voted for Brexit,' he tells her.

No response.

'Young people don't understand why people who have had peaceful lives and have been able to go where they liked should now want to stop their children doing the same.'

Nothing.

'Someone gives you a postage stamp and a pen and asks you to write down everything you love about football. You can't even fill the paper.'

A slight twitch in the corner of her mouth.

'You wear high-heeled shoes sometimes but, if it was up to you, it would be men who had to wear them.'

Is that the trace of a smile at the corners of her eyes?

'Daniel told you he was OK and not to worry.'

She flinches slightly at the abrupt change of subject but remains impassive. She gets it; Gert is giving her a way of communicating without betraying Daniel's trust. It's cheating.

'Things happened in that castle when he was abducted that have changed him and he no longer trusts himself.'

I love you, that's what he told me. And other stuff. None of your business.

'Daniel has seen things he cannot explain and he is returning to the castle to …'

She shakes her head.

Gert pauses. They are on the flyover now with London spread out below and around them. What has Daniel told her to keep to herself?

'He knows that he is a danger to others. A killer.'

Tiffany shakes her head slightly but Gert judges it to be involuntary. She doesn't want to consider the possibility.

The minutes pass. Tiffany stares out at the scenery. Tall apartment blocks rise like stalagmites. A helicopter passes between them as if on a high wire.

'Women prefer circles to squares,' Gert starts again.

'Idiot,' Tiffany laughs.

Gert puts his finger to his lips. 'Keep that to yourself.'

They smile.

'He gave you something.'

She is like an open book. Denial. Hesitation. Recollection. Concealment. Finally a shake of the head. What did Daniel give her? Out of nowhere Gert realises that Daniel is an anagram of Denial. The flyover is dropping back to earth.

Edgware Road. Marylebone Road.

'How long did he ask for?' Gert says.

Tiffany's look says those aren't the rules. Gert stays silent. Euston Station. King's Cross. The taxi pulls up on York Way.

'You'll tell me if Jordan calls?' Gert asks as Tiffany grabs the door handle. He rummages in his jacket pocket. 'I picked this up earlier. Thought you might ...'

He places something in the palm of her right hand. A badly painted eyeball stares up at her. A small torch in the shape of a fish.

It can't be, can it?

The torch she gave Daniel the evening they met. Her selling him chips. Him heading off on foot, in the rain, in the dark. Up the hundred and ninety-nine steps past Whitby Abbey.

'Where?' she asks.

'In the garage. It's the torch you gave him.'

'No. He lost it.' But the coincidence is too much and she dares to dream. She must have told Gert about the torch. Maybe Daniel bought another one. But if he did and if he was in the garage where a dead Rasta man has been found then ...'

'I swear to you, Tiffany, I *will* find him,' Gert says, following her train of thought. 'However long it takes.'

'You think Thor Lupei has him again?'

'People keep telling me Lupei is dead.' He glances at his watch.

Commuters push past the taxi. Tiffany accepts the nightmare isn't over. Will she recognise the danger when it reaches her? Are all the scravir emaciated monsters who lick along the shadows or do some breeze into a room as charmingly as Lupei?

'Do you think Daniel is still in the country?' Her voice is small.

Gert shrugs. 'Your train.'

'He's gone, hasn't he?'

Gert shows Tiffany the time on his watch. It is four minutes to the hour. She pushes open the door and steps out. The station entrance is straight ahead.

'You'll ring me?' she shouts. 'If you hear anything.'

He nods. 'Of course. And you'll ring *me*?'

She purses her lips and turns away.

CHAPTER 12

London

Wednesday, 18th January 2017

Daniel hasn't gone anywhere.

As Tiffany's train heads north it passes just a couple of cold miles from where Daniel is sitting, shoulders hunched, on the edge of a simple iron-framed bed in a homeless shelter in Camden. His hair is wet from having a shower. He has finally stopped shivering.

Resting on his lap are the unbound vellum pages of the book he has killed to keep. The book that holds the key to his future.

If he has one.

'Need company, Dan my man?' RJ sticks his grinning face round the door. Thirties, jeans, long hair, broken glasses, gap tooth smile, parka jacket, and a chess set. RJ is Daniel's roommate and has been at the centre on and off for six months. He is making an effort to take new boy Daniel under his wing. It is hard work.

Daniel snaps the pages shut and stuffs them in his sports bag.

RJ steps into the room. There are three beds: Daniel's, RJ's and a spare one, unoccupied since Monday night when its occupant was turfed out for verbally abusing a member of staff.

'Maybe later?' RJ rattles the pieces in the box.

'Maybe.'

'Did your stuff turn up?'

Daniel shrugs.

'We all know who did it,' RJ says. 'Bloody tea-leaf.'

Daniel looks up.

'I told Kelly,' RJ continues. 'He's also nicked Alfred's fags.'

Daniel says nothing. Is nicking phones the same as nicking fags? Everyone talks crap in the shelter. There are the ones who are so wasted they have no idea what they're saying, the ones who say whatever they think you want to hear, and the conspiracy nuts who genuinely believe whatever shit is put in front of them. Oh, and there's the bastards cynically exploiting everyone else and taking everyone for what they can get.

Just like outside.

RJ is in the trying-to-make-everyone-happy category. Not that it does him any good. Anyone a little bit different gets picked on.

Just like outside.

'You stopping in tonight?'

Daniel shrugs.

'Catch you later. Might be some takers downstairs, eh?' RJ rattles his chess pieces again.

Daniel waits for RJ to have gone then fishes the pages back out of his backpack and gets back to work. In a different world RJ might be a good friend but not here. Not now.

The top page is charred along one edge; how close Jonah Tallman came to destroying this fragment of a book of secrets. Thirty-six pages. In one direction the pages contain dense lines of text, in columns and written in various languages including English, a ledger detailing some eight hundred names and addresses of individuals who received Lupei's help.

Turn the document over and upside down and there are the pages the Rasta quizzed him about in the lockup garage; five sides covered in that jumble of strange letters that continue line after line without paragraphs or breaks of any kind. The letters remain as unintelligible to Daniel now as on the day he stumbled away from the Romanian castle where he had ripped the pages from the large leather-bound book. In truth, he does not even really know which way up the letters should be.

The list of names has not proved any more useful. Three times Daniel has selected a name and address in a bid to find someone who might be motivated to help him. All in London. Three times he has failed; person no longer at this address, or no answer at all.

Daniel is desperate. He is the sorcerer's apprentice, the servant who peered round the curtain that shields human beings from the stuff of our existence. Somehow he must make use of his knowledge or die trying.

He picks a fourth name and address, four miles from Camden.

Human sanity is built upon not looking behind the facade. We look in a mirror and we see a face staring back. Not a skull. Our eyes are almonds, not golf ball-sized gelatinous spheres. Our mouths open, talk, and chew; we pay no thought to the cartilaginous hosepipe behind our epiglottis, the drainpipe that ferries a lumpy puree down to an irregular balloon that pulses an acid soup towards a slippery stretch of plumbing encrusted in a lacework of a thousand blood vessels.

Our bellies are soft palpable surfaces beneath which we occasionally experience hazy discomfort; we do not visualise the snaking sausage coils of shit, the gently rippling detritus trundling towards the puckered sphincter between our legs.

Mention hearts and we do not see a blind sanguinated pumping fist clenching an octopus of veins and arteries in the pits of our chests. We see empathy and romance. A scarlet Valentine.

Brain is the abstract repository of memory, intelligence, reason, language and art, a tool for passing exams; not the wrinkled mousse encased in a bone sandwich and perched on a stick above our shoulders.

In short we are, to ourselves, surfaces into which we insert things and from which things emerge. Everything else is too much information.

But for Daniel the facade has melted. Through the instruction provided him by his captor and master, Thor Lupei, Daniel's consciousness now caresses the curve of his bladder, trails the tributaries of his bronchioles, and surfs the sinews that swing his skeleton. With the deftness of a potter drawing a vase up from a spinning lump of clay, he feels every crevice and nuance of his physical being. He feels, for example, the four hundred grams of muscle he extracted from Jonah's neck, meat that now coats his own muscles like the batter on a fillet of cod or the mucus on a wheezing windpipe.

And he senses this physical reality of flesh and blood in every person he meets.

Humanity is becoming a glorious charnel house.

'Cup of tea, love?'

Daniel jumps, slamming shut the pages of the book a second time and stuffing them into his sport bag in a single movement.

It's Kelly Heaney, a member of staff, standing in the open doorway. A slim red-haired woman with the kind of warm smile and generous spirit that simultaneously makes you glad to be alive and depressed that you haven't earned it.

Kelly is familiar with the body language and behaviour of her clients, from the defeated slouch and drooping shoulders to the extreme possessiveness they display for those few possessions they carry with them. So many broken people.

'I need to go out. Can I do that and still come back?'

'You know the rules, sweetheart. No booze. No drugs.'

'Yeah, understood.' He gives her his sweetest smile. He stands.

'I'll hold the room till ten but after that …'

'I tried to tempt him with the beautiful game,' RJ says, appearing beside Kelly in the doorway, still clutching his chess set. 'It's freezing out there, mate and I still haven't drawn your picture.'

'Football,' Kelly corrects RJ. 'Football's the beautiful game, isn't it, Daniel?'

Daniel shrugs.

'I'll give you a game if you want,' Kelly tells RJ.

Daniel gets up off the bed and grabs his coat and slings his bag over his shoulder. 'Back in a bit.'

Kelly and RJ step aside to let Daniel leave the room.

'Ten o'clock, remember,' she calls out after him.

It's the young ones that get to Kelly most; walking ghosts, futures fading with every sorrow step.

CHAPTER 13

Thurloe Square, Central London

Wednesday, 18th January 2017

At the top of the expensive steps is an expensive front door. Black and encrusted with gleaming brass knockers and knobs.

'Can I help you?'

Framed in the doorway, lit with the manicured perfection of a diva on a West End stage, is a man in a dark suit and tie. Hair slick, nostrils flared. The sharp angled face and hard jawline somehow ring false; like a watch that reads six o'clock when you know it must be past nine. A surgeon's knife has sliced flesh from skull, teased nerves, probed veins and buried all the evidence beneath the hairline.

Over the man's suit an apron sports a cartoon representation of someone's idea of Mr Universe. A bulging hairy chest sporting a huge gold medallion. Below a taut six-pack, and a slender waist that would flatter a wasp, a zebra skin thong poses and bulges suggestively.

The black shoes, as slick shiny as the door, carry distorted reflections of the street, revealing the dreary box-shaped lines of a Range Rover and the skinny young man standing at the top of the steps.

Mr Universe looks disappointed. 'Can I help you?' he asks a second time. Hoping the answer is no.

'I am looking for Mr Jonathan Finch-Porter.'

The raised eyebrow sneers at the young man. Music is playing; the regular thump thump of a bass drum.

'Is he in?'

'Who shall I say is … occupying the porch?'

'Thor Lupei.'

The nostrils flare again. The door starts to close.

'Nice thong, by the way. Makes you look … almost …'
Lost for ideas, Daniel abandons his sentence unfinished.

Has he just had the front door slammed in his face or is
he expected to wait? He can see his breath in the chill air,
interlacing with car fumes from the Cromwell Road. From the
other side of the door a drunken laugh. Daniel shifts foot to
foot.

*Wasted journey. Get back to the shelter before they close.
Too cold for another night on the streets.*

Daniel is stepping back down the expensive steps as the
door swings open behind him, spilling light, creating shadows.

'I'm sorry, Mr Lupei. We cannot find you on the list so I'm
afraid …'

'Dorothy,' shouts a second voice. 'We're still waiting for
those olives. Do I have to prostrate myself and wail like a
Banshee? Who's that?'

'No one. He was just leaving.'

Daniel turns. What list? Behind Mr Universe is a second
man, dressed as Bo Peep. With bouffant orange hair and fat
moustache.

'Who is *this*?' Bo Peep enquires, pointing a dramatic finger.

'Thor Lupei. Apparently.'

'Really? Oh, what fun!'

Daniel is confused. 'Forget it,' he mutters. 'I'll just …'

'Nonsense, let him in,' orders Bo Peep, his pupils so dilated
that Daniel can almost see through to the back of his skull.
'We need a few more bright young things. And fetch those
bloody olives. We're all absolutely parched.' He looks directly
at Daniel. 'Dorothy will find you somewhere to climb into
costume. Toodle Pip.'

A flutter of the fingers and Bo Beep is gone. Dorothy, aka

Mr Universe, sighs theatrically and throws the door wide open.

'I don't know where he picked you up, darling, but I hope he used tweezers.'

Three heavy duty and very shiny brass locks click into place as the door closes behind Daniel. Dorothy's nostrils flare, as if catching the whiff of something disagreeable. The muffled music is louder now. A couple of young women in tutus and carrying trays bearing miniature food and a sugar bowl cross the hall giggling, stilettos clicking on the white marble floor. One knocks on a door. From the other side a male soprano sings *Enter!*

The tutus push open the door and disappear across the threshold.

'Aaah, Cassandra, you little temptress!' someone gushes.

'Woof woof! All mine I believe,' barks another voice.

Dramatic sniffing noises are quickly followed by crazed giggling.

A theatrical cough. Daniel turns.

'You can use this,' Dorothy opens another door. 'To freshen up.' Through the doorway Daniel sees a room painted emerald green. A life-sized swan, wings outstretched, hangs on the wall. 'Shall I take your coat?'

'Yeah, OK.' Daniel slips his sports bag off his shoulder, removes his jacket and hands it over to Dorothy who holds it pinched between forefinger and thumb as if handling a plastic pouch of poodle poop.

Daniel keeps the sports bag. He turns the key in the lock. Has he done the right thing? Should he have turned heel while he had the chance?

The swan on the wall is in fact a porcelain urinal. A garland of naked cherubs flashing their bums frame the mirror. The gold toilet roll holder carries a roll of paper printed in various currencies. The bathroom is a temple to kitsch.

Daniel thinks of Jonah, the Rasta, lying dead in a lockup

garage. Eight miles or a million miles away, take your pick. He thinks of the cardboard boxes that have protected him from hyperthermia the past few days while people here wipe their bums on fake banknotes.

A gentle knock at the door followed by the sound of running steps and wild party laughter.

'Out in a minute,' Daniel calls out.

He uses the urinal. As he washes his hands, he studies his face in the mirror and sees a sucker out of his depth. Is Bo Peep the Jonathan Finch-Porter listed in the ancient pages hidden in his sports bag? Is it possible to hold a quiet chat about Thor Lupei with a man off his face on whacky dust?

Daniel slings his sports bag over his shoulder and unlocks the door, resolved to tell Dorothy or Mr Universe or Captain Thong – whatever his name is - that he wants his jacket back. Leave while there is still time.

The entrance is empty except for one of the blonde waitresses, tutu shimmering and ample cleavage pouting over her bodice. On seeing Daniel her face breaks into a festival of unfettered joy.

'Oh! I love the look. It's so … it's so … she grabs her chin in what she imagines to be a pose that conveys intelligence. 'Got it! It's like … so *NOW!* Clapham Cowboy meets Greenwich Grime. Hyper real, you know? Yay!' She snorts happily and claps her fingertips together. 'Selfie! Selfie!' she chants, pulling a mobile out from somewhere.

She snuggles up close to Daniel and fires off a few shots, her face frozen in her very best selfie rictus. Her false eyelashes have more bristles than a toothbrush. 'Where do you even find a costume like that?' She strokes the side of his face while checking her poses on her phone. The favoured photo gets sent off. 'Yas will love it! Here, give me your bag, Cowboy. I'll take you up.'

He hands over the sports bag he has promised never to let

out of his sight and watches her open a door beneath the stairs.

'It will be quite safe in there,' she coos and he nods stupidly. Ten minutes and he'll be on his way, he tells himself.

He tails the shimmying tutu up a staircase that twists and turns with the grace of a vulture ascending a thermal. He follows her through a set of double doors into a long room thick with hedonism, couples and triples entwined, a few in states of undress, tongues searching and probing, eyes as wide as curiosity, gay and straight, laughing and leering. And at the centre of it all, backlit by strobe lights, is the master of ceremonies, Bo Peep, spread-eagled on a throne of red velour, champagne glass in one hand, vaping vial in the other, exhaling huge scented clouds with the industriousness of a Farringdon Fabric Funk Nite smoke machine.

A waiter is offering Bo Beep a seafood canapé from a silver tray. Bo Beep makes his choice and beams at the waiter.

'Absolutely marvellous! You, Sir, are a gentleman and a scallop.'

He opens his mouth wide to allow the waiter to pop the tartlet in, spots Daniel and beckons him close. Closer.

'I hope you love scrambled eggs.'

Daniel is confused.

'We always have scrambled eggs for breakfast, Darling. As a pick me up.' Bo Peep pouts and winks conspiratorially. 'So, Mr Lupei, what brings you to London and what happened to your lovely pink eyes?'

Daniel glances left and right. So Bo Peep knows that Lupei is, or rather was, albino. Daniel has found his man. Although the room is packed, no one is paying any attention to them. Daniel has to seize the moment or drown in it. 'You're going to help me, Mr Finch-Porter.'

'I am?'

'Because I know things,' Daniel whispers. 'About your transplant. Your pancreas.'

Bo Peep is befuddled, too wasted to call his sheep to the rescue, but he cannot conceal his surprise.

'I just need a few thousand to leave the country.'

'A little bird told me that Thor Lupei is dead.'

'But his memory lingers on.'

'Who are you?'

'It's not important.'

'And I thought you were just another cheap trick, a tawdry little whore. Should I call the police?'

'No, you won't. Did Lupei tell you about the young woman he killed to get you your transplant?'

'How much?'

'This is Lonnie Liston Smith, isn't it? A friend of mine has it all on vinyl. 80s jazz funk. It's OK but I prefer the blues. Like Lupei.'

'How much?'

'Ten thousand,' Daniel suggests. He spots a waitress. 'Want another glass of bubbly, Jonathan? Can I call you Jonathan?

'And then you'll go away?'

A woman in bondage gear is waving from across the room. Bo Peep waves back with his fingertips, making best efforts to muster a smile. Daniel copies the gesture. The woman appears satisfied.

'What would the masterful Thor Lupei want with riff-raff like you?' Bo Peep hisses.

For a brief second Daniel ponders telling Finch-Porter his life story, then changes his mind. Waste of time. Take the money and run.

Finch-Porter reads him like a book. 'Why should I give you anything?'

Daniel grips the older man's shoulder and concentrates. Finch-Porter's eyes grow wide with surprise then terror; he feels it, he feels the power flowing from Daniel's fingertips.

'Who *are* you?'

'Help me out and one day I'll tell you,' Daniel whispers.

Finch-Porter scans the room desperately, no longer seeing the erotic couplings that were weeks in the planning, no longer enjoying the laughter or the jazz funk rhythms, the shifting kaleidoscope of coloured lights, or the aphrodisiac smoke of wafting incense. At last he spots his butler by a window, gently whipping a pair of unidentified buttocks while someone else films everything on their phone.

'Dorothy,' he wails at the top of his voice.

Dorothy aka Mr Universe abandons his flagellation duties and hurries to his master's side. Whispers are exchanged while Daniel looks on.

'No, I *don't* mean that,' Finch-Porter hisses. 'Fetch the money and bring it here. In something discreet.'

'But if we found somewhere quieter ...' Dorothy starts.

'I am not soliciting your opinion, just do as I ask.'

Dorothy clenches his jaw. A tight involuntary shake of the head betrays his anger. He spins on his heel, throws Daniel a glance of utter contempt, and marches off.

Daniel's heart is racing. Can it really be this easy? What has he forgotten? How will he escape if, by an invisible signal, everyone in the room turns on him?

His sports bag. Have they guessed what is in it? Is Dorothy stealing it right now?

Relax. He felt the power you possess, that's why he wants you gone. He won't dare pull a stunt.

Like a concertina, time is stretching and distending. The seconds hang loose like the paper garlands above his head. Where is the sodding money? Why is it taking so long? Surely in a house like this they keep a few thousand quid sitting in a pot? Dorothy's not staggered off to a cashpoint in his zebra skin thong apron for fuck's sake. Why does the room smell of vanilla? Daniel wonders where he would land if he throws himself through the window.

You're on the first floor, dipstick.

Daniel senses Finch-Porter's eyes on him and gets a grip on himself. He stares back insolently and quite deliberately raises his hand, clenches it and unclenches his fingers.

'Did Lupei ever tell you about the scravir?' Daniel asks, leaning forwards a little to ensure that his words are not lost in the hubbub. 'The power to do good is always balanced by … something else.'

Finch-Porter's gaze darts away to Daniel's right. Dorothy appears beside them, carrying a paper carrier bag. Finch-Porter nods and the bag is passed to Daniel.

'Some cakes and sweets for your journey, Darling,' Finch-Porter declaims loudly. 'So sorry you can't stay.'

'Step back,' Daniel tells Dorothy. 'Further.'

When he is satisfied Dorothy is far enough away, and keeping one hand on Finch-Porter's shoulder, Daniel puts the carrier on Finch-Porter's lap and reaches inside. Tucked between various cakes is a single thick wad of banknotes. Fifty pound notes. How many should there be? Fifty times twenty times ten. Two hundred notes. Daniel flicks through them. Takes a few out of the bag. They look real.

'Enjoy whatever shithole country you end up in, darling. And don't send a card or bother coming back. Next time we'll be ready for you,' Finch-Porter says.

'Look after your stolen sweetbreads,' Daniel replies. 'She was a young woman Lupei seduced in a Soho bar. Didn't die straight away. You can survive a few years without a pancreas. But then you knew that didn't you? Must be a comfort being able to buy other people's body parts.'

'Let's leave it there. You've got what you came for. So just fuck off out of my life. If you please. Show him out Dorothy and don't do anything silly, dear, it's only money.'

Finch-Porter turns away. The audience is over. Daniel follows Dorothy's mincing hams towards the door between the coupling bodies and brittle canapés, snorting quiffs and quaffing coves, lickspittles, hangers-on, roués and libertines. He wonders idly how Finch-Porter acquired his millions, where he buys his friends. Does anyone ever earn such wealth, is anyone really worth so much more than the rest of us? On the winding staircase they pass a waitress, carrying another tray of miniature food. Daniel feels his shoes bending the thick pile of the carpet, he absorbs the artworks hanging on the walls, catches the fake scent of summer flowers, and clutches the paper carrier bag to his chest. He can see the front door.

His footsteps ring out as he steps onto the marble floor of the hall.

'You left your coat,' Dorothy observes as he sashays round to the door beneath the stairs.

'And my bag.'

'Of course. Is this it?'

Daniel peers through the open doorway.

Dorothy has his back to the door and is moving various bags around on a shelf. 'There are three here and I'm not entirely …'

Daniel steps forward quickly, keen to retrieve his bag and the precious pages it contains, keen to get out of the house and out onto the street. Is it already too late to reach the safety of his homeless refuge? How long will the tube journey take? He crosses the threshold and peers around Dorothy's shoulder. Still hunched over in front of the bags, Dorothy suddenly pushes Daniel violently to the right. Daniel staggers to regain his balance but his left foot finds not floor but air. He tumbles, realising too late that he is at the top of a flight of stairs. He smacks his shoulder, then his head as he rolls helplessly down into a dark void.

CHAPTER 14

Crow black shadows smother me. Cold as callous kicks in kidneys but not as harsh as on the shivering street. I smell cleaning products and drip dank dark. And something else. Have I pissed myself? Blind as corners, I cannot move. I am not afraid. Does a man who has slept and sulked in a coffin lose the feel for fear?

My shoulder aches, my head throbs as urgently as the lights on a passing ambulance. I can fix that. I think. I am not like before. Nothing is like before.

I can wait.

I sleep.

I am no longer alone. A wafer of light hangs high then vanishes in the envelope of a creaking door. A lacklit afterglow, faint as the sickening sickle moon. Boots whisper and scuff stone steps. Something is kicked, rolls then silence then crashing on a floor. Glass shatters. Steps approaching.

My limbs are bound.

'What do you want?' My voice is hoarse, sandpaper over rough brick.

No answer. Movement disturbs the texture of darkness. Scuffed scratches. For lack of serious input my mind wanders. Disassociated images jumble. The labyrinth beneath a castle. The stiff gait of a scravir hunting on stick thin legs, his fingers reaching opportunistically like the tentacles of an anemone. A carved wooden door springs to life and tries to bite. Something creeps outside my tent. Sniffing the air.

'What do you want?' I repeat.

'A deal.'

I cannot put a face to the voice but feel I should.

I wait.

'I hadn't really understood what Lupei meant to him,' the voice says finally, 'until he whispered why I had to give you the money.'

The sound of a rubber seal popping is accompanied by a flood of directional light. I blink as my eyes adjust. A fridge door behind me perhaps?

I remember now. Tumbling down a set of stairs. That is why my body aches. Straining against my bonds I can just make out rows of shelving units stuffed with shoes, aerosol cans, boxes, suitcases and a tumble of what look like masks.

He leans into view, twisting the wire on a bottle of champagne.

Dorothy.

'So Finch-Porter told you to throw me in the basement and grab back his money? Tell him I want to see him. He has no idea how ...'

'That old tart?' Dorothy laughs. 'Captain Thick as Thursdays? Doesn't even brush his own teeth. Drowning in money he never earned. Anyway, no, you can't see him. He isn't here. Left straight after the party with a couple of his little whores. He'll be on Cable Beach in Nassau with his trotters up.'

The cork pops, smacks the ceiling and falls back to the ground. I try to lift my neck but I am trussed, wrist, ankles, neck, and pelvis.

'The boss has no idea and won't be back for three months. You are here because I decided to keep you here and I have a proposition that will earn you your freedom and earn me a fortune. You see, whatever business you think you are in, you are in the wrong business. Want some bubbly?'

'What I want is to sit up. A shower, clean dry clothes and some food.'

'In which case you'd better shut up and listen.'

PART 2

CHAPTER 15

Europol headquarters, The Hague

Monday, 11th April 2017

Fast Forward.

Antoine Hoek is determined not to rise to the bait; the coffee machine has to be kept clean and if the bastard does not understand that then he is to be pitied.

'I asked you if you ...'

'I *enjoy* cleaning it,' Antoine replies calmly. 'It gives me time to think. The ability to think is useful, don't you agree?'

'You were late again this morning.'

'I make up for it at weekends.'

'Twelve minutes late today. Eleven minutes late two days ago ...'

'You want an investigations specialist or a watch?' Antoine turns to face team leader François Winders.

Winders' face is flushed, Antoine guesses the man drinks too much. With his thin tie tight around his neck, Winders' bald head resembles a red party balloon.

Beyond the kitchen area half a dozen operatives are glued to their computer screens pretending not to be listening to the verbal sparring. The large open plan office is half full today. Winders and Antoine stare each other out; the rapidly rising middle manager and the jaded professional who cannot be bothered to negotiate office politics or the humiliating brown-nosing it necessitates. Insolence rests easily on Antoine's face. Winders cracks first.

'Hervé wants to speak with you.'

'If it's about coffee then …'

'Forget coffee for a couple of minutes. It's a missing person lead. He seems to think you might be interested. A Mr Cappuccino.'

'Ha ha. I am laughing so hard.'

Winders walks away. 'And I want that extradition report on my desk by six.'

Antoine doesn't need the last word. He makes coffee, pours two cups, and strolls over to D Section where he puts one cup in front of Hervé.

'Smells good,' Hervé says without looking up. 'This your famous new blend?'

'Winders says you're itching to see me.'

'And I thought he had short term memory loss.'

'A missing person.'

Hervé shakes his head. 'I couldn't tell him, you know what he's like. No, a London news story has come in and I remembered something you said last December. Take a look.'

Hervé swings his computer screen round. The screen shows an article from the Southwark News website.

Tragic death highlights rise in anorexia

Health professionals have warned that NHS cuts are putting lives at risk following the discovery of a body in a flat in Peckham.

Identified from her driving licence, Nadine Boucher, 25, is believed to have died several weeks ago, her body only being discovered after the alarm was raised by neighbours who complained about a 'foul smell' in the communal hallway.

A source has revealed that the woman had a strangely withered arm that was so thin it was "like an Egyptian mummy, just skin and bone." The source speculated that death was maybe the result of thrombosis caused by a blood clot in the collapsed brachial vein.

"Vulnerable young people are increasingly left isolated and alone in the community. This tragic incident highlights the need for a rethink; we cannot go on like this," said a healthcare worker at King's College Hospital.

Police have released a photo of the young woman and are appealing for friends or relatives to come forward.

'Why me?' Antoine asks.

'Keep reading. The comments.'

majorincident   *7 hrs ago*
It's all hospitals ever do, blame other people. If they had more English speaking staff none of this would happen.

3littlebirds   *8 hrs ago*
Can't believe it. Nadine didn't have a withered arm. This is a cover up. RIP sweetheart.

Antoine's expression changes.

'Aha, I thought that might interest you,' Hervé smiles, reaching down into his backpack. 'And our old friend.'

'Gert?'

'Yes, him.'

Antoine shakes his head. 'Find someone else. Please.'

'Why would we do that?'

'I thought I had finally persuaded him to step away from this in January. Then just a week later he's pestering Scotland Yard, impersonating me, pissing people off. Someone had tipped him off with a lead. I don't want to find him dead in a ditch, OK? He's an obsessive.'

'That's why he's good,' Hervé observes. 'It's a bit late in your career to start worrying about informants.'

'He's not an informant, he's an ex-employee and this is too personal. Gert's a friend, find someone else.'

Hervé stares thoughtfully at Antoine as he sips his coffee. The Frenchman is one of the best analysts in the building, nothing gained from antagonising him.

'You know what? Heaven is missing a barista.' Hervé smiles and places his empty cup on the desk. He claps Antoine on the shoulder. 'You're working on the Paris case, aren't you? Good. Keep me in the loop, OK?'

'Yeah, sure. Thanks, Hervé.'

It is Saturday night and he should be at home playing with his kids. Instead Antoine is still at his workstation having made his apologies and promised to take the whole family to the zoo tomorrow and take his wife Marijke on a romantic evening out (if she sorts out the babysitter).

Night has fallen and cold rain flecks the windows. Antoine has pulled three screens together and is alone with his databases and a fresh pot of this week's star bean: a Yirgacheffe dried in the entire fruit in Southern Ethiopia.

Against his better judgement he has been double-checking Hervé's London news item and deep diving from there. Nothing much he did not already know. Which is a relief. The ugly events of last December still haunt him. He knows that most of his colleagues would write his old friend Gert Muyskens off as delusional, but Antoine has known Gert for years. He's not mad. Like many police officers Gert has a demon on his back, driven by an unquenchable thirst; the desperate need to solve his brother's death. Gert will not stop until he has the answers even though they will not undo the past.

Antoine drums his fingers. Let sleeping dogs lie. But isn't that what everyone says? Isn't that how bad things happen?

Scotland Yard are no help. The pathologist's interim report on Nadine Boucher contains nothing to trigger alarm. A sad but unremarkable death. No evidence of a crime so no resources to investigate it. No break in, no signs of assault, no violent boyfriend, no emergency calls to the scene of a domestic.

You don't set the hounds running until you see the fox.

But no history of anorexia either, no medical record detailing a withered arm, so what really happened to the young woman in Peckham?

The open-plan office is quiet, no sign of life. Antoine leaves the computer monitors on as he takes his dirty cups to the kitchen area then decides to visit the toilets. Five minutes later he's back at his desk, sending Hervé his résumé of his search into the London story along with his recommendation that Gert is kept out of it. He logs out, switches everything off for the night and shoulders his backpack.

Before midnight he is at home, sprawled across the sofa, beer in hand, a mindless chat show on the television and Marijke at his side, asleep phone in hand in the middle of doing her Duolingo Spanish.

Two in the morning, six kilometres away. Gert Muyskens is packing an overnight bag. He's been on sick leave for three months so he doesn't need to tell anyone that he will be in London. There is just a chance that he finally has the useful lead he's been hoping for.

CHAPTER 16

South London

Tuesday, 12th April 2017

The day is warm. Trees are in full leaf. Frisky blackbirds, dreaming of a second brood, exhaust themselves serenading their mate above the thunder of the traffic. A ransomware cyber-attack is causing headaches across the capital.

Fifty minutes after arriving at St Pancras station, Gert steps off the 63 red London bus in Peckham. He strides down St George's Way, blocks of flats on one side and Burgess Park on the other. The flat he is looking for is on Dragon Road. He finds it, presses the intercom button and waits.

'So you knew Nadine well?'

'I still can't believe it, you know I mean?' Charice tugs one of her braids.

Gert nods and smiles sadly, he wants to tell her about the disappearance of his brother Pim and the subsequent discovery of his mutilated body, but the simple act of remembering still brings a welling up of emotions still so raw that he knows his voice will abandon him and he will be unable to speak about it or anything else. He scans the room for something to distract him.

High on the wall, above a large photo of a group of children playing football on a beach, is a novelty clock mounted on an old Stevie Wonder Motown record. Gert guesses the photo was shot in the West Indies.

'You OK?' she asks.

He nods.

The windowsill is thick with potted plants. Charice is staring through the succulent leaves towards the park. 'No offence but why aren't the British police investigating? Why you? I mean what's it got to do with the Netherlands?'

Gert has recovered his composure. 'The newspaper report said she had a withered arm.'

'Rubbish. Her arms were both fine. Thinner than mine, which isn't difficult, but not skinny. Nothing freaky. We used to hang out, go clubs and gym. The girl was fit. You can't lift weights on a withered arm, can you? Sure you don't want a coffee?'

'A glass of water, thank you.' The flat is really warm and Gert, who has travelled through the night, is worried he'll fall asleep.

He follows Charice into her kitchen. 'Did anything strange happen in the weeks before she disappeared? Had she met new people? A disagreement at work? A death in the family?'

'Not to my knowledge,' Charice says, handing him his water and wandering back into the lounge. 'Life was sweet.'

Gert follows her. They sit down at the table.

'Oh.'

'Oh?'

'Well there was one thing. She threw five thousand quid at her nose.'

'Drugs?'

Charice shakes her head and laughs. 'No, no that! A nose job. Which was madness because ... her nose was fine. But some people get like convinced ... know I mean? Five thousand quid. What you could do with that money! You can fly round the world for that.'

'Where did she go for the operation? A private clinic?'

'That was the problem. We argued. I was only looking out for her. At least she didn't go to Thailand or something. She found this place in Central London. On the internet.'

'Do you remember what it was called?'

Charice shakes her head, 'Perfect something. She showed me on her phone. I thought the website looked fake. Random pretty people but not real, like reality television. You know I mean? Anyway she went. Next day, when I heard nothing, I knocked on her door, to check she was cool and to ask if she needed anything. No answer. Same the next day. I'm thinking she's embarrassed about all the swelling and stuff, so I breathe easy a few more days then try again, to check she's OK. And this time she answers.'

Charice pauses. She stares absently up at the clock.

'You must have been relieved.' Gert prompts gently her.

'What? I'm off to work in half an hour by the way.'

'To see she was OK.' Gert ignores the deflection, sensing that Charice's battle is with herself and not with him.

Charice sighs. 'She kept the door on the chain. Opened it up just enough.'

'Young woman alone at night.'

'This was mid-afternoon. And she could see it was me.'

'So how did it look?'

'What?'

'Her nose. Or were the bandages still on?'

'It's just like the crack in the door I'm looking through, you know?' Charice says irritatedly. 'I say *do you need me go shops* and she says no. I say *is everything OK?* and she nods. I say *how's your nose? Does it hurt?* And she says no, the operation was cancelled. She change her mind. Which is mad because I can see her nose is a different shape. No scars or stitches but I swear it's different. So I say *check you later*.'

'And?'

'And that's it,' Charice continues. 'Apart from seeing her across the road from the bus a couple of days later nothing until the news she died.' Charice buries her face in her hands.

'She was fine,' she mumbles through her fingers. 'What they say about her is crap. Nothing wrong with her arm.'

Gert sits and waits then asks quietly, 'Do you know who reported the … who contacted the police, Charice? Was it you?'

'Why would she lie? I should have checked on her.'

'You did.'

'I mean gone inside.' Charice stands up and takes a step towards her front door, signalling that the discussion is over.

'You have a key?'

Charice stares at Gert as she processes what he is saying. 'We gave each other a spare. In case we got locked out. Her family are four hundred miles away. In Scotland.'

He smiles sympathetically.

Three minutes later they are two floors up. The door still carries marks from the police tape. Gert turns the key and pushes the door open. The air is thick with disinfectant but it doesn't quite mask the underlying odour of death. Charice looks fearful and takes two steps back.

'I can't,' she apologises. 'Sorry.'

'She was your friend. You'll notice things I would miss.'

Charice shakes her head but does not walk away. She fights her fear, eyes closed, taking deep breaths.

Gert feels guilty and is about to call it off when the young woman opens her eyes and steps forward, past him and straight into her friend's apartment. Gert follows her.

The kitchen is clean. Crockery on the draining board as if the washing up has just been done. A small orchid sits on the windowsill, tiny white flowers forming a halo. Instinctively, Charice fills a cup from the tap and waters the plant.

The lounge is tidy but Charice senses someone has moved everything and then put it all back. There is a dark stain on the wooden floor and the chairs by the dining table are stacked up. The smell of decay lingers. Charice grabs the table to steady herself. Her eyes drift towards a cork board above the television where a bunch of smiling photographs show her friend in life: at a party, with an older couple, in a park with Charice.

'They've moved everything,' Charice observes. She feels an overwhelming sense that Nadine's spirit is still here. If the policeman weren't with her she would leave immediately.

'Can you see anything that shouldn't be here?'

Charice shrugs.

'Did she have a laptop or a tablet? An address book? Anything on which she might have a record of the operation?'

Charice is about to say no when she remembers. She walks back into the kitchen and opens the tall cupboard beside the fridge. On the inside of the door hangs a calendar.

And there it is. 1st March. 4pm. Perfect Look, Thurloe Square.

'That's it!' she says. 'Where she went for her operation. And something else. The surgeon contacted her. Like the day before. Nadine said he was really fit: expensive clothes, super neat beard, wavy grey hair. The kind of suntan you only get sitting on your yacht, was how she put it. She said it proved they were good at what they did. I said it only proved they were good at ripping people off. That's me; always tactful.'

'So it was a video call, yes?'

'Must have been.'

'Did the guy have a name?'

'Doesn't everyone? Sorry, it's not your fault. The name sounded churchy. Pulpit, Sermon … no, Sanctus. David or Damian Sanctus. Something like that, I'm sure of it.'

Gert nods his thanks. 'I'm taking up your time.' He leaves the kitchen.

'Wait, you still didn't tell me what Nadine has to do with a Dutch cop.'

'I'm looking for a friend. I just hope I'm not too late.'

CHAPTER 17

Kensington, London

Tuesday, 12th April 2017

Gert Muyskens fantasises that on a different day he might have been popping into the Natural History Museum, enjoying a day off with his young family. Lotte wants to see the dinosaurs with her mother. Luuk is going with him to look at insects, especially the gruesome ones that eat dead bodies.

Except Lotte and Luuk don't exist. Gert doesn't have a family, young or otherwise. Or a wife. Or time for a bout of mid-afternoon self-pity. He walks past the museum entrance and on down the Cromwell Road towards the London offices of Perfect Look.

Charice was right, the website is a generic off-the-shelf exercise in anonymity. None of the many photos represent either clients or the owners; they are all readily traceable as coming from photo libraries. The contact information is beyond vague, only a mobile number – now dead - and a reference to *discretion assured at our London offices*.

Gert has checked all this while the 345 bus from Peckham to South Kensington crawled westwards through Brixton and Clapham. As soon as the bus turned north towards the Thames he switched off his phone and removed the battery; no one can track his movements.

Gert steps into the road and turns to stare up at the properties in Thurloe Square. Wrought iron railings painted black, four steps up and a short walk between identical white colonnades to a dozen identical front doors also painted black. Miniature trees in terracotta pots on balconies. Six storeys if you count both basement and attic rooms. A gated park in the centre of the square surrounded by a grey black metalled moat of BMWs, Range Rovers, and Mercedes. A row of £10 million townhouses. If Perfect Look has its offices here then it is discrete to the point of invisibility.

The car horn causes Gert to leap backwards. A black taxicab rips past.

'Hey! Wotcha! You looking for something?'

Gert finds himself face-to-face with a short stocky woman in a blue nylon housecoat. In her sixties, her face somewhat out of step with the flame of pink hair poking out from the side of her headscarf. In her left hand she holds a couple of leads, in her right a plastic bag and a bunch of keys. The dogs at her feet are little larger than hamsters. Gert realises that she has just stepped through the park gate behind him.

The woman tilts her head as if to check he has understood her.

'Yes, sorry. Thank you,' he says. 'I have an appointment at the clinic but I am confused, there isn't a plaque. Perfect Look. Do you know where ...'

'You're not the first to ask, dear. Not so much lately but back in February, March. I said to Bert I should organise tours. Bring in a little extra lolly.'

'So you know where the clinic ...'

'I know where it isn't, if that helps. You see, we're at number 30. You don't need to look at me like that, I didn't say I owned it. Just keep things tidy and fresh for them. They're never here, you see. Like most of the houses. Lords and ladies, rich foreign, stars, slippery ne'er-do-wells, the jet set. We all know each other; the housekeepers and staff. Marjory at number 27, Simon, Tiny Tim, the Blackstones.'

Gert realises this is a performance that could go on all day. 'So Perfect Look?'

'Hold yer horses, I'm getting there.'

One of the tiny dogs barks.

'Oh, do shut up,' the woman hisses, 'or you're both going in a toad-in-the-hole.'

The dogs' brows wrinkle anxiously. Gert has no idea what she is talking about.

'Spoilt little mongrels,' she confides to Gert with a wink. 'Not enough meat on either of them and daft as brushes. Where was I?'

'Perfect Look,' Gert prompts her.

'You foreign?'

'From the Netherlands.'

'Thought so. Can always tell. So, all I can tell you, dear, is that one of the young men who enquired as to the location of your clinic, I saw him later the same day stepping out of a house down the far end. The one with the privet. So, as Doctor Holmes would say, don't spoil the pie for the sake of using yer leftovers. If you follow me.'

Gert resists the temptation to point out that it is Doctor Watson and *Mr* Holmes, and that Sherlock Holmes could not even boil an egg never mind using a culinary metaphor.

The woman is already crossing the road, dragging her dogs behind her. 'Can't miss it, it's the one all shuttered up. Old money. Spends most of his time in the tropics. Come to think of it, he has a butler. Adam, though between you and me he looks more like an Anthea. And far too la-di-da to mix with the likes of us riff-raff.'

The house with the privet is shuttered on the inside, its windows blank and white. Gert knows that to hesitate is to draw attention to yourself. He walks straight up to the front door, rings the bell and rattles the door knocker.

If the woman is right then it is likely that the owner is away and that the butler will open the door.

When it is clear that no-one will answer, Gert walks back

onto the street, opens the side gate that leads down to the basement and hurries down the steps, having closed the gate behind him. Shielded from the gaze of anyone in the street above, he produces his lockpicking tools and grabs the door handle. The door swings open; it wasn't even locked.

He is immediately on high alert, expecting an alarm to kick in.

Nothing.

If Nadine Boucher's flat in Peckham carried a lingering odour, here the smell of death is a slap in the face. He has told himself he is here to rescue Daniel but already he is thick with apprehension . Gert closes the door to ensure that his presence does not attract attention from the street. The door fits snugly into place sealing in the sickly miasma that haunts the air. He is at a crime scene. Behind the shutters the windows are triple-glazed and leak-proof.

Using the torch on his phone Gert finds a light switch.

A large storeroom. Through an archway he can see to the back of the house, and beside this archway are stone steps that lead up into the rest of the building. The walls are lined with shelving units stuffed with shoes, cleaning products, boxes, suitcases, and kitchen equipment.

But the focal point is the object in the centre of the room. The large table appears to have come from a torture chamber, with shackles at all four corners and two candle holders close to where Gert imagines the head of the victim must lie.

Without thinking, Gert reaches into his overnight bag for the vial of peppermint oil he has kept since he occasionally attended autopsies as part of his police detective work. He rubs the oil along his upper lip to mask the smell in the air. He takes short shallow breaths through his mouth to keep the gravebloat stench from fouling his nostrils and dons a pair of latex gloves and scene of crime shoe covers.

Beside the table are a couple of buckets, one of which

contains a puddle of urine. On the floor at the far end of the room at the foot of the steps is a large box overflowing with carnival masks. Gert rummages in the boxes and sees a range of sex toys along with bondage gear.

Stepping past the stone steps and under the arch Gert finds more furniture lined with red or black velvet and fitted with straps, chains and handcuffs. Black bondage costumes hang from a rack, bodices, corsets, latex suits with full face masks, all reinforcing the idea that sex and not plastic surgery are on sale here. Is he in the wrong house or was Nadine Boucher traumatised because she had been conned into attending a sadomasochist orgy? Maybe Charice knew her friend less well than she imagines? Maybe Boucher attended an orgy willingly but met someone there who terrified her or threatened her.

Gert's chain of thought is disrupted by his next discovery. Tucked away beside the clothes rack is a small table on which lies a tray that carries the remains of a meal, a soup bowl, a crust of bread. The bread is stale and dry. He looks back at the torture table. Has someone been kept prisoner here?

Leaving the basement, he climbs the stone steps and reaches a door lined with thick padding, presumably acting as sound insulation. Gert pulls open the door and finds himself in the main hall. For all its opulent marbled splendour, this space carries the heavy miasma of death. It is hard to believe that neighbours and pedestrians on the street have not called the police to complain but, as the housekeeper explained, most of these houses are unoccupied; they are investments and occasional pied-à-terres for the super-rich rather than homes and no doubt designed to prevent any movement of persons, microbes, weather, heat or cold, or odours, in either direction without the express permission of the owners.

If there are birds in the trees of the park outside, their voices cannot be heard indoors. Nor can the traffic.

Gert works quickly and methodically. The emerald-green

downstairs bathroom, a temple to excess with its garish swan-shaped urinal, its plump cherubs gathered round the mirror above the sink and its gold fittings, is empty. So too are a cloakroom and a kitchen, marble lined and fitted with dark mahogany cupboard doors, lit with pencil-thin recessed beams of light. A clutter of dirty coffee cups are clustered in the grey granite sink like limpets awaiting a spring tide. In an office, Gert finds a stack of mail addressed to a Jonathan Finch-Porter: art magazines, hotel brochures, island getaways, Private Eye, a couple of envelopes carrying the crest of the House of Commons.

Before venturing upstairs, Gert opens the door of the vestibule. Unopened mail fans out beneath the letterbox.

As he climbs towards the upper floors, he hears and then sees his first flies. Huge bluebottles, bloated black Zeppelins, meandering lazily.

There are over 7000 species of flies in Europe and many have a nose for death. Gert is tense. This house may be empty. Or maybe not. He is torn between his desire to throw on all the lights and banish the shadows in this shuttered morgue, and the awareness that he might trigger attention he would prefer to avoid. He steps onto the first floor landing. All the doors bar one are closed. Faces leer from oil paintings, a bronze statue seems poised to leap from its pedestal. The thick carpet muffles his shoes.

Through the open doorway, light from the outside world seeps between the slats in the window shutters. The first signs of chaos. An upturned chair, a mess of paper scattered across the floor and, from behind the corner of an imposing desk, an expensive brown brogue pointing at the ceiling.

Up there, that's where you need to look.

Why is the shoe not lying flat?

There's a foot in it.

In a corner of the room, away from the window and beside

a closed set of four bifold room dividing doors, is a hospital screen on casters. Partially visible behind the screen a coat hangs on a hook.

On the desk, a bonsai tree in an olive-green ceramic pot, a plate of biscuits and two coffee cups. Gert daubs an extra smear of peppermint oil on his upper lip.

The body is lying by the window, face up. In phase two; bloated as if about to explode. Alive with maggots. Caucasian. Grey hair gathered in a halo of waves around the head, smart suit, hand-painted silk tie. It is tempting to read an expression of shock in the features but far too late to make such an assumption; death has distorted everything. Nauseous, Gert leans forwards and carefully rifles the pockets, jacket first then trousers. He puts everything on the desk behind him. A key fob bearing four keys and a memory stick, a couple of credit cards in the name of Steven Dixon, an unopened pack of chewing gum, an Equity card in the name of Steven Chard, a small Swiss army knife, and an iPhone. Could this be David Sanctus, the man Nadine Boucher spoke with? Gert switches on the lights and takes a few photos on his phone then slides the items into one of the plastic evidence bags he always carries. He takes further photos of the room and the body.

No sign of robbery. The desk drawers are all shut and so are those of the small filing cabinet beside it.

The desk drawers contain a pencil sharpener, letter paper and envelopes, a magnifying glass, a receipt for curtain cleaning services, holiday cruise brochures, an expensive fountain pen, a bottle of whisky, a DVD remote control and a photograph of two men standing in Thurloe Square in front of the house. One is dressed as Marie Antoinette, complete with powdered wig and handlebar moustache, and the other as a butler, dickie bow, bowler hat, white gloves.

Gert takes a photo and scoops everything back into the drawers.

The filing cabinet is similarly dull: utility bills, a box of Christmas cards containing a printed greeting: "may all your Christmases be white. With best wishes from Jonathan" and a family crest, two poodles rampant above a swirling sash bearing the legend:

'Finch-Porter - Partout Je m'Amuse'.

A couple of auction house catalogues of Art Nouveau collections going under the hammer and a folder containing restaurant menus.

The window is locked. He picks a sheet of paper up off the floor; a small flyer advertising *Perfect Look – where art and medicine embrace*. There is no address or phone number on the flyer; just a few generic photos of beautiful people, a list of procedures, the assurance of total discretion, and an email address.

Gert crosses over to the hospital screen and pulls it back. A blue hospital gown lies like a sloughed snakeskin on the chair. Like the desk, the chair looks expensive. The maroon longline trench coat is in a unisex size but the bra hanging on the next hook seems to confirms the last patient was a woman. Instinctively Gert leans forward to smell both items and to note the sizes. All he gets is peppermint oil and the thick stench of death, if there is a perfume he cannot smell it in this place. He reaches into the coat pockets. A tissue, a receipt from a coffee shop in Elephant and Castle. And that's it. How far is that from Peckham? Gert has no idea.

Why would anyone leave behind their coat and bra? Had the death already occurred when they left? Were they the murderer?

Back on the landing Gert checks the other first floor rooms. A bathroom and, through a pair of carved wooden doors that look Japanese in style, the space beyond the dividing doors in the previous room. It seems set out for a party, decorations hanging from the chandeliers and three chaises longue sofas against the walls. Erotic art sketches line the crimson walls. Half a dozen coffee tables littered with sex toys.

Gert wanders back to the landing. If this is indeed a cosmetic surgery clinic then it is the strangest version of one. Nothing adds up. The last door, oak-panelled like the others, doesn't open. What he took to be a light switch is the button for a lift. He presses the button and waits. There is no noise to suggest a mechanism coming to life and, after a few seconds, he decides to climb the stairs.

For half his life Gert has been drowning in murders and mayhem, investigating the carnage humanity gathers about its skirts. How often have people partied while disaster swirled around them, like the Londoners dancing in the rain-soaked streets while the Great Plague of 1665 rampaged the gutters and alleys? He remembers the news clipping from the Whitby newspaper just a few months ago, where the discovery of emaciated corpses in the street did nothing to quell the public appetite for enjoying the fake gore of a Goth weekend. Have the events in Whitby and his brother Pim's death distorted his capacity to keep a clear head and made him prone to seeing evil where none exists? What if Nadine's death has nothing to do with the mayhem in Whitby? What if this crime scene has nothing to do with either Daniel or the scravir? On the other hand he isn't here by accident; unfortunate incidents don't gather randomly like raindrops on a window.

As on the floor below, there are four doors on the second floor, including the lift. One door, on which hangs a sign reading Theatre – authorised personnel only', is partially open. Gert pushes the door with his foot. The stench increases exponentially.

The room beyond is not an operating theatre. A carpeted floor, a designer sofa in aubergine purple, pretty floral curtains sashed at the windows, a bowl of fruit festering on a dining table. None of which belong in a sterile environment.

He continues to push the door open. A box with flashing light comes into view. An anaesthesia machine. Still switched on. The reservoir bag hangs like a punch ball in a boxing gym. There are bellows, flow meters, vaporisers, a display unit to show breathing rate and pulse.

There is an obstruction on the other side of the door; to see more he will have to cross the threshold.

Twenty years a detective before being shunted away to transport police duties in Rotterdam, Gert has witnessed many crime scenes but he has never become immune to the horror of them. His mouth sharp with bile, he steadies himself and takes a series of photos on his phone.

The air is ringing with flies, the carpet crawling with maggots. In front of him are two operating trolleys, side by side. On the nearer of the two, hanging from the handrails, are two sets of handcuffs.

Gert tries to think about the handcuffs but is distracted by what lies behind the trolleys. Leaning against each other, their backs supported by the wall behind them, are two decomposing bodies. Both Caucasian. At a guess one man would, in life, have been of normal build and height, the other is a head taller and built like a heavyweight boxer. One is in jeans and a t-shirt the other in a shirt and tie, and both are wearing outdoor shoes. The heavier man has his hands on the shoulders of the shorter man. The faces and bodies are both grossly distorted and bloated by the process of death but Gert is convinced that their features register pain and horror. The shorter man's arms are out in front of him, fingers and thumbs bent as if grasping something or maybe pushing it away.

Could an operation have been taking place at the very moment the men met their deaths? If so then what happened to the patient or patients? Could either of these men have been one of the patients or the surgeon? What possible explanation can there be for the presence of two trolleys in a plastic surgery operating theatre? And why the handcuffs?

Could the dead woman Nadine Boucher have been here? Had she witnessed something she should not have seen? Is that her bra and coat downstairs?

He scans the room. No sign of a break-in, no broken windows, no damage to furniture or fittings. Gert crosses towards the bodies, avoiding the damp patch spreading across the carpet. Still wearing the gloves he donned on entering the building, he delicately retrieves items from the bodies, as he did in the room below, and places everything in a second evidence bag. Bank cards, phones, keys.

Behind him the anaesthesia machine bleeps. Gert flinches involuntarily; time to leave.

When eventually the British police do enter the building Gert knows that his fleeting presence will raise further questions for them but that is not his concern for now. Back on the landing he hesitates, he wants to leave but he knows he will only visit this building once. He has no choice.

On the next floor are two large bedrooms, both en-suite. One is submerged in a polite cacophony of Laura Ashley floral prints. The other bedroom is all gold and cream panelling. The bed, large enough for a fairy-tale princess and several overweight suitors, has a carved and gilded wooden bedhead, plum-coloured drop drapes festooned in gold lattice and fleur-de-lys embroidery. The bulging belly bedside tables resemble portly servants on stubby legs. Gert wonders idly whether the master of the house sleeps in a wedding dress.

He runs up the last set of stairs to the attic floor and finds a locked door.

Locks are no match for Gert's toolkit.

Here the décor is simpler and he guesses he must be in the butler's quarters. Kitchenette, a small lounge, bathroom, bedroom and office. The milk in the fridge is two weeks past its sell-by date, the raspberries have a hairy coat, but the spinach and ricotta tortellacio from Camisa in Soho look fine. The bed is made. The wardrobe contains mainly work clothes, dark suits, black socks, two silk dressing gowns, underwear from a shop in the Burlington Arcade on Piccadilly. The mahogany dressing table speaks of a man who loves tidy and expensive; a tortoiseshell comb and brush, an onyx bowl containing three sets of gold cufflinks, a bottle of *Le Parfum de Therese* by Edmond Roudnitska.

But nothing linking to Perfect Look or plastic surgery.

Gert leaves the apartment and races down the first flight of stairs to the third floor. He decides to try the lift again and presses the button. This time the doors open. Gert reels back.

A fourth body.

A black male dressed in surgical gown is slumped forwards, his chin on his chest, smart phone in hand. The lift carpet is sodden with his body fluids. The skin of his face is beginning to slip from the bones. Death hangs thick as sickly-sweet candyfloss. Gert gags. He pushes the body. It tilts and collapses heavily against the rear wall of the lift.

As he leans forwards to prise the phone from the corpse's fingers, Gert notes that, as with the other bodies, there is no obvious sign of any wound or external injury and no blood. Summoning all his mental focus, he takes half a dozen photos on his phone then turns and races down to the main entrance hall, through the door beneath the stairs and down the steps to the basement. One minute later, having removed his latex gloves and overshoes and closed the exterior door behind him, he is back up at street level where he strides purposefully away without looking left or right in case the woman with the hamster-sized dogs is peering from behind her employer's curtains.

CHAPTER 18

Paradigm Shift Café, Rotterdam

Wednesday 13th April 2017

'Most suckers don't know to put a PIN on the iPhone SIM,' Stefan chuckles, slipping the SIM he has retrieved from the phone Gert has handed him into a second iPhone that is lying in front of him on the table.

They are in a booth at the back of the coolest café in the Katenrecht district close by the harbour. The place is empty. It is raining strings outside; the sunny streets of London seem far away and long ago, even though it is only fourteen hours since he caught the Eurostar from Paddington. Gert is dog-tired.

Stefan, beard, ponytail, beanie hat, rust-coloured t-shirt, leather waistcoat and jeans is on his fifth cup of coffee, his spliff still hanging unlit from the corner of his mouth. He is one of Gert's *eyes and ears* in the Katenrecht district.

'My phone's unlocked so all I do is slip in the SIM, grab a SNS code, reset the password and presto presto, she opens like a flower. Beautiful, eh?' Stefan hands the phone and a fourth SIM card to Gert. 'Phone security is bullshit. Shame one of them had brains or I'd have opened them all. You owe me one.'

'I owe you nothing. You are a parasite and a klaploper. I'm saving you from yourself.'

Stefan has never seen the tall policeman look so pre-occupied.

'So who are the lucky sods who lent you their phones?'

'You really don't need to know.'

'Do I keep this one?' Stefan asks cheerily.

Gert holds his other hand out and waits for Stefan to hand over the goods.

'If I let you keep it you'll be found floating face down in the dock in less than a week. Which is tempting offer but no.' Gert stands to leave and drops a couple of banknotes on the table. 'Buy yourself a drink. I'll return this,' he waves Stefan's iPhone in the air, 'when I've finished with it.'

Which doesn't worry Stefan overmuch; he's got dozens of iPhones and has never paid for any of them.

CHAPTER 19

Phone One: Mouthbites message exchanges
Dorothy Makepeace

Leroy Thompson
You're friends on Mouthbites
Anaesthetist and personal fitness trainer

21 JAN 2017 AT 19.13
I hear you so no more CAPITAL
LETTERS OK? Not cool. Checked with
Bonito and he can be here tomorrow
round midday. You sure F-P away for three
months? It is good location but not at any
price. I've got mate who can knock up
website cheap as chips. Kit will be harder.

> 21 JAN 2017 AT 19:23 you wrote:
> NO. NO CONTACTING MATES. Worry
> about kit, I'll sort website. Does Bonito
> come with own gear? We need to be
> able to finish situation off quickly if things
> get out of control.

21 JAN 2017 AT 20:25
B is crossing frontiers, Dorothy Dear. He
says he'll get what he needs in London. Is
patient sleeping happily? We can always
wrap him in clingfilm.

21 JAN 2017 AT 21:03 you wrote:
Need you here at 9am. TAKE THIS
SERIOUSLY. He is DANGEROUS.

22 JAN 2017 At 11:43
Bonito arrived Terminal 2. With you in an
hour.

Holly Broadfingers
You're friends on Mouthbites
Web designer and exomorph

20 JAN 2017 AT 20:04
Found spesh template. Responsive. Funky
carousel and divine animation. Can have
everything ready this time tomorrow. Need
all contact details, pix, biogs etc. to charm
the punters. Where are you setting up? Might
have my nose done too. Chance of a fat
discount? Haha ;-)

20 JAN 2017 AT 20:17 you wrote:
All I want is an email address and
some glam photos of the idle rich.
Perfect smiles, lab coats, cutesy
noses, expensive looking theatre, lots
of white bground, six packs, porn star
cleavage, cupcake butts, all ULTRA
WHOLESOME, blah blah. NO PIX OF
ME. Just copy one of those dreadful
Californian sites.

20 JAN 2017 AT 20:19
Understood. I'll keep my nose out for now.

Cassandra Beamish
You're friends on Mouthbites
Dancer

22 JAN 2017 AT 10:17
(photo of Cassandra in tutu, and low cut strapless bodice)
This what you mean?

> 22 JAN 2017 AT 10:20 you wrote:
> No, Cas, the look is SOPHISTICATED and PROFESSIONAL. Think Cruela Deville meets Angela Merkel. NO THIGHS. NO BUSY BALCONY.

22 JAN 2017 AT 10.33
Boo hoo. Fenella Frump it is then. Did I tell you my mum used to be a receptionist?

> 22 JAN 2017 AT 10.35 you wrote:
> Why am I not surprised?

J F-P
You're friends on Mouthbites
Collector and bon viveur

20 JAN 2017 AT 04:29
Don't forget to cancel flowers from the Vestry. Rufus will arrange pick up of party accessories. Don't be sulky.

20 JAN 2017 AT 08:05 you wrote:
He already picked up yesterday
afternoon. Shall I say flowers from end
April? They like to know.

20 JAN 2017 AT 09:56
End April suits. Pool pump gone again and
Caspian AWOL. Paradise Lost … or spoiled.
Call Timothy. They must have someone …

20 JAN 2017 AT 10:07 you wrote:
Palmdale Pools off Madeira Street in
Nassau usually pretty good. Surely
easier than sending Tim on 9000 mile
round trip?

20 JAN 2017 AT 10:11
Why didn't Adrian think of that? Bless you,
Dorothy. Toodle pip.

25 FEB 2017 AT 13:40
Adrian tells me he's popped round with some
things for me several times but you are never
there. Worried.

25 FEB 2017 AT 14:05 you wrote:
Still here, Sir. A must be calling at 3am,
you know what he is like. He can always
drop package outside basement door
and leave message.

1 MAR 2017 AT 13:04
Another call from Adrian. Says he saw pretty
man leaving house as he parked car. Then

you took package at door and wouldn't let him in. We're all upset. What am I paying you for?

> 1 MAR 2017 AT 17:43 you wrote:
> Someone in to fix plumbing. Downstairs swan leaking and tsunami across floor. Didn't want anyone sliding about. It was dreadful. Afraid I was a little short. I'll send orchid basket and note.

1 MAR 2017 AT 18:20
Prefers vegan chocs. That's why he's such a bear! News from Christie's? Might leave it a couple more weeks if auction is delayed.

> 1 MAR 2017 AT 18:35 you wrote:
> Chocs away. Auction still 25 April.

CHAPTER 20

Phone Two: Mouthbites message exchanges
Leroy Campbell

Bonito
You're friends on Mouthbites
Security consultancy services

20 JAN 2017 AT 08:50
Wim says you called.

> 20 JAN 2017 AT 08:52 you wrote:
> Job in London if you're free. 10 weeks.
> Residential. Safe confinement of
> individual.

20 JAN 2017 AT 08:56
Sounds boring. Is pay good? You still going
to the gym?

> 20 JAN 2017 AT 08:57 you wrote:
> Individual is unique. Secure confinement
> essential. Job linked to a clinic so good
> money. Centre of London so plenty of
> nightlife. And gym has had an upgrade.
> My last contract finished before
> Christmas so I am signed up.

20 JAN 2017 AT 09:45

OK. Malta's dead right now. Will you fix accommodation? I'll have to travel light so need equipment budget. Who is contractor?

20 JAN 2017 AT 13:24 you wrote:
Busy morning … You can doss at mine. Met contractor at a party 2 years ago. See him from time to time. Seems sound. He spotted short-term opportunity to make fortune. We get bonuses.

20 JAN 2017 AT 17:01
I'm in. Call you later.

CHAPTER 21

Phone Three: Mouthbites message exchanges Stephen Chard

Angela Brookes
You're friends on Mouthbites
Actor, University of Life

23 JAN 2017 AT 01:50
Sounds well dodgy. You sure?

> 23 JAN 2017 AT 01:51 you wrote:
> Beats working in that fucking call centre.

23 JAN 2017 AT 01:53
Yeah, but six months in Wormwood Scrubs
might not be so funny.

> 23 JAN 2017 AT 01:56 you wrote:
> I'll be careful. I'm bored BTW. Can I
> come round?

23 JAN 2017 AT 01:57
What? Now?

> 23 JAN 2017 AT 01:59 you wrote:
> I'll be about fifteen minutes.

> 28 JAN 2017 AT 00:12 you wrote:
> Shit. Forgot the time. You still up?

29 JAN 2017 AT 09:40
I was in bed. Asleep. How's it going?

29 JAN 2017 AT 19:03 you wrote:
Just got in. Going good. My name is
Dominic Sanctus. Early 40s. Yacht in
Seychelles. Connoisseur of fine wines.
Specialist in rhinoplasty, boob jobs,
tummy tucks, facelifts, you name it. To
look the part they've given me a clothes
budget and super white dental veneers
(for that million dollar smile) ... and a
hobby! I now love bonsai trees. (which
are actually pretty cool). Oh, and I've
dyed my hair grey. Very sophisticated,
you'll love it!

29 JAN 2017 AT 19:09
For Christ's sake, Stephen, you know sod all
about medicine.

29 JAN 2017 AT 19:13 you wrote:
Panic ye not. I've done my homework.
It's all front of house. To put the
clients at ease. I don't actually use
the circular saws ... or bread knives.
(joke). They just want someone
who can look expensive and sound
reassuring. Quite a lot of them want
to take photos of the staff but we tell
them no. I'm there to give the spiel.
Fifteen years experience and a deep
understanding of facial structure and

anatomy enables us to offer you the
highest standards of accredited services
all linked to an individualised care
plan blah blah. Show them pics of an
operating theatre somewhere and bla
about famous people I have enhanced,
naming no names of course. How we
are harnessing the latest scientific and
technological innovation blah blah and
can promise the finest care before,
during and after surgery. Sorry, post op.

29 JAN 2017 AT 19.30
But you can't, can you? What about the
patients? Who exactly is butchering them
while you spout shit?

29 JAN 2017 AT 20:07 you wrote:
Just had takeaway from Chez
Jules on the High Street. Pretty damn
good IMHO! And yes, OK, fair point.
The skinny guy doing the ops is
actually pretty weird. That's why I am
on contract. He looks like a student
and, get this, they keep him shackled
to a trolley. This big guy called Bonito
(fish tattoos all down one arm) is with
him at all times. Even carries a gun.
Fuck knows what they're doing and
still don't know what makes student so
dangerous. But punters leave happy
enough. TBH you wouldn't even know
the patients had been operated on
except for the changes to shape of

their bodies. I have to put bandages on them before they come round so I see everything. Can honestly say I haven't seen any scars. Even close up.

29 JAN 2017 AT 20:40
That sounds sick or evil or both. I'm worried.

29 JAN 2017 AT 20:43 you wrote:
Shall I come round and comfort you? A quick boob job perhaps?

29 JAN 2017 AT 20:44
Grow up. I'm not joking, Stephen. It's freaking me out and no, you can't come round. Call me when you quit.

16 FEB 2017 AT 20:45 you wrote:
Am I forgiven yet? They're paying me a grand a week and I need someone to spend it with.

19 FEB 2017 AT 19:45 you wrote:
Did you get my message, Angela?

26 FEB 2017 AT 23:56 you wrote:
I know you're still blanking me but I need someone to talk to. I met the surgeon today. Adam (that's the boss) left him in the room with me because they had some kind of emergency downstairs. Someone trying to get into the building I think. So he is asleep on his trolley then suddenly his eyes open and he asks

who I am. I tell him I'm just doing a job. He rattles his shackles and asks what I think about kidnapping. At which point Adam reappears with Bonito and they wheel him out of the room. What do I do?

4 MAR 2017 AT 00:24 you wrote:
Popped round after work but no one in. Where are you? I'm worried what they'll do to me. Today I found out that they keep our mystery man locked in the basement, shackled to a table. Should have told you this next bit earlier, soz. Got the gig because the boss, Adam, hired me a few months ago. It was for a sex party type thing and I didn't want you to do a number. They wanted performers (no, not sex) and he'd seen me in a show at that community theatre in Shepherd's Bush. Anyway, when Adam is not running a plastic surgery clinic, he's a butler. The whole thing runs from this house in Kensington. They must be raking in millions. There's 6, sometimes 9 operations a day and it's been going on for weeks now. I said I wanted to quit and he said no. I really need to speak with you, Angela.

4 MAR 2017 AT 00:34
What did you expect, you bell end? You use your Equity card to take a job pretending to be a surgeon in a cosmetic clinic and now

you're worried that something dodgy is going on? Your mess, you sort it.

> 4 MAR 2017 AT 22.16 you wrote:
> If I don't get out of this alive you need to know this. The prisoner's name is Daniel. I snuck in and asked him this afternoon. Also tried to talk with Adam but he fetched the big bruiser Bonito in to show me his gun. Should I call police?

4 MAR 2017 AT 22.30
Oh yeah, great idea. Don't forget to tell them what you like for breakfast so they can tell the prison. Or the morgue.

CHAPTER 22

Rotterdam, Netherlands

Thursday, 14th April 2017

Gert saves his notes and shuts the laptop. It is the middle of the night. His body is exhausted and it is all he can do to stand up but his mind is racing.

Dorothy Makepeace, aka Adam Allen according to the credit cards in his trouser pockets, has to be the butler.

F-P and J F-P are the same person, Jonathan Finch-Porter the homeowner, for now in the Bahamas struggling with a dodgy swimming pool. Left in January, back in a few days, and in for an ugly surprise.

Actor Stephen Chard, aka Dominic Sanctus, is lying behind the desk on the first floor. Dead. Bonito, the operation's muscle, is up in the operating theatre exchanging body fluids with the butler. Leroy Campbell, anaesthetist, must be the body in the lift.

Two of the cast are missing: Cassandra Beamish, possible exotic dancer and receptionist; and the man Gert is looking for. Daniel.

If Gert has harboured doubts those are now gone; he must put pressure on Tiffany to find out what she is hiding. He types a text:

Hi Tiffany, we have to meet. I now
have proof of what has been
happening. I am sorry it is very bad news.
Daniel is in a bad place and must be helped

or stopped. I need your help. If you are in contact with him please keep this message secret from him. We are both in great danger and have no time to waste.

A small voice in his head warns him that he is in no fit state. The mind plays tricks in the middle of the night, amplifying fears, over-dramatising situations. He is too tired. He should read it again in the morning to check the wording before sending it. He cannot afford to alienate Tiffany.

But the situation is already out of control. Daniel has a three or four week head start. God knows what other horrors have already occurred. He can't wait. He presses send and prays she will finally listen.

There is one more thing to do before he can sleep. Adam Allen's phone also contains an accounting app and a bunch of files, but first things first.

A fresh pot of brew.

An hour later, surfing a caffeine high, Gert has finished. Having forwarded Adam Allen's client database to his email address to view the file on the larger screen of his laptop, he now knows that 300, maybe more, clients passed through the doors of Perfect Look, each paying many thousands of pounds to receive treatment from someone who is possibly becoming one of the most dangerous people on the planet; Daniel Murray.

None of those clients knew how their cosmetic procedures were carried out. None of them would have known there was no operating theatre and no safety net in the event of an emergency.

Dominic Sanctus, the fake surgeon with an Equity card, greeted them at front of house and satisfied their need for a reassuring expert. He soothed them, mouthed meaningless molasses, then handed them over to anaesthetist Campbell who knocked them out so that Daniel could assault them in their sleep. Finally, a smuck-smiled Sanctus would be there to wave them off when they woke up.

Gert has also found the confidentiality agreement barring the clients from disclosing the precise location of the clinic, along with the fees each client paid for their procedures, and the names and photos of the staff.

The range of procedures is dizzying: rhinoplasty, chins, cheeks, breasts, facelifts, brows, eyelids, liposuction, ears, scar removal, buttocks, thighs. How could Daniel, barely out of his teens and totally unqualified, be messing around in people's bodies shifting fat and tweaking muscles and tendons with, presumably, enough competence to perform successful plastic surgery on hundreds of patients? It is insane. Was that the problem for Nadine Boucher? Was she hiding away because something had gone wrong? Had the cartilage in her nose collapsed? Had Daniel destroyed a nerve and left her with a frozen face or no feeling in her cheeks? Had he damaged her liver? How many patients died?

Where is Daniel? Having killed upwards of six people, he has to be found. The killing must stop.

Having sent the bare bones of what he has learned to Antoine's dark web address via the Tor Browser, and grateful that Antoine has kept communications channels open in spite of everything, Gert closes his laptop.

Pre-dawn light seeps through the edges of the blinds as Gert collapses exhausted onto his bed. Head throbbing, ears roaring with tinnitus, neck muscles tight as tension ties, he succumbs to a dreamless sleep.

CHAPTER 23

'Under-eye wrinkle removal and earlobe reconstruction.'

I guess that the patient is in his forties. Receding, dyed ginger hair. Overlarge ear tunnel plugs have left his earlobes hanging as limp as spaghetti hoops. He has big bags under his eyes.

'You've got twenty minutes. We've a busy afternoon.'

I am no longer really listening. Though I am a prisoner I am also the master of my own world. Unwittingly, my captors have created the perfect opportunity for me to hone my skills and realise my potential.

My eyes are closed. It is like static electricity, like when you rub a balloon against your jumper then float it above your arm and watch the hairs spring to attention.

Creierul anticilor

In the primal centre of my brain - medulla oblongata, midbrain and pons - the ember awakens and glows in the wind whisper of another soul. Mind within a mind. I feel the energy in my fingertips. Touchdown onto the patient's skin comes in a rush that overwhelms my senses. A lynx-like leap and I have crossed the void and I am surfing the physical reality of another individual. Every journey is easier than the last. My consciousness follows tiny blood vessels to find a vein then races in a sea of platelets heading for the heart, on through the beating valves and up towards the sleeping face. Reaching the earlobe is like walking to the end of the pier; a sense of narrowing, fragility and extremity. I think the aperture to heal, drawing flesh towards flesh until skin fuses with skin and the hole disappears. Like raindrops coalescing on a windowpane. No scar, no pain. Then shrink the skin, absorbing spare tissue into myself. Following the skin around the back of the skull, sensing ten thousand hair follicles trembling at my passing, I reach the other ear and start again.

I imagine my captor looking down as I work. What does he see? Art, science, medicine, magic? Certainly he understands that the world has changed in ways that Thor Lupei, my master, never did.

For centuries Lupei's bread and butter was organ transplants. Trawling over battlefields removing internal organs from the dying in order to save the lives of princes and a few paupers. Backstreet muggings to snatch a sweetbread. Cynical seductions that ended pre-dawn with the theft of a couple of heart valves.

For Adam, this is the twenty-first century and there are other forces at play. Vanity trumps medicine. Monetise the desire for tighter eyelids, new tits, bum lifts, a chisel jaw, the removal of a few kilos of yellow belly fat, a perky nose job.

The second earlobe restored to its original form, I move on, following the line of the skull to the front of the face. I know what eye bags look like and I can "see" the pockets of fat and the wrinkled skin. I shift half the fat to the upper lip, shrink the skin and remove the bigger wrinkles.

But there is something else; a subtle sense that something is wrong elsewhere in the body. The feeling grows as I fix the second eye bag. I'm learning that bodies are a continuum, a collective, an ecosystem. The bloated eye bags are the product of a blockage; the puffiness is not down to fat alone. I pause to form a picture and sense a radiating pain emanating from down in the abdomen.

I still do not know why he picked me, but in those few days that he spent teaching me his secrets, Lupei spoke to me about pain and the human condition. The scabies that crawls beneath a lifetime's itching skin. The nits and bugs festering in the hair. The wounds that will not heal. Abscesses that eat the face behind rotting teeth. Cancers that are not even identified let alone treated. In Lupei's medieval world a person suffering from kidney stones would accept almost any treatment to alleviate their suffering; even a fist shoved up the anus to allow the 'doctor' to massage the throbbing kidneys from within. Pain was everywhere and on a scale which we simply cannot imagine today.

I feel it here in this body, a hibernating bear stretching stiff-limbed in its slumbers. In a few months this man who thinks only of the selfie trivia of eye bags will be howling in agony as his failing organs abandon him to a dark dystopia.

'He's only fallen asleep.'

The spell is broken. I withdraw from the patient's body in a retreating tide, the top of the thorax, skirting the shoulder and down the arm until finally I step back into my own fingerprints. My chest heaves at the shock of my return. Four deep breaths and I open my eyes.

'What the fuck was that about? What were you doing?'

'He loves it,' Leroy calls out from across the room. 'He's a pervert. Rapes them from the inside. Disgusting bugger.'

I stare back at Adam, still gathering my strength. Soon he will make a slip and I will destroy him. He is smart enough not to let me touch him. Finch-Porter must have put him on his guard; that's why they tie me down and why they keep a gun trained on me but time is on my side. Every operation hones my skills, over three hundred by now. Five to eight operations a day. Where once I struggled to find focus and made stupid mistakes now I am a greyhound at the starting gate, a predator primed and ready.

'While you were working, there were tears rolling down your face,' Adam observes as we wait for the next patient to be wheeled in.

'I could teach you, Dorothy,' I say softly.

He shakes his head. He is no fool.

Neither am I; this venture does not end with my freedom.

'Why were you crying?'

'I see things. That man's problem is not his eyelids, it's his liver. Lupei saved Finch-Porter's life by …'

'Save it. Do I look like Mother Theresa?'

Today's last patient, a woman in her twenties, is pretty and as skinny as I am. She is wheeled in unconscious and positioned beside my trolley. She is here because she is worried her nose is out of proportion with her face. It isn't, it looks absolutely fine. But who am I to say?

She was recommended Perfect Look by a friend who had two kilos of belly fat removed a couple of weeks ago. I remember that one, I was bloated with it for a couple of days until I could offload much of the yellow gunk into the butt cheeks of a stockbroker from Kent who imagined that rounder buttocks would draw in the crowds.

How does this work? Why is the tissue not rejected? Science says it must be but somehow this method Lupei has taught me bypasses all the rules.

The young woman smells of perfume, the same scent Tiffany wore when we walked to the Whitby Pavilion. Emotion wells up.

'Daniel.'

An object prods my shoulder from behind. Adam steps into my line of sight. In the background Bonito has a gun pointing at my face. Adam holds up a board carrying various photos: to the left is the woman's nose from the front, from both sides, from below, from above and, to the right, are photos of another slightly narrower and shorter nose. For which operation she is paying thousands of pounds.

I wonder where Tiffany is right now and what she is doing.

The second prod is calculated to hurt. In an hour I will be back in the basement, having had a quick wash, stretched my legs, studied a cosmetic surgery video (supplied by my gaolers), and eaten something. A night in chains followed by another day at gunpoint.

'Get on with it, Daniel. I have a busy evening.'

My fingertips brush something hard; a small diamond solitaire on her ring finger. I take a deep breath, focus, and invade another body, penetrating its plumbing with effortless ease.

Cleaner arteries, a younger body not yet bruised by the passing of time. Slender, supple, clean. I guess that she does not drink and that she takes regular exercise. I skim beneath the surface of her skin, imagining her in in a garden holding a yoga pose beside a wholesome bowl of natural yoghurt. The muscles of her neck flutter at my passing. Which is a little odd, usually my patients are unresponsive to my presence. Her jawline is firm, her cheeks soft. I feel the tiny almost invisible hairs on her face, soft as Sundays, a mist gathering over a damp lawn at dusk.

Her nose twitches as if ready to sneeze. Something is not right. I work quickly, forming a sense of length and width, skin and cartilage. The foot, the bridge, dorsum nasi, apex, ala nasi, septum. This is my fifth nose, I have studied and learned the terms. A second twitch.

'Leroy. Leroy!' Adam sounds agitated. 'Something wrong here, mate. You sure she's under?'

'I'm on it.' Leroy always calm.

I pause, divide my attention between the patient's body and my own sensory input. I sense Leroy pulling up one of the unconscious woman's eyelids, a flood of sensory data fires her cerebral cortex.

'Should've been enough.'

'Well, it fucking isn't,' Adam snarls. 'Sort it out.'

Footsteps. A door opens and closes. I guess Leroy has left the room.

The patient coughs and splutters.

'Christ. Sort this shit out,' Adam shouts.

With Leroy gone, and Bonito holding the gun, there is no one but Adam to sort anything out.

A groggy female voice burbles. 'Where is the …'

'You have to …' Bonito's voice, baritone Italian.

'Shut the fuck up,' Adam snaps.

A slight jolt to the trolley, as if someone has flinched.

'Shit, shit, shit.' Adam kicks something.

And suddenly there it is. The moment I have spent weeks waiting for. To calm her down while he awaits Leroy's return, Adam has taken the woman's hand and is stroking it gently. He has made the biggest mistake he will ever make.

In a helter-skelter rush I hurl my inner self through her torso towards her right hand and, in a single heave, leap her hand and enter his.

I am rage, destruction, revenge. Adam jerks back, wrestles frantically as he tries to release the patient's hand but it is too late. I am blocking the nerves in his arm; his fingers are locked.

Think pain is history, Adam? Let me medieval your world.

I want to flood his nervous system with wave after wave of agony so rich so full he will beg for death.

I rampage like a rash, siphoning muscle from the young woman's arm to smother Adam's throat, compressing his trachea, choking him. He gasps for breath.

The woman groans.

Bonito steps forward. Has he sensed my involvement? A surge of fear; will he shoot me dead?

But Bonito will not shoot because, in truth, he has never internalised what Adam told him about me. Bonito does not believe in magic or mysterious powers and I am still strapped to the trolley and not even close to Adam. The security man's imagination does not allow him to construct a narrative for what is happening before his eyes. He races round the trolleys, catching Adam and steadying him.

'Alright, mate?' Bonito asks. He waves a foot towards the leg of a chair in an attempt to drag the chair towards him. 'We'll sit you over here. OK? Just hang on in there. You're OK. Almost there.'

The patient rocks back and forth agitatedly on her trolley as the anaesthetic wears off and consciousness returns. Adam slumps forwards, the colour draining from his face. His heart thumps erratically. Bonito grabs Adam's shoulders, lifts him back, off the patient and sits him on the chair. I feel Adam fade away, like a dying flame, his brain activity confused and chaotic. He is still gripping the young woman's hand.

A last flutter and his heart stops. Sensing catastrophe, Bonito puts two fingers to Adam's neck to feel for a pulse and I seize the moment of flesh-to-flesh contact to cross over into him. I am a cornered beast locked in a life-or-death struggle. I turn my head to the side and open my eyes. I see what I have been experiencing through my Creierul anticilor, my primal being; the slumped Adam, the gasping Bonito, and an increasingly agitated patient.

Opening my eyes brings too many sensory distractions, my concentration and focus start to collapse. It is harder work, wading through two bodies to reach a third. As my eyelids close I catch sight of Bonito turning towards me. Our eyes lock. I transfer all my energy to crushing his voice box, taking flesh from the young woman, carrying it through Adam and into Bonito. His legs kick out. His free hand claws at his own throat, trying to clear the obstruction that is suffocating him.

He falls heavily against the wall, dragging a table over with him, scattering papers across the floor. A twitch and he is gone.

A rattle in Adam's throat and he too is gone. I let go of my patient's hand, reopen my eyes and stare up at the ceiling. I feel relief and disgust in equal measure. I don't have to see them; I know they are dead. What have I become? In less than a minute I have killed two men. Men I have every right to despise for enslaving me, abusing me, and obliging me to invade the bodies of others for nothing more than to satisfy their greed. But they were human beings all the same. Perhaps I should be grateful to them for creating the perfect platform for me to hone my talents. I have progressed from hesitant novice, fearful, clumsy and hamstrung by self-doubt and become an adept able to project my consciousness almost effortlessly into another human being. They have gifted me a growing sense of the power that Thor Lupei awakened in me.

Who can I become if I harness all my talent?

A groan brings me back. I turn my head to find myself looking directly into my patient's eyes; both of us still lying on our trolleys.

'Who are you?' she whispers as she takes in the room, the lights, the portrait hanging on the wall of Finch-Porter lounging in orange trunks beside a turquoise sea.

'Help me,' I say. 'Please.'

Her gaze returns to me, drifts downward, sees my wrists shackled to my trolley. Her body arcs in spasm, desperate to escape but not yet fully in control of her motor functions. She sees the two bodies slumped against the wall. Gasps.

How long has Leroy been gone?

'We're both in great danger,' I tell her. 'Help me.'

She shakes her head and pushes herself up into a sitting position, confused at the weakness in one of her arms, which looks painfully thin. She looks towards the door, then behind her at the two bodies, then back at me. Carefully swinging her legs over the edge of the trolley, she keeps as far as possible from the bodies against the wall.

'The keys. In his pockets,' I explain. 'The smaller guy.'

She rummages and find the keys, unlocks one of my handcuffs, drops the keys on my chest and flees the room without saying a word, her hospital gown flapping behind her.

Did I just damage her?

Thirty seconds later I am off the trolley. My wrists and ankles ache as I hobble towards the door without a second glance at the bodies but I am not quite quick enough to avoid trouble. I reach the landing at the precise moment the lift bell pings and the doors open to reveal the anaesthetist, Leroy.

He is even more surprised to see me than I am to see him; it is the first time he has seen me standing. I seize control of the situation, because I have to. Leroy is still doing his double-take as I take three steps towards him.

'They're losing her, they sent me to find out where you had got to,' I lie. 'Do you need any help moving this stuff?' I indicate a stack of imaginary equipment beside him and Leroy turns involuntarily, as people do, to see what I am pointing at.

Before he has a chance to turn back I am on him, hand on his throat, focused on squeezing the arteries in his neck. The power comes easily to me now but the surge is as shocking to me as to him. In my rage my abilities have escalated. In a couple of seconds he is unconscious, crumpling to his knees and falling backwards into the lift. It is all I can do to maintain a grip. He looks up at me ... and is gone.

A slamming door.

A shout rings out. A woman's voice. I descend the stairs; whoever is attacking her could also threaten me.

'Easy mate. Let's talk about it.' The guy with the wavy grey hair is standing by his desk, making calming movements in the air with his hands.

I still have no idea what this man actually does apart from look pretty. In the periphery of my vision the woman is in the corner of the room adjusting her clothes.

'I haven't touched her,' the man mutters. 'Is there a problem upstairs? I'll call Bonito, OK?'

He is scared witless. I step towards him. A woman is crying. She seems familiar. Not the woman from upstairs. Someone else. Where have I seen her?

'It wasn't me. I'm just an actor. OK? Look, these aren't even real teeth.' Chard pulls the veneers out of his mouth. 'I won't breathe a word. Oh, Christ. I'm sorry, man. It's Daniel, isn't it? We were only … I'm just here to put the patients in …'

'Shut the fuck up,' I say.

'Yeah, sorry. Sorry.'

The woman flees the room on high heels. Rushing steps on the stairs. She is a victim like me; like the patients. Let her go. Wavy grey hair man looks to the door then back at me, calculating the odds. We hear a door slam. I realise that I cannot let him go, and he knows it too.

Afterwards I go down to the basement and, ignoring the piss bucket and the table I've been strapped to, I rummage in a shadow corner of the room between the wall and a box of carnival masks, hoping against hope that I am right.

I am!

The first good thing to happen to me for as long as I can remember. My sports bag! Adam, aka Dorothy, aka poisonous little bastard who locked me up and finally got what he deserved, just dumped it in a corner and forgot about it. Finch-Porter's ten thousand pounds is still in there and, at the bottom of the bag beneath my clothes, so are the vellum pages from the castle! I feel a wild exhilaration so intense that I almost scream for joy. Shouldering the bag, I throw open the bolts and locks on the basement door and step outside.

Back in the world again.

The late afternoon air brushes my face. It's warm! Sounds and smells barrage my senses. Birds shout over the traffic rumble, car horns, stiletto footsteps rattling along the pavement. The smell of diesel fumes. Dirty blue sky. A cherry tree in full bloom, its bright petals drifting above the road, catching the sunlight like a bloom of tiny jellyfish. Hyperreality.

I'm free.

CHAPTER 24

London

Thursday, 16th March 2017

For two months my eyes have seen only a few metres, the length of a room, the height of a stairwell. Weak from lack of exercise, I walk past the tube station, no more going underground. I consciously stretch my legs, feeling my body physical filling space and time.

The London air is stale. It always is, no one ever opens the window on this great city, we all just breathe in each other's exhausts, car fumes, farts, early morning mouths. We do it and we get on with it, even on the tube, crammed together close enough to rinse our teeth in each other's spit. We are stoical creatures. Sloane Square is admittedly a posher class of stale: last night's poulet au gratin, the spent gases of Ferraris, diamanté encrusted halitosis. But stale for all that.

Beyond the square the road is heading towards Buckingham Palace. I am euphoric.

I have survived.

My muscles are rust, my body has absorbed and disgorged morsels of flesh, fat and fibres from hundreds of random strangers, but I am stronger, more confident than I could have imagined possible. The future awaits. Everything Thor Lupei once was I can become if I can find the keys to my new life.

'Yo! Daniel, my man! Where have you been? At the shelter everyone said you'd died. You owe me a game.'

And there he is, out of nowhere. Like the unexpected station on a train journey. The extra crisp when you thought you'd finished the packet. RJ, the random guy I played chess with a couple of nights at the homeless shelter before my flawed decision to attempt to squeeze ten thousand quid from Jonathan Finch-Porter.

'Looks like we both had the same idea,' he says, running his fingers through his greasy shoulder-length hair. 'Queen's rich. Big house, thoroughbred horses, private ship, blah blah; she must be good for a few smackers. Please Ma'am, I'm starting a new life and I was wondering if you might …'

'I tried that a few weeks back, RJ. Didn't go so well.'

'What? Her Maj?' Rajesh grabs my arm and spins me round, his eyes wide. 'Scamarama at the palace? You did that? Take a prize from the top shelf, my man; that is big time upfront cojones. How much was she good for?'

I sweep a hand up and down to help him focus on my attire. 'This look like a man who has hit the jackpot?' I ask.

He wrinkles his nose.

'Could be a cover up. I know, it's the new *I ain't got shit* range from Saville Row to throw people off the scent, right? To mingle effortlessly with low life.' He arches an eyebrow. 'I went to the same place for my new jimajams!' He gestures towards his filthy jeans.

'Do you want a coffee?'

'Yeah! All right! Dan the man is in the lolly. The only way is up, baby,' he sings and does a little dance shuffle thing. 'Where are we going, rich boy?'

'To the top. The very top,' I grin.

The very top is a fleapit café in Soho a mile and a half beyond Buckingham Palace. The china teacups are made of polystyrene. So are the cakes. RJ seems unphased, though he has struggled a couple of times along the way when the heel fell off his right boot and had to be banged back into place on the pretty pavements of the Mall.

RJ spills the news from the homeless shelter: who died, who got into drunken brawls, why the red-haired Kelly broke down in tears over a stolen photograph. In return I spin him a load of nonsense about meeting up with an old friend and spending quality time on this houseboat in Camden near London Zoo and being woken up by the roaring lions. He knows it is all bullshit but is too polite to call me out. Everyone in the shelter talks bullshit.

'You like music don't you?' says RJ out of nowhere. Changing the subject. 'Blues, isn't it?'

I must look confused.

'I could tell back at the hostel. Seen you retune the radio at breakfast.

'You don't miss anything, do you?

'Trouble with the blues is it's like Indian music.'

'What?'

RJ is full of surprises.

'No key changes. I like the modulations,' he continues. 'C to A minor then back again. Old style. You know? Old Beatles songs and the Pet Shop Boys. I love them so much I have them on my apple pie, instead of custard.'

Then just as suddenly he goes quiet, staring at a couple laughing at the other side of the café.

'Another cuppa?' I offer in the pause.

RJ nods and shrugs simultaneously like he can take it or leave it. 'Try one of the other cakes, yeah?'

'They were shit, weren't they?' I stand up and head for the counter. As I reach it I hear the café door open. Spinning round, I see RJ heading out. 'Give me a couple of minutes,' I say to the waitress and charge after RJ. 'What was all that about?' I ask him after I have dragged him back inside and seated him at the table.

He stares at his broken boots and for a moment looks like he is about to burst into tears. 'Sorry, man,' he says finally.

'I'm a waste of space. You got better things to do with your mash. Don't spend it on me.'

I catch the waitress' eye. 'Two coffees and two croissants.'

'Were you born here?' I ask RJ.

In his eyes is the pain of a thousand accusations: taking our jobs, abusing our women, go back to your own country …

'I don't mean that.'

His eyes tell me he doesn't believe me.

'What I'm trying to say is, *I've* only ever known London. Except for once, a few months back when I've gone to Whitby, this town up north. Practically at the North Pole. It's like all boats and …'

Why do I say nothing about my time locked up in a castle in Romania?

The waitress arrives with the coffee and croissants. Out of nowhere I remember the sound of a woman's stilettos across the stone floor. The waitress at the party. She took my bag. Not a victim at all. And I let her go. Damn.

RJ is talking.

'Sorry? I missed that.'

'My uncle took me to Whitby. Dracula, fish and chips, kids fishing for crabs in the harbour. Like Brighton but darker. What?' RJ looks disappointed. 'You can't believe that I had a life before this shit?'

'It's not that,' I start but cannot think of anything else. It is that. 'What I mean, RJ, is that I have to leave. Get away. Out of London. Out of the UK. I'm in a heap of shit.'

I open my sports bag and give RJ a glimpse of the wad of money nestling in the paper carrier bag. His eyes come out on stalks.

'I know exactly who you need to meet!' he says, getting to his feet and heading for the door.

'The cakes, RJ. The bloody cakes!'

'Forget them. The world is full of cakes, Dan my man!'

EVENING NEWS

Traffic signals not to blame for rush hour death of pedestrian outside Natural History Museum
By Art Holmwood - 23 hrs ago

Londoner, Cassandra Beamish from Finchley, was hit by a westbound bus on the Cromwell Road right outside the Natural History Museum at around 17.45 on 16th March. She died instantly.

South Kensington police said: 'a phone recovered at the scene suggests the woman was texting as she stepped the onto the road. We would remind everyone to avoid using mobile devices while crossing busy streets.'

The tragic accident during the afternoon rush hour led to two-hour delays for traffic heading west. Unconfirmed reports suggest that the recovered phone may have carried an unsent text indicating the woman had been attempting to catch a No.74 bus heading east towards Baker Street. The same message also showed the woman was concerned for her life having (allegedly) just witnessed two murders in the vicinity.

Police have declined to comment.

CHAPTER 25

Rotterdam, Netherlands

Thursday, 14th April 2017

Gert wakes up sprawled across his bed still in his clothes. His head is buzzing, humming.

No, that's not it. His phone is ringing, somewhere beneath the carpet of scribbled papers scattered around his torso like autumn leaves. What time is it? What day is it? He isn't even sure what country he is in until he recognizes his own bedroom.

'Yes?'

'It's like waking the dead,' says a familiar voice.

'More than you could ever know,' Gert answers. 'Antoine.'

'Do you want to tell me all about it?'

Gert swings his legs over the side of the bed and staggers across the room to open the curtains. The bright light hurts.

'I'm guessing you need fresh air. See you at Paradigm Shift. Forty minutes?' Antoine says at the other end of the phone.

'You know Paradigm Shift?' Gert asks.

'Unless you want to avoid your stooge Stefan.'

'Why would I want to …'

'Don't be late.'

'So the bastards have won?'

'If that's how you see it.' Antoine sighs.

An uncomfortable silence hangs heavy between the two men in the otherwise empty coffee bar. Rain flecks the windows. Cool Runnings by Bunny Wailer is playing on the sound system.

A Saab pulls up outside. The woman in the purple coat who was leaving as Gert came in, and has since been standing on the pavement, climbs into the back of the car. It heads off towards the city.

'You've got a choice,' Antoine continues. 'You walk away and rebuild your life or …'

'I've been trying to find out what happened. You've set me up.'

'I have not.'

'So why send me all that stuff?'

'What stuff?'

The two men stare at each other.

'The news clippings.'

Alarm bells are screaming in Antoine's head.

'I haven't sent you anything. Nor did I tell you to go to London and pretend you are a serving police officer, or suggest that it is OK to break into buildings and trample around crime scenes. You're looking at five to ten years. Do you know how the other inmates treat police officers?'

'Make your mind up. I'm a civilian remember?'

'Don't get cute. I'm your friend and God knows you need one right now. What did you receive and how?'

'Same as last time. Dark web account.'

'Last time?'

'The clipping about the Rasta in the garage.'

Antoine shakes his head. 'Someone is way ahead of us. Shit, Gert! I've been telling you to walk away. For months.'

Gert's knees are bouncing up and down, almost knocking over the low table between him and Antoine. A cup tips over, spilling coffee across the tabletop. Antoine mops up the mess with a paper napkin.

'So I just go back to counting passengers on and off the ferries?'

'No. You're sacked from that too. Just pack your bags and

go. While you still can. If you don't, you will be arrested.'

Gert's eyes are black with fury. 'So I find Daniel and proof of how dangerous he has become and …'

'STOP!'

'It's Hervé, isn't it? It must be. Maybe a member of his family …'

Antoine gets to his feet and slaps a twenty euro note on the table beside his empty coffee cup. 'I have to get back. Good luck, Gert. There is a new life waiting, if you're smart. Buy a plane ticket and fuck off. You've 24 hours. I'm done.'

The front door swings back slowly on its piston.

Gert's phone vibrates. A message from Tiffany.

Message from Tiffany Harrek
to Gert Muyskens
14th April 2017 at 08.13
Please stop. Not interested.
I don't believe you. I can't take
any more of this crap about Daniel.

Gert Muyskens is a big man, a proud man. He hasn't cried since discovering Pim's body in a skip over thirty years ago but now, with his promise to bring his killer to justice in tatters, with everyone turning their backs, the strain and the stress overwhelm him. The waitress stacking cups behind the counter worries whether she will be late for her evening yoga class.

CHAPTER 26

Mikăbrukóczi Castle, Romania

17th April 2017

Half a dozen huge logs are spitting and crackling in an open fire large enough to roast an ox. The flames from the fire and a dozen beeswax candles positioned around the Great Hall cast shifting light across the tapestries that hang on the stone walls. The air is thick with the sweet honey of the candles and the aromas of the burning logs; cherry and oak.

The large wingback armchairs gathered around the fire are empty but beside them is a large bed. While the hall and much of its furnishings belong in older and darker times, the bed is the very essence of modernity as are the machines and monitoring equipment positioned alongside it.

An early electric guitar blues gurgles from the sound system hidden behind a tapestry, the cadences rising and falling like a murder of rooks chasing and tumbling in a chill sky.

The frail finger of a hand that rests upon the mattress taps time imperceptibly to the music. Plasma leaks from horrific burns, the body so raw it hums with pain. The patient has no lips. For months now he has not slept for more than twenty minutes at a time, enduring a litany of nightmares interspersed with the misery of consciousness. With eighty-five percent of his skin burned it is a miracle that he is alive at all.

Occasionally the crackle of the burning logs alarms him, reminding him of bones drybrittle snapping in the flames in the oubliette, but he no longer smells the cooking bodies. In truth he smells nothing at all in the stump that was once a nose.

A squeak of heavy hinges. The carved oak doors at the far end of the hall swing open to reveal a large woman with an aquiline nose and a raptor's eyes. Her starched white uniform rustles as she strides briskly towards the bed, clipboard in hand, her shoes clicking a tattoo across the stone floor. At her side is a nurse, the pilot fish accompanying a shark.

The doctor leans forwards and talks into what is left of the patient's ear. Only she is close enough to hear the response, her ear almost touching the patient's face. Words so weak, so slow, so guttural and so fragmentary they barely make a whisper. She listens carefully, draws back, shakes her head. Knits her brows. Leans in and listens again, scribbles the instructions on her clipboard then reads them back to the patient for confirmation that she has understood correctly.

Radu Felini, the staff manager, waits in the open doorway, stroking his grey moustache, a nervous tic fluttering beneath his left eye. Pepene, scravir, stands beside him. The doctor beckons Felini forward.

'He wants to talk to you but keep it brief,' she advises Felini. 'He is very frail and the chances of survival are still very low. The eyelid grafts appear to be stabilising but I need more cadaver skin.'

Felini leans forwards. 'I am here, master.'

The eyelids open painfully to reveal bloodshot eyes.

It hurts Felini to see the boss like this. In other circumstances he would surely be healing himself but for now he is more vulnerable than a newborn baby with cholera.

Lupei is trying to speak.

Felini leans right in close.

'Ha you oun Danier?'

'No, but we have some news,' Felini answers.

'Dell ne.'

Felini explains what he has learned and stops only when the doctor intervenes to tell him to stop. Felini steps back and watches as the doctor checks the various monitors by the bed.

'Hind he.'

Felini cannot make sense of the guttural sounds.

The doctor leans and asks the patient to repeat what he said. He then turns to Felini.

'He says find him.'

Felini nods.

PART 3

March 2020

CHAPTER 27

Europol headquarters, Rotterdam

4th March 2020

A grey grim geometry that takes the fun out of functional, Europol's Rotterdam headquarters makes no effort to soften its image. The stacked concrete boxes occupy space; that is the best you can say. A fortress with a job to do.

Airport terminals have more charisma.

'Sorry to leave you in no man's land.' Antoine strides forwards hand outstretched. 'We're up to our eyeballs in pandemic scenarios.'

Gert waves away the apology. 'No worries. I'm warm and dry. It's raining cups and saucers out there! I had forgotten how miserable winter is in Rotterdam.'

'How have you been? What's with the haircut? You look tanned. And fit!' Antoine steps back to look at Gert. 'My God, are you living in a gym! You look great!'

'Sorry, you are ...?' Gert turns to the tall and elegantly-dressed young black woman who has followed Antoine through the doors and is now standing beside him.

'Floriane Onyemachi,' she smiles. 'It's OK. I'm not coming with you. Antoine said he was meeting an old friend and I was nosy. Another coffee connoisseur?'

Gert shakes his head. 'Onyemachi. That's a Nigerian name, isn't it?'

She smiles again, impressed.

'I just about know the difference between an espresso and a latte,' Gert grins, 'but beyond that ...'

'Don't listen to him,' Antoine laughs. 'He could be a Q grader.'

Floriane arches an eyebrow.

'Professional coffee taster,' Gert explains. He slaps Antoine on the shoulder. 'This guy talks such shit. Anyway, let's go.'

By the time he returns to work, nearly two hours later, Antoine is exhausted.

The lift doors open. As he steps out he collides with a wall of files coming in the opposite direction. Folders flap open like butterflies and a hundred pages float to the floor.

'Do you know how long it took me to ...'

Antoine drops to his knees to help Floriane gather her papers.

'So how was Captain Q Tip?'

'It's Q grader,' Antoine corrects her, 'and to answer your question, tiring. You know what it's like with obsessives.'

'We're all obsessives, it's in the job description. He used to work here, right? Seems a nice guy. You're dripping on my papers by the way.'

'Yeah, sorry.' Antoine runs a hand through his wet hair. 'Still raining. Gert was a policeman. Got transferred here then demoted to harbour police when he burnt out. Brother died when they were teens, joined the police to put the world right.'

'Not that unusual,' Floriane takes the papers from Antoine, puts them on an unoccupied desk and starts refilling her folders.

'Right. Except this had some weird angle to it. A music festival. Brother found emaciated in a skip. It all kicked off again three years ago and I think it was my fault. I was trawling data and came across reports of a number of emaciated corpses found at a Goth festival in Whitby. It's a small town in the UK and ...'

'Correct. It's in Yorkshire. I've been there, it's beautiful,' she interjects. 'It's where the Dracula story started, right?'

'I told Gert and he packed his bags and went. Didn't even tell his boss. Came back with this mad story about flesh-sucking evil. I shouldn't have encouraged him. There were a bunch of students at the festival, some died and two were kidnapped. A couple of police also died, half a dozen vagrants and a pathologist. Anyway we eventually found one of the missing students in Romania, wandering about on a mountain. Murray. Daniel Murray.'

'And?'

'And nothing. The whole thing came to an end. Gert disappeared into a bottle. Whitby police interviewed Murray and released him. A couple of months later we got a tip off, can't remember who from. I didn't tell Gert but someone did. Off he went again. To London this time. Annoyed the local police. Then again a few months later. More bodies, in an illegal cosmetic surgery clinic. Gert convinced himself that Daniel had become possessed by evil. Only this time he was treading on too many toes; the local metropolitan police demanded that Gert was put in jail for impersonating a police officer.' Antoine pauses to take a breath. 'So I told him to go, for the twentieth time, to build a new life far away. And finally he listened! Fast-forward three years and here he is, tanned, ten kilos lighter and looking better than he has in years. He's setting up a diving business, even though the locals tell him it isn't a great place to do it. Typical Gert. In Suriname, which is in South America near …'

'I know where Suriname is,' Floriane interjects. 'And I know it was a Dutch colony before you tell me.'

Antoine takes a breath, know-alls can be tiring.

'Great, so you'll know that there are two hundred times fewer people per square kilometre there than there are in Netherlands. It's a heaven for sleepy laid-back people. Anyway, Gert is catching a flight back to Latin America tomorrow. He's only here to clear out his flat and put it on the market and to say his goodbyes to Europe. It was good to see him even though he is still an obsessive. I now know more about turtles and sea grass than any human being ever needed to know.'

Floriane laughs. 'Sounds like you need a coffee.'

'Pass. I had four at the café and I'm already on the ceiling. What are you working on?'

'That trafficking case. They're using luxury cars now. Not lorries. Twelve people crammed into a Mercedes, three in the boot, can you believe it?'

'I'll believe anything. Except Sweden winning the Euros.'

'I thought they had excellent bands.'

'The football not the song contest.'

Floriane gathers up the folders. 'Oops! Better get going.'

'You know what's amazing?' Antoine calls out as she walks away.

'Go on.'

'He told me a joke. Why do turtles sleep all day?'

Floriane shrugs.

'They're noc-turtle.'

'Ouch!' Floriane winces.

'Yeah,' Antoine grins. 'But the first time since I've known him - fifteen years - Gert is happy and telling bad jokes!'

Rain smears the windows as afternoon drifts by in a deluge of spreadsheets, a minor diplomatic incident involving speeding tickets, and an arrest warrant. The coffee high has gone. Antoine is dead on his feet. He goes online and orders a pizza and is pulling on his jacket when he feels the tap on his shoulder.

'Guess what?'

'We're moving offices to a beach hut on the Cote d'Azur?'

'Wrong. I've found something very interesting.'

'That's great, Floriane. Can it wait until after my Mexican hot with added peppers?'

'You bastards. You always assume you're the only ones who can …'

'It's not you. It's me. I'm sorry. What's it about? The contraband case? Do you want to share my pizza?'

'No. I have to go. It's my niece's art exhibition open day. She's had a tough time these past few months so I want to be there for her. Anyway, rewind a few hours, that student, the one who went missing. What was his name?'

Antoine is confused.

'The one who turned up in Romania,' she says. 'David? Damian? Donald?'

'Ah, OK. Gert's evil Goths.'

'Correct. Can you give your friend this?' Floriane fishes a report from her bag and flicks through the pages. 'Here you go. Daniel Murray, wasn't it? Good news. He has been arrested in Briançon, France, close to the Italian border.'

'Not a good idea, Floriane.' It winds him up the way she says *correct* like she is marking his homework.

'Why?'

'Gert has finally sorted out his shit. The last thing he needs is to be dragged back to …'

'Isn't that for *him* to decide?'

'I'm not doing it. Just put it back where you found it.' Antoine makes a show of looking at his watch. 'Ancient history. Look, I have to go collect my pizza. See you tomorrow.'

Antoine heads towards the lifts, leaving Floriane rooted to the spot, report in hand, feeling like an idiot.

'Allô, oui. Commissariat de police.'

'Ah bonjour. Floriane Onyemachi, Europol.' She slips into French as effortlessly as she speaks English, Dutch, German, Italian, and her mother tongue of Igbo. 'Le Commandant Marinette Proust s'il vous plaît.'

Seconds later the captain answers the phone. Floriane

wonders idly what the weather is like in Briançon, a small town of 11,000 people in the French Alps close to the Italian Border.

'If you think we're simply handing this case over to Europol I can tell you now that …' The voice at the other end of the line sounds tired and irritated.

'Hello Commandant. I am sitting here with your report and I have a couple of quick questions.' Floriane speaks briskly and authoritatively.

'Go on.'

'You are holding a British National; Daniel Murray on charges of human smuggling.'

'And?'

'We need his photo and a transcript of any interviews you have conducted.'

'Why is Europol interested?' Proust fires back.

'Missing person dating back to 2017.'

'Unless we go back to the judge we have to release him midday tomorrow. Send someone down.'

'The photos?'

'I told you, send someone down.'

'Got it. Let me talk with colleagues and get back to you. Thanks, Commandant. By the way what have you done with the immigrants he had hidden in the car?'

'Only one survived the fire. He has been sent to the hospital in Gap. From there he will go to a CRA, Centre de Retention Administrative. If he survives the next twenty-four hours.'

'I know what CRA stands for, thanks.'

Floriane sits at her desk for a minute, drumming her fingers, lost in thought. If Antoine isn't interested, is there any point in pursuing the matter? Her phone pings. Her sister reminding her not to be late to the art exhibition.

CHAPTER 28

Schiphol airport

5th March 2020

Kilometres of corridors. A limbo land of waiting. Rows of individual plastic seats, designed with armrests to prevent anyone from sprawling out. Dozens of shops selling crap you don't need at ten times the normal price.

Gert has visited every shop within a kilometre at least three times, resisted the executive toys at €140 each, and the watches that cost more than time itself, but has fallen for the three fun-sized gouda cheeses – red orange and green like a traffic light – all in a festive sleeve for €33. Like the ones he gave Tiffany, three years ago he realises. A taste of the old country to take with him back to Latin America. He is on his fifth coffee in his third café.

It is 07:43.

His flight to Paramaribo leaves at 09.25. He scrolls his phone, half-reading news stories about viruses and international travel. In his mind he is already back on Galibi beach, sitting in the moonlight beside a leatherback turtle as she lays her eggs. They can shove their pandemic.

When his phone vibrates he almost drops it.

A text.

> Flo On
> Important news. Ring me

Flo On? Who? Floriane, that woman who appeared beside

Antoine at Europol, perhaps? If it is her, it cannot be personal. If it's not her then it's a wrong number. If it *is* her it is still a wrong number; Antoine must have told her he is no longer a cop.

He ignores the text, stares out of the window at a plane taxiing outside, breaks the fancy packaging and the wax and starts eating the green gouda.

The gate number for his flight appears on the screen above him. Gert grabs his hand luggage, shoves the other cheeses into the front pocket, and heads off to find gate E24.

That quiet buzz of anticipation from a hundred people who are sort of still in Schiphol airport and sort of already on their way. The desk by the gate is unoccupied. Not surprising; departure still over an hour away.

Why call flights so early?

Gert wishes he had bought a newspaper. Sure, you can get all the stories on your phone but there is something tangible in holding sheets of paper. The rustle. The physical geography of turning real pages. Is he becoming an old fart?

The woman sitting beside him is snoring. He returns to café three, orders a glass of orange juice and reads the menu six times, including the small print.

It was good to see Antoine one last time but he shouldn't have gone.

'Mr Gert Muyskens to Gate E24 please,' says the tannoy speaker.

He glances at his watch. Still early. They never board sooner than thirty minutes before departure. Damn the waiting. And the orange juice. He'll have a sixth coffee. An espresso. His phone vibrates in his pocket. He ignores it and takes his coffee back to his seat. He sips from the tiny white cup with his eyes closed, it may not be a prize-winning blend but it's not bad. Funny to think he has friends for him in a forest clearing over seven thousand kilometres away.

'Mr Muyskens?' says a voice at his back.

He turns.

'Your flight is boarding, Sir,' smiles a bright-eyed blond woman in a sky blue KLM uniform. She is holding a clipboard. 'It's a little early but we are hoping to take off ahead of the delays that are forecast for later on.'

'OK. I finish my coffee, right?'

She ticks him off her list and is already thinking about the next person.

Gert returns to the gate and joins the queue, head buzzing with caffeine.

'Do you not check your phone, Mr Muyskens?' says a voice behind him.

'I am *in* the bloody queue.' he says exasperatedly. 'I told you, I'm finishing my coffee. What more do you want?'

'We met at Europol.'

He turns. It isn't the KLM woman.

'Floriane Onyemachi. I have left you a dozen messages.'

'I know who you are. Whatever it is, I am not interested,' he snaps. 'I am about to board a flight home.'

'We've found Daniel Murray.'

Thirty-two minutes later they are taking off from Amsterdam Schiphol in a small jet, destination Aérodrome de St-Crépin, in the Hautes-Alpes of southern France. 1100km. Flight time of two hours.

Floriane has tried small talk but Gert is distracted. She has explained the bare bones: apprehended on the French-Italian border, between Montgenèvre and Claviere, running away from a crashed vehicle found in flames. A Mercedes E-Class Saloon containing eight bodies, including two in the boot. Positive identification found in backpack. Murray denies having been in the vehicle and claims to have been 'out jogging'. Lack of evidence means he will be released at midday local time.

Unless something turns up.

Gert stares blankly out of the window, watching France slip by. Like the plane, he is on autopilot. At least there is decent legroom, unlike on the Airbus back to Suriname.

The flight I should be on.

He barely registers the tap on his shoulder, takes the glass of water and drinks it as automatically as a houseplant. The humwoosh of the jet cocoons him in emptiness.

Someone removes the empty glass from between his fingers.

So many trees down below; he has never really thought of France as a forest until now.

A ping.

'Your seatbelt, Sir. We are landing in a couple of minutes.'

His ears ache then pop, ache then pop, the sound of the ventilation increases its roar, the mountains are suddenly above the plane and, with a bump, they have landed and the deceleration throws him forward.

In the back of the squad car Floriane assures the driver that, yes, it was a pleasant flight. She glances at Gert, eyes closed, head back, hands on knees, and wonders if he will be of any help.

Twenty minutes later they arrive in Briançon, drive up the steep Avenue de la Republique and park at the back of a nondescript concrete building. The French flag hangs over the entrance of the police station. It is 11:24.

'Bonjour.'

Commandant Marinette Proust is a short stocky woman with closely cropped red hair. She ushers Floriane and Gert into her office. Her desk is tidy. A photo of a ski run, mountains and a blue sky hangs on the wall behind her.

'We have very little time,' Proust explains. 'I am surprised you have made the journey.'

'This is Gert Muyskens …' Floriane pauses, wondering whether to call Gert a policeman. Decides not to. 'Gert has helped us with a previous case and knows more about Daniel Murray than anyone. Off the record, we want to interview Murray about a series of crimes that are of long-standing interest to Europol,' Floriane says in perfect French. She turns to Gert. 'I was saying that ...'

'It's OK, I understood enough. We're running out of time.'

'We will help you as much as we can,' Proust says in heavily accented English.

Gert nods.

'Par ici, this way, please,' Proust says, ushering them out of the room. They use the stairs down to the basement. 'Cell 4, the gendarme will accompany you.'

The gendarme's expansive stomach leads the way. He produces a chain of keys and unlocks the door to Cell 4.

'I would rather you stay in the corridor,' Gert tells Floriane. 'For your own safety.' He turns to the gendarme 'Lock me in, Murray is a very dangerous man.'

The gendarme shrugs and pulls the door open.

He is sitting at a desk at the far end of the room, his back to the door. Thin, casual clothes, dark messy hair.

Gert crosses the threshold. The door is locked behind him.

'Hi Daniel. It's been a long time, hasn't it? Nearly three years since Whitby.'

No response.

'So how did you end up here, ferrying illegals over the border? Can't say it is what I expected. Are you still in touch with Tiffany? She's a nice girl,' Gert continues talking calmly and he advances slowly. 'I've been meaning to contact her again but I went away. Left the country. A bit like you. The whole thing got too much. Those murders in London. It's bad, Daniel, very bad but I think I understand what happened. I could help ...'

'I'm out of here in an hour. They got nothing.'

The words are so soft that Gert almost misses them.

'Not many Londoners wandering around on a mountain pass on the Italian border, down the road from a burnt-out car, Daniel,' Gert suggests.

'What do you know?' he snarls and turns to face Gert.

Gert returns to the cell door and knocks. 'Let me out.'

'Are you sure?' Floriane asks him.

'Of course, I'm sure!' Gert is furious. 'Whoever that is in Cell 4, it isn't Daniel Murray. How could you not do the most basic checks?'

'Who is it then?'

'I don't give a fuck who it is! I should be halfway to Latin America, with my luggage! Are you flying me back to Schiphol or do I have to take a train?' Gert grabs his backpack and heads for the door.

'Mr Muyskens, please,' Commandant Proust intervenes. 'We have papers, bank cards, an Oyster Card from London ...'

'Anything with a photo?' he sneers. 'Did you bother checking whether any of that stuff belonged to the man you have arrested?'

'We have his driving licence.'

Gert holds his hand out. 'OK. Show me it.'

Proust grabs the file from her desk and opens it. 'Here you are.'

A provisional driving licence. The photo isn't great but it is a photo of Daniel Murray. There is a superficial resemblance but you would have to be drunk or half-asleep to see it as a photo of the man in Cell 4.

'So who is in the cell?' Gert asks, getting his temper under control. 'Have you checked his fingerprints. Is he on the database? Why does he have Daniel Murray's ID?'

'We'll do it now.'

Proust walks out leaving Floriane and Gert in uncomfortable silence.

'Look, I'm sorry. I thought that ...' Floriane starts. 'Provincial police force ...'

'Forget it.'

'You're thinking he stole Daniel Murray's cards?'

'I'm thinking I should have ignored you and got on my plane.'

'You didn't because you're a good cop.'

'Was. Was a cop. Now I look after baby turtles and life is infinitely more meaningful.'

'Where was Daniel Murray last seen?'

'I lost his trail in London. April 2017.'

Commandant Proust re-enters her office. 'His prints have been taken and sent.'

'Give me the details and I can get them to hurry up,' Floriane tells her.

'Can I take you to the café for a pastry while we wait?' Proust asks.

'And our mystery man stays in his cell?' Floriane asks, looking at her watch. It is ten to twelve.

Proust nods.

They don't have long to wait. In Gert's case, two chocolate éclairs and two double espressos. For Floriane, a pain au chocolat and a café au lait. For Commandant Proust, a madeleine and a cup of tea; she is making up for lost time.

Floriane's and Proust's phones buzz almost simultaneously.

'London. Our man here was arrested in a homeless shelter in Camden. March 2017,' Floriane tells Gert. 'Gave his name as Kevin Moore. Accused of beating up two other customers.'

'The customers' names?' Gert cannot hide his interest any longer.

'Albert Little, sixty-seven years old. Later died from his injuries. And someone called Colin. No surname. Kevin Moore escaped while being transferred from Charing Cross Police Station.'

Gert is visibly disappointed.

'I think we have enough for the judge,' Proust smiles. 'But you will need good luck with extradition; Brexit makes everything more complicated. It could take months.'

'In the meantime Kevin Moore stays here?' Floriane asks.

Commandant Proust shrugs, 'unless someone instructs otherwise.'

'I found them,' Kevin answers, rocking back on his chair and putting his boots up on the table.

Gert and Floriane are sitting opposite him in his cell, on chairs provided by the gendarme.

'I'm not interested in how you stole the cards but where. In London?'

Kevin smirks. 'Can't remember, mate.'

'Here is something to think about, Kevin,' Gert says. 'Right now, here in Briançon you are under arrest, suspected of involvement in the deaths of eight individuals.'

'And smuggling of illegal migrants across frontiers. Four to twenty-seven years imprisonment,' Floriane tells Kevin. 'Expect twenty minimum.'

'In London you will at least be on home soil,' Gert adds. 'Providence Mission in Camden, you were there how long?'

'Doesn't bother me, pal. Might as well stop here. Whatever.'

'And Murray was there with you? At the shelter. Is that where you met?'

Kevin shakes his head pityingly and says nothing.

The journey back to Amsterdam takes longer; a three-hour journey in a squad car to Geneva and a passenger flight from there to Amsterdam Schiphol. As with the earlier flight, Gert is in no mood to talk. He crawls into his smart phone to explore diving holidays in Venezuela. Floriane leaves him to it and gets on with her work. They are flying over Paris, just an hour from Schiphol airport, when she attempts to chat with him.

'I can help you, Gert,' she says. 'And you can help me. We will need to establish who is controlling Kevin Moore. He didn't turn up on the French border in a car full of illegal immigrants by accident.'

'I don't need to establish anything,' Gert answers.

'Your experience will …'

'They spat me out, kiddo.' Gert fixes Floriane with a cynical stare. 'Surplus to requirements. I told them things they didn't want to hear.'

'Do you have proper coffee?' Floriane asks a passing steward.

'Of course, Madame,' comes the reply.

'Black, isn't it, Gert?'

Gert nods.

'Two please.'

The steward smiles and heads off.

'You think you are the only one who has ever had a hard time?' Floriane asks Gert. 'You don't think I might also get shit from the suits and paperclip riders on the fourth floor? Like who's that foreign black bitch think she is stepping in here and rocking the boat? Or, since when do Africans tell us what to do? That's the way it is. It's what puts the cis in system and the crass in bureaucracy. Get over it.'

'OK,' Gert cuts her off irritatedly with a wave of his hand. 'You win the eternal suffering stakes and I am a self-indulgent loser running away to lie on a beach.'

The coffees arrive. Wrapped in the roar of the air-conditioning, they sip and ignore each other. But Gert is thinking about London; the bodies sprawled across the floor in Thurloe Square, the garage in which the Tallboy the Rasta took his last breath, and where Daniel had gone after fleeing his flat. It was winter and very cold out on the streets. Could Daniel have gone to a homeless shelter and, if he had, who else might he have met there, besides Kevin? Would someone remember him? Might there be clues as to where he had gone? Or why he visited Thurloe Square? How deep is the link between Daniel and Kevin?

Forget it and go back to your beach.

Three years have passed. Staff will have changed, the homeless will have come and gone. It would be like trying to identify an individual ant by the trace of its footprints across a tablecloth.

'They won't stand a chance without your input,' Floriane says gently, second-guessing his thoughts.

CHAPTER 29

Europol, Rotterdam

5th March 2020

Antoine Hoek stares team leader François Winders in the eye. The two men hate each other. Antoine hates Winders for his pettiness, his pretentious cravats and loud skinny ties, his lack of imagination and the casual misogyny, racism and homophobia that exude from his every pore.

Winders for his part detests Hoek's smug air of superiority, his social ease, his disregard for rules, his brown shoes with a blue suit and, more than anything, his refusal to accept that, as team leader, Winders has the right to expect obedience from all his staff. Including Hoek.

'You engineered his sacking. Twice. From the Korps Nationale and then from the harbour police. Why on earth would he listen to a word you say?' Antoine asks. 'He doesn't even live here. You drove him out of the country.'

'Draw up the paperwork, give him whatever he needs and alert the Metropolitan Police in London. I want him in Camden by this time tomorrow.'

'No, you tell him. He respects you,' Antoine scoffs. 'And while you're at it you can explain why ...'

'Get the fuck out of my office!' Winders roars, 'or leave your badge on the table and see if anyone else will employ you.'

Antoine likes it when the veins on the younger man's forehead throbs.

The flight from Geneva arrives some ten minutes late. It's dark. Hard rain hammers thousands of square metres of flat roof as the passengers run down the aircraft steps and onto waiting buses. Flashing lights reflect in puddles across the tarmac. Airline staff in cheerful uniforms brandish smiley teeth and clutch umbrellas to accompany the arrivals on their short walk into the terminal building.

Floriane and Gert are waved through passport control. Antoine is waiting to usher them to a taxi and a conversation that only hours earlier seemed implausible.

By the time they reach Europol the matter is settled. They're even taking care of Gert's luggage that was already on the plane to Suriname and has now arrived in Paramaribo.

Through security and into the lift.

'Where is Winders? I want to hear it from him,' Gert says, looking around the open plan office.

'Doesn't do grovelling, it creases his suits,' Antoine answers. 'But we can all sit in his office with our feet on his desk while we sort out the paperwork. If that helps.'

Gert likes the sound of that. 'Someone should tape him behind the wallpaper.'

Floriane looks confused.

'A Dutch saying,' Gert explains, 'meaning get rid of the bastard.'

'Oh, OK,' Floriane smiles. 'Can I choose the wallpaper?'

'Cups of solace?' Antoine heads off towards the espresso machine without waiting for an answer.

By the time they leave the building an hour later, muddy bootprints on Winders' desk, they have a plan. Gert has funds in euros and sterling, and Floriane and Antoine have endured a thirty-minute briefing about Whitby, Daniel Murray and Thor Lupei. If they have not believed every word, they have hidden it well.

Gert dares to hope that he is no longer alone.

Standing outside, beneath hard-working umbrellas, Gert voices the thought he would not utter inside the building.

'Why has Winders changed his mind?'

'Yeah, it bugs me too,' Antoine admits.

'Don't overthink,' Floriane urges them. 'Could be anything and probably above our pay grades. Maybe the French and Italians want to blame the British for the human trafficking on their border. Or a decision from the top to employ an outside operative to keep the heat off Europol. You know that Brexit means no more access to the Schengen Information System? Maybe someone wants to teach the British what it means to no longer have data on the movements of criminals, missing persons and objects of interest before it kicks in fully.'

'Or a distraction,' Antoine suggests. 'Wouldn't be the first time. I hear Winders wants to become a politician. The important thing, Gert, is that you have the opportunity and the funds to try to report on how Kevin Moore obtained someone else's identity. And, with luck, find out what happened to Daniel.'

Gert nods thoughtfully. 'If I am being set up, I swear Winders …'

Antoine pats his friend's shoulder. 'We've got your back. Call me if you have any problems.'

'Yeah, OK.'

They watch the big man walk away, silhouetted against the streetlights reflecting up from the pavement.

'What do you think?'

Floriane turns towards Antoine. 'The challenge will be to pull him out of there in one piece.'

CHAPTER 30

Camden, London

6th March 2020

London is a contradiction. Always changing. Always the same. Gert stands at the exit to Camden tube station and stares out at a familiar urban geometry. Bricks, buildings, bins, benches. Streets splayed like spokes on a wheel. Yellow red brown black white surfaces interspersed with the jelly mass of humanity spreading like mould over a Petri dish, corralled briefly by traffic lights then pitching purposefully forward once more.

Sure, there's a veneer of change, new gadgets to be clutched and stared at, new pantones to wear and carry.

Brandscape, blandscape and, aside from a single pigeon and two sickly sycamore saplings, no trace of the natural world.

Just days ago Gert's toes were soft sinking into warm sand, a gentle breeze draping his shoulders, a turquoise sea lapping a green continent, crystal clean and thick with the cries of insects and birds. Now here he is back in a blue suit, bought just an hour ago to look the part he has to play. He is even wearing a white shirt and a skinny green tie. But still in funky black trainers.

'Oi, pal. Get a move on.'

A hard poke in the ribs.

Gert presses himself against the wall to allow the stream of late commuters, bottle-necked in his wake, to surge out of the station.

It is shortly after ten. Providence Mission is a three-minute walk. A repurposed Victorian factory, three storeys of sand-yellow brick squatting in a street of five-storey red brick. Aside from the Gothic arch above the entrance, the street and everything in it is an orgy of straight lines encrusted with signs advising that there is only ONE WAY. No parking, no loitering, no hawking, no feeding the birds, no nuisance, no standing in this area.

A fresh slash of graffiti advises:

Gentrification zone
POOR PEOPLE PLEASE LEAVE
Quietly

'You've caught me at a good time,' Nika Shakarami smiles brightly as she steps out from behind the reception counter. Her eyelids are puffy, her eyes red, she has already put in a full shift at University College Hospital on the Euston Road and should be in bed asleep but she has four hours volunteering before she will go home. She wears a large purple jumper over her nurse's uniform. She wishes she had put some moisturiser on her hands, the cold and all the handwashing have exacerbated the cracking and itching, but she is nothing if not committed. 'Our clients are all out during the day. The Pathways Coordinator may be able to advise you; when she gets in.'

Nika takes Gert on a tour of the building. A smell of cleaning products lingers in the stairwell. Everywhere is bright lights and cheerful orange or green walls. A practiced eye notices the absence of metal or glass objects; chairs, cups and cutlery, all plastic.

'We provide short term respite, over the winter months, for up to 16 people, Mr Muyskens.'

'Would Kevin Moore have stayed for a few days or several months?'

'No one stays months, the need is too great. We have over 600 rough sleepers in Camden alone. We help people back on their feet, put them in contact with other agencies and ...'

Nika stops and opens a door. The room beyond is no wider than the corridor they are standing in. The external wall is whitewashed brickwork, the other walls are plastered. A larger room has been subdivided into three, providing just enough space for a single bed, a bedside table and four hooks for clothes.

'Our clients prefer their own space. These pods are small but cosy and safe. We only welcome men from 25 to 65 years of age.'

'You get larger rooms in prison.'

'We do our best, Mr Muyskens.'

'Yes, I'm sure. Quite a few of them are coming from prison?' Gert keeps his voice light. 'It must be difficult to ...'

'For them and for us,' she agrees.

'Are there many fights?'

Nika's phone vibrates in her hand. 'Excuse me.' She takes the call. 'Yes. Yes. He has some questions about ... In your office. Yes, of course.' She smiles at Gert. 'Our co-ordinator can see you now.'

'That's not what I am asking,' Gert interrupts, pushing the photo across the desk. 'The records show that a Kevin Moore was arrested here following a fight that led directly to the death of Albert Little, aged sixty-seven years. I am asking you whether this photo shows the man who was arrested. Yes or no.'

Megan Oxbow, pathways co-ordinator, mid-forties, in her usual navy-blue trouser suit, shoulder-length hair the colour of a rich tea biscuit, a woman who prides herself on process. 'I cannot release confidential information without a ...'

'At the moment I am asking you informally, but if Europol

feel the need to escalate this you can expect the shelter to be closed for a couple of weeks while the teams go through everything, the rooms, the paperwork, interviewing each staff member and …'

'May I see the photo?'

Gert turns to see Nika is still standing in the doorway.

'I've been here since the beginning of the year before the team expansion and the building works so perhaps …'

'I'm sorry Nika, don't you have things to do?' Oxbow snaps.

Nika flushes, nods and hurries away.

'We like to do things properly here in England,' Oxbow declares. 'We have enquiry processing procedures and we are exceptionally busy. I recognise that might seem odd to you and I am sure you think you have good reasons for disrupting the …'

'Forget it. Let's do it the hard way,' Gert stands up. 'I hear too much bullshit. You'll have more time to process my enquiry when the shelter is shut for two weeks. Thanks. I'll find my own way out.'

He strides out of the office and finds his way out onto the street. Mission unaccomplished. Coffee shop, rethink. In that order.

'Excuse me.'

The voice comes from the alley to his right. Gert turns to find Nika vaping in the shadows. She beckons him to join her.

'Bert Little was a lovely man and he didn't deserve to die.'

'No one deserves to die,' Gert replies. 'Well, almost no one.'

'Megan Oxbow only arrived in August so she won't know anything. May I see the photo? Yes, that's him. Everyone was afraid of Kevin. Kelly recognised him and warned me the minute he arrived. I shouldn't say this but some of them are more homeless than others.' Nika returns the photo to

Gert. 'This was before the pods; some of the clients were still sharing rooms.'

Gert eyes light up. 'Kelly is a co-worker?'

'She left. Didn't get on with Megan.'

'And she'd been working at the shelter for a while? Do you have a phone number?'

Nika shrugs. 'I might be able to … but she wasn't there that night, didn't work weekends. Nor do I normally but …'

'Sorry to cut you off, Nika. Won't you be missed?'

'It's OK,' Nika picks at the cracked skin on her left hand. 'My uncle ended up homeless. For Oxbow it's just a job.'

'I understand. Here's my number.' Gert scribbles his number on a scrap of paper from his pocket. 'If you can persuade Kelly to contact me …'

He watches the young nurse walk back up the street and re-enter the shelter and wishes someone like Nika had been there to for his brother Pim.

He is sipping a passable Americano when his phone rings.

'Mr Muyskens?'

'Yeah.'

'I'm Kelly. Whereabouts in Camden are you?'

Ten minutes later the coffee shop door opens and a slender red-haired woman with green eyes and a big bright yellow scarf steps in. She walks straight over to Gert and shakes his hand.

'Nika told me to look out for a huge man who looks like a Dutch farmer,' she smiles.

'Do we all look the same?' Gert laughs as he shakes her hand.

Kelly laughs. 'Big hands, broad open faces. And I guess it's the accent.'

'I didn't even tell her my nationality! What can I get you to drink?'

They sit at the back of the café where their conversation can be private.

'We see many things, Gert. So many wasted lives, especially the young men. The ones who haven't even begun to live when everything comes crashing down around them.'

'It must have been hard for you, walking away.'

Kelly shakes her head. 'Regrettably, Providence isn't the only shelter in London or even in Camden, not by a long chalk. I found a new job in a few hours. Couldn't stand that woman, Megan. She wouldn't know compassion if it bit her fat arse. After a couple of days I said to myself Kelly Heaney time to pack your bags and hit the road. Anyway, this isn't about me, is it? How can I help you?'

'Kevin Moore. To start with. The French police arrested him on their border with Italy. I understand you know him.'

'Devious little shit. Pardon my French,' Kelly sweeps her hair away from her eyes. 'Sometimes you have a gut feeling, you what I mean? People who aren't what they claim to be. Kevin was like that. Right little Uriah Heap. Obsequious and grovelling to your face then, behind your back, manipulative and mean. I don't doubt he had a tough background like the others but we take our hardships differently, don't we? Look at Mandela and Mugabe. Both thrown in prison for years by bastard racist governments but one comes out positive and forward-looking, the other is eaten away with the desire for revenge.'

'So you think Kevin was responsible for Albert Little's death?' Gert asks, steering Kelly back towards the point.

'I think so, but who knows? The police went through the motions but never really investigated. Victim and suspect were both vagrants, you see? Perfunctory is what I'd call it. Four days later charges were dropped and Kevin was back knocking on the shelter door. No one gives a fig what happens to these men.'

'He had eight people in the car,' Gert tells her. 'Smuggled them over the border. All dead in the burnt-out wreck. They arrested Kevin close to the scene on a deserted road.'

'My God! And how does that link to Providence Shelter?'

'Good question. When Europol ran his prints through the database, the arrest popped up. That's all we know.'

'And you want to hear more than Scotland Yard's side of the story?'

'We want to ensure Kevin doesn't slip through our fingers like he did in London. We want to find out who is paying his bills. And there's something else.'

'Oh.'

'Nika told me that you had worked at the shelter for several years.'

'Since 2015. Why?'

'When Kevin was arrested in Briançon he gave false ID and this is a long shot but I am wondering if there's a link.'

'Go on.'

'Does the name Daniel Murray mean anything to you?'

Kelly shakes her head.

'Could he have been at the shelter? It would have been the start of 2017. A young man, nineteen years old. Tall and skinny. Brown hair.'

'I'd need more than that,' Kelly smiles.

Gert reaches into his pocket and pushes the photocopy of the oyster card and provisional driving licence across the table.

Kelly stares long and hard at the image. 'Shame the hologram is obscuring the face.'

'My guess is that he would have only been there a few nights. He had a flat in West Ealing that he must have left in early January. He may have acted paranoid.'

Kelly arches an eyebrow. 'You could be describing half of my clients. Are you thinking the two were friends?'

'Not really. I just want to know how Kevin Moore ended up

with Daniel Murray's papers.'

'And Murray is part of the ...'

Gert changes tack. 'Do they keep client records? Would there be a way of checking back, all the way to January 2017? To find out when Kevin Moore was at the shelter and whether Daniel was ever there?'

'Good luck with that. You'll have to negotiate with Odious Oxbow; the database is on the computer in her office. And with her being new and a cow, there's no guarantee that she will have kept records going back ...'

'OK.' Gert sighs. 'It was a long shot. Sorry to have pulled you away from your work, Kelly.' Gert gets to his feet. 'I'll settle the bill. It's OK take your time. You have my number if you think of anything. And for the record I met Megan earlier and I share your assessment.'

Gert pays at the counter. He turns as he opens the door, gives Kelly a wave.

'No wait,' Kelly calls out. 'I may have a plan.'

CHAPTER 31

Camden, London

6th March 2020

It is 8 pm when they meet again outside a pub on Camden High Street, from which they can see the entrance in the narrow street opposite. Bang on cue, the door to Providence Shelter opens and out steps Megan Oxbow. In a few seconds she has disappeared down the road.

'She catches the train at Camden Road,' Kelly explains. 'Never stays late, even in an emergency. Just dumps everything on the other staff.'

Kelly is carrying a large shopping bag from which delicious aromas are drifting. Gert follows Kelly across the road and onto the side street.

'Hey, Kel. How are you, my love?' a large white-haired Irish man shouts from a doorway. He is wearing two coats, both very much the worse for wear, and carries an assortment of carrier bags. It is many weeks since he had a comb and a shave.

'Conor!' Kelly stops while the old man shuffles across the road. 'Long time no see!'

'The place went downhill when you left, my heart. New rules, skinny cubicles you can't even turn around in, and a matron in league with the devil himself.' He gives Gert the once over. 'See you've a new class of clientele at the shelter.'

'He's not a client and I'm not back at Providence, Conor. But we *are* dropping in so, if you want, I can put a word in.'

'It's my luggage, Kel. Two bags max they say. New rule.

What am I meant to do with all my treasures?'

'They should be in the British Museum!'

'The Murphy collection is already too expansive, they tell me. I'm eating away at the space they set aside for those pharaohs and Romans.'

When they reach the entrance Kelly presses the bell. Two long and two short blasts; Gert guesses it is a way of messaging staff about who is outside. In a few seconds the door opens part way. A large round face with thick glasses appears.

'I've told you, Conor. We're full tonight so ...'

'Mark, how are you?' Kelly says brightly, stepping in front of Conor.

Mark's eyes light up.

'I know, I know,' Kelly says. 'I promised to pop by months ago but I'm here now and, to celebrate, I am bearing gifts.' She raises the carrier bag. 'I want you to squeeze our good friend Mr Murphy in somewhere and then I'll introduce you to Gert.'

'He's Garda,' Conor interjects. 'Past 9 pm they're always policemen.' The old Irishman turns towards Gert. 'No offence.'

'You watch too much television,' Kelly tells the old man.

Mark opens the door and lets all three of them in, locking the door behind them. 'Give me ten minutes to sort Conor out and I'll put a kettle on.'

'Or plan B. You open the office and we'll sort out drinks and snacks,' Kelly suggests, patting her shopping bag.

Seconds later Mark is walking up to the second floor with Conor, leaving Kelly and Gert alone in the office.

'Plates are through there,' Kelly tells Gert as she switches on the office computer. 'Mark loves his food.'

By the time Gert has found the cups and plates, put the kettle on, and re-emerged from the tiny kitchen, Kelly is already downloading files onto a memory stick.

'Fancy that! Nika gave me the old passcodes,' she explains, 'and they haven't changed. Megan, a woman obsessed with rules and protocols at the expense of everything else, has zero understanding about digital security. Tragic. Anyway, don't just stand there, there's samosas and pakoras in the bag along with pilau rice and three curries.'

'I owe you big time,' Gert says.

'Indeed you do. I like it when people owe me favours. Gives me a warm feeling right here.' Kelly pats her chest. 'Like putting money in the bank.'

An hour later, bellies full, Kelly and Gert are back on the street and waving goodbye to Mark as he locks the door.

'Well here you go. I hope it brings you joy and good fortune. Let me know how … or …' she hands Gert the memory stick but at the last second holds on to it. 'Here's a thought. It's still only nine o'clock. I'm just around the corner. You can come to my grand apartment and explore the data there. With a coffee. That way, if you have any questions …'

Gert grins, 'Sounds perfect.'

Just round the corner turns out to be a kilometre walk north to a tiny attic flat on Pasthull Road. By the time they arrive Gert knows the history of Kelly's entire extended family, in Dublin, London and Chicago. And Kelly has learned almost nothing about Gert other than the fact he used to live in Rotterdam but now lives in Suriname.

He follows her into the kitchen, notices the photos of exotic locations on the corkboard by the fridge, while she closes the curtains and puts the kettle on.

'Second thoughts,' she says. 'We'll probably do with something stronger. Make yourself comfortable in the front room. It's that way.'

He sits himself down on a sofa that is covered in a bright batik throw. There's a dining area with Ikea chairs, a shelf with travel books, scented candles, and an embossed metal sign praising Irish Guinness hanging above the mantelpiece that has no fireplace beneath it. Gert takes the laptop from his backpack and gets to work.

'Do you know the name of the Property Management System they use at the shelter?' Gert asks when Kelly enters.

'Better than that. I have it installed from when I was working there,' Kelly sits down beside him at the dining table and powers up her laptop.

'Holy Mother of God but it takes forever. I swear my brain must be an internet browser. 13 open windows, 10 of them frozen, and no idea where that damn music is coming from.'

Gert smiles. 'So you already have all the data?'

'No. I only had access to the portal, to help from home in emergencies. But my passwords were cancelled the day I left. She's lax but not that lax.'

Gert messages Floriane the details in Rotterdam and minutes later has a password to access to the software courtesy of Europol. The memory stick is inserted and, rather than waste an hour learning how the system works, Gert lets Kelly do the hard work while he prompts her.

'Start around the 12th of January 2017,' he tells her, 'and we'll move forward from there.'

'It's simpler than it looks,' Kelly explains as she types. 'Most of these boxes are irrelevant. Would you believe that the shelter doesn't have minibars or room service!'

The screen shows a calendar with a row of headings for the week commencing Monday 9th January 2017 with days along the top. Beneath them are boxes showing occupancy rates – almost always 100% - number of guests, number of staff and volunteers. Beneath that are listings for the individual rooms. Kelly clicks on one of the rooms and two and sometimes three sets of initials appear.

'This is before the rooms were split into individual pods. That happened in ….'

'Nika explained.'

'That glass is yours, by the way,' she tells him. 'Redbreast, single pot still, smooth and sweet as sticky toffee pudding.'

'So those initials are the clients?' Gert sips his whisky.

'Yeah. We're looking for D.M. Is that right?'

'Assuming he used his real name.' Gert says.

Kelly scrolls and clicks the rooms, the days, the week. No D.M. appears. Kelly clicks on the initials listed in one of the rooms to show Gert how the database links to other pages. C.F. becomes Colin Fenton along with a brief description: early fifties, originally from Durham, served in the army, lost home in house fire, sleeping rough since 2013, diabetes, scabies, MHI.

'MHI?'

'Mental Health Issues,' Kelly explains. 'Shouldn't really be listed like that, it's too vague. Must have been one of the volunteers. A lovely fella, Colin. Wouldn't hurt a moose, except when the demon drink was thumping around in his head. Died in the summer that year, hit by a delivery lorry on Great Portland Street. Deserved better. They all do.'

She moves onto the week commencing 16th January. Full occupancy every night. No D.M listed anywhere. Kelly clicks forward again.

'No, wait! Go back. Your mouse just highlighted something when you hovered there. What does that do?'

Kelly hovers and clicks. After a brief wait another box opens with an image of the client.

'Perfect. Let's go back to the 9th and start again. Check all the photos.'

'Pretty please?'

'Sorry yes, please. And this whisky is excellent.'

And there it is. Under a false name is a photo of Daniel Murray. He is listed as David Jordan, sitting on a chair in the office of Providence Shelter. They go back a week and discover that he made his first appearance on Saturday 7th January. Age

25. White. No distinguishing marks. No family. No religion. Likes: music. Dislikes: football, rich kids, and camping.

'Now the monkey comes out of the sleeve!' Gert is delighted.

Kelly turns away from the screen to gaze bewilderedly at Gert.

'Sorry, a Dutch expression. We're getting somewhere!' Gert hugs Kelly and kisses her cheek. He lets go immediately. 'I'm sorry. Forgive me. I have waited so long for this moment.'

'Keep a grip, Sir, this could be a long night,' she grins. 'And, now we have a decent photo, I recognise him.'

'Tell me about him.'

Kelly is lost in thought. Nearly three years gone. Days cascading in a kaleidoscope. Spent souls and sad-shadowed faces. Whiskered wandering old men abandoned in piss-stained trousers, shuffling the pavements of shame. The middle-aged, still in shock, fallen between the crack-filled days and nitazene n-bomb nights or curled up in the pits of a bottle. The young sofa-surfers who missed their wave, thrown out of the family home, shell-shocked, numb but with Bambi still loitering in their sweet pleading eyes. And the feral dodgers high on rage, punching out at everything that moves.

'He's not twenty-five,' Gert is saying. 'Not even now. In January 2017 he was just nineteen years old.'

'They lie to get in,' Kelly says, still staring at the photo on the screen. 'The minimum age is there to protect the kids but some are so desperate to get off the streets, particularly in winter. It's a game. We know they're lying but we make a judgement call.' She turns to look at Gert. 'He had a sports bag. Curled around it when he slept, like it was his nucleus. I put him with RJ and Tommy. David told me that ...'

'Daniel,' Gert corrects her.

'Sorry, Daniel. Told me he didn't belong in the shelter. Just sorting himself out. Needed a few days. They all say that.' She blinks slowly. 'You know, it's the young ones that get to me most; the kids whose futures fade with every sorrow step.' She takes a deep breath and a sip of her whisky. 'Right, let's find Kevin Moore.'

'No, park him for now and focus on Daniel.'

'I thought …'

Gert shakes his head. 'How long was Daniel at the shelter? When did he leave? Has he been back this year? Presumably you can do a client search now we have a name?'

'Yes, of course. As long as he has used the same name.'

In no time they establish that David Jordan, AKA Daniel Murray, stayed at Providence Shelter just seven days, from the 7th to the 10th of January then from the 15th to the 17th. Never came back. As Kelly reads, further memories trickle back.

'Said he'd been rough sleeping for three or four days. I say sleep but most of them cannot sleep at night, especially at the start. Too much fear. They sleep in the day, hidden under boxes in shop doorways. It's easier if they have a dog to protect them but then, if they do, they cannot come into the shelter. Anyway, I could see he wasn't twenty-five but we took him in. Persuaded him to have a shower to warm up. He even took his bag into the shower. No idea what was in it. Mementos from home probably. No, tell a lie, that's not quite right. One evening, the evening he left I think, I came into the room and saw him shove a pile of old papers into the bag. Quickly, as if he didn't want me to see them. Yellow they were, you know, like parchment.'

Kelly pauses. Gert sips his whisky, says nothing, doesn't want to break her train of thought.

'He was sitting on his bed. RJ was there, suggesting they play chess. RJ was or is mad about chess. Super bright guy. Come to think of it RJ called him Dan the Man, I should have picked up on that, shouldn't I? Anyway RJ was always trying to get a game. Daniel wasn't interested. Asked me if he could go out for a couple of hours. They can't do that because the need for rooms is so great; if they are not back by ten o'clock the bed goes to someone else. Simple as that. It would have been the Wednesday.'

'The eighteenth? How would you remember that?' Gert prompts her.

'I had my leotard on under my uniform and felt sweaty. Dance class on a Wednesday afternoon before work.'

'Did he say where he was going or why he had to go out?'

Kelly shakes her head. 'If he did then I've forgotten. Nearly three years ago.' She pauses again. 'There was something about him. You know? Beneath the little-boy-lost exterior there was also a steeliness. When people crossed him. They were eating dinner one evening when Ted Showem went straight for the table Daniel and RJ were sitting at and started having a go at RJ. Ted was a big East End bruiser, wore his prejudices like barnacles. Pleasant enough when sober but not sober often enough. Out of nowhere Daniel has grabbed Ted's arm. Ted raises his other fist but Daniel looks him straight in the eye. Doesn't say anything, mark you. And suddenly Ted's lowering his fist, like all the bravado's sucked out of him. He shuffles away to the other side of the dining room, eats his food and leaves.'

'That certainly made an impression on you,' Gert observes.

'It was a surprise,' Kelly agrees. 'Of course we didn't know at the time that Big Ted was ill.'

'Oh?'

'Cancer, organ failure or something. He died a few weeks later. In the shower. There was a … no, it's not important.'

Kelly returns to the database. Gert watches her as he processes what he has learned. He tries to remember the dates on the Mouthbites messages he retrieved from the smart phones in Thurloe Square. They started on the twentieth or twenty-first of January, messages about security and creating a website. The dates almost match. So it is possible that Daniel went straight from the shelter to Thurloe Square. Why? Was he invited? Did he invite himself? Were the papers in his sports bag important? Despite his best intentions Gert is being sucked back into the world of Thor Lupei and the scravir, as if the jungles of Suriname have never happened.

'There you go! That's Kevin, isn't it?' Kelly is triumphant, pointing at the photo on the screen. 'You were right, they were both at the shelter at the start of 2017. Like I said before, a devious little shit. Doesn't surprise me one bit that he would have stolen from Daniel. He stole from dozens of people. But you see here, in January he was going under a different name.'

'Does anyone register under their real name?'

'It's a mixture of shame or to stop others from finding them, the police perhaps or relatives they wish to avoid. To be fair, there are plenty who do use their given name. We do our best.'

'As far as I am concerned, you are all angels. Except Megan.'

'So what now, Mr Europol?' Kelly finishes her whisky and shows Gert the bottle.

'If I have another I will probably not find my way back to my hotel,' he confesses.

'Who says you have to?'

It has been a long time since Gert shared a bed with anyone. He's not even sure he understands what she is really saying.

'I don't want you to think that …'

'I'm not and I don't want you to think that either. Think of it as two ships passing in the night. My guess is that we both need time out and human company as much as the other. Loneliness doesn't only consume the men in that damn shelter, now does it?' she says, taking his hand. 'You've bags under your eyes the size of travelling trunks.'

'I'll just message my colleagues the news about Kevin. And there's more I need to know about …'

'Of course,' she says, tilts her head to one side. A strand of red hair falls playfully across her cheek. 'But how about we leave the *more I need to know* stuff till the morning? So whisky or coffee?'

On balance, he thinks that whisky might be safer.

The sex is good. They are secretly both surprised at just how good and how straightforward it is, given that neither of them has had a partner for longer than they care to remember. Somehow the context of their meeting, the common bond of humanity and caring for others, has simplified everything and allowed their bodies to do what bodies do. No angst, no self-doubt, no performance anxiety. They touch, caress, move in an escalating crescendo as animals do, and are spent.

Afterwards Gert lies there beneath the skylight, looking up at the orange sky that passes for night in London, Kelly curled up asleep against him, her warm back ebbing and flowing to the rhythm of her breathing like gentle waves rolling on a beach. He is a man reborn. Deep in the core of his being he is overwhelmed by the realisation rush that he can still walk away from Daniel Murray. He might even persuade Kelly to come to Suriname with him. There is perhaps a version of the world in which he is finally fulfilled and happy.

Meanwhile Gert's messages to Antoine and Floriane have been received.

And intercepted.

CHAPTER 32

Camden, London

7th March 2020

'I'll be back around 4pm. Stay as long as you like,' she shouts as she does up her coat. 'There's food and drink in the cupboards. Good luck!'

'Thanks, Kelly.' Gert is propped against the pillows, hair tousled, eyes full of sleep. 'For everything. I've been thinking. We know that Daniel knew Kevin Moore, and that Moore has been arrested smuggling people across frontiers, and Daniel disappeared, probably in April of 2017. Now all we need to do is …'

'All *you* need to do, lover. I have to get to work. Catch you later, perhaps. I'm back around five. Just pull the door to when you leave. And keep in touch!'

Kelly grins as she crams a beanie hat over her red curls, blows Gert a kiss and with that she is gone.

Over a bowl of muesli, Gert reviews the previous night's work and scribbles the timeline starting in January 2017: the conversation he had in Whitby with Tiffany, the discoveries they made in London, the records showing Daniel had met Kevin Moore in the homeless shelter just days before the communications started between the people who ran the cosmetic surgery in Thurloe Square, the bloated bodies. The Mouthbites messages clearly show that Daniel was at the heart of Perfect Look. They kept him prisoner until someone made a catastrophic mistake then Daniel was gone.

Someone has to know how the pieces fit together. Daniel

must have met up with Moore later and asked for help to get smuggled out of the country.

Let others do the work.

He hasn't previously been able to step back but right now Gert is still in a better place. There is a life awaiting him across the ocean. He has just spent the night with a beautiful woman who took him as he is, no questions asked, no backstory unpacked. He can still walk away. He is far enough away from the event horizon to escape the black hole.

Tease out a few more fragments, hand everything over to Antoine, then rebook his flight and leave.

It is twenty to four when Gert steps out of Whitby station into the chill air at the end of a long train journey. Past the swing bridge and along St Ann's Staith. Sunshine bathes the cottages across the harbour on the East Cliff. The gulls shriek as they dive-bomb a hapless tourist, forcing her to drop her fish and chips. The air brisk and bright, the sky peppered with stars that cannot yet be seen. But they are there all the same.

'She left,' the youth behind the chip shop counter tells him. 'We can't give out addresses.'

'No problem, I think I have it,' Gert takes his chips.

His phone identifies the sleekest steepest snicket up from the harbour. On Cliff Street he presses the doorbell and, as he waits, wonders how it is that the sea is woven into the fabric of his life. Loitering, watching him. In Rotterdam, on the beaches of Suriname, and here in Whitby.

The door opens behind him.

'Oh.'

Her disappointment is tangible, even before he turns round.

Time has moved on. She is different. Still as young and as pretty as before but more self-assured. Brunette again instead of blonde. On her hip she carries a toddler, a boy packed into a tiger onesie, blue eyes wide as oceans. Her face is a mixture of emotions, surprise, pleasure, weariness, anxiety, discomfort.

'Gert.'

'Tiffany. Long time.' He looks at the boy. 'Maybe I shouldn't have come.' He feels she is judging him, pitying him even. Three years past and he is still stuck in the winter of 2016. 'I've moved to Suriname. In South America. Like here but hotter. Lots of turtles.' He is jabbering. 'We're setting up a diving school. For tourists. There's a whole world out there, you know. Sorry, you know that. Of course you do.'

'Do you want to come in?'

'Meet the father? I am so pleased for you, Tiffany but I'm not sure that ...'

Tiffany's eyebrows crease. 'Oh? Oh! No, Gert.' She laughs. 'I thought you were supposed to be great at reading people! You can't meet the parents; they're both out. I'm babysitting. Oh God, you thought that ...'

'I just dug a hole and jumped right in!' Gert gasps. 'What an idiot! I thought she's settling down, making a new life, moving on ...'

'I *am* making a new life, maybe not the way you think.'

The boy is beginning to wriggle.

'Come in, before Ethan starts bawling. I'd offer you a drink but ... Do you drink tea?'

He follows her into the flat. In the kitchen Tiffany lowers Ethan into his playpen and puts the kettle on.

'Did you know that turtles existed before the dinosaurs?' Gert says as he watches her drop teabags in the cups. 'Brown hair suits you, by the way.'

'This is the Jurassic Coast, Gert. Have you not read the tourist guides? There are turtle fossils in the cliffs, we learn about them at school. But you didn't come here to talk turtles.'

'You're right. I wanted to see you before I leave Europe.' Gert takes the cup from her, sniffs the contents, wrinkles his nose.

'It's Tina's. Lady Grey. She's all airs and graces that one, now she's a mum and works in insurance.'

'I've cleared out my flat in Rotterdam and put it up for sale. Goodbye to the Old World and …'

'It's about Daniel, isn't it?' Tiffany cuts to the chase.

Gert nods gratefully. 'After he vanished I was desperate to find out where. I wanted to make sure you were safe.'

'I can look after myself.'

'He did give you something, didn't he? He meant the world to you but you were so confident and calm. Before I go I would like to …'

'Don't go there. I won't betray him.'

'Is he still in touch? Has he called you?'

'He doesn't have to. He'll be back when he's ready.'

'So you're just waiting while your life drifts by? Looking after other people's children.'

'Don't make assumptions. Back in 2017 when I understood he were gone for a while I realised that if he's making something of himself then so can I. I went to college, got my A-levels and now I'm in second year of my nursing degree. In Middlesbrough. Plus … I'm learning martial arts, lifting weights, and I've been on an adventure of my own. This girl spread her wings! Last summer I even got my jabs and flew off to see my dad's cousins, in Bali. My uncle Ted sorted my mum out, she were having kittens. It's what she does. Anyroad, Daniel's not coming back to a girl stuck behind the dead-end counter in a fish and chip shop. I've even been diving!'

Gert puffs his cheeks. 'You are amazing! I am a fool.'

'Thank you.' Tiffany does a little bow. 'And don't be too hard on yourself.'

Gert tries a sip of his tea. Pulls a face. 'I think Daniel was smuggled out of the country.'

'That's funny, all we ever hear are stories about people trying to get in.'

'Did he have a passport?'

'How would I know that?'

'He had to show ID to buy drinks at the bar, or something.'

Tiffany shrugs. 'Can't remember.'

'Did he say anything about going back to Romania? The police in France arrested a man they said was Daniel Murray a few days ago.'

Tiffany's expression drops, she cannot help herself.

'Turned out to be a man carrying Daniel's Oyster Card. A man caught smuggling people over the French Italian border. The car was burned out, eight bodies still inside.'

Tiffany gasps.

'I'm not saying Daniel was in the car,' Gert quickly adds. 'This is about the man they arrested. Does the name Kevin Moore mean anything to you?'

Tiffany shakes her head.

'Kevin and Daniel stayed in the same homeless shelter in London. They were there the day you and I were in London trying to find Daniel's dad. By the way,' Gert says, changing tack. 'I went back to see Daniel's dad two months later when I was investigating what had happened in Thurloe Square and I spoke with him. Can I play you the interview? It's on my phone.'

'You're wasting your time. Daniel is not evil.'

'How many people have to die before you accept …' Gert says, losing his composure.

'Enough!' she cuts him off mid-flow. She can see where this is heading. 'I think you'd better go.'

'At least I tried.' Gert says, handing her his cup. 'And remember this, if I am still looking for him then so are other people.'

She shakes her head in despair and escorts him to the front door.

'Look after yourself, Gert. And the turtles,' Tiffany smiles then steps forward and hugs him. 'I know you mean well.'

'Can I at least send you the audio file? You can listen to it when you're ready.'

He is smiling with his mouth but not with his eyes. She nods; she can always bin the files and block Gert's messages later. As he heads off down the street, Tiffany finds herself remembering watching Daniel walking away; over three years ago now.

She shivers. With Daniel she knows in the core of her being that one day she will see him again but, somehow, watching Gert disappear into the snicket, she is overwhelmed with sadness. She senses this is the last time she will ever see him. Tears in her eyes she closes the front door. Ethan is bawling in the kitchen.

Gert feels like a pilgrim as he climbs the 199 steps up towards the church and the Abbey. Penitence and discovery. At the top he stares down at the town spread out like an animated scale model. The Pavilion across the harbour, a boat entering the harbour jaws, the flashing lights of the amusement arcades. A pheasant on the field beside the path shrieks like a car horn as it flies up from a thicket.

Gert goes back down and, as the sun fades in a winter sky, he cobbles along Henrietta Street, passing the cottage that became a focal point for the horror of that weekend in November 2016.

Then back to Church Street and across the swing bridge and along Pier Road until he stands on the west pier at the very end of the harbour jaws above a heaving sea where he finally accepts that Tiffany will never betray Daniel no matter what. She trusts him and that is enough. Yes, she possesses a secret, something he has given her, but she doesn't understand its significance.

Gert envies her. He thinks of Kelly and tries to imagine

himself trusting another human being as completely. It is ridiculous, he has known Kelly little more than 24 hours, but then Tiffany had only known Daniel for a few days.

Unless they have been in constant communication.

No, the body language all pointed in one direction: she does not know where Daniel is.

As the train leaves Whitby station, Gert is still not entirely clear why he came, except maybe to confirm that his quest is futile. He already regrets sending Tiffany the audio file; she doesn't need an extra burden.

Tiffany's phone vibrates on the worktop. A new message.

> **Gert Muyskens**
> Today at 19.23
> Train leaving soon. Had a long walk round
> your wonderful Whitby. Here is the audio
> file. Really good to see you. If you ever
> want to swim with turtles …
> Attachment: Int.WayneM12APR17.mp3

She puts her phone down and gets Ethan's food ready.

Hours later the intercity train is approaching Peterborough when Gert's phone wakes him up. His first thought is that Tiffany has listened to the audio file. Now she understands why it is so important that they find him.

It isn't Tiffany, it's a message from Kelly.

> **Kelly Heaney**
> Today at 00.13
> Hiya. Just got in. Bit of an emergency at
> wk … Hope you had a great day. Sarah
> downstairs said you called round earlier
> with another fella, but she described you

as having a fat moustache and your friend
as 'tall and skinny', looked very unwell.
Prosecco talk prob, the woman drinks like
a fish. Anyway, I said 5 and it's 6.30 now.
Can't find shame emoji :(Should have left
you a key. 8pm is gd if you want. Popping to
shops. Do you like fish? Oh and I've been
thinking … I know, it happens :-(… You
need to talk with RJ. See you L8r.
GIF: Cute kitten, Here's Hoping!

Gert stares at the phone. She sent the message nearly six hours ago! He replies immediately.

That wasn't me, Kelly. I've been out of
London since 10am. Leave the flat now. I'll
call you from Kings Cross in 50 min.

His knees are bobbing up and down.
It's gone midnight, she'll be asleep.
He cannot take the risk. He messages again. Waits 30 seconds then decides to ring her.

'The person you are calling is unavailable. Please leave a message after the tone. When you are …'

He cuts the call, temples throbbing. He smashes his fist against the toughened glass. A couple down the carriage stand up to see what is going on. Gert waves; everything is fine.

It isn't. With every fibre of his body he knows that everything is not fine.

When they finally reach Kings Cross, Gert punches the button to open the doors, charges down the platform and dives into the nearest taxi.

'Pasthull Road, Camden. As fast as you can.'

'Thirty miles an hour, pal.' the driver drawls as he switches on his engine. 'That OK?'

Gert rests his head back and closes his eyes, fists clenched, trying to control his breathing. It is one in the morning and the journey takes little more than seven minutes. He throws fifteen pounds at the driver, jumps out of the car and races to the front door. Three bells. He leans on the top bell: *K Heaney*

What was her neighbour called? Sam, Suzie ... Sarah! Middle bell.

'Hello?'

Not Kelly. Another woman's voice.

'Is that Sarah?'

'Who is this? It is half past one in ...'

'Gert, Kelly's friend. I need you to listen really carefully ...'

Thirty seconds later there is a shift in the tiny reflection on the security viewer set into the front door. Gert holds up his passport, it's meaningless but shows willing.

'Have you seen or heard from Kelly this evening?' Gert asks the middle-aged woman who opens the door.

Sarah is groggy with sleep and alcohol, her grey hair in disarray, her outdoor coat thrown hastily over pink pyjamas. Gert strides into the house and hurries upstairs with Sarah in pursuit.

'So who was it pretending to be you this afternoon?' Sarah says behind him. 'He called himself Gert, said he had forgotten the keys Kelly gave him. And the very thin man, didn't look at all well.'

'Did he sound foreign?' Gert shouts over his shoulder.

'Can't remember. Oh God, what have I done?'

'Nothing, Sarah. You did nothing wrong. Did you see them leave?'

They reach the second floor. Kelly's door is ajar.

'It's best you stay outside,' he advises her.

'Shall I call the police?'

'Yes, but just wait a moment, OK?'

'Kelly! Kelly,' Sarah cries.

'Shh. Please. Wait here.'

Gert steps into the flat. He is sick of the fear, the sadness, the anger that haunts him. The hall is fine. Maybe he has misunderstood everything. Maybe she has a lover. Maybe he has made a mountain out of a mole. He would be perfectly happy with being embarrassed.

Fire door closers seal every room away. Gert pushes open the first door. The bedroom. Everything is fine; the bedclothes in disarray just as they were when he got up. Why didn't he at least tidy the bed, rearrange the quilt?

Doesn't matter.

The second door opens onto the empty bathroom, everything in its place. The kitchen next. Two unemptied carrier bags of shopping on the table. A bottle of prosecco beside them. Why are the curtains open? Last night when they arrived, Kelly switched on the light and drew the curtains as soon as she stepped into each room.

Back out into the hall. One door left.

'Hello?' Sarah's voice from out on the landing sounds tentative and fearful, and fragile as gossamer.

'Nearly done,' Gert calls out.

He pushes open the last door.

It is as if he were in a plane flying high over a patchwork landscape. The woosh in his ears like a jet engine. Scattered shapes make features on the green rug. A magazine, a bunch of flowers, the shiny blue-grey lid of her laptop reflecting light like the surface of a lake, a yellow scarf spread out like a field of wheat … Partially hidden by the upturned table, lying on her side, a wave of red hair spread across the rug like blood leaching around a corpse.

Gert staggers forwards, a clumsy bear of a man, an involuntary groan emanating from the deepest corner of his soul. He grasps the table and hauls it aside as if it weighed nothing and he sinks to his knees.

Behind him Sarah, the neighbour, steps into the room, unable to wait a second longer on the landing. She gasps and collapses. Gert spins round and checks Sarah for a pulse, and finds one. He positions Sarah safely on her side and turns back to Kelly.

He rolls her gently onto her back and recoils. She is skin and bone; sunken cheeks, a look of horror in her dead eyes.

Scravir.

Gert strokes her hair tenderly, his tears dripping onto her face.

'Oh God, Kelly. Sweet Kelly. You didn't deserve this.'

His body shakes uncontrollably. He is leaving his DNA all over the place but he couldn't care less; it is way too late for that.

If he had simply taken his flight back to Suriname two days ago,

… if he had simply ignored Floriane at the airport,

… if he had done what Antoine had told him to do a thousand times

… if … if … then none of this would have happened and this beautiful woman would still be alive. He flashbacks. Twenty-four hours ago he and she were lost in each other's arms and he was experiencing physical contact and healing he had given up believing in. He had dared to let go of all the hurt that has clung to him for all his adult life. Her gift to him, freely given.

His gift to her. Death. There is nothing left. He isn't a fixer, he is a conduit for misery.

Just go to Heathrow, get on the next flight and go.

CHAPTER 33

Whitby

Thursday 8th March 2020

Grey clouds squat in the dour landscape, reflected in the thick waters of the Scaling Dam Reservoir. A third of the way to Middlesbrough, Tiffany stuffs her case notes back in her backpack and looks around at her fellow passengers. Lauren has missed the bus again which is bad because the lecture starts at 10.30 and they've been warned any more absences and they're off the course.

Tiffany hesitates, her hand hovering over her phone. Why did Gert stir everything up again? She was happy in her bubble, ticking along, everything predictable, ordinary. Then he shows up and everything kicks off, and now she has to, doesn't she? She tucks her air pods in her ears and presses play.

Sound of knocking three times.

Gert: 12th April 2017, 9am. I'm outside the home of Wayne Murray. He was out when we visited in January. Hoping for better luck today.

Sound of knocking.

Gert: Here we go.

Latch turns, door opens.

Voice: Yeah?

Gert: Good Morning. Mr Wayne Murray?

Voice: Why?

Gert: I'm a friend of your son, Daniel. Can I come in?

Voice: What's the little bastard done now?

Gert: Best if we speak inside.

Sound of walking. Footsteps echoing in a hall.

Wayne: Through here.

A door opens.

Wayne   Shift that junk and park yourself on the sofa.

Gert: So you are Daniel's father?

Wayne: Yes. Waiting for Dan to collect his crap. What do I
         want with computer games, a broken bike, old
         school books? Told him I'd skipped it all but I'm all
         heart me.

Gert: You keep the place very warm, Mr Murray.

Wayne: You can take your coat off if you're too hot. And
         when you leave you can take his shit with you.

Gert: Must have been tough when his mother left.

Wayne: What's that to do with you?

Gert: How long have you lived here?

Wayne: Fifteen years. No, tell a lie. Sixteen. You've still not
         told me what …

Gert: I'm told your son is a good man. Honest,
         courageous, and kind. You must be proud of him.
         His girlfriend Tiffany says that …'

Wayne: Oh, I get it. Daughter's up the duff. Angry dad come
         to extract some wonga to pay for nappies. That it?
         Should have guessed Dan was out shagging
         foreigners. Where you from?

Tiffany pauses the recording and stares out of the bus window
at two crows fighting on a stone wall. No wonder Daniel hates
his dad.

Gert: Tiffany is from Yorkshire and I am not her father.

Wayne: North of Watford. That's foreign to me, mate.

Gert: Your wife left you when Daniel was just seven years
         old. She found you and Daniel too boring and

	wanted a better life, according to your son. Where did she go exactly?
Wayne:	None of your bleeding business.
Gert:	Please assume it is my business, Mr Murray.
Wayne:	What's that card?
Gert:	Europol. European Police Force.
Wayne:	What's he done?
Gert:	Please allow me to ask the questions. Your wife, where did she go?

The pause is so long that Tiffany checks to see if the audio is still playing.

Wayne:	She wanted excitement. Living in a terrace in West London with a regular bloke and a nipper didn't cut it.
Gert:	Why did you let your son grow up feeling that it was his fault?
Wayne:	Look, pal, she left and I had to deal with it. The best I could. We survived. Alright? If I had to …
Gert:	She returned to Middlesbrough?
Wayne:	What?
Gert:	To Middlesbrough?
Wayne:	If you already know everything why are you asking me? Yeah, I guess. Her family's from down there.
Gert:	I am not trying to catch you out, Mr Murray.
Wayne:	And there was me worrying.
Gert:	It is unusual for Roma to settle in one place.
Wayne:	What?
Gert:	Roxana's family came from Romania.
Wayne:	You didn't come here about Daniel. It's not about him, is it?
Gert:	It is very much about him. Daniel has disappeared, like his mother, and I want to hear your explanation

of what has happened.

Wayne: ARE YOU ACCUSING ME?

Gert: Should I be?

Gert remains calm even as Daniel's dad is losing his temper. Another pause.

Wayne: You want a cup of coffee?

Gert: Water or tea is fine.

Sound of a chair being pushed back. The acoustic changes as footsteps leave one room and enter another. A tap squeaks and water pours. Something (a kettle Tiffany guesses) is filled and placed on a surface. The silence is slowly replaced by an escalating whistle as water comes to the boil.

Wayne: (in a whisper) She didn't leave.

Tiffany pauses the recording, uncertain that she can bear listening to the rest. She stares blankly at the surrounding moorland, remembering what Daniel had told her about his mum, about her leaving, about how it made him feel. Abandoned by his own mother.

She can't stop now, and she taps the arrow on her screen.

The kettle stops boiling. Sound of water poured into cups. Neither man has spoken for thirty seconds or more.

Wayne: She died.

Tiffany can see Gert, in her mind's eye, say nothing, leaving a space for the other person to fill when they can no longer bear the silence. He's done the same to her and must have done it thousands of times when interviewing suspects. Daniel's dad must have no idea that Gert is recording the conversation.

Wayne: She adored him. Close as clams, the pair of them. I

hardly got a look in. Car that hit her had false
plates. He wasn't seven, he was six. A week after
Daniel's sixth birthday. Party balloons still hanging
on the fucking stairs. The police said it was just a hit
and run but ... you know ... (the sound of sobbing)
They took her down Ealing Hospital. She's in a right
mess. God knows how long they operated. So I tell
the boy she's gone away for a few days. Can't let
him see her like that.
(another long pause)
One thing leads to another. She's hung on for
nearly three weeks and I'm thinking when she's
over the worst of it I'll take Danny down and he'll
see her on the mend. But instead of getting better
she just slowly ... you know. And then it's too late.
That's the trouble with bleedin' lies. You can't go
back ... I'm sorry, I can't ...

Gert: It's OK, Mr Murray. Take your time.

Tiffany is wiping away tears; partly for Daniel and partly
for herself as the memories of David's death flood back. She
watched her brother fade away in the hospital and has felt grief
eat her away from the inside. Those weeks lost in that stupid
fog of hope that reality could for once be just a dream and
cancer could be like a headache; here today gone tomorrow.
The anger, the self-pity, the sadness and, finally, the acceptance
that he had gone. He was just sweet sixteen and she was still
at primary school.

Wayne: I had to tell her family. They come down from up
          North and ask to take the body. Like a coward I
          says yes and that's it, she's gone.
          Didn't even go to the funeral. Did it to protect him.
          Told them he wasn't ready. He didn't really know

them, her family. After a few months I told Daniel she's left us. Walked out. Thought it would explain everything. Avoid telling him about the accident. Keep him safe.

(a pause)

All a fucking waste of time because he hates me like a dose of the clap and I can't look at his face without seeing her and thinking how I let him down.

Gert: (very gently) I'll take the cup before you drop it. Thank you for your candour, Mr Murray. Did Roxana ever tell you where in Romania she came from?

Wayne: Never asked. I'm not prejudiced.

Gert: So it wasn't true that Daniel's mum thought he was boring?'

Wayne: She loved him to bits. It was like watching the petals falling from a flower.

Gert: I needed to know what had happened to Daniel.

Wayne: Is he DEAD!

Gert: I don't think so. But he is in great danger. And not just him.

Wayne: What have I done?

Sound of cups placed on work surface. Shoes echo in the entrance hall. Door swings open.

Gert: I'll be in touch when I have news. And thank you.

The sounds of an urban street. A door closes. The microphone is dragged loudly against fabric then silence.

The recording has ended. The bus is still heading towards Middlesbrough. Tiffany sits in the cloud of her thoughts. Daniel has his own childhood trauma completely wrong. Until now she has been happy to wait but not any longer.

CHAPTER 34

Flight KL4021

8th March 2020

Sleep doesn't come to the guilty. There is no peace for Gert who is still amazed that he wasn't arrested at Heathrow, having taken the underground straight from Camden to the airport and paid cash for the first available flight out.

The turbulence that is upsetting everyone around him is of no interest to Gert. He couldn't care less if the plane slumps and falls from the sky. He has lost interest in himself, his safety and his future. Over and over he asks himself why he allowed Floriane Onyemachi, a woman he had barely met, to reach into his past and tease him out of retirement. If only he had resisted he would already be in the tropics, reunited with his luggage and walking along a golden beach beneath an innocent sky. And Kelly would still be alive.

Floriane is just doing what Antoine does or what he himself would have done, sniffing through data, spotting a detail, setting the hounds running but who is orchestrating everything and why? The obvious candidate at Europol is Winders, a man obsessed with promotion and influence. What does he gain from all this? Has he intercepted Gert's messages to Antoine and Floriane? Antoine is expert at covering his tracks, as Floriane must be.

Round and round the whirlpool, dragged inexorably downward. Who knew about Kelly? Only Antoine, Floriane, and the staff at the homeless shelter. What were their names? Why would any of them have spoken with the police? Is it the

Metropolitan police? That Oxbow woman? Is someone there as compromised as that detective inspector in Whitby when the bodies piled up during Goth Weekend? What was Kelly wanting to tell him? Are Europol liaising with Scotland Yard?

Let it go.

A crackle and the in-flight communications cuts in.

'Good afternoon, ladies and gentlemen, this is your captain speaking. We apologise for the bumpy air earlier on. As you will have noticed, the problematic weather is now behind us.'

'We are approaching our destination and have already begun our descent. We will be landing in fifteen minutes, at 12:13, so please return to your seats and follow instructions from the on-flight team. Apologies for the slight delay; restricted visibility has caused a few traffic challenges on the ground. The temperature in Bucharest is just 2°C so those gloves and hats will come in handy! Thanks again for travelling KLM, we hope you have enjoyed your flight and hope to welcome you aboard again soon.'

The plane lands in a white winter wonderland. With no luggage to collect from the carousel, Gert is quickly on his way but, in his blue city suit, he is not dressed for winter. Two hours later, having stopped at a hunting shop to buy boots, clothing, binoculars, a long hunting knife, and other equipment, he is sitting on a train heading north.

The train cannot be said to be an express; three hours to travel just 180 kilometres. The wide Romanian plains eventually give way to the foothills of the Carpathian Mountains. The temperature outside is now well below zero. Snow hangs heavy in the pines and muffles the fields.

At the back of the compartment, Gert sits head back, eyes closed. He has sent couple of messages to Antoine and is trying to rest. Now his decision has been made, he is at peace with himself.

His phone rings.

'Gert, listen to me very carefully,' says Antoine, side-stepping all the usual pleasantries. 'And start by understanding that everything that I have worked out in a couple of minutes others can also work out.'

'Have you got my messages?'

'Don't talk, just listen. Either you are too old school to understand the world or you're rusty. I was glad you left the UK, you were just hours away from arrest for murder. Unfortunately you made a bad decision. The worst decision. You are not on your way to Suriname, you are in Romania. When this call is over, as soon as you have downloaded the information I have just sent you, remove the SIM card from your phone and throw it out of the window or destroy it.'

'Understood,' Gert says, sitting up straight and kicking himself for being so stupid.

'I know what you are trying to do but you are way out of your depth.'

'If you know that then why …'

'Shut up and pay careful attention to what I have sent you. If we don't see each other again I want you to know that I have counted you as one of my few true friends in this world. You are honest and your heart is pure. Or tries to be.'

'I am being set up. I couldn't possibly have killed Kelly. She was killed by scravir. She had the life sucked out of her; her neck was no thicker than a scaffolding pipe.

'For your information there are two bodies not one in the flat in Camden. The second woman died of a heart attack before she could ring the police. That's the only reason you weren't stopped at the airport, they didn't find the bodies until an hour ago.'

'Someone at Europol or in the Metropol …'

'I know and I'm on it. Look after yourself. Bye.'

Gert checks his messages. A couple of pdf files and a set of video clips. He downloads them all then prises open his phone and removes the SIM card. A minute later the thumbnail-sized card is broken and lying in the falling snow between the railway tracks having been flushed out of the toilet and Gert is no longer broadcasting his whereabouts. Until he buys a cheap burner phone he is now cut off from the world and on his own.

As he scrolls through the files he is furious with Antoine for hiding so much from him. Way back in early 2017 Europol was assembling evidence that pointed to the continuing presence of evil in the neighbourhood of Mikăbrukóczi castle. And it is clear from the ever-shifting explanations that came from the local police that they were fatally compromised and unreliable.

Keen for some practical information Gert turns to the video clips.

The first shows what appears to be an operating theatre. Trolleys covered in gleaming instruments, computer screens and medical equipment. The camera pans across the scene to reveal a scene of chaos. An overturned cabinet with papers strewn across the floor. Scalpels and broken bottles and a broken operating table on its side. At the back of the room is an open door. Lights are flashing in a corridor that appears to be lined in stone. A body lies half in and half out of the corridor and it is this that is preventing the door from closing. The face isn't visible.

But just as interesting, more interesting, is what the video has captured inadvertently. There must be a glass wall between the camera and the operating theatre because, zooming in, Gert is able to form a sense of a second room, behind the person shooting the video, caught in fleeting reflections. He sees the ghostly echoes of chairs and sofas scattered about, minimalist modern in style. He also glimpses the filmmaker holding the phone, a young woman with brown hair. She appears interested and maybe surprised, but not fearful. And that last detail matters because of the other person in the room with her.

Caught in the reflections is a tall man standing behind the young woman. He has massive hands and is dressed like a medieval peasant. Beneath the flaking grey skin on the top of his head is an unkempt comb-over. His face is a mess. A gaping open mouth, as if its owner is struggling for breath. Discoloured teeth set in expansive gums. One of the man's nostrils is missing.

Most people would be displaying extreme anxiety so why is the young woman unphased by the presence of this man?

Does she know him?

Gert returns to Antoine's notes. She is called Maria Mayer. Sweet sixteen. Worked at the castle for just a few months, until her body was found in the forest a kilometre down the mountain on the 10th of December. Her body had been partially eaten by wild animals, wolves in all probability. The video clip was apparently sent to her boyfriend along with a couple of others on 5th December 2016, the day she failed to return home after going for a walk. Maria lived on a nearby farm. The family reported her missing shortly after dusk. Mother said her daughter had been at home for a few weeks on full pay. She had been going for long walks and had complained about the older staff, saying they were picking on her. Mother also claimed to have been unaware that her daughter had been seeing a local boy Dumitru, until he turned up on the doorstep to show the video clips Maria had sent him. The family reported the matter to the police who had done nothing with them. Dissatisfied with the response, the mother protested. According to her, the local police had threatened her and the girl's boyfriend with talk of unfortunate traffic accidents, at which point she had sent the video clips to Europol along with the observation that the local police and politicians were corrupt and probably involved in the conspiracy over her daughter's death.

And Europol had sat and done nothing.

The second clip is taken from within a room looking out

into a corridor. The footage is shaky and accompanied by the sound of heavy breathing and then talking. A girl's voice pleading, presumably in Romanian, repeating the same words over and over, the panic rising as she speaks.

'Vă rog. Salveaza-ma! Mamă. Usile. Vă rog! Doamne Fereste, Doamne Fereste, Doamne Fereste. Salveaza-ma. Vă rog!'

The corridor is lined with photographs, a number of which are no longer on the wall but in pieces on the floor. Suddenly the sidewalls move towards each other and Gert realises they're not walls but doors and the filming is taking place within a lift. As the doors close the video clip ends.

Where were the clips shot? Gert guesses the castle, even though the rooms are not what you would expect in a medieval building. The tall skinny man must be a scravir. Why was she not frightened of him? Did she know him? How many are there like him at the castle?

He tries to remember everything he has learned about the scravir. Aren't they meant to be like slaves, animated by the will of their master? Which would mean that Lupei is still alive.

Dusk arrives. Shadows bleed from the trees, the train now an illuminated bullet plunging through a fading landscape. Gert's reflection stares back at him, tired and miserable, in the carriage window. Pressing his face against the glass, he shields his eyes. High above, a starless indigo sky straddles the mountain tops.

Gert imagines how Thor Lupei might have turned the castle into a place that suited his needs. Any construction work would have required an architect and builders. Will he find someone in the village willing to talk to him?

The provenance of the second set of video clips is less clear though Antoine has supplied a plausible backstory. Some two weeks after the girl's body had been found, a second body was discovered in thick forest some four kilometres away. A policeman called Nistor Pichler, age 43, also partially eaten. The official story was that Pichler and Zamfir Vulpe, a second policeman, age 36, also reported missing on 14th December, had assaulted or raped the girl. When the girl's body was found, the two policemen realised it was just a matter of time before they were caught. One of them, Vulpe, vanished, presumably left the country and the other committed suicide aware that he had brought disgrace to his family. Antoine had established that Nistor Pichler's children were the same age and in the same school as Maria.

The story promoted by local police makes sense but is it correct? And it doesn't explain how the video clips ended up with Antoine.

The first frame of the video clip shows a forest road, shot through the windscreen of a car. Gert presses play.

The vehicle is advancing up a mountain thick with snow. A man speaks. The rhythm of his voice suggests he is talking formally, giving a context to the video clip perhaps. The car noise is intense and Gert guesses the vehicle is fitted with snow chains. The road ahead is virgin snow, no tyre tracks, no footprints.

A second voice interrupts the first speaker. Very quickly the two men are arguing. Occasional glimpses of dark blue sky and sunlight piercing the trees. The car starts to slip across the road. A hand comes into frame and grabs the steering wheel as the camera, a smart phone presumably, is dropped face up onto the dashboard where it slides back and forth. The two voices are shouting at each other now. For some twenty seconds the visuals are only sky and tree tops skating back and forth then the movement stops. The phone is picked up.

The view ahead is now quite different, the forest of trees parts to reveal a high stone wall. The car slows and stops. The first voice utters a few more words in the formal tone he used at the start of the clip. The second voice offers what sounds like a sneering throw-away remark and the clip finishes.

There are four other people in the train compartment, two middle-aged women, an old man and a young man. Gert studies each of them in turn. He picks the young man, mid-twenties perhaps, wearing a baseball hat and a thick puffa jacket, playing a game on his phone.

'Excuse me,' Gert says sitting in the table seat opposite. 'Do you speak English?'

The man shakes his head.

'German? Deutsch?' Gert doesn't mention Dutch since the odds of finding a fellow Dutch speaker are low.

The man shakes his head a second time. Gert sighs then has an idea. He pulls his phone out of his pocket and grimaces to indicate that it is broken then points at the man's phone and gestures to indicate he would like to borrow it. The young man smiles and hands it over. Gert finds a translation App and starts typing.

I would like help to transcribe some Romanian please.
As dori ceva ajutor pentru a traduce niste romana in engleza, va rog.

The man smiles and nods. Gert produces his phone and locates the start of the video clip. Gert types:

My SIM card is broken not my phone. OK?
Cardul meu SIM este stricat, nu telefonul meu. OK?

The man nods again, satisfied with the explanation.

Gert hands over his phone and watches as the young man extracts a pencil a sheet of paper from his bag and proceeds to watch the clip, type the words on the phone, scribble the English translation, rewind, type, scribble and rewind.

At first he seems almost amused by what he is hearing. Gert can still hear the clip while the young man watches across the table. At the point where the shouting starts the young man looks genuinely alarmed as the car starts to slide across the road and looks up anxiously at Gert.

'It's OK,' Gert reassures him. 'No accident. No bad.'

The young man continues to watch and scribble as the two voices shout at each other.

'Bad words!' he tells Gert. 'Very bad words.'

The shouting subsides, the vehicle is emerging from the forest, Gert guesses. Suddenly the young man grimaces. He looks Gert in the eye.

'Police. No more translate.' He puts the phone on the table and pushes it across to Gert along with the piece of paper then glances around the compartment to see if they are being observed. The old man is asleep and so is one of the middle-aged women; the other woman is on her phone chatting with someone.

Gert hands the man back his phone and collects his own from the table along with the sheet of paper.

'Thank you. Thank you,' Gert smiles and returns to his seat to read the translation.

12.34 on Wednesday 14th December 2016.
Myself and Zamfir are on the road from the village up to the castle.
Did you go to the restaurant?
Yes, of course
So she did not tell you to …
She doesn't dictate my life, Nistor.
OK, OK. Sorry I asked.
How long do you think this is going to take, and can you stop dumping stuff on the floor?
If you really want to keep the car clean, stop smoking.

Do not start.

You started. The ashtray's overflowing, the car stinks and you are banging on about a crisp packet. Really? How about …

Fuck off, Nistor. So what are we going to tell him?

If he's there, we ask about Maria.

She was a naughty little prostitute, from what I hear.

For God's sake, Zamfir, she was a child. Sixteen years old.

Watch out. We're sliding all over the road. Dump the bloody phone, Spielberg. Jesus. Into the skid. Turn into the skid.

Take your hand off the wheel.

Oh fuck. Shit.

I know what I am doing.

Yes, yes, that is fucking obvious.

There you are. See? Wasn't even close.

Making a bloody film while driving on an ice rink. Remind me to avoid ever being in a car chase with you.

Says the man who has written off three cars. I am keeping a record, that's all. OK, we park outside. I do not want to be locked inside that castle.

We are not arresting him. Agreed? We will get so much shit if you try to arrest him.

We are questioning him and then…

Gert is not hugely the wiser but he does now know the date and time the film was made. The two policemen, Pichler and Vulpe, were acting on their own authority, clearly anxious about what their superior officers might say if they attempted an arrest. Did they park outside Thor Lupei's home, Mikăbrukóczi Castle? Gert won't know that for sure until he sees the place for himself as he has been unable to find photos of the castle online. Antoine's notes confirm that the last stretch of the journey is on a private road.

The setting of the last video clip is immediately clear; it is the same operating theatre that the girl videoed a week or so earlier. Only this time the room is tidy, no equipment scattered across the floor, the operating table upright. Voices talking as two men walk away from camera towards the door that Gert has seen in Maria's video clip. One appears to be in uniform and must be one of the two policemen, the other policeman is presumably holding the camera. The door is opened to reveal the corridor beyond. No body on the floor.

As the camera steps out of the operating theatre and into the corridor the acoustics change. The walls are lined with cut stone blocks. Gert wishes he could understand what is being said. He glances down the train compartment at the young man then decides against bothering him again.

After a few metres the cut stone walls give way to rough rock as the corridor or tunnel drops down into the ground. The man leading the way stops and begins to turn. The camera is hastily dropped out of view and the video clip ends.

Gert checks his watch. He packs everything away, closes his eyes and tries to rest.

Outside, the feral night licks the flanks of the passing train.

Sixty minutes later, the train's two-tone horn blasts a plaintive cry that ricochets off a hundred buildings. The brakes skreal and grind and the carriages slow in a sea of sparks.

Busteni station south of Brasov.

Cold air pours in through the open doors and prowls the floor of the carriages. Beneath one of the seats is a pile of sloughed city clothes. Blue suit, white shirt, skinny green tie, black trainers.

CHAPTER 35

Hotel Floare de Colt

8th March 2020

The small town has two seedy two-star hotels and Gert has picked the wrong one. As he closes the curtains in his first-floor room he sees the snow swirling in the wedge of light beneath a lamp post across the street. The radiator is stone cold, his breath hangs in clouds. Gert dumps his few belongings and walks back down the squeaking wooden staircase to find something to eat.

A short walk down the street, the door of the bar opens in a rush of hot, beery, smoke-filled air. Shaking the snow from his coat, Gert finds a table and orders pickled cabbage rolls with polenta, washed down with two bottles of an excellent local craft beer. The place is packed, mainly locals plus a drunk American couple wearing baseball caps, taking selfies.

'Do you speak English, German or Dutch?' Gert asks the young couple to his left.

Fingers intertwined across the table, the lovers gaze into each other's eyes, oblivious to the noise around them.

Gert repeats his question.

'Yes, little,' says the young woman in English, pushing a strand of black hair from her eyes to get a better look at Gert.

'I am here in your beautiful country to walk in the mountains and the forest. Where can I find a guide?'

'What for you want one?' she asks.

'I want to see wildlife, animals and birds. I am a naturalist. For three months I have been working in a team studying

Meyer's naked mole-rat in the Pannonian Basin. Which is good but the land is so flat. I want to walk in the mountains before I go home to Netherlands, which is also flat. Too flat!'

The young woman laughs. 'Here we have many mountains!' She translates what Gert has told her for her boyfriend's benefit.

'Petru is happy to be your guide. He knows mountains. But there is too much snow.'

'I have proper boots and clothes and sticks,' Gert tells her.

The lovers chat some more.

'Where you want walk?' she asks him.

'I hear there are many birds and jackal and lynx to the north. In the forests by Mikăbrukóczi Castle and ...'

The young woman's face drops. Her boyfriend is no longer smiling either as he spits his words across the table at her.

'Not possible,' she tells Gert. 'South is better.'

Petru has stood up and is frowning suspiciously at Gert. He picks his phone off the table and mutters to his girlfriend, who collects her coat from the back of her chair.

'I'm sorry. Have I said something wrong?' Gert asks.

The young woman shakes her head and follows her boyfriend out of the bar.

'You having a tough time with those there locals, my friend?' one of the Americans shouts across the room.

Gert crosses the bar to sit with the Americans and explains his mission to see the local flora and fauna.

'Says in the guide they're a superstitious bunch round here. Some voodoo thing I guess. I'm Tyrel.'

'Gert.'

They shake hands.

'I'm Annie. As is *git your gun!*' the woman says, also offering her hand.

The couple are in their forties; he is overweight and bearded in shapeless jeans and check shirt, she is slim as a bird, all blond curls and curves in a figure-hugging turquoise dress.

'We're doing the grand tour,' Annie explains. 'Ten weeks to see Europe. Seen some lovely old places, haven't we, Tyrel? And the food! Well, not all the food but …'

'Turned her pretty nose up at the tripe soup,' Tyrel explains. 'We call it variety meat back home. Prefer a steak myself.'

'Oh, Tyrel!' Annie interjects. 'I've just had a thought!'

'She does that occasionally. Always ends badly!'

'Oh, don't. He's always teasing me,' Annie tells Gert. 'You *are* always teasing me.' She pouts then bursts out laughing. 'Anyway, my idea.' Annie mimes a drum roll and cymbal strike. 'Baboom Kischhh. Why don't we take you to your mountain? Huh? Good idea? Oh YEAH!'

Gert is confused.

'Wow! Not a bad idea, girl.' Tyrel admits. 'If it's on the satnav, and if the satnav can be bothered to work, we can mosey there tomorrow. I hired us the best four by four in the entire country,' he boasts, picking a set of keys off the table and dangling them in Gert's face, 'and it's been sitting in the damn parking lot for thirty-six hours in its snow chains going no place. *She* has cold feet about driving into the mountains.'

'I DO NOT!' Annie beams at Gert. 'Don't listen to him. I'm practically a snowbird. I'd LOVE to see a lynx! I guess they're smaller than the cougars we have in Arizona but it will still be like WOW, right? Go Wildcats!'

'10am sound good to you, Gert?' Tyrel asks.

Annie claps her hands together. 'Oh, this is SO exciting! Thank you Gert, what a wonderful idea!'

'Another drink, Gert?'

'Thanks, Tyrel, a beer would be great.'

Tyrel climbs unsteadily to his feet. 'Must be the mountain air.' He staggers to the bar waving a fist full of banknotes.

'Hey, young man,' Annie shouts after her beau. 'Out of order. What am I supposed to do? Wait until you're snoring later and raid the minibar?' She turns to Gert. 'Tell him I want a beer. The little girl's powder room is expecting a visit.'

Gert watches her go and joins Tyrel at the bar. 'Forgive me but it's been a really long journey today. I need to sleep.'

'Cool, buddy. Ten o'clock in the car park across the road.'

Gert nods. 'What colour's the car?'

'Electric Blue Dacia Duster, can't miss it.'

Gert claps Tyrel on the shoulder and walks slowly to the door. As soon as he is out in the open air, his demeanour changes. He strides to his hotel, collects his belongings and hurries to the car park. He'll be on his way towards the mountains before Tyrel even notices his keys are no longer on the table.

In minutes, Gert has left the town and is driving up a single-track road. He switches off the radio; country music is a distraction. A couple of small hamlets and a few isolated farms later the car enters the forest.

Conifers and huge walls of rock crowd the roadside on the left, the land plunging away to his right. Lit for an instant in the headlights, the landscape glows red in his tail-lights then disappears black into the ink of night. The engine roars and he weaves his way upwards. The road hugs the contours of the valley as tightly as Annie's turquoise dress clung to her curves.

Beneath the car the snow chains rattle and roll; the blizzards have barely penetrated beneath the overhanging trees.

Another snatch of open land, snow-swaddled in deep drowsy drifts. Garden walls, a small village, all of thirty houses, a church and a tavern. No lights, everyone in bed.

Gert is at peace, not the peace and healing he felt in Kelly's arms, more a quiet acceptance; whatever happens in the coming hours he will have lived purposefully. He does not hesitate at the crossroads, the route memorised earlier on the train. Stealing the car has simply saved him from waiting until the morning to hire a vehicle.

Suddenly the forest stops and the road passes a narrow field with white muffled hedgerows at the end of which is a farm. The sign reads Ferme de Munte, Mountain Farm.

The home of Maria, the girl who worked at the castle.

Back into the gloom of the forest, steeper now, the wheels spinning in last autumn's leaf litter. A dozen kilometres from the town and approaching Gert's destination. Driving more slowly now and on sidelights not full beam.

A patch of brightness up ahead.

Gert parks off the road among the trees. He cuts the engine, lets his eyes acclimatise to the lacklight then steps out into the cold clean conifer-scented air. A dead branch serves to sweep the leaf litter about behind the car and blur the tracks of the tyres. Shouldering his backpack, Gert heads up on foot towards the castle, keeping under the trees where his footprints can remain hidden.

Beyond the treeline, tyre tracks on the snowbound road reveal the passing of several vehicles.

The castle takes Gert's breath away. To the east the castle walls grow out of the bare rock, leaving a vertiginous drop of sixty metres or more from the ramparts down to the valley below. Behind the castle, to the south, the mountain surges upwards in a dense dark forest of conifers clinging to a gradient too steep to climb without crampons and ropes. To the north and west is the forest he has just driven through.

The castle ramparts are some five metres in height and incorporate windows and the roofs of various outbuildings, enclosing an area that, Gert guesses, must be half the size of a football pitch. Directly in front of the gatehouse the land, cleared of trees, is relatively flat and cloaked in a thick blanket of snow. Mikăbrukóczi castle is a medieval fortress.

Gert sits down, safely hidden in the trees, to think. His winter clothing, balaclava and fur-lined boots are keeping him warm for now but a frost breeze drifts malevolently between the trees. He will die of exposure before dawn if he doesn't find a way in.

He imagines the staff. Do they live in the castle grounds or climb forest paths to reach it every morning? Surely not every morning. Especially in winter. There are wolves and bears. And what about the scravir? The local tales about the scravir go back centuries; he read about them in the account he found on the Whitby pathologist's computer. The villagers will surely not venture these wild forests after dark.

Gert shifts his position to put a large tree at his back. Faint animal yelps and grunts to his right, away among the trees. A hooting call echoes forlornly. He pictures the girl arriving at work. Just sixteen. Does her father drop her off at the gate? Is there a path up through the trees that she would climb safely after daybreak?

And suddenly he knows what he must do.

Retrieving the binoculars he bought in Brasov from his backpack he looks towards the gatehouse and is still trying to focus when his eyes are blinded in a supernova of light. Night becomes day. He drops the binoculars.

In the glare of powerful lights an eagle-owl is swooping down, gliding just above the road then up over the snow drifts and away into the forest on silent wings.

Nature has come to his aid, tripping the security systems for him. For a moment he sees the surveillance camera above the gate. From its placement, Gert guesses it offers a wide shot of the road and that it must be possible to stand at the gate unseen by the camera. Maybe a person on foot can approach from the side without triggering either lighting or camera.

The light cuts out and darkness returns.

The snow comes halfway up his thighs as he approaches the castle close to the lip of the cliff and out of sight of the gate. No hope of covering his tracks, he has one shot at this. He hugs the castle ramparts as he advances towards the gate praying that the owl will not only have triggered the lighting but also have put the gatekeeper on alert. His plan relies on it.

Beside the massive wooden gate, Gert retrieves his phone, scrolls his apps, finds what he is looking for and sets the volume to full.

The heavy iron chain dangling from a hole in the rampart is chill, drawing the heat from his fingers even through his gloves. Gert rolls up his balaclava, he needs to hear the slightest noise on the other side of the gate. He pulls the chain. Bells rattle obligingly on the other side of the metre-thick wall. He waits. Nothing. Pulls again.

This time he hears footsteps. Gert presses play and slides his phone forwards in front of the gate.

'Vă rog. Salveaza-ma! Mamă. Usile.'

Maria's voice pleads in the darkness. The video clip the girl took while standing in the lift.

A shuffling on the other side of the gate.

'Vă rog! Doamne Fereste, Doamne Fereste, Doamne Fereste.'

The dead girl's cries hang in the chill air.

Why are they not opening the gate? Have they no conscience? Gert grips his hunting knife.

'Salveaza-ma. Vă rog! Pepene!'

'TACI NAIBII!' shouts an angry voice on the other side.

More shuffling behind the gate.

'Salveaza-ma!'

Suddenly a frenzy of activity as bolts are torn back.

'DIAVOLU!'

The small door set within the gate is wrenched open and a man leans out. He has recognised Maria's voice and senses the devil's work. The little bitch must be right up against the door out of range of the camera. Ghost or no ghost, he will give her a beating she will never forget.

Ovidiu, the old fool who claims that wolves lay eggs, the

servant who has never done anything more challenging than chop wood and peel vegetables, has made his last mistake. He is still registering the lack of a human presence in front of the gate and still trying to make sense of the square of light in the snow when his jacket is grabbed from his blindside, yanking him forward. As he falls, a massive blow from the hilt of a hunting knife smacks the back of his head. He is out cold before his temples hit the snow.

Gert drags the unconscious old man back inside the gatehouse and leaves him bound and gagged in the side room he was sitting in before he heard the bell at the gate.

The shadows beneath the gatehouse arch provide perfect cover as Gert considers his next move. The owl returns to land silently in the empty branches of the tall tree in the middle of the grounds. High over the serrated crest of the mountains, a bone yellow moon emerges from behind the clouds.

In the depths of the forest a lone wolf howls her respects. Across the valley others of her kind awaken and climb to their feet, shaking the powder snow from their backs, and look up. The chill air quickly swells with a febrile bestial chorus of devotion.

Though safe within the sanctuary of the medieval fortress, its circular towers and high-pitched roofs blanketed by moonlit snow, the hairs on the back of Gert's neck stand on end.

If it weren't for the car tracks running from the gatehouse towards the main buildings, he could have slipped four centuries back in time. The internet has next to nothing on the castle. It was in ruins for centuries and not even a tourist attraction, visited only by walkers keen to enjoy the view of the valley from the northern edge until that vista became obscured by vegetation. The current buildings look ancient but Gert knows that Thor Lupei has had the whole place reconstructed to his own specification with only a cursory nod towards planning regulations for historic structures.

Money talks.

As if on cue, the moon disappears, plunging the castle back into deep shadow. Gert steps out from under the arch, knife in hand. The setting is so intense and strange that, if it weren't for the bitter cold on his face and the faint aroma of the pine forest, Gert might imagine he was playing a computer game.

His boots squeak the snow as he hurries through soft silent flakefall towards the main buildings. The eagle-owl in the tree slowly rotates its head to track his passing.

The massive door is not locked. It swings open on silent hinges without Gothic fanfare and Gert steps inside.

Uninvited.

He pushes the door shut and stands immobile. His pupils dilate slowly until his irises have all but disappeared.

Three figures loom before him. Kerbing his instinct to flee, Gert stands his ground and studies them. Sloughed skins, like the shed shells of moulted tarantulas. Suits of armour. One clutches a long sword, the second a metal-headed mace, and the third a battle axe.

Hanging on the walls in the stairwell beyond the suits of armour are animal heads: two wolves, a stag and a chamois. And half a dozen guitars.

Gert has to imagine the colours because there are none to be seen in the monochromatic gloom.

Where should he go? Should he climb the stairs? If Thor Lupei is in the building, where will he be? In his mind Gert rehearses opening a bedroom door, creeping towards a huge four-poster bed knife in hand, but he knows he must avoid the trap of imagining his opponent an easy prey. Lupei has not survived so long by accident.

He opens a door to his right and steps into the Great Hall. Embers huddle and glow within a mantle of ash in the huge fireplace, casting a feeble orange light. Beside a shuttered window, a large beeswax candle flickerflames in the air currents Gert agitated by opening the door.

In front of the fire are three high wing-backed chairs. The room, warm and smelling of honey and aromatic woods, is a curious blend of ancient and contemporary. Thick tapestries alongside slick steel lighting stands. An ornate wooden chest in dark oak, thick with history and banded in iron, serves as a table upon which rest two stunning pieces of modern ceramics – a large bowl beside an abstract human figure – and a golden West African lost wax figure of a cow.

A semi-acoustic guitar straddles one of the wing-backed chairs, its rippling lacewood grain gleams in the fireglow.

The room exudes refinement and taste and, momentarily, Gert finds himself envying the master of this domain.

There are doors to either side of the fireplace. Gert opens the left-hand door and can see nothing. He pulls a torch from his backpack and cupping his hand over the lens, switches it on, allowing only the faintest slither of light to escape. The walls of the narrow passage are painted black, as is the ceiling. He proceeds cautiously, burdened by the feeling that he is entering a tomb. After a couple of corners the passage ends in a door that he opens. He steps out into a wider corridor with grey stone walls. The door he has just passed through swings shut behind him with a soft click. Turning round he sees only a mirror without a door handle.

Ahead of him is a banqueting hall the walls of which are covered in geometric designs in blue, orange and green painted directly onto the stone. The long table is covered with a rich purple cloth. Between five large candelabra, squats a curious object; a large black spider the size of a cat. Gert approaches cautiously. The creature's body is quite flat. One of the eight legs is extended straight ahead and appears to have wires upon its upper surface. Only when he reaches the edge of the table does Gert recognise the object for what it is: a guitar, the extended leg the fretboard. As if sensing his presence, the spider's legs collapse slowly, leaving the body to sink to the table, then clench again and lift the body up off the table. Gert shakes his head in astonishment and walks away, backwards.

He continues down the corridor, reaching a rough-hewn door that opens in a rush of tumbling snowflakes.

On the other side of a small courtyard an even older door creaks and sighs like an ancient beast turning in its sleep. Gert crosses the threshold into a space as cold as the forest. His breath blooming in the slither of light emanating from his torch, Gert ascends a stone staircase, its worn steps sagging the song of seven centuries. Empty suits of armour stand sentinel along a long corridor, at the end of which he reaches the large carved wooden panel.

Shadows dance in the shivering torchlight. The chiselled animals appear almost alive. Contemptuous. Malevolent. Evil lurks in the crow's gaze. The jay longs to stab out his eyes. The wild boar glares up from its carved undergrowth of ivy and thorns, tusks sharp in its ugly gaping maw.

Besides a carved robin, its beak slightly open as if frozen in the middle of an alarm call, is a door handle.

Gert reaches out a hand.

The sound of something breathing.

A hollow creak.

Gert shivers involuntarily and decides to retrace his steps. He will return in daylight. His quarry, if he is alive and if he is in the castle, will surely not be sleeping in rooms as cold and dank as the grave.

He turns away to the sound of scraping and shuffling. Spinning back, he knows the animals have turned towards him. He could only see one of the crow's eyes before. And the robin's beak was open!

Unnerved, his boots echoing in the whispering dark void, Gert hurries back towards the staircase. The uneven steps are treacherous underfoot and he rolls his ankle. Hobbling, he pulls open the exterior door and staggers back out into the flake-swirled courtyard, dropping both torch and hunting knife in the snow. As the door groans shut behind him, a heavy presence hurls itself against the other side with bone-shattering force. Furious feet scuffle the stone floor trying to push the door open or smash it down.

Gert retrieves his knife and torch and steps back into the main body of the castle, pushes the door closed and looks for a bolt he can slide to secure it. Nothing. He will have to hope the other door holds. Past the banqueting hall doors and the mirror he cannot open, he seeks a route back to the main entrance.

Elsewhere within the metre-thick stone walls of Mikăbrukóczi castle the warning cries of the carved menagerie have not passed unnoticed.

It is ten degrees warmer in this part of the castle. With every step Gert feels safer and better able to think. Self-doubt is gnawing away. Did entering the castle armed only with a hunting knife ever really constitute a serious plan?

The corridor does eventually lead back to the main entrance where Gert switches off his torch and stands silently in the lacklight clinging the stairwell, weighing up his options.

To his left is the door that leads outside.

He still has choices.

A race to the gatehouse. Get out of the castle, find the car and drive away. Even if he cannot reach Suriname, arrest on suspicion of the murder of Kelly and a long prison sentence are perhaps preferable to confronting the evil festering within these walls.

But the flames of rational thought burn too weakly; he is too far in. His fate is sealed.

Gert Muyskens looks up the stairwell, half-expecting the stuffed animal heads on the walls to turn towards him.

How many floors are there? Three or four? From his memory of looking across from the gatehouse, he thinks three as he puts a foot on the first step. It bears his weight without creaking.

But there is a sound.

A soft tapping sound.

Mechanical and repetitive.

Water in a central heating system perhaps?

Long hunting knife in hand, Gert starts to climb. On the landing he lifts the knife to his eyes, tilting the blade to serve as a slender serrated mirror to reveal the view behind him down the stairs.

Nothing.

But the clicking noise remains, just audible above the tinnitus fog in his brain.

Even less light at the top of the stairs. Gert senses that shining his torch, however faintly, will bring bad consequences so he leaves it off and fumbles forwards into the gloom, his left hand brushing the wall to keep him grounded, his right hand sweeping the hunting knife round in a series of arcs, in front of him, to the side, behind.

The corridor turns left, effectively killing any last hint of light from the stairwell and plunging him into a pitch as total as a deep-sea trench.

There will be a window soon.

You can't let him know you're coming, surprise is the only thing in your favour.

There! That tapping sound again …

Behind me …

Shh. Swing the blade!

If there's anything there you can slice its head off. Stab its eyes out.

See? Nothing. You're OK.

No, it's breathing …

IT'S BREATHING!

That's you, you idiot.

No one else here.

Relax. You'll give yourself a heart attack.

There, that click. Don't pretend you can't hear it.

WHOA!

What's that?

Something different beneath my fingertips.

That's not the wall!

Control your fear. Stay calm and think.

Some kind of ridge. Feels slightly warmer. Oh God!

A door? A door frame.

Yes, that's all it is.

There. Now smooth. Like wood.

That's why it's not so cold.

Now the frame again.

Cooler now. That's stone.

That's the wall.

Yes, that narrow gap between one stone and the next.

You're OK. Keep going.

Don't rush. You can turn and come back.

Count the doors first then decide what to do.

Safer running towards the stairs if you have to.

That's it.

That clicking is my shoelaces, they must have come undone.

IT'S NOT.

It IS. You're just freaking yourself out.

See? The noise stops when you stop.

Should have checked them, or double-knotted them.

Wait! What's ...

WHAT HAVE I HIT?

Maybe the corridor is narrowing.

Don't drop the knife. DON'T DROP THE KNIFE.

Keep left hand on the wall.

It's curved ... maybe a vase ... on a table.
Yes, that's it.
OK.
WHAT??
It's moving!
DON'T LET IT FALL.
It will break and you'll wake the whole castle.
You don't even know what it is ...
Your finger not the blade ... use your finger.
OH, FUCK.
It's warm.
It's not a vase.
NOT A VASE AT ALL.
It's got fucking eyebrows!
Oh, please no! NO!
There. Have a bit of that. YOU LIKE THAT?
Sharp enough for you?
Slice it in half ... Kill it.
KILL IT!
Let go!

'LET GO!' Gert shouts.

Strong fingers wrap round his ankle. Nails dig into his flesh. Sweat is trickling down the small of Gert's back. His body is shaking. He tries to pull his leg away but the vice-like grip is too strong. He loses control of his bladder. Nerves screaming, Gert stumbles backward and falls, the knife spilling from his hand as his elbow smashes excruciatingly on the hard floor. The option of flight has gone, only fight remains. Gert kicks out wildly, his boot connecting with his assailant.

But it is too little too late.

As tightly as the muscle-bound embrace of a boa constrictor, the darkness smothers and squeezes until Gert loses consciousness.

CHAPTER 36

Whitby

9th March 2020

Thurloe Square? Where have I heard that before?

Tiffany is still up and working on her laptop. It is nearly one in the morning. Ethan is teething and has been crying most of the evening. Tina doesn't seem to mind the noise.

Tiffany checks her messages again, on the off-chance of a reply from Gert, as she has done every fifteen minutes for hours. Nothing. It's like he has vanished off the face of the Earth. She wants answers to her questions about his interview with Daniel's dad, and she wants to confess finally about the micro SIM card Daniel sent her three years ago.

Gert's interview has tipped the balance. The knowledge that Daniel is out there somewhere convinced that his own mother left him when he was a small child because she found him boring is too much to bear. Tiffany wants Daniel to know the truth even if he is mad at her for tracking him down. That is why she has broken her promise to herself and is exploring the contents of the SIM card.

There are forty photos of pages of an ancient book written on rough yellow paper that seems to have veins in it.

According to Daniel, when they spoke up by the whalebones after the police had finished interviewing him., he found the book in the castle in Romania. He said it was packed with thousands of names going back centuries, lists of organ recipients. She hadn't asked what he meant but remembered something about the head of police in Whitby being on the list.

Why didn't I ask him what he meant?

Maybe this is what Gert is trying to get from her.

Daniel said he had torn some pages from the book and handed them over to the police. Which police? In Romania or in Whitby? What if he *hadn't* handed them over? Why would he do that? Why did he keep photos of them?

The names and addresses come from cities across Europe, thirty or more names to a page, with notes in different languages. All written by hand. The entries are not random; there are clusters in a particular town then a different town then a new country, weeks and months passing by as if the writer were travelling slowly from place to place. Beside a name is an address followed by a brief description of the individual, the name or names of internal organs and a sum of money.

10th May 1857. Joseph Stairs, bank manager of London Road, received a kidney. £24

The list isn't contiguous. A series of names and places visited in the 1850s switches abruptly to the 1970s and then to the 2000s. Presumably this is down to Daniel having torn out pages at random from the book, or was he only copying some of the pages? In 2008 there are fifteen entries in Paris and Rouen in France, all written in French, then over to London.

Oxford Street, Marylebone Road, Baker Street, Old Kent Road ... and the address that has leapt out at her.

11th November 2009. Jonathan Finch-Porter, a wealthy waster, Thurloe Square. Pancreas and kidneys. Fee: £93,000

Why does that address leap out at her? It isn't famous for anything: West End shows, posh shops, museums, fictional detectives ... Then it hits her. Gert mentioned it, just two days ago when he turned up on the doorstep. He was investigating in Thurloe Square. That's what he said, she is sure of it. And here it is in the pages of the book that Daniel stole from Thor Lupei in Romania!

She picks up her phone and messages again. Where is he? She dials his phone number, who cares what time it is? Nothing. She has to be up at seven to catch the bus to Middlesbrough. She'll try him again in a few hours. Or have to think of something else.

Antoine has just arrived at his workstation, still has his coat on and is in his eight-thirty pre-meeting with three junior analysts when his phone rings.

'External call for you, please hold.'

Followed by musical doodling on an acoustic guitar. The music cuts.

'Hello?'

'Are you Antoine Hoek? Friend of Gert Muyskens?'

A woman's voice. British, maybe from the north of the country.

'Who is this?'

'Yes or no?'

Antoine braces himself for bad news. 'Yes.'

'He told me I could trust you.'

Antoine looks around him and indicates to his junior staff that he needs some privacy. They return to their desks.

'Who is this?'

'Gert is not returning his messages. Something has happened.'

'Tell me who you are.'

'Tiffany Harrek. I have information about Daniel and …'

Tiffany? Isn't she a friend or girlfriend? Antoine tries to get his head in gear.

'When did you last speak with Gert, Tiffany?'

'He came to Whitby two days ago.'

'Please give me fifteen minutes to set up a secure remote conference call? I'll contact you on this number, OK?'

Antoine gives the team their assignments then leaves the building, avoiding Winders and Hervé. He crosses Scheveningseweg and enters Van Stolkpark, stopping only when he is more than 100 metres from the nearest human being. He sits on a bench surrounded by trees. The air is damp, it will rain soon.

Seconds later he can see Tiffany on his phone and she can see him. She is young, brown hair, blue eyes, a freckle or beauty mark on her left check. Behind her a large window looks out onto a narrow street with red brick terraced houses.

'Thank you for waiting, Tiffany. I wanted to be away from colleagues.'

'Where is Gert? I'm worried,' Tiffany says.

'So am I.'

'I have something that Daniel gave me. I told Gert I had nothing but it weren't true and I should have given it to him three years ago. To be fair, I were protecting Daniel.'

'Here is my problem, Tiffany. Someone has betrayed Gert. Here at Europol.'

She looks gutted.

'Can we meet?' she asks.

'That may not be a good idea.'

'I don't want to talk over the phone.'

'OK. Are you prepared to travel and do you have a pen?'

It is mid-afternoon. The pigeons and lions are fighting it out over dominance of the square, even though the lions cannot eat, being made of stone, and the pigeons cannot be fed, it being illegal.

Antoine is confident no one is tailing him. He has chosen a public space where Tiffany will feel safe. As long as Nelson's good eye keeps gazing south towards the Admiralty and not down into the square, they won't be overlooked.

He spots her by one of the fountains, wearing the turquoise mini backpack she said she would be carrying, staring at the tumbling water.

'Tiffany.'

'Are you sure we're safe?' She starts to turn towards him.

'Don't look at me, carry on enjoying the fountain. Nothing is hundred percent but, yes, I think so.'

'I managed to reach Jordan, Daniel's friend,' she tells Antoine. 'He's up there, watching us, ready to be my knight in shining armour.'

Is she telling the truth? Antoine pretends to be reading something on his phone while keeping an eagle eye on the comings and goings around them. He spots three people looking out over the square from up on the plaza in front of the National Gallery.

'You have a file for me,' he says.

'Is Gert all right?'

'Your friend and mine keeps doing stupid reckless things. He is currently in Romania, when he should be in Suriname cuddling turtles.

'Romania?'

'I think he has decided to be a superhero. He wants to kill Thor Lupei, if Lupei is alive, something that the Romanian police deny.'

'Are you helping him?'

'If by that you mean am I in touch with him, the answer is no. He is safest if no one, including me, knows where he is. I did persuade him to ditch his mobile phone to prevent anyone from tracking him.'

'Gert were right, there is a link between Daniel and Thurloe Square.'

'Where the murders took place?'

Tiffany glances up towards the National Gallery then leans

forwards to look at the water rippling. Antoine knows about Thurloe Square.

'Daniel sent me copies of the pages of a book he stole from Lupei's castle. On a SIM card. I kept it in a box. I swear I never looked at it until last night.'

'Do you know where Daniel is, Tiffany?'

'I hoped that Gert knew and I were trying to exchange the SIM card for an address.'

'Gert was in London two days ago. Did he tell you that? He visited a homeless shelter and met someone called Kelly.'

'Does she know what he is doing?'

'She's dead. He met her on Wednesday and she died on Thursday.'

Tiffany's face drops.

'There is worse. I think someone in my department at Europol is responsible. We are running out of time. Have you got the SIM?'

'Yes.'

'Can you drop it discretely as you leave.'

'What about Daniel?'

'All I can tell you is that the name RJ is important. Daniel met a man called RJ at the Providence Homeless Shelter in Camden. But be careful, Kelly told Gert and she is now dead and Gert's message to me was probably intercepted so you won't be the only one looking. If you are foolish enough to want to look and I somehow think you are. Love is a strange thing. Good luck, Tiffany.'

'Thank you.'

'Don't thank me. I just hope you won't regret it. And I've left a slip of paper with a secure email address on the dark web if you need to reach me. It's on a chocolate wrapper by the bin near the toilets over there. Set one up yourself on the same service and email me on it. Now go, and make sure you are in a crowd until you are absolutely sure no one is following you.'

Antoine shifts his shoe to cover the tiny SIM card Tiffany has dropped and keeps a casual and discrete eye on the young woman as she walks away across the square. She pauses to put rubbish in a bin, drops her keys and retrieves them with the sweet wrapper in a single movement, she could be a professional. She climbs the steps to the plaza in front of the National Gallery. One of the three people he spotted earlier, a black man, mid-twenties crosses towards her. They head off towards Charing Cross Road together.

In a couple of hours, as soon as the Eurostar is back on French soil, Antoine will call the office on a burner phone that cannot be traced and learn that, no, Winders has not been in the office today and no one knows where he is. Having cleaned off his prints, he will drop the phone in a bin at Rotterdam Central Station the moment he alights from the train.

'Thanks, Jordan. I'm sorry we lost touch. Your mum said …'

'She was trying to protect me, that's all.'

'My mum's the same. I were worried about coming to London and meeting Antoine, you made all the difference.'

'Totally Spy v Spy,' Jordan says then, when he sees Tiffany doesn't have the faintest idea what he's talking about, he explains, 'some old American cartoon from the 1980s. There's a black one and a white one, both carrying bombs and then shit happens and … whatever.'

'You mean meeting in Trafalgar Square with an agent from Europol?'

'There you go, girl.'

'Let's hope it doesn't end with bombs then.'

'You know.'

Tiffany and Jordan are walking up Tottenham Court Road towards Camden from Trafalgar Square. Seems safer than taking the tube.

'You heard from him?'

She shakes her head. 'Apart from the letter and the SIM card, no. Have you?'

'I dinged him a few times, left messages, went round his yard and even shouted through the letter box. Nothing. Guess he was depressed. I wanted to help but then my mum steps in, reads the riot act and sends me away. She was convinced I would get picked up by police, or worse …'

'Did she tell you Gert and I had been round to find you?'

Jordan shakes his head. 'Pure chance you reach me. She's off in Jamaica seeing her aunties and aks me to look after the house. I move in, find my old phone in a drawer and charge it up just to transfer phone numbers and thing, and your message pings up! Insane!'

'How long will it take to reach Camden?'

'Half an hour maybe a bit more.'

'I'm going to try to tell you everything I know before we get there.'

'How's Whitby?'

'Whitby can wait.'

By the time they reach Camden High Street, Jordan is up to date on Daniel and the daily grind of a nursing degree and Tiffany knows about the Transport for London graduate scheme.

The door to Providence Mission is opened by a hard-faced middle-aged woman in a blue trouser suit with sleek beige hair who does not let them in.

'Hi, we are looking for RJ,' Jordan says, flashing his Transport for London card. 'We believe he left some personal property on the Northern Line a couple of days ago and I'd like to …'

'You can leave it with me,' the woman says.

'So you know RJ?' Jordan asks.

'We aren't at liberty to discuss clients with the public, sorry. Is there anything else? We are very busy.'

'I need to talk with RJ and arrange an appointment,' Jordan says, trying not to let the woman get to him.

'Leave your card and he can contact you, if he wants to, when he arrives.'

'Let me get this straight. You won't tell me if there is a RJ at the centre but, if there is, then you will give him a card.'

Megan Oxbow is looking increasingly irritated.

Tiffany tugs Jordan's sleeve. 'Let's leave this cow to stew in her own juice.'

The door closes.

'I was doing OK, Tiff. A couple more minutes and …'

'She's a bitch, it's written all over her face. Forget it, we'll think of something else.'

'You looking for someone?'

They turn to find themselves face to face with Nika Shakarami. 'From what I overheard you have just met Megan Oxbow. Hair the colour of a biscuit and a face like a prune sandwich? I'm about to go in, she's my boss.'

'We're looking for someone called RJ.'

'Never met him.'

'Oh, well. No worries,' Jordan says. 'Come on, Tiff.'

'I said I never met him, before my time, but I know about him. Rajesh was what you call a character.'

Tiffany's eyes light up. 'Rajesh?'

Nika nods. 'Most of our clients are sad cases, broken by trauma. Rajesh Anvit was different. People still talk about him. The Dali from Delhi. Obsessed with chess and a bit of an artist. Always drawing people. Proper portraits and mad cartoons. There's still one up in the office.'

'What was he doing in the shelter?' Jordan asks.

'His uncle and his dad threw him out and …'

'Out of Delhi?' Tiffany is confused.

'Delhi and Wembley. His dad threw him out of India and his uncle threw him out of Wembley.'

'This make sense to you?' Tiffany looks at Jordan, who shakes his head.

'I'm sorry, I'm not explaining it very well.'

'You're not explaining it at all,' Jordan smiles.

'OK. The story that he told is that he rejected the caste system, he was high caste himself, and he made so much noise his family banished him,' Nika explains. 'When the uncle threw him out he became destitute. Oh, and he was a manic depressive I think.'

'So Rajesh and Daniel were friends?' Tiffany asks Nika.

'Daniel?'

'Daniel Murray. He was here in January 2017.'

Nika does a double-take. 'Someone else was looking for a Daniel. A big foreign guy. '

'Gert?'

'Yes! You know him?' Nika asks.

Tiffany realises she has said too much. 'Sorry?'

'You know the foreign guy? Gert.'

'Oh, sorry. No, I mean Gert,' Tiffany grabs Jordan's arm and smiles up at him. 'How strange is that, love,' she laughs. 'Not like it's a common name, is it? You and this other man both being called …"

'My grandfather was Dutch,' Jordan explains to Nika.

Nika appears satisfied with the explanation. 'OK,' she says, 'so the other Gert asked me about Kevin and I put him in touch with Kelly then she messaged me and said he was also looking for this Daniel and I was meant to get back to her but she's not answering her calls and …'

Nika hasn't heard about Kelly's death and Tiffany decides not to complicated matters. 'Does Rajesh still visit the shelter?'

'This is three years ago. Kelly or one of the old boys here will know. Look, give me a number, if I find anything out I'll message you. I'm Nika.'

Tiffany gives Nika her contact details.

'I can't get deep into this,' Jordan says as they walk away. 'You get that, don't you? Daniel and me we go way back and thing but I've got a life now Tiff. Did I tell you I've got a daughter? The baby mother and I don't live together but I've moved on. Got a job. Can't be disappearing back into that dark shit, OK?'

'They found that body in the lockup garage you and Daniel and Alex played in. I went there with Gert and saw the words Gristle Gang sprayed on the wall outside. That was you three, wasn't it?'

'We were kids. That's all,' Jordan cuts her off. 'You got a life too, you know?'

'You sound like Gert.'

'Just saying …'

'STOP!' Tiffany shouts then immediately feels bad. 'Sorry, this is stressing me out, Jordan. Are you any good with setting up a dark web email account?'

'I'll have a go,' he answers, keen to build bridges not walls. 'You going back to Whitby now? If not, my mum's is …'

Tiffany phone wakes up. A message from Nika:

> It was March 2017. Connor – one of the old men here - remembered because he says two amazing things happened that month: He won £50 when Ireland lost to Iceland in the football, and he beat the mighty Rajesh Anvit at chess. The only time he ever did in 40 attempts! He says Rajesh disappeared the next day. A sore loser according to Connor.

Tiffany forwards the information to Antoine who is up to his eyeballs, catching up, when the message comes through. He'll deal with it later on.

CHAPTER 37

Mikăbrukóczi Castle, Romania

9th March 2020

Gert Muyskens is no coward. Twenty years in various police forces have exposed him to danger, mayhem, and death.

But it is one thing to enter a boxing ring, adrenalin coursing, muscles tight, anticipating the first pummelling flurries of blows, armed with your own strength and capabilities. Quite another thing to be immobile, like a moth pinned to a board, a helpless witness to your body's fragility.

He is on his back in a cavernous space. Not on the floor. A table perhaps? The ceiling above his head appears rough-hewn from solid rock. His body, aside from his ears, eyes and mouth, are unavailable to him. He assumes he must still be in his body but he feels absolutely nothing. Even his neck muscles have abandoned him, he cannot turn his head. The space is large, he knows because he has shouted and heard the echoes. The air feels cool on his cheeks.

Is he restrained or paralysed? If paralysed, has his body been damaged or is this a chemical induced condition? What drugs do they give you in the operating theatre to keep your body quiet? An anaesthetic or a muscle relaxer? They block your nerves, don't they? Or has his spinal cord been severed?

Am I dead?

Not dead.

Where is the light coming from? All he has to go on are the shadows on the ceiling. A monochrome rocky surface like photos of the Moon landings. How far above his head is the ceiling. One metre? Five metres? The shadows suggest that the light source is behind his head.

A sound. The rhythm of walking.

Not one person, more than one.

Gert's breathing accelerates. He can hear air entering and leaving his nose but why can he not feel his chest? A pathetic whimper catches in his throat. The feet are closer now. In the space with him. Where were they before?

Doesn't matter.

The floor is solid but crunchy. Maybe rock like the ceiling. The feet approach then stop beyond Gert's line of sight.

Silence.

No, not silence.

The sound of breathing. His own and someone else's. How many people?

Say nothing. Wait. There are two of them, maybe they will speak to each other. Maybe he thinks I am unconscious.

Ten, twenty seconds pass. The feet turn. Walking away now.

Bastard. It's Lupei! It has to be. Shh, say nothing. Wait …

Gert's heart is thumping in his ears, his body bracing for pain. But he is paralysed. Will he feel pain?

A face looms into view above him. The man is huge and skeletally thin. His eyes stare down with the dark dullnumb disinterest of a tiger shark on standby. Clumps of hair cling to the flaking pockmarked skull, the skin of his face pulled tight as clingfilm over a bowl of offal, so tight that his mouth cannot close to hide the tombstone toothfest within. A nostril has abandoned his face for good.

Scravir.

'Go and find Radu. He has another job for you,' says a rich baritone voice.

The scravir nods and withdraws.

Footsteps leave the cavern clumsily; their owner is limping.

'It is funny how obsessions maketh the man, is it not?' the

baritone voice says, now just an arm's length from Gert's head.

'You have had so many opportunities to walk away. So many chances to choose life and make the most of your brief moment in the universe. But instead you return, time and again. K'keleb shuwb al keseel shanah ivveleth. As a dog returneth to his vomit, a fool returneth to his folly.'

Thor Lupei sighs. 'How you have squandered everything.'

Silence. Time slows and waits.

'Your surname, Muyskens, means little mouse.' Lupei says eventually. 'Why would a mouse throw itself at the wolf?'

'You killed Pim,' Gert wheezes, his voice as weak as tissue paper. 'My brother.'

'Your brother?'

'Schaesburg park during PinkPop festival. You left him in a skip. He wasn't even twenty.'

Another pause.

'Ah,' Lupei says. 'I remember. Vaguely. And now, judge and jury, you want your pound of flesh in return?'

'You bring only death, darkness and destruction. Daniel thought he had killed you but he was wrong. And now he is as evil as you are.'

'The failed policeman turns dragon slayer. I should thank you for your help in finding my protégé, by the way. I am not sure anyone else could have done it. It requires an obsessive's determination.'

'Why did you kill Kelly, you psychopath. Show yourself!'

Thor Lupei ignores the instruction.

'I have not left the castle for some time. My convalescence has been protracted, the circumstances in which Daniel left me were serious even for an individual with my esoteric aptitudes. Propitiously there are many beneficiaries of my good deeds who are more than willing to act on my behalf. Over the years thousands have owed me their lives or the lives of their loved ones.'

Another long pause.

'If you hadn't approached that woman at the shelter she would still be alive. But you know that, don't you? It eats at your vitals. And so it should. Daniel is mine. Tell me, what good has come from your existence? What have you added to the sum of human happiness, little mouse?'

'Who is the traitor at Europol?' Gert asks.

'Ah, the noble art of maieutics. We will leave that to Socrates, with your blessing, and I will ask the questions. If you were to choose your own epitaph, what would it be?' Lupei's baritone asks gently. 'Something about saving turtles, perhaps? But that is unfinished work. Exposing my friends in Whitby? That too ended in death and failure. You brandish your hatred of me, Mr Muyskens, but what have *you* done to atone for your sins? Anyway, we are wasting time. You want your pound of flesh and here it is. Choke on it.'

A shadow looms fleetingly into view over Gert's face as something warm touches his neck. A sensation like an electric charge surges within him. His neck swells like a balloon, pressing down on his oesophagus and constricting trachea.

Gert tries to protest but he can only inhale and is unable to speak.

'I mustn't keep you,' Lupei is saying. 'I cannot pretend that you have not been an irritant but your dogged determination has served its purpose. Thanks to you I have reason to believe that my Daniel may now be in the subcontinent. You have been a great help. And now that wide sea of human souls awaits your arrival. Sleep well.'

Another surge of smothering passes through Lupei's fingers and blossoms in Gert's neck as he tries desperately to exhale. And the lights go out.

CHAPTER 38

West London

9th March 2020

'I'm off. You can come too if you want,' Jordan tells Tiffany. 'It's in West Acton. At the Conservative Club. I promised I'd be there at eight.'

'You're a Tory?' Tiffany is surprised.

Jordan shakes his head. 'Nah. We just joined to use their snooker tables. They're the best in West London.'

'I have to ring my mum or she'll go spare. She's still stuck in that *I must protect my baby* loop.'

'Yeah!' Jordan laughs and clicks his fingers. 'I hear you. Listen, check you later, right? You know where the kitchen is. I'm back around eleven.'

'Thanks, Jordan. For everything.'

Tiffany watches him leave then goes to make herself a cup of coffee.

She messages her Uncle Ted. The bond between them is as strong as it's ever been, something to do with them both having survived great danger; him when his fishing boat was smashed to pieces in the harbour jaws in the storm and her when … well, she doesn't want to revisit those events. She has always felt able to tell him things she cannot express to her parents. Uncle Ted understands that Tiffany needs to breathe and have a life.

> Hi Uncle Ted. I'm in London and I'm OK.
> Back tomorrow, I think. Mum doesn't need

to know. Have you been out on the new
boat yet? Shall I buy you a 'My niece went
to London and all I got was this bloody
t-shirt'? Haha.

The opening titles of Casualty are still playing on the television
when her phone vibrates on the coffee table. She hopes it is
Uncle Ted. It isn't. A message on the dark web email account
that Jordan helped her install.

> About your guy: Full name Rajesh Anvit
> Pandit. Age 32. Education: Modern
> School in Delhi. Universities: Delhi
> College of Arts & Commerce, and Royal
> College of Art in London.
> Your source is right. Father threw him out
> of India into the hands of uncle. RJ was
> causing trouble in Delhi. He joined the
> anti-caste system protest in April 2018
> to protest against treatment of Dalits
> ('untouchables') and was arrested. Father
> bailed him out then he alleged that RJ
> stole money to support activism against
> his own family's textile business.
> Uncle is Fanindra Namburi, cautioned
> by Inland Revenue in UK for tax evasion
> and suspected of human trafficking by
> police. So we may now know how Daniel
> escaped the country, if he has … there is
> no record of Daniel leaving through ports
> or airports. But no records of Daniel using
> any bank in the UK since Jan 2017 either.
> Current whereabouts of RJ also unknown.

Tiffany sits there, her eyes glued to an argument happening on the television screen in a hospital corridor while her mind is far away. Could Daniel really be in India? Why? To escape? Unconsciously, she rummages in her mini backpack and produces the lidded brass disc she keeps there.

She opens the compass and flicks the catch to release the crow needle. It spins to point north. She pushes the black spot on the base of the case and the crow turns slowly round and round without stopping. No scravir about. How would she react if it did stop? She shivers at the thought. Is that why Daniel fled? What is he doing? Is he safe?

Her phone vibrates again. She drops the compass. A second message from Antoine Hoek.

> I have spoken with NCB in New Delhi.
> They can help us find Rajesh. Finding
> Daniel will be harder, if he is there. Are
> you willing to come with me to India? I
> know that is a big ask. Forgive me asking.
> Do you have a passport? Respond ASAP.

The search engine tells her that NCB is an acronym for National Central Bureau. Everything is moving too fast. For years nothing except Gert's wild accusations then suddenly Antoine (is he Gert's boss or just an ex-colleague, she can't even answer that) is asking her to go to India. And where is Gert?

Get back to Whitby and keep out of this.

But can she keep out of it? That woman from the homeless shelter, Gert met her and thirty-six hours later she was dead. If Lupei is alive and if he is looking for Daniel then sooner or later he will hunt her down, if only to use as a hostage. In fact it's a miracle they haven't already found her.

Tiffany tries to remember who she was three years ago.

Working full time at the chip shop. Five GCSEs to her name and the ambition to one day become the restaurant manager.

Suddenly she's back there behind the counter. It's the end of a long shift in the spring of 2017, a few months after she last saw Daniel. A boring Thursday night. It's been raining all day, hardly any tourists, and her boss, Dave, is waxing philosophical.

'Hey, Tiff, here's a poem for you,' Dave shouts over the fryer. 'The moving fish finger writes and having writ moves on. Nor all thy something something nor all thy ... Oh, sod it, I can't remember, but the point is: you only get one shot at life, you can't change the past, you can only move forwards. Don't forget that. I'm just pissing my life away here stirring bits of fish and potato and half of that's gone in the bin today.'

'Are you all right, love?' she asks.

'Listen to me. For God's sake, don't waste your life behind that frigging counter. Spread your wings, Tiff. Fly away while you're young enough,' he tells her. 'And I don't mean become a sodding seagull. Miserable squawking twats! No sense of adventure. Follow a boat four or five miles from the harbour and then fly straight back and dive bomb poor sods walking on the pier; to nick their chips. Bastards.'

Back in the present, Tiffany smiles. Maybe she can persuade Jordan to go with her to find Daniel. They have travelled abroad together before. Admittedly it was only on the ferry to Rotterdam while they were looking to save Daniel and Alex but maybe ...

She is on the sofa, in front of Match of the Day, when Jordan arrives back.

'Didn't know you loved football,' Jordan jokes as Tiffany sits up and rubs her eyes.

'I don't. I fell asleep.'

'Do you want a drink?'

Tiffany makes herself a coffee while Jordan cracks open

a beer. He sits down beside her on the sofa and she tells him what she has learned since he went out.

'India's miles away. You need jabs and a guide. You can't just turn up,' Jordan says, his eye half on the football. 'Oh, look at that! Offside!'

'We don't have much time,' Tiffany says. 'Can we switch the TV off?'

'It's OK, I'm listening. Sure you don't want a beer?'

'Who organised the murder of that woman? Kelly. If Lupei can kill her, then he can kill us. And Daniel's lived his whole life thinking his mum walked out on him when it's not true. He doesn't know that she's dead or that she loved him. We have to find him, Jordan.'

'Yeah, OK. Let me think about that.' Jordan sits back, spilling some of his beer. 'Shit. Can you fetch a cloth?' On seeing her expression he changes his tune. 'OK, I'll get it.' He forces himself up off the sofa and disappears into the kitchen and returns with a roll of paper towel that he presses onto the damp patch he has created on the sofa. Dropping the sodden mess on the floor he drops back onto the sofa and drapes an arm round Tiffany.

'I've been thinking, Tiff. You and me. How about we …'

Tiffany pushes him away. 'You're drunk so I'll pretend you didn't say that. Where's my bedroom?'

'Hey! I'm just saying that maybe, you know, we could …'

'There is no we, Jordan. Not like that anyway.'

'You're beautiful,' he smiles. 'Even when you're mad at me and …'

'Just STOP!' Tiffany speaks more decisively and firmly than Jordan has ever heard her speak. She stands up, towering over him. 'Where's my room or, if this is my room, can you please leave? Now.'

'OK. OK. Shit. I was only …'

'Come on. Out.'

'Fucking hell, man.' Jordan prises himself up off the sofa. There is still the glimmer of hope in his eyes.

'OUT!'

The wind leaves his sails and he staggers out of the room. Tiffany hears him trudging heavily up the stairs. A door slams and she relaxes just a fraction. She pushes furniture in front of the door to the hall and finally sits down and wipes a tear from her face and hopes she doesn't need the toilet in the night.

Did I give mixed signals? Don't blame yourself. It's his fault, if he weren't drunk none of this would have happened?

Find a hotel. Get away.

You can't, it's too late. You barely know where you are.

She's angry. She frustrated. She's annoyed with herself, she's annoyed with him. She sends Antoine a message and reads his reply. And after two hours staring up at the ceiling, she's asleep.

It's eight thirty and the sun is shining as Jordan comes downstairs, hung-over, embarrassed and ashamed, and dreading having to explain himself. The door to the front room is closed. Should he knock? He decides to put the kettle on, make them both a cup of coffee. Then he knocks on the door. No answer. He waits in the kitchen for ten minutes then knocks again. Finally he turns the handle.

He has to push the door open. The room is empty. No sign that anyone was ever there.

'You useless stupid shit, Jordan,' he says, kicking the sofa.

His mum is right, why does he always fuck things up? He sits down and sends Tiffany an apology; he wouldn't blame her for never talking to him again.

PART 4

2020

नई दिल्ली

New Delhi

CHAPTER 39

New Delhi

8th March 2020

Halogen Jones, he thinks of himself by this name now, has his dark and favourite places in the dense concrete lattice where the song of jostling traffic never slows.

Like other cities, Delhi loves shadows. Just as well because no one remembers when they last saw the stars in this joss stick smog thick air sick metropolis; unless by stars you mean the Bollywood glitterati, those foxy divas and hunky heroes who swoon and strut beneath lacquered jet-black hair helmets.

Even the sharpest sickle moon can no longer scythe the blanket brown haze to catch a glimpse of the ground.

Jones sees those shrinking angles where flyovers plunge into the dust of Delhi where, backs to the wall, human beings slink in the smallest gaps, eyes watchful in the lacklight. He sees the fleeting fires of waste paper over which thin-ribbed waifs cough and spit. He sees the crouched slender sanctuaries of those who live without a safety net.

He frequents the slums where everything is for sale, where those with money take advantage of those without, where lives are wrecked and then wrecked again, and where body fluids run like treacle in the dirt dust below bare tungsten bulbs hung by the neck from cheap plastic cables strung between dampwept shacks.

Within days of arriving here he understood that sanity for all, rich and poor alike, depends on the capacity not to see those things that bring no advantage in the seeing. But the scale of it still overwhelms; sometimes it seems that half the view is a chimera, shimmering half here and half nowhere.

This morning, as he sat in the back of a rust-ravaged tuk-tuk, a mask shielding his nose and mouth against the harsh hot diesel air, Jones studied the fruit sellers opposite the bus station. Bodies, clothes, wooden barrows, leaves on trees, road, kerb, earth, sky, railings, exhaled air; everything dust grey except for the pyramid piles of fruit. Oranges, bananas, apples that sang with colour so vivid and intense you might imagine they shone through a window from another universe.

Now, ten hours later, after a long day at work, he is heading in the opposite direction on the back seat of another tuk-tuk behind another malnourished barefoot driver with respiratory problems. The traffic lurches and spars in juddering splutters. He understands it now. While in Europe roads are made up of long lanes that drivers follow, here in India roads are made up of short spaces that demand to be filled as they appear.

Bathed in a puddle of yellow sodium light, a man lies asleep in the dirt beside the traffic lights. One leg propped up against a railing to form a living triangle of stick-thin flesh. One arm fallen away from him, the hand trailing over the edge of the kerb, vulnerable to any passing vehicle. How easily will that trailing arm be ripped off and tumble away through the cacophony of rolling wheels? Will the man wake? Will he have the energy to cry out? Who will mourn him?

A hundred metres on, four grubby children squat empty-eyed on skinny haunches under a bush. Beside them discarded newspapers tremble in the fumes of a passing bus.

All this is as unremarkable and invisible as the dust to all but the most curious. A sweaty casual fatalism clings to everything that moves and everything that does not.

Jones taps the driver's shoulder and points. The driver nods, coughs, spits onto the road, and throws the tuk-tuk wildly to the left across the honking flow of traffic towards a side street.

Past the small shrine with its faded flowers and the lantern lit ramshackle snack stall leaning against the banyan tree.

For a moment Jones worries he has miscounted and picked the wrong street. Then he spots his quarry: the pot-bellied middle-aged jack-the-leering-lad scratching his groin as he studies the slender frame of a girl passing by alone after dark.

'OK. Achaa. Good. Stop,' Jones tells the driver fifty metres further on. He presses 100 rupees into the old man's hand, climbs out, and walks back towards the main road.

The cloud of diesel fumes is still swirling in the wake of the departing tuk-tuk as Jones taps the pot-bellied man's shoulder.

'Excuse me.'

The pot-bellied man turns.

'Cigarettes?' Jones mimes lighting up and putting a smoke to his mouth. 'You know where I find them?'

The other man's eyes move quickly, measuring Jones up, clothes, shoes, haircut, face.

'I have just arrived in Delhi,' Jones lies effortlessly as he leafs through a wad of greasy rupee notes. 'I need smokes. Can you help?'

The pot-bellied man smiles and bobs his head sideways, that Indian nod that means both yes or no and a thousand nuances between. His eyes linger on the money. 'Yes, Yes. Come.'

Jones smiles back, the epitome of the gullible innocent abroad. 'Thank you so much.'

The man strides forwards towards the snack stall. Jones taps his shoulder.

'No, not stall. Shop. I want good cigarette. Understand? I can pay.'

Crass as clickbait. The careful eyes try not to show either contempt or greed. They fail. The half-smile is as happy to molest a twelve-year-old girl as fleece a gormless tourist. They walk in single file. A rickshaw piled high with hessian sacks squeals past on its rusty bike chain. A languid cow ankle deep in plastic waste masticates her carrier bag cud like a southern rancher chewing tobacco. What comes out if you pull on the udders? Gelatinous gobbets of clingfilm, perhaps.

Crossing the threshold into the gloom of the corner shop, Jones observes the pot-bellied man and shopkeeper haggling. He takes care to give the impression he understands not a word of Hindi. 850 rupees for twenty India Kings is a rip off but of little significance in the grand scheme of things.

Emerging back onto the street clutching a pack of cigarettes he has no intention of smoking, Jones seizes the moment. He presses 100 rupees into the pot-bellied man's hand.

'You know where I find girl? You know jiggy-jiggy?' He thrusts his pelvis back and forth.

The pot-bellied man smirks. He knows jiggy-jiggy, he thinks of little else from dawn to dusk. He grabs Jones's arm.

'Come. Best girls. Young, clean. You like.' The smirk fans open into a smile of ugly yellow teeth and bad breath.

In seconds they are pushing through the grey-brown maze of alleys behind the shop. A man pissing against a wall. Punjabi rap echoing in a room. A young boy struggling to carry a bucket of slopping liquid. An old woman sitting in a doorway, her sari lit by the flickering fluorescent tube in the bare room behind her. The pot-bellied man walks quickly. If Jones had not visited these alleys before, in disguise, he would be lost in seconds but he is not lost. He knows exactly where the pot-bellied man is leading him, he is here to avenge the man's victims.

A few more steps. A girl is crying nearby. Raised voices. A couple arguing. The sweet smell of cooking and the acrid honk of human shit. There is the side alley shortly after the butcher's shop. One longer stride and Jones is at the man's back, grabbing his shoulder, energies focused, pulling him off-balance and sending him tumbling headlong and unconscious into the shadows.

Jones glances around him. No-one has seen a thing. In a second he has stepped from the light and disappeared from view. He kneels beside the pot-bellied man. The wet ground soaks his trousers. He wonders briefly what he is kneeling in. Without hesitation he yanks the man's shirt up and places a hand directly on his belly; skin-to-skin contact makes what comes next much easier.

Ten minutes later he is on his way, leaving by a different route, moving more slowly, burdened a little by the extra weight and tired from his labours, the inhabitants of the slum none the wiser.

At dawn, the body is found and flung onto the back of a truck.

The police knock on fourteen doors. Only the old woman in the doorway remembers seeing anything but, since she hated the pot-bellied man who preyed on children almost as much as she hates the uncle who sold her into prostitution for a packet of cigarettes four decades earlier, she says nothing of the European who walked the alley last night. To her, he is an avenging angel.

Weeks later the body is removed from the morgue and disposed of without ceremony or autopsy; they need the space and the police have more pressing things to worry about. Without an autopsy they will never know what happened to him.

CHAPTER 40

Aesthetic WonderSlim Clinic, New Delhi

9th March 2020

How much loose skin is there?

How much extra fat is there?

Chloe swipes the questions away and waits for her phone screen to refresh. She knows they have to ask but she hates them for it, hates the invasive nosiness and the smug implied criticism, and hates the pretty young things who created the form while sitting in their airy open-plan office laughing at the pathetic overweight people who will have to fill in the answers.

The woman in the elegant turquoise sari tidies the magazine and brochures on the table. Different country, same waiting room magazines.

'Shall I bring you coffee? Or chai?' she asks with her perfect-toothed smile.

'No, I'm fine,' Chloe replies, then immediately feels guilty that she has sounded brusque or rude.

The sari woman does that Indian head bob thing. 'Everything is good at your hotel? Not too jet-lagged?'

'I picked one of the hotels on your list.' Chloe makes the effort to sound interested. 'The Excelsior, not far from the airport.'

The other woman smiles. 'Very good hotel. Have you filled in ...'

'I'm still doing it.'

'Don't worry. I also have paper registration form if you prefer.'

Chloe smiles, tight-lipped and shakes her head. The woman leaves.

How much loose skin is there?

The question doesn't look any better the second time round. How much loose skin is there? Chloe shrugs; it is years since she has viewed the mirror as her friend. She quickly types in her answers, presses send, closes her phone and turns to the magazines. With the air-conditioning it's possible to forget the heat and pollution outside. She almost wishes she had brought a cardigan.

The magazines are as bland as those on the flight. Page after page of handbags, jewellery, shoes, spa packages, hotels. Contemporary kitchens in Singapore, Sydney, Buenos Aires, Mexico City, Chicago, Delhi. Same brands right across the global village. Except it isn't true because the magazines make Manchester look like New York; they obviously haven't taken a walk in Ardwick or Oldham.

'Miss Hodson?'

The woman in the turquoise sari is back.

'Please to follow me.'

Chloe grabs her handbag. The corridors beyond the door are lined with a mixture of Indian art and the faces of what must presumably be happy customers. A mixture of Asian faces and white ones. In one photo a dozen children with beaming smiles pose in front of a large pink building.

'This way please,' says the woman in the sari, ushering Chloe into an office.

Chloe sits beside the vast mahogany desk opposite the doctor. He is younger than she expected, slim and with dark hair. He wears fashionable glasses with dark blue frames, an open-necked shirt beneath the crisp white jacket. Hipster beard. Quite young, thirty maybe. Maybe not even that old. On the walls are various charts and certificates. An ornate wooden screen covered in carvings of maybe a hundred elephants fills a corner of the room. The doctor types on his laptop, seemingly oblivious to her arrival. Despite his rudeness she relaxes a little, because his is the first white face she has seen in India. Not that she is racist in any way, she assures herself.

'What's the weather like in Manchester?' he asks, without looking up.

Chloe clears her throat.

'Raining. As usual.' She laughs nervously, as if his knowing that she is from Manchester is a little too personal.

'It will be raining here soon, though here in Delhi it's more a waterfall than a shower.' The doctor glances across the desk and flashes a brief smile. 'It's not for a couple of weeks. Don't worry, you'll be back home long before then.'

His eyes are light blue, almost grey. Chloe's hand goes unconsciously to her neck, feeling the fat that obscures her jawline. Even a fleeting look from a man and there she is, embarrassed and ashamed.

If she had money, Chloe would be in Harley Street instead of hunting down a cut-price deal in Delhi and she wouldn't have had to dump her kids on her sister for a week. Nor would she have had to witness the extreme poverty that flanks the journey from the airport. Whole families in cardboard shacks propped against the dust-dirty trees inches from a chocking sea of cars, lorries, motorbikes and three-wheeled rust buckets that weave in and out like flies over cakes at a picnic.

Stupidly she wound her window down as the taxi passed over a river and gagged as a thick miasma of fumes, particulates, and human excrement slapped her nostrils. *Please, air conditioning* the driver said, telling her off. She pulled the button and the window closed and the smell faded, leaving only the muffled music of the car horns.

The doctor moves his laptop aside and studies her form. Chloe recognises her own handwriting; is it really eight weeks since she filled it in?

'This is rather a long list,' he observes, turning the pages.

She says nothing. Finally, he reaches the back page and looks up, studying her for a few seconds. It feels like eternity.

'We have to prioritise,' he says gently. 'Your body is …'

'Your website said that you do everything,' she says.

'Yes, but not at the same time. We have to give your body time to recover.'

'I can't come back and forth. I've got kids and a job and …'

He sighs. 'OK, let's examine you and take it from there.' He presses the intercom button on his desk. 'Karuna. Could you come in?' He turns to Chloe. 'I always ask one of the female staff to attend the examination, so that you may feel one hundred percent safe.'

'Thank you.'

The woman at reception enters the room and moves the carved screen to reveal a hospital couch.

'Please,' she says.

Chloe steps behind the screen and strips off, feeling a rising shame and sadness as she allows another person to see her imperfections. Karuna smiles pleasantly; there is nothing to be ashamed of. Chloe resents the compassion of the beautiful. She brushes aside the offer of a blue hospital gown, this is not a moment for modesty, she has come to get fixed and hiding away the rolls of excess skin will serve no purpose. Let him see everything. She lies back on the bed and nods at Karuna.

'I'm ready,' she says simply.

He steps round the screen. Chloe lies, eyes closed, fighting back the tears, feeling his male gaze on her, imagining how repulsed he must be by the ocean of hanging pink, the sagging pillowcases where once she had breasts, the thighs that look like they have melted in the sun, the living drapes that fall over her genitals. She prays that at last someone will help her out of the hellhole she has tumbled into. She hears low voices and keeps her eyes closed. Suddenly his breath is close to her ear.

'Ms Hodson, I must ask you to consent that I touch you,' he says gently.

'Just get on with it. I doesn't feel like me anyway,' she answers, eyes tightly closed, voice and lips trembling.

Fingers lift her skin and move it back and forth. She feels a pinching and probing where once she had a waist.

'Forty-six centimetres,' he is saying. 'Eleven point five.'

Her thighs, her arms. The folds of flesh are both a part of her and as separate as if someone were tugging at a sleeping bag she happens to occupy.

'Would you stand, please?'

She opens her eyes for less than a second, just to get her bearings as she swings her feet round and stands up. The probing continues, as does the calling out of measurements. In a curious way she almost finds it comforting; it is the first time she has allowed anyone other than her children to touch her for over five years.

'All done. You may get dressed, Ms Hodson.'

Chloe opens her eyes. He has gone. Karuna stands, clipboard in hand.

'Please come through when you are ready.'

Dressed again, Chloe steps out from behind the screen and sits down opposite the consultant.

'What about my face? You haven't measured my face.'

The doctor looks up from the screen of his laptop.

'As I said earlier, I must consider the demands that surgery makes on your body. When your body has had a chance to heal, we can consider further work. Now let us discuss the programme for the next couple of days.'

Ten minutes later the consultation is over.

'So, tomorrow afternoon at three o'clock,' he tells her.

Chloe nods. The woman in the sari is already waiting in the doorway.

'Karuna will show you out.'

At the threshold, Chloe turns. 'Doctor?'

'Yes.'

'I'm sorry. You didn't tell me your name.'

His gaze is so intense that she blushes, suddenly feeling she has been rude to ask.

'Please,' he says. 'I should be the one apologising, not you. My name is Mr Jones. Halogen Jones. See you tomorrow afternoon, Miss Hodson,' he smiles pleasantly.

A minute later Chloe is in a taxi on her way back to the hotel. By the time the driver has screeched the wrong way round a roundabout, narrowly missing a motorbike carrying an entire family, parents and three small children, Chloe has closed her eyes again. She keeps them shut until the driver opens her car door some forty minutes later.

Her hotel, like the clinic, is clean, modern and anonymous. Safe in her room. The lullaby hum of the air conditioning, and the heavy curtains shield her from both the heat and the kaleidoscope of sights and sounds outside, Chloe throws off her clothes and settles herself among the dozen gold and pink scatter cushions that are spread across the large double bed. She lies there exhausted, waiting for her body to cool.

What is there in the minibar? What will she do for food?

I'm not hungry.

She is hungry. Does the hotel have a restaurant?

Where is the minibar? There is a kettle on a table in the corner of the room, and what looks like packets of crisps.

How much extra fat is there?

A drink then. What time is it in Manchester? Too early to ring. A glass of white wine would be nice. Can you even get wine in India? Of course you can. She is in Delhi not some remote village in the middle of nowhere.

The minibar contains fruit juices, cola, lemonade. Beside the kettle are two bottles of complimentary water. She puts one in the fridge and drinks the other while flicking through the pages of the plastic leatherbound 'Welcome to the Excelsior' book beside the telephone. Turns out she can order any of thirty-five different curries from her room for less than three pounds each. All vegetarian, nearly all involving cheese.

How much extra fat is there?

She has come to India to lose weight not to stuff her face with curry. Why is eating such a bloody battleground? Chloe sighs heavily and returns to the bed, lies back and closes her eyes. It is going to be a long night.

She wakes to the sound of the telephone ringing. For a second she has no idea where she is. The digital clock below the television across the room reads nine twenty-two. Day or night? Chloe rolls over and grabs the receiver.

'Yes?'

'Hello, This is Chloe Hodson?'

'Yes.'

'Reception please. Your guest is waiting in the lobby.'

'What?'

'Your guest. He is waiting please. With taxi.'

'Who?' She rubs her face. Her throat is as dry as an evening with Tutankhamun. 'Who is it?'

Four thousand miles from home, who can possibly be waiting for her? In her earpiece she hears the receptionist talking with someone.

'Mr Jones, Madam. To visit the finest restaurant in New Delhi.' There is a slight pause. 'He says better even than Rama's on Wilmslow Road.'

What could go wrong? Anyone who knows Rama's on Wilmsow Road cannot be that bad she thinks to herself, climbing off the bed. The marble floor is cool beneath her feet as she crosses over to her suitcase to find something to wear.

It is not Mr Jones waiting in the lobby, but his elegant

assistant, Karuna, brandishing another shimmering smile and sari two-piece.

'Please to follow me,' she says.

'Where is Mr Jones?'

'Waiting in the car.'

The hotel doors hiss apart and Chloe steps from air-conditioned cocoon into a smack of sound, smell, heat and humidity. The car, a large green Audi, is surrounded by forty commuters on motorbikes, stop starting stuttering, every inch of road submerged in a tailpipe haze, horns burbling busily like courting frogs. Does the traffic never stop? The hotel guard braves the traffic and opens one of the rear doors. Halogen Jones is sprawled across the back seat, limp leafing a magazine. Chloe climbs in beside him.

'What if I told you that you could have all your surgery for nothing?' Jones asks nonchalantly, putting the magazine on the seat between them.

'Dumb northern woman will do anything for money, is that it? I'm not an idiot, Mr Jones.'

'Neither am I, Miss Hodson. You turn up in my surgery, miles from home and wanting every plastic surgery procedure under the tropical sun. All to be done in one visit. You not only want to lose twenty kilos, you also want your body and face changed out of all recognition. Eye bags, nose, jawline, neck, lips, cheek bones.'

'I want to look beautiful again. What's wrong with that?'

'Is the new passport waiting in a drawer?'

'What do you mean?'

'I mean that if you are going to such lengths to change your identity you must have prepared meticulously,' he smiles casually. 'How will you re-enter the UK on a passport with a photograph that will no longer bear any resemblance to you? Are the police after you?'

Chloe says nothing.

'I am not judging you,' he says softly, barely audible above the engine noise. 'Simply proposing a deal, a favour perhaps.'

The freeway is crazy. The driver, a huge man as broad as an ox, slams the brakes. Walking towards them, in the fast lane, are half a dozen cows. Karuna, in the front beside the driver, is on her phone. The car circumnavigates the cows. Chloe curses herself silently for having left the hotel. Jones has read her like a book; he holds all the cards.

'What do you want?' she says finally.

'That's great.' He folds his arms. 'Let me explain …'

Ten minutes later the car leaves the freeway and enters a maze of narrow alleys thick with pedestrians. Street food cooking in doorways and on the backs of carts. Raised voices compete with the gravel growl of motorbikes and the horns. The streetlights have had a punch-up and most of them are broken.

'I'd rather pay,' Chloe says when Jones finally stops to take a breath. Her voice is calm and measured but inside she feels anything but.

'OK. Entirely your choice Miss Hodson. Karuna will draw up an invoice in the morning, to cover all of the procedures you have requested. I would expect a final bill of around twenty-six thousand dollars and …'

'Ten thousand pounds,' Chloe cuts him off in exasperation. 'I have your email quotation.'

'You are asking for a series of procedures that, carried out together, add hugely to the complexity of the surgery. To ensure your safety I will require additional staff and you will require extra post-operative care.'

Chloe turns to the window. A couple of youths, their faces painted in fluorescent colours, are harassing a young woman who is waiting patiently for an old man to exit the corner shop. Suddenly the old man is pushed aside by a skinny boy who runs away down the street clutching a bag of cakes. The shopkeeper appears in the doorway to scream a shaking fist in the direction of the fleeing boy. The young woman waits patiently, her eyes cast down.

'I need to get back to the hotel,' Chloe says.

'The quickest route is on your right. Can we stop please?'

The car stops.

'It is just a short walk to the tuk-tuk station, Miss Hodson. Turn right and follow the alley, just after the café. You can't miss it, there is always a blind man sitting outside singing religious songs. I'm afraid I have to complete my charity work.'

Chloe is wide-eyed, no way is she stepping out onto the street.

'You are welcome to stay in the car if you prefer. What time will we back at the hotel, Karuna?'

The driver glances at Chloe in his rear-view mirror. 'Eleven o'clock, Sir.'

Chloe is incandescent. How could she have been so stupid? She has no choice; she stays put. Ten minutes later the driver pulls up hard against the wall of a rundown building.

'Won't be long,' Jones reassures her, pushing open his door.

Karuna and the driver are also getting out. Chloe slides across as Jones is about to close his door. She says nothing, she doesn't have to, he knows why she does not want to sit alone in the car.

Jones and the driver retrieve backpacks from the trunk of the car.

In the building's lobby a single bulb dangles naked on a wire. The air is thick with the odours of food and damp rot. Like a tramp's shirt, the walls are blotchy with sweat.

On the first floor Jones stops in front of a door and knocks. A young girl answers, her face breaking into a huge smile as she recognises him. As they follow her down the narrow hall, two more children appear. They shout for joy and disappear back into the room at the end of the hall. Karuna calls after them in Hindi.

Both adults in the room are sick. The man lying on the bed is skin and bones, his chest juddering as he sleeps. His thin skin is translucent. On the floor beside the bed, his wife shakes with fever. Chloe is torn between compassion and the fear that she might catch something.

The driver hands his boss his backpack, from which Jones extracts a large jute bag. He hands it to the mother. The children gather round, chattering animatedly as she produces a mountain of bread, curry, cakes, mangos, bananas and eggs. She divides the food between the children and her husband.

'Why isn't the mother eating?' Chloe asks.

'She thinks only to save her husband and her children,' Jones explains, producing a second smaller bag from the backpack.

Karuna takes the bag, which also contains food, and squats down beside the mother, whispering gently to her. The woman shakes her head but Karuna insists and the woman relents. Soon mother and children are all eating. The father's food lies untouched at the foot of the bed.

Jones opens his own backpack and places various medicines beside the sleeping man. Chloe is feeling guilty for questioning Jones' motives and thinking only of herself. It turns out he really is carrying out a charitable mission to bring comfort to a desperately poor family.

'What's wrong with the father?' she asks.

'Their illness is poverty,' Jones tells her, without looking round. 'Their lives are stunted by pollution. Ask yourself how many tall people you have seen since you arrived. So many respiratory illnesses. When they fall ill there is no safety net. No work, no income. Vithal has acute kidney failure. Aged only forty he has given up. His wife Meena is sick with malaria, but she knows that without Vithal the struggle for survival will overwhelm her. The whole family is weak with hunger. What little she has she gives to her children.'

Chloe is on the edge of tears. Nothing she has known in Manchester has prepared her for this. She knows about food banks, wheeling and dealing, life on welfare, drugs, dodging the rules, but nothing like this. She weighs more than both parents put together.

'This favour, does it hurt?'

'No, not at all. It's less painful than surgery,' Jones reassures her. 'It is the perfect solution. For them and for you.'

He doesn't press her. Instead he joins Karuna on the floor beside Meena. Between mouthfuls of dhal and rice the mother listens attentively, occasionally glancing over her shoulder to check on her husband.

'So what brought you here?' Chloe asks Jones, playing for time. 'From London to India?'

'It's a boring story,' he answers, while handing Meena a couple of pills and a water bottle.

Chloe is sure it isn't, but she makes up her mind. 'OK, I'll do it.' The words are still leaving her mouth when her phone rings. She is suddenly very tense. 'Do you mind if …?' she starts.

'Absolutely fine,' Jones replies.

'My ch…children,' she stutters. The call lasts only a minute. "Everything is fine … Yes he is … I'll be back in five days. Love you."

A minute later she is lying on the floor, eyes closed and trying to relax. Meena is also lying down. Halogen Jones sits between them, holding Chloe's left hand and Meena's right. Karuna and the driver have taken the children away into the flat's single bedroom. Vithal is wheezing in his sleep.

Chloe feels nothing at all. She is not surprised because what Halogen Jones has proposed is ridiculous. Chloe is a child of the Enlightenment, even though she does not know the word.

She gets most of her opinions from social media. She finished school with just 4 GCSEs, all poor grades, but she believes in a rational world where there are laws that govern how things work. There has to be otherwise how would anyone trust doctors and scientists? What Jones is promising is just mad cult guru nonsense, conning vulnerable people with false hopes. Why doesn't he stick with the food and the medicines? She hopes the mumbo jumbo will be over quickly.

The sensation is so subtle, so delicate, like no more than someone touching a single hair on the back of her arm.

Jones relaxes every muscle as he searches within himself for the spark that will kickstart the process. To the uninformed he is meditating but his assistant Karuna, who pops her head round the door to check everything is going to plan, knows meditation does not begin to describe what will happen. Her own daughter owes her life to Jones.

It begins as a single moment in the primal centre of his brain. Creierul anticilor, the brain of the ancients: medulla oblongata, midbrain and pons. In his mind's ear his erstwhile mentor, Thor Lupei, is telling him to focus his thoughts prior to projecting them along his synapses.

'To acquire my craft you must learn to travel at will through the human body,' whispers the imagined soft rich baritone. 'You must become as familiar with its contours and edifices, its lumps and conduits, its treasures and repositories, as one might be at home with the rooms and possessions in a house. Imagine the veins and nerves to be the electrical system or plumbing, the stomach is the dining room, the bladder the bathroom, and so on. We are currently in the library, if you will. Now come with me.'

Jones has learned his lessons well. He fans the spark, feels it growing until it is like a fingertip lightly stroking the inside of his brain. Satisfied everything is primed, he launches himself like an underground train penetrating a tunnel, coursing the conduits of his own body until he reaches its extremities. The familiar surge of adrenalin and the dark threshold make him gasp. Again he hears his master's voice in his head, *'You are quite safe. Relax and follow the flow.'*

One moment he is feeling the tingling in his right hand and the next he is feeling the same sensation within Chloe's left hand as his consciousness crosses from his body and into hers. Her hand twitches violently as if she wishes to pull away. But it is already too late. Loitering in her fingertips, resisting the urge to explore, Jones focuses another thread of his consciousness, this time to leap his life force from his left hand and into Meena's right.

How differently they feel, the podgy well-fed fingers of one woman and the thin, compliant, waxy fingers of the other. With the grace and agility of an ice-skater Jones now slides away, leaving behind the safety of the shore. He feels the underside of Chloe's tattoo as he surges along her arm and through her body, probing, evaluating. A moment later he is ready to begin.

A fly on the ceiling would tremble at the curious phenomenon at either side of the sitting man. One woman is slowly deflating, her clothes gently subsiding around her, as the face of the other fills out. Between them the man's face is tortured in concentration. Ripples crawl like parasites below the skin of his hands and arms. Beneath a grubby sari, skinny limbs are swelling as first muscle and then fat accumulate like flotsam on a beach. For one woman the loss is a relief, an opportunity to rid herself of the weight of her unfettered appetite, for the other the gain is the arrival of a thousand missed meals and the chance to survive long enough to raise her children.

His breathing steady, Jones continues his work, transferring Chloe's extra flesh with the finesse and craft of a sculptor, reducing the thickness of her calves, thighs, and buttocks.

Skin, fat, muscle, sinew. Absorbing the extra weight within himself for a few seconds as he transfers the excess flesh onto the frame of the small mother, building layer upon layer like a forensic sculptor creating a body of clay over a collection of bones. Much more than muscles; arteries and veins, lungs, the chambers of the heart, the whole body must be able to sustain its new substance. When he is done some nine kilos of living flesh have moved from one woman to the other.

Slowly he extricates himself from his hosts until, like a suction pad releasing its grip, he suddenly pops back within his own body. He hears the swing of the door hinges and opens his eyes. Karuna is back.

'Now the father,' Jones says quietly, letting go of Meena's hand.

Karuna closes the door on the children's voices; they are playing a counting game with Rajesh, the driver. She shakes Meena's shoulder. Meena opens her eyes, smiles and takes a deep breath. Surprised by the energy of her breath she tries to sit up but Karuna pushes her gently back and whispers that she must rest.

Chloe sleeps.

Karuna withdraws and Rajesh appears. He looks anxiously at Jones who nods reassuringly.

Rajesh lifts Vithal from the bed. His clothes are stiff with sweat and the pungent smell of urine. Placing the father carefully on the floor, Rajesh turns to the mother. It takes him a couple of attempts to lift her in his arms.

'Watch your back,' Jones advises.

With Meena on the bed and her husband occupying her place on the floor, Jones takes Vithal's hand, closes his eyes and immerses himself again in the world of creierul anticilor.

The process is repeated but this time Jones has a decision to make, one he has not discussed with anyone. Vithal's failing kidneys will soon kill him, and his body is so weak that it will not cope with the extra demands a few kilos of extra muscle and fat. Jones wishes he had kept the kidneys he harvested from the pot-bellied man, but they have already been of service. Two street children are alive tonight thanks to the old abuser's organs.

With luck Chloe Hodson will be delighted with her weight loss, her tightened jawline, her youthful breasts, and will never discover what she is about to lose. Sweat trickling down the small of his back, Jones reaches deep into her vitals and uncouples her left kidney. It blooms, searing hot within him, as the cells surge along his arm across his thorax and out into Vithal's sickly frame. Delicately, lovingly he positions it, disconnects one of the failing kidneys and connects the new replacement it its place. Immediately Vithal's body is sighing with relief. His consciousness racing from point to point, Jones directs flesh, fat, capillaries, lung tissue and skin to their new homes. Jones absorbs the failed kidney into himself, to discard later on. When he is done, Vithal is no longer at death's door.

Rajesh places Vithal on the bed beside his wife. Karuna brings the children into the room and, with Meena listening attentively, explains that everyone must rest.

Jones, his body aching with exhaustion, wakes Chloe who stares around her wildly. Who are these people? Where is she? The smell and the heat and the sound of the children chattering in Hindi frighten her.

'Everything is fine,' Jones tells her. 'You did really well. Rajesh will carry you to the car. It is vital that you remain relaxed, your body needs to recover.'

Chloe slowly lifts an arm and is stunned to see how much thinner it is. And lighter too. She tries to lift her head but her body feels so tired.

'Please trust me,' Jones says gently. 'Karuna will help you to your bed in the hotel. Just sleep. I will be there tomorrow shortly after nine.'

'Are you not coming with us?'

'I have a few things to do here,' he smiles.

'What about the swanky restaurant?'

'Tomorrow. I promise.'

She manages a half-smile.

Rajesh and Karuna help Chloe to her feet then the driver sweeps her up in his arms. The children gather round the white woman who has given them the ghost of a chance of survival. They put their hands together in a namaskar and bow in thanks. Meena lying on the bed also offers a namaskar.

'Thank you,' she says in English.

The youngest child, a four-year-old girl with grown-up eyes throws herself in her mother's arms and bursts into tears.

Halogen Jones watches Chloe, Karuna and Rajesh leave. He resists the urge to sleep. Out of nowhere he remembers the words of the pathologist dying at the foot of the cliff in Whitby in the north of England: *"He moves slowly when he is full"*. What would Thor Lupei make of what Jones has become?

A police siren. It is time to go. Using the bed for support, Jones hauls himself to his feet. He has one more visit before he can go home. He takes Vithal's hand and squeezes it gently. The man's eyes open.

'God bless you sir.' Vithal whispers.

Jones explains the various medicines, what to take and when. A skill he has learned over the past two years.

The boy walks Jones to the door.

'Look after your parents,' Jones says in Hindi, ruffling the boy's hair. 'I'll be back tomorrow.'

The boy nods.

Jones takes the stairs slowly. Rajesh's car has gone. There is the hint of a breeze and the smog has lifted a little. With luck the wind will drive the pollution from the city and everyone will enjoy a couple of days without coughing.

CHAPTER 41

10th March 2020

Tiffany awakens in a modern minimalist room that could be anywhere on Earth. The room is quiet and comfortable. Neutral prints hang on a magnolia-coloured wall. Biscuit-coloured floor-to-ceiling curtains. On the table beneath the blank face of a large television is a kettle and a small wicker basket containing sachets of teas and coffees. For a moment she lies there relaxed and dreamy then she remembers where she is and leaps out of bed.

It is already eight-thirty. She dresses quickly, jeans and the retro turquoise t-shirt with a daisy she picked up in the departures lounge at Heathrow, brushes her hair, neon pink scrunchies it, and washes her face. Before leaving the room she pulls back the curtain. The window looks out on a drab concrete wall in a space the size of a bathroom. Somewhere, high above, there must be sky but she cannot see it.

The corridor is as neutral and characterless as her room. She presses the lift button to the top floor. Having arrived in the middle of the night in an air-conditioned limousine that dropped them of in front of an air-conditioned hotel a mile from the airport along an empty freeway, Tiffany has no sense of where she is.

The lift doors open and she …

… steps into India.

The sun is bright and hazy. A explosion of tropical plants clambers across the warm walls of the hotel terrace, eight floors up. Two small birds with long curved beaks and dark iridescent plumage, flutter gracefully between the flowers, sipping nectar. A row of parakeets, green with plum-coloured heads, chatter in the branches of a small tree. The air is thick with traffic noise and petrol fumes. The sky is a dusty brown blue.

Five other hotel guests are already having breakfast. Antoine sits alone, scrolling his phone, a cup of coffee and a croissant beside him on the table.

'Sorry, I overslept.'

Antoine smiles. 'Don't worry. What do you want to eat?'

'Those beautiful birds! What are they?'

He shrugs. 'There's continental food and curries. All vegetarian, I think. The coffee's not too bad.'

At the buffet, Tiffany fills a plate with vegetables, paneer and Indian bread and joins Antoine.

'We have an appointment in an hour with someone from the NCB,' he tells her. 'They are as keen as we are to find Rajesh Anvit Pandit.'

'This is really good!' she tells him, tasting spices and flavours as bright as the parakeets.

'Pace yourself, Tiffany,' Antoine grins. 'Here you can have curry morning, noon and night.'

Her mouth full of paratha, Tiffany gives a thumbs-up.

'Good morning. They told me I would find you here. Please forgive me for intruding on your breakfast.'

Antoine and Tiffany turn to find a short and very overweight man in Khaki uniform.

'Johar Varma, National Central Bureau, at your service, I thought I should come to you. We have a busy day.'

'Please, join us,' Antoine indicates the spare chairs at the table. 'Antoine Hoek, Europol, and this is Tiffany Harrek who is assisting me.' Antoine beckons a waiter. 'Coffee?' he asks Varma.

'Thank you but no, we must leave straight away, the traffic is very bad.'

Tiffany barely has time to wolf her food. Minutes later they are in the back of an air-conditioned Mercedes locked in a coughing sea of motorbikes and tuk-tuks, Antoine and Varma glued to their phones.

Tiffany stares out of the window at a bewildering spectacle of people wandering about with what looks like powder paint splashed all over their faces and clothes. A motorbike carrying three youths overtakes the car; red face in front, blue face in the middle, and a wild zebra stripe confection in green and yellow on the face and torso of the youth clinging on at the back. The street itself is a dayglo spatterfest of colour as if paint-bombs have been dropped from the sky.

'What's going on?' Tiffany asks Varma.

'Holi Festival. People are celebrating Radha and Krishna, divine love and the coming of spring,' Varna explains without much enthusiasm. 'It involves a lot of colour, and an equal amount of alcohol and public disorder.'

Tiffany thinks of the Goth festival in Whitby. Top hats, bodices, masks ... and the mayhem hidden within the merrymaking. The bodies, the scravir and Thor Lupei. Despite the bright sunshine and vibrant colours, she shivers.

Antoine hasn't even looked up as he trawls his phone messages.

'Where are we going exactly?' he asks.

'It must be important for you to travel here at this time,' Varma observes also scrolling his phone. 'With this virus, it is unclear how much longer international travel will be permitted. Tell me, what has this troublemaker Pandit been up to? We thought we had got rid of him; if his family had not sent him to UK the scoundrel would have been arrested years ago.'

'Do you have cases of emaciated bodies being discovered on the streets?' Antoine asks, by way of starting the explanation for their visit to India. 'Unexplained and maybe ...'

Varma emits a hollow laugh. 'Do Europol not brief you?

Let me educate you. India population: 1.3 billion, 180 million below the poverty line, 18 million street children. Maybe 3 million homeless in Delhi alone.'

Around them on the Mahipalpur Mehrauli Road the motorbikes and tuk-tuks are the mortar between the mass of cars and lorries, all locked together like Lego bricks.

Beneath grey dust-laden trees on the roadside a group of children squat in the dirt beside a shutdown shack daubing each other with bright powder paints they have picked up off the road.

'Do we have cases of emaciated bodies on the streets?' Varma repeats Antoine's words back at him. 'Look around you. This isn't Amsterdam. Or Zurich. If that's all you have, we will struggle to help you.'

Antoine and Tiffany say nothing.

'There is death everywhere. And hunger. Every night,' Varma almost relishing the misery he is describing. 'No burials, no autopsy or …'

'OK, thank you,' Antoine cuts Varma off mid-flow; it is going to be a long day.

For a few minutes no one speaks. Tiffany is a swirling mess of excitement and anxiety. Her rising anticipation of seeing Daniel again, of telling him about his mother, of seeing him smile, is tempered by the realisation that she understands almost nothing about India. The young woman from Whitby has seen city traffic in London, and experienced a short holiday on the small island of Bali, but nothing like this.

An elephant appears, coming straight towards them on the wrong side of the road, its face and ears a kaleidoscope of colours. Behind the huge animal are people waving banners.

'Do you keep track of foreigners?' Tiffany asks the Indian policeman.

'This isn't North Korea. Only the ones who give us problems, like you do in UK. I am taking you to someone who may help us find … Stop! STOP!' Varma shouts at his driver.

The driver slams the brakes. In a flurry of car horns, Varma leaps out of the car and weaves between the cars towards the pavement where a youth in a green t-shirt, having spotted the policeman, is racing towards an alley. The youth disappears into the shadows pursued by the police officer.

Car horns chorus their complaints as the driver steers towards the kerb. The elephant and its handlers have now drawn level. The animal is at the head of a procession. Hundreds of people, men and women, are shouting, waving placards and banners, all written in a script Tiffany cannot read. Some of the men are armed with sticks. She glances at Antoine. He looks as nervous as she feels.

Twelve hours in India and they are caught up in a street protest.

Thank God for the tinted windows. No one can see us.

'Where's that idiot gone?' Antoine mutters.

Tiffany spots eyes glancing at Antoine in the rear-view mirror.

'Why are they protesting?' she asks the driver.

He looks around at the situation around the car before answering.

'They are Dalit, scheduled caste, untouchables. People are angry. This virus is spreading fear and the Dalit know that they will soon be abandoned. They will be forced to do the dirty work and receive no protection. Already some higher caste are shouting corona corona at them, blaming Dalit for the virus.'

The driver's tone suggests he is sympathetic to the protestors' cause. What are untouchables?

'That man Mr Varma is chasing, is he Dalit?' Tiffany asks him.

The driver nods. 'Probably. He ran to escape beating. Please not to ask me more questions.'

Out on the road tempers are rising. People are climbing out

of their cars to shake fists at each other or to hurl abuse at the protestors. Two young men climb out of an expensive 4x4 and cross over to a kerbside fruit seller's cart where they grab oranges and hurl them at the protestors over the sea of traffic. Beside them the stall keeper, dressed in rags, is shouting and trying to push them away; his livelihood is being destroyed. He gets a slap across the head for his troubles. The young men laugh as one of their missiles strikes a female protester on the back of the head. A group of the protesters breaks away from the march, dodging between the cars, sticks raised, to confront the fruit throwers.

'Take us away,' Antoine orders the driver. 'Now!'

'I must have instruction from my boss,' the driver explains.

'This will be an international incident and your boss will end up in prison for abandoning two members of Europol in the middle of a riot.' Antoine's tone is hard. 'I am ringing my office in five seconds if you do not do as I ask.'

The driver is caught between a cyclone and a tsunami. In desperation he throws open the car door and disappears into the crowd, abandoning the vehicle and his passengers to their fate.

Antoine throws himself over the front seats. It is too late; the open door has already been spotted and a group of the marchers are racing towards the car. Antoine closes the door but before he can identify the lock switch on the dashboard all four doors are pulled open. Brightly coloured hands reach in and haul Tiffany and Antoine from the vehicle. Someone has already started the engine and is thumping the car horn to clear space for a getaway.

Tiffany understands just one word in the mayhem as they are bundled towards the kerb: hostages.

CHAPTER 42

10th March 2020

They haven't even reached the kerb when everything changes again. Tiffany and Antoine are dragged back to the Mercedes and thrown back in the car. Two men climb in with them, one on either side, blocking access to the rear doors. Three men in the front, including the driver. Paint powder smears the seats and doors. The men chatter animatedly in what Tiffany assumes must be Hindi as the protest marchers make space to allow the car through.

The Mercedes speeds away to the next intersection where they turn off the main road into a maze of narrow streets. The buildings are four or five storeys high. Shops piled high with sacks of rice. Street vendors trundle stacks of snacks on the backs of old bicycles. Over their heads, electric cables are strung about chaotically, like lianas in a jungle. Washing hangs bright from a hundred windows and balconies. Pedestrians and motorcyclists press themselves against the shop fronts to avoid being mown down. A stray dog yelps as the car slaps its haunch.

Tiffany is thinking about her mum, cursing herself for being so stupid. She doesn't need to be here. She is not responsible for Daniel. How many times will she put herself in danger for a guy she barely knows?

One of the men on the front seat turns and leers at her.

'Antoine,' Tiffany says, without turning towards him. 'What do we do?'

'Stay calm. The theft of the car will already have been reported. It probably has a tracker and the police will be mobilising a response unit.' The flat tone of his voice suggests he isn't even convincing himself.

One of the younger men, a slim youth with a big green moustache, laughs. He repeats in Hindi what Antoine has just told Tiffany. They all laugh.

The journey ends in front of a roll-up garage door. As soon as the gap is high enough, the car enters the shadows and the door drops back to the ground.

The driver cuts the engine. More chatter. The doors are opened.

'Come,' orders the moustached youth.

The air in the garage is thick with exhaust fumes. The two foreigners are led down a passage with bare breeze block walls and no natural light. A heavy steel door is unlocked and they enter a storeroom piled high with cardboard boxes.

The oldest of their kidnappers, with dyed jet-black hair and beard over a seventy-year-old face, indicates the open door with a turn of the head. Antoine and Tiffany step forwards. The old man shakes a finger, not the two of them, just the man.

'No,' Antoine defies him. 'We stay together.'

The old man steps forwards and slaps Antoine across the face. One of the younger men, in jeans and a yellow t-shirt, looks nervous and mutters something to the others. The old man barks at him but the younger man stands his ground and speaks again, his voice stronger this time. He speaks earnestly and the others listen and nod. The old man snarls something while staring contemptuously at Tiffany and strides away.

'Please to both go in,' says the English speaker with the green moustache.

Without really having the time to consider why she should trust him, Tiffany seizes her moment. 'Thank you. Please help us. We are looking for someone. Rajesh Anvit Pandit. Do you know him?'

The man's eyes narrow momentarily. 'Go inside, please.'

Tiffany and Antoine enter the storeroom and are locked in.

'At least they forgot to take our phones,' Antoine says as the footsteps recede on the other side of the door.

His face is lit up in the darkness as he keys in a phone number. He waits. Tries again.

'Damn! No signal. Bastards.'

Six hours later Johar Varma's driver arrives at the National Central Bureau headquarters to report the theft of the Mercedes. He is escorted to the Deputy Inspector's office.

'You expect me to believe this reprehensible nonsense?'

'Yes, Sir. Sorry, Sir. It is the truth. Assistant Superintendent Varma instructed me to stop and set off after the vagabond. I parked my vehicle and advised my passengers to wait, Sir. But they left the car. They are foreigners, Sir, and I felt obliged to get out and tell them to return to the car and wait for Assistant Superintendent Varma. That was when we were attacked by the protesters. I myself was knocked out. When I regained consciousness the vehicle and the two foreigners were gone. I have not seen Assistant Superintendent Varma since he gave chase, Sir. I give you my word that ...'

'Stop dribbling!' the Deputy Inspector shouts. He drums his fingers on the desk. Rs. 44 Lakh, or 4,400,000 rupees of limousine stolen. Two foreigners abducted. Will Europol pay 50,000 euros to get their people back, to cover the loss of the vehicle? Unlikely. The culprit is self-evidently that buffoon Johar Varma but, since they have yet to find him, the driver will have to suffer in his place. 'Throw him in the cells,' he instructs the two constables by the door. 'And if he gives any trouble, you have my permission to teach him some manners.'

It doesn't take long for the situation to deteriorate further. At dusk Assistant Superintendent Varma's body is reported found in an open sewer in Sangham Vihar slum, eighteen kilometres east of the airport.

CHAPTER 43

11th March 2020

Tiffany awakens to the sound of a key in a lock. She is lying on the floor. The room is black and stuffy. Is it night? Is it day? She smells food. She is famished. She also desperately needs a toilet. Close by, someone else is groaning.

Panic.

'Tiffany?' says a voice with a European accent.

It's OK. It's Antoine.

The door opens. The light hurts her eyes. Three men in silhouette. As her irises adjust, Tiffany realises the light in the corridor beyond the doorway is actually quite dim. She recognises two of the men from earlier. The third is an old man wearing white robes and a turban.

'Come,' says the young man she spoke with earlier. His moustache is no longer green.

Tiffany and Antoine climb to their feet.

'Please, I need a toilet,' she tells him. 'And we are hungry.'

The young man nods. 'My name is Nikit Chamar. What is your good name?'

'I am Tiffany and this is Antoine. What happened to your green moustache?' she adds, trying to build a rapport.

'Regrettably Holi lasts only one day,' he answers, good-naturedly.

They follow Nikit, with the other men taking up the rear. A remark is made, accompanied by ugly sniggering. She shivers in spite of the heat.

The toilet is a hole in the ground in a stinking room devoid of furnishings except another two-watt light bulb and a bucket containing rank discoloured water. Tiffany waits in the corridor while Antoine takes his turn. Why are there no windows? She dare not check her phone to learn the time. Through the flimsy toilet door they can hear Antoine throwing up. Were they listening when she was in there? When Antoine emerges his face looks whiter than ever. He looks haggard.

They are escorted through a maze of corridors until eventually they reach a large space lined with shelves that are crammed with food; in jars, tins, bags, sacks, crates and boxes. In the middle of the room is a long table seated around which are five men and two women. The women are both middle-aged and wearing saris. Seeing them Tiffany relaxes just a little; they must surely understand how she feels.

'Sit,' says the old man with dyed red hair, sitting at the head of the table.

Someone needs to tell him the coloured paint festival is over, Tiffany thinks to herself. As she and Antoine take their seats, the old man beckons to a youth standing in a doorway.

'Bhojan aur paanee.'

The youth disappears and reappears with a tray bearing bottled water, two glasses and a plate of samosas.

The old man beckons Nikit and says something to him.

'My grandfather says eat and drink. He also asks why you are looking for Rajesh Anvit Pandit.'

'It is a complicated story,' starts Antoine.

'Not you. The girl,' says Nikit. 'He wants to hear the girl's explanation.'

Tiffany finishes her samosa and drinks from one of the bottles before replying.

'I believe that Rajesh may have helped my friend to escape the UK,' she says. 'My friend Daniel were kidnapped by bad people but he made friends with Rajesh in a homeless centre in London. We learned that Rajesh is a good man, he paints and plays chess and helps people. We think he helped Daniel.'

Tiffany stops, worried that her Yorkshire accent will make her hard to be understood. Should she have avoided the word kidnapped?

'Have you met Rajesh?' Nikit asks.

Tiffany shakes her head.

'And you?' the young man asks Antoine.

'No,' Antoine replies. 'but we know he is an important figure in the anti-caste movement, standing up for the rights of the Dalit community, and that he was sent to the UK by his own family to prevent the police from arresting him. I am from Europol. I am not here to arrest Mr Pandit or to reveal his whereabouts or activities to anyone, including the Indian police. It is Daniel that we are ...'

The old man holds up a hand to stop Antoine in mid-flow, then exchanges words with his grandson.

'He asks when did you arrive? Have you been in quarantine?'

Antoine and Tiffany shakes their heads.

'We arrived yesterday in the night,' Antoine answers.

Angry words are exchanged in Hindi. The old man barks an instruction and everyone falls silent.

'Why would your friend come to India?' Nikit asks Tiffany.

'He came to escape from bad people.' Tiffany pauses, wondering how much to say. 'Maybe he is working with RJ.'

She is intensely aware of all the eyes on her, weighing her up, listening intently to the young man's translation of her words.

'Eat while we speak,' Nikit tells Tiffany and Antoine.

Aside from occasional outbursts of disagreement, the conversation around them is calm. One of the women is particularly vocal and is listened to respectfully by all the others.

Tiffany wonders if she has said enough, or too much. She looks around her. Are all shops like this in New Delhi; without windows to keep the building cool in the heat of the day?

'Describe Daniel,' Nikit says, interrupting her thoughts.

The conversation around the table has ceased and all eyes are on her once again.

'Tall and thin. A kind face with thoughtful eyes. He is not an extrovert or loud. About twenty-three years old. Messy brown hair. Blue eyes, a bit green. Oh, he loves blues music and plays the guitar. He has a London accent, not like mine.'

'What does he do? What is his profession?'

She is stuck. She cannot say an assistant for an estate agent though that is the only job he mentioned to her. That was more than three years ago. She looks around the table, wondering what she should say. She doesn't want to talk about Thor Lupei; they will just think her mad.

She considers how she has changed in the past three years, from chip shop apron to nurse's uniform, learning new skills, making something of herself. Can she really guess what Daniel has become? She thinks of the pages torn from Lupei's book. The lists of organ transplants. What did Daniel say in his letter? Something about Lupei teaching him things and Daniel wanting to prove that Lupei's powers could be used for good. What does that mean?

'He helps people,' she says vaguely.

The conversation around the table resumes. Tiffany pours herself another glass of water and offers one to Antoine.

The old man claps his hands together and there is silence.

'We have decided,' Nikit translates for his grandfather. 'First you leave your phones here. We will take you to Rajesh. You will be blindfolded. Our movement is in danger from the police and from this virus. If you bring the virus then we are all already dead. You must not approach Rajesh. If you attempt to do so you will be shot, is that understood? One of the women will accompany you so you will feel safe. We go now.'

Antoine and Tiffany stand up.

'No! Only girl,' the old man says in broken English. He

turns to his grandson and says a few words in Hindi.

'You must stay here,' Nikit explains to Antoine.

Tiffany puts her phone on the table.

'Are you sure, Tiffany? We can refuse and await here together.'

'I think they can help us,' she tells Antoine, 'as long as we don't risk their safety. To be fair, I would be just the same.'

'Once we are separated then …'

'I get it. But you said this would be risky. I'll be alright.'

'You're an amazing young woman, Tiffany.' Antoine smiles.

'My nan says I'm a total wazzock! Anyroad, best get on with it.'

She follows Nikit out and one of the women of the room. On the threshold she looks back. Antoine is emptying his pockets onto the table. He smiles tiredly; that same look that Gert gave her before he walked away in Whitby.

Another corridor, a door and she is back in the open air on wasteland between tall housing blocks. It is much warmer than inside. A hint of light in the sky. Dusk or dawn?

Time will tell.

Parked beneath a tree with leaves the size of dinner plates is a battered red car in which two men are waiting. The woman who has accompanied Tiffany outside produces a blindfold.

'Sarika says you have beautiful hair,' Nikit tells Tiffany as her eyes are covered.

He is saying that to stop you panicking.

She is helped into the back of the car. Nikit sits on one side and the woman on the other. She knows this because there is enough light to see a yellow sari through the gap at the bottom of her blindfold. And she can smell the woman's perfume.

The car rocks and judders over the rough ground. Punjabi rap music is playing. Tiffany surrenders to the experience, she can do no other.

Time passes. The slither of sari brightens; it must be dawn. The car joins a better road and the speed picks up bringing cooler air through the open windows. After a while the car stops. Words are exchanged and moments later Tiffany smells spices. Something warm is put in her hands.

'Breakfast,' Nikit explains. 'Vegetarian, good snack.'

It is, feels round, the size of a satsuma. The crisp outside gives way to a chewier centre. It is delicious and she finishes it quickly. At her side the woman laughs.

'Sarika says you have good appetite,' Nikit tells Tiffany.

It is hard to be sure but Tiffany guesses the journey takes around twenty minutes before the car stops a second time and the engine is cut. Car doors open. The sound of shoes on a hard dusty surface. The others wait. The shoes return.

'OK.'

'We can get out,' Nikit says, 'but keep blindfold on.'

Tiffany does as she is told. The woman, Sarika, helps her out of the car and escorts her some thirty steps across open ground. Tiffany feels the sun on her skin.

'Three steps.'

They climb them and a door closes.

'Remove blindfold now.'

They are in a passage with natural light coming in through a long wide window set high up on the wall. A door opens. A man in bare feet steps out to greet them. Slim, medium height, mid-thirties, long black hair. His hands together, fingers pointing upwards in a namaste, he nods to each person in turn.

'You are most welcome.' He says formally, then his face breaks into a big gap-toothed smile. 'Yo! What's happening in the U of K? Come on in. Do you play chess? No one here will give me a game anymore. Call me RJ, by the way.'

Rajesh Andit Panvit's accent is weird, London with more than a hint of Delhi.

'Hi RJ, I've come a very long way to find you.'

'That's a Yorkshire accent,' RJ tells Nikit. 'I'm guessing Whitby?' He pronounces it Whit-beh like a local. 'Let's grab a pot of tea. Can't promise fish and chips though.'

Everyone follows RJ inside, taking off their shoes as they cross the threshold. Tiffany does the same. The apartment is minimalist and cosmopolitan in its décor and furnishings, like the hotel room she woke up in twenty-four hours ago.

The main room is bright with sunshine pouring in through the skylights. They all sit on two large sofas with a long low table between them. An elegantly dressed woman in a blue sari arrives with teas and cold drinks.

'I'm here to find Daniel and …' Tiffany starts but is cut off in mid-flow by a shake of RJ's index finger.

'I want to know about *you*,' he says pointing at her. 'What makes Tiffany tick? I've heard honest, brave, beautiful, cuts through crap, works in a takeaway, the first person who ever really noticed me. Is all that true?'

Tiffany sips her tea and takes her time to compose herself. It is strange to hear Daniel's description of her, if those are his words, spoken here in India by a man she has never met before. Is Daniel nearby? Is he listening? She wants to call out his name.

'I don't work in a fish and chip shop anymore; I'm training to become a nurse.'

'Sorry about the blindfold, the locked rooms and all that shit. We have many enemies and have to take precautions.' RJ turns to the others in the room. 'Tiffany and I will talk privately.' He repeats the words in Hindi.

Everyone exchanges namastes and the others leave.

'Don't worry, they're waiting outside,' RJ tells Tiffany. 'So listen, before we start, the name Daniel means nothing to anyone here.'

Tiffany is alarmed.

'No, you misunderstand. It is just that here in Delhi he uses a different name. OK? For three years we have avoided the attention of the police. I want to keep it that way.'

'I need to see him.'

'I hear you. We'll sort something.' RJ smiles. 'In the meantime, tell me about the square in the suit. The guy you arrived with. I need backstory. You don't mind me drawing you while we talk, do you?'

While RJ pencil sketches Tiffany on a drawing pad, she tells him about Gert and Kevin Moore and Daniel's stolen Oyster Card and how RJ turned up in the homeless shelter records.

'So the guy in our warehouse is Gert?'

'No, Gert is in Romania. I'm travelling with Antoine Hoek, Gert's old boss.'

'Why is everyone digging this old shit up all over again?'

'Has Daniel told you about Thor Lupei?' Tiffany asks.

RJ's hesitation is enough; by the time he shakes his head she knows he is lying.

'Lupei is dangerous. He killed two of Daniel's friends in Whitby,' Tiffany says. 'And many others. Daniel told me Thor Lupei were dead. Everyone except Gert thought it were over. At Europol they thought Gert were insane; no one believes in the supernatural anymore. I didn't want to believe either. But they're wrong. Lupei is out there and he wants revenge.'

Tiffany stops, aware that RJ is saying nothing, waiting for her to fill every pause. Just like a police interview, just like Gert. She has said enough. Has she made any sense? She won't tell him that Daniel loves her. Is it even true anymore?

Of course it's true.

She can't tell him that she and Daniel are bound up together forever because of what happened in Whitby. Or that ever since her brother died when she was just a kid she has known deep in her soul that nothing is ever casual or throwaway, that everything matters.

You're not telling him because you don't trust him.

'… you *know* that or you *think* that?' RJ is finishing his pencil drawing as he speaks.

'What?' Tiffany realises she hasn't been listening.

'How do you know Lupei isn't dead. Why does he want revenge?'

'I just know and I want to talk with Daniel. Lupei may already be here in India. We may not have much time.'

RJ puts his sketchbook down beside his smart phone on the table between them. He studies Tiffany very carefully.

'OK, thanks for coming,' he says finally. 'We're very busy here helping people, people with serious real-world problems, helping the sick and the poor and the hungry, but I have been listening. I promise I will pass everything on if or when I see your friend. Do you need a lift back to the airport?'

Tiffany has had enough. 'You think I came all this way just to be bullshitted? Are you listening?' She grabs the sketchbook off the table. It is a very good likeness of her, which just makes her angrier.

'Daniel needs friends right now. I've seen what Lupei does to people. Have you? Are you listening because if you …'

She is interrupted by a loud psychedelic trance groove.

'Excuse me,' RJ takes the call on speaker phone

'We have a problem!' A woman's voice.

'Go on,' RJ replies.

'Suspected heart attack. What do I do?'

'What does he think?'

'There was no warning, nothing in the notes. It's looking bad and …'

'What does *he* think?'

'I don't know, RJ. He is very tired, we've been up all night,' the woman says. She continues in Hindi then finally says, in English, 'The past few days have been very difficult and …'

'OK, hang in there. I'm on my way. Nikit can bring me. You're at the clinic, right?'

'No, we're in Kusumpur Pahari near the …'

'Send Nikit directions. Bye.'

RJ cuts the call and looks up at Tiffany. 'I am sorry; a bit of a crisis. You can wait here.'

'I am a nurse,' Tiffany says. 'Take me with you.'

RJ drums his fingers on the tabletop.

'Forget all the other stuff for now. Just let me help.'

RJ studies her and nods. 'OK, let's go. I can have you dropped off at the airport on the way back.'

RJ's car, a silver 4x4, makes good progress initially. Nikit drives with Sarika, the woman in the yellow sari at the back beside Tiffany. RJ sits in the front passenger seat with his feet, in funky blue trainers now, up on the dashboard. The radio plays Indian hip-hop. The street is wide and lined with beautiful trees and flowering bushes. The sun is warm and, in spite of everything, Tiffany feels excited and glad to be alive.

And so it goes until they reach Kusumpur Pahari slum. Shortly after entering the narrow winding lanes they are stuck behind a water tanker. Surrounding the tanker are a hundred women and girls, and a sea of blue plastic jerry cans.

'Isn't there another route?' Tiffany asks after a couple of minutes.

'Look at the traffic,' RJ tells her, leaning back in his seat, eyes closed. 'We are hemmed in on all sides.'

It is true, behind them is a long line of cars and trucks.

'Now you see why the arts of meditation and developing inner peace are so highly prized in India,' RJ jokes. 'Relax, Tiffany. We have air-conditioning. Imagine that you are lying on a mountain in your beautiful Yorkshire and let this moment pass.'

RJ says something to Nikit in Hindi and he changes the radio channel to the slow serenity of an Indian raga played on a dusty bamboo flute accompanied by the slow shifting drone of a tanpura.

'But there is someone with a heart attack,' Tiffany protests. 'Can't we do something? Won't they move if we tell them there is an emergency?'

'These women have been waiting since dawn for the tanker. Some have slept outside all night to protect their spot in the queue. There is no running water here. The entire slum, one hundred thousand people, rely on these tankers for their drinking water.'

Outside two women are shouting at each other. It is not yet spring and barely 25°C. Tiffany tries to imagine the scene in mid-summer when the temperature is over 45°C.

'What happens if the tankers break down?' Her voice is tight and she is beginning to hyperventilate.

'I need to rest,' RJ says. 'I suggest you do the same, babe. Relax. We'll be moving soon.'

Tiffany closes her eyes and imagines she is standing at the end of the harbour jaws in Whitby. Sunrise is coming. The sky is purples and oranges, the sea a vast carpet of whispering wavelets, criss-crossing back and forth. Early seagulls silhouette a fading night while water laps and licks the sandstone piers.

Everything is OK.

Her panic subsides. Her breathing slows to the lazy tempo of the tanpura drone.

Careful, Tiffany. You'll end up in orange robes, handing out flowers and chanting like a hippy.

Her frown fades. She will help RJ deal with the medical emergency and then maybe he will help her find Daniel. Tiffany is trying to imagine how ambulances access the slum when fingers touch the back of her hand. She jumps.

Sarika smiles. Something in the woman's eyes remind Tiffany of the look her mum used to give her to console her when she was a child. The plastic jerry cans are all full, the crowd is dispersing and the tanker is moving off.

RJ and Nikit reanimate like polar bears coming out of hibernation. A hundred metres further on, along increasingly bumpy ground, Nikit floors the brakes and slams his fist on the horn. Within seconds two young children, Tiffany guesses they must be around eight years old, appear around the side of a ramshackle building. The young boy and girl are squabbling. The girl wins and steps up to the car while her brother stays back, arms folded, glowering grumpily. RJ opens his door and the girl clambers in over him to sit in the middle at the front. Nikit asks her something and she nods and points. The car sets off and takes the next right turn, with the girl giving Nikit a running commentary as they negotiate the labyrinth.

'Welcome to our low-cost hi-tech living satnav,' RJ explains to Tiffany. 'Google Maps knows less about this slum than the Mariana Trench.'

A dead end is reached and the car stops. There are four narrow alleys leading off in different directions. Within seconds, three men appear from one of the alleys. RJ gets out of the car and talks with them then leans in through the open car window.

'OK, it's a short walk from here. One of the guys will take us; the other two will guard the car. Let's go.'

Tiffany turns to Sarika, who nods and replies in Hindi.

'You can chill. She's coming with us,' RJ explains.

RJ presses money into the girl's hand and she scampers off happily. RJ, Tiffany and Sarika follow their guide into the labyrinth. Tiffany is reminded of a psychology lecture she attended in her first year at Middlesbrough. Rats in a maze, learning different routes to earn a reward, a piece of fruit or a broken biscuit. She is already lost five times over: she couldn't find the car if she tried, the car is lost in a bewildering lattice of narrow streets, the slum is somewhere in Delhi (but where?), she cannot understand a word of Hindi, and she has no idea where the airport is.

They push past rusty bicycles and handcarts and under clotheslines heavy with washing. The alleys are swept clean, but the realities of an absence of running water are impossible to escape. One minute the air is thick with the delicious aromas of cooking and spices, the next they are rattling across wooden boards over an open sewer, assaulted by the fetid miasma of human sewage.

A small hotel, implausibly named *Paradise*. An even smaller shop with no windows, selling plastic bottles and buckets visible through the open door guarded by an old man in blue shorts.

There are signs of the indomitable human spirit; plant pots painted in bright colours out of which spring all manner of flowering plants, their blooms bright against the concrete. For thousands this is home and it needs to be its best version of itself. On walls and paths everywhere there are traces of the previous day's colour festival.

A blue and battered wooden door, the top half intensely lit in the late morning sun, the bottom in deep shadow. The door opens to reveal a tired middle-aged woman, her arm draped over the shoulder of a slender tearful girl. The woman is visibly shocked at the sight of Tiffany.

'Hi Karuna,' RJ steps forward. 'How are things?'

'Not good,' the woman replies. 'Halogen-Ji is tired and upset. He says grandmother is too weak but if he cancels then things may get worse. We are stuck. I urged him to wait for the nurse but you know what he is like.'

'Are you sure she has had a heart attack?' Tiffany asks.

Karuna turns to stare at Tiffany.

'She is a nurse,' RJ explains.

'We have no equipment. Normally the nurse is …'

'Let's go inside,' RJ says.

Karuna and the girl step aside to let RJ and Tiffany in. The man who has guided them to the house stays outside.

The passage is dark and stuffy as an armpit. The cloying sweet smell of burning joss sticks hangs heavy. They squeeze past a stack of containers and find themselves in a brighter space where the overhead light comes from water-filled plastic bottles that have been pushed through holes cut into the roof over their heads, trapping the refracted sunlight above and providing as much light as an electric bulb.

It is darker in the room. Tiffany has only lived in houses and flats where there are multiple rooms with different functions: kitchen, bathroom, bedroom, front room. Here the whole house fits in one room. The brick walls are ultramarine blue, but you can barely see them beneath a sea-clutter of pots and pans, coat hangers and clothes, photos and paintings of gods, food containers, dustpan and brush, and a spaghetti of electric cables. At a corner a few bricks have been punched out to create a lattice of tiny glassless windows through which the sun seeps. On small patch of bare wall someone has pressed handprints, black on blue, to ward off evil spirits.

Clothes hang from wooden poles mounted on the ceiling along with an assortment of large and bulging plastic bags and wicker baskets. There's more stuff scattered across the floor: boxes and crates covered with brightly printed fabrics, a broken fridge without a door. A tatty rug with a red stitched hamsa hand.

And then there is the bed.

Iron-framed like a hospital bed, it is mounted on bricks to lift it high enough off the ground to use the space beneath for further storage. There are two people on the bed. Ducking beneath the hanging washing Tiffany approaches. The man has his face turned away and is holding the old woman's hand. The woman is on her back, contorted in pain. Her grey hair hangs loose and lank.

Tiffany tilts the woman's head back to open her airway by pulling the tongue forward. She feels for a pulse while lowering her face towards the woman's mouth. Tiffany can feel the woman's breath, faintly brushing the skin of her cheek; she is alive. She turns to Karuna.

'Please help me roll her over onto her side. Is there aspirin?'

Karuna shrugs.

'We'll fix it,' RJ calls from the doorway.

Tiffany and Karuna roll the old woman gently over onto her side. A little blood and vomit fall from the woman's toothless mouth.

'Can you please ask the gentleman to let go of his wife's hand?' Tiffany says to Karuna.

'I am not sure that is safe.'

Tiffany is confused. 'She will be more comfortable if her arm is not twisted back. Then we need to crush aspirin in water as soon as RJ returns. It will thin her blood and relive the pressure on her heart. Please.'

Karuna nods and goes round to the other side of the bed. They talk in Hindi. Tiffany feels the old woman's brow; it is cool and clammy and strangely tingly to the touch. The woman's eyes open slowly and she stares up at Tiffany in some confusion. The tingling stops.

'You can move her arm now,' Karuna says from the other side of the bed.

'Nani-ji!' calls the little girl from the doorway, stepping into the room. She hurries forward and stands by the bed smiling down at her grandmother.

RJ appears with aspirin.

'Can someone find a glass and some water please?' Tiffany asks Sarika who is sitting quietly at the back of the room.

'You can move her arm,' Karuna says again.

Tiffany reaches over and lifts the woman's arm and places it in front of her. The man has rolled over on his side away from the woman. The girl pops up at Tiffany's side, holding a cup containing water and the aspirin RJ has given her. Tiffany pops a couple of tablets from the blister pack and drops them in the water. She stirs them round with her finger to dissolve them, it is too complicated to ask for cutlery.

'I need you to drink this,' she tells the woman. 'Can someone translate please?' Someone obliges, the woman nods slightly and Tiffany gently lifts and turns her head to ensure the water doesn't spill. Drop by drop the aspirin is drunk. Exhausted by this small act, the woman manages a flicker of a smile then closes her eyes. The girl, who has been watching everything intensely, flinches.

'It's OK. She's tired, that's all,' Tiffany reassures the girl. 'She needs to rest.'

RJ translates from the doorway and the girl relaxes and rests her hand lightly on her grandmother's fingers.

Emotionally drained, Tiffany steps back.

'Is the old man all right?' she asks Karuna.

Karuna is confused. She goes to the other side of the bed and speaks softly then offers her hand and helps pull the man up into a sitting position. He has his back to the old woman as he takes several deep breaths. Tiffany wonders if the young girl has lost her parents. Will the old man be able to cope?

'This lady needs to go to hospital,' Tiffany says. 'How does that work here in Delhi?'

'We can get her to Ayushman Bharat - Health and Wellness Centre but what happens to her grand-daughter?' says Karuna.

'She'll be OK,' the man says in perfect English. 'We'll look after her.'

The man stands and turns.

Both he and Tiffany do a double-take.

CHAPTER 44

11th March 2020

Tiffany and Daniel stare at each other, open-jawed, across the iron bed as the room and everything in it blur to fog.

The hipster beard and handlebar moustache are weird but sort of work, she decides. He is transported to another time and place. He hears waves smashing against a pier and the cries of seagulls; she is as beautiful as in his dreams.

Beside Tiffany, Sarika is sitting on the floor, holding the young girl's shoulders, comforting and reassuring her. The girl listens intently to instructions and nods. RJ stands in the doorway as Karuna explains to him how the crisis unfolded.

Daniel and Tiffany hear and see none of this.

'What …' they both start simultaneously then stop.

Again the words reach their lips at the same time.

And are aborted.

'You first,' Daniel smiles.

Tiffany grins. 'This is weird!'

'Yeah,' Daniel agrees. 'You on holiday?'

'WHAT?'

'Joke. It's like …'

'Yes, it is, isn't it?'

'How did you find me?'

'Long story.'

'I can believe it.'

'What's with the moustache?'

'Long story.'

'I can help. I'm a nurse.' Tiffany blushes, 'I mean help here, not help with your moustache.'

He laughs.

'Halogen-Ji, you have been up all night,' Karuna says. 'Go home and rest, we can finish here. I will wait with her until we take her nanny to hospital.'

Daniel nods. He crouches down beside the girl and speaks softly to her in Hindi. Her face resolute and serious, she alternates between staring at him and glancing at her grandmother. Tiffany watches in awe at the girl's courage, what can it be like to become the carer at just eight years old? Abruptly the girl's face crumples, and she throws herself forward to wrap her arms around Daniel's neck.

'Bahut dhanyavaad! Thank you!'

'Swagut hai,' Daniel replies, hugging the girl back. 'You're welcome.'

He prises himself gently from the embrace, stands up, produces a wad of banknotes from his trouser pocket and hands it to Karuna.

'Can you make sure she's OK for food, water and everything?' Daniel turns to RJ. 'OK, let's go home.'

'Am I staying here?' Tiffany asks, unclear as to what is happening.

Daniel does another double-take, still in shock at Tiffany's presence. 'Of course not. You're coming with me. With us. If you want. Karuna and Sarika will look after the girl.'

Tiffany nods.

They follow their guide through the alleys to RJ's car, the sun hot on their backs. Sitting beside Daniel in the car, Tiffany no longer smells the slum. RJ has jacked up the Punjabi rap on the radio and that sort of suits them both. Daniel smiles tiredly, puts his head back and closes his eyes. Tiffany reaches out to touch his hand lightly with her fingertips. She sees a faint smile cross his face, beneath the moustache. Within seconds he is asleep.

The traffic ebbs and flows.

'RJ?'

'Yes.'

'Am I going to get my smart phone back?'

'Yeah. I'll drop you and Halogen-ji off then go and collect your stuff and that guy you came with. Anthony?'

'Antoine.'

'Great. And can I have Karuna's phone number and the name of the hospital she's taking the old lady to?'

'Sure, why not?' RJ says as the car stops in traffic. He pulls a business card from his trouser pocket and scribbles. 'There you go.'

He passes the card back to Tiffany. She looks at the front of the card.

'What's the Aesthetic Wonder Clinic?'

'You'll see.'

The slum is way behind them when RJ turns the car off the main road and onto a wide tree-lined side street. Halfway down, he stops in front of a pair of large gates and toots his horn. A security guard, a youth in an oversized uniform - jacket sleeves covering his hands, trouser legs rolled up, cap falling over his eyes - appears on the other side and opens the gates to let them in.

RJ cuts the engine beneath the leathery dark green leaves of a tall jamun tree. A couple of black drongos hop from branch to branch in the tree canopy, shrieking and complaining, their calls echoing off the walls of the pink concrete apartment block.

Tiffany gently shakes Daniel.

'We've arrived,' she says. 'Somewhere.'

Daniel blinks. 'Tiffany, hi!'

'You OK, Bro?'

'Yeah, I'm good, RJ.' Daniel stretches. 'Let's go.'

There are several brass plaques by the entrance to the building, including one that reads:

Aesthetic WonderSlim Clinic ®
My Perfect Look

They take the lift to the second floor and RJ opens the door to the clinic. The blinds are closed so he flicks on the lights.

'I'll leave you,' RJ says, 'I am picking up Tiffany's phone and then sort out Antoine. This guy we locked up with Tiffany,' he tells Daniel. 'He's from Europol. Not a great move, kidnapping a blessed cop, is it? So I'll sort that and ... oh, anything else you guys need?'

Daniel shakes his head.

'OK. Check you later. Cool.'

The door closes behind the departing RJ and finally, for the first time in over three years, Daniel and Tiffany are alone.

'I'll show you round,' Daniel smiles, opens a door and leads the way.

There is a reception desk and a waiting area with half a dozen chairs. On the wall behind the desk is a photograph of Daniel, in hipster beard and handlebar moustache, flanked by the smiling faces of beautiful clients. Down a corridor to another waiting area, with a water cooler and a table stacked with magazines in half a dozen languages. More photos.

'We worked so hard to get all this organised,' Daniel says proudly. 'RJ, Karuna and me. Really tough at first.' He pauses to look at her again. 'Wow! I still can't believe you're here!'

'This is my office,' he says, opening another door. 'Felt all wrong at first, like I was an imposter, but you have to make people feel at ease. Give them confidence. Same with the beard, they say it makes me look older.'

'Dead ringer for ZZ Top.'

'Who?'

'My uncle Ted's favourite band. Look them up.'

Tiffany stares at the big mahogany desk, the bookshelves

stacked with serious-looking books, the reclining couch, the screen behind which, presumably, people get changed.

Framed certificates on the walls complete the picture.

`Five-star accreditation`
`for facial rejuvenation`

This Association recognises your selfless service and devotion to the betterment of plastic surgery.

This is to certify that Mr Halogen Jones of Aesthetic WonderSlim Clinic, New Delhi has been independently assessed and is compliant with the requirements of ISO 9001:2015 applicable to

PLASTIC SURGERY, BREAST SURGERY, HAIR TRANSPLANT, & COSMETIC SURGERY

'I wish we could bring all our clients here, to the clinic, the people who really matter, but it isn't possible. Some are too weak to leave their homes so we go to them. Sometimes, like today, there are children to think about or other family members. And RJ thinks it would freak some people out. All this stuff is for the rich, we have to look like the kind of place they expect to see.'

Even the way Daniel is talking is confusing Tiffany. His voice is the same but not the same, like those films where the hero discovers he has a twin brother who has grown up in a millionaire's mansion. It's been disorientating enough finding him holding an old woman's hand in a slum.

'Are you OK?' Daniel asks. 'Do you want to sit down?'

Tiffany shrugs and nods simultaneously, unable to marshal her thoughts. 'I don't know.'

Daniel finds her a chair and a glass of water.

'The air-conditioning gets to me sometimes,' he says. 'Like it's 35 degrees outside and then in here ... In July, Delhi can reach 44 degrees. Everyone just stays inside.'

'He's coming, Daniel,' Tiffany interrupts him gently.

'When we first arrived RJ said ...'

'He's coming.'

'What?'

'Thor Lupei.'

Daniel nods, as if what she says is obvious, then does a double-take. 'What?'

'He is coming here to kill you.'

'He can't. He's dead. I saw him fall into the flames three years ago.'

'So why did you run away? Why are you here? Why hide in India?'

Daniel says nothing.

'Gert told me Lupei is alive,' she continues.

'That Dutch policeman? I never met him, did I?'

'Lupei killed Gert's brother. He's been hunting Lupei for years. And ever since you disappeared, he's been ...'

'OK,' Daniel holds up a hand. 'Let's forget the tour for now and go upstairs. We can sit down, grab something to eat and you can explain everything.'

The apartments are reached via an internal staircase; the lift and main stairs do not give access to the second floor.

'This is home,' he announces, hoping the change of scene will help Tiffany.

It's a large open-plan apartment. Sunlight floods a room tastefully decorated in a mixture of Indian and minimalist furnishing. It speaks of money and power.

'I didn't pick any of this beautiful stuff, before you ask. Karuna's done it all,' Daniel says.

Tiffany dies a little inside. 'I don't suppose you miss your bedsit in South Ealing. Bit more space here.'

'You went to Ealing?'

'Gert took me when we were looking for you.'

Daniel fetches various soft drinks and snacks from the kitchen area and places them on the low table in front of the huge turquoise sofa. They sit down.

Daniel's phone rings.

Tiffany stares about her, feeling utterly at sea.

'Hi. OK, good. Yes, of course we pay. Tell her not to worry. Yeah, OK.' Daniel turns to Tiffany. 'That was Karuna. They've reached the hospital.'

Tiffany wants to ask about Karuna but isn't sure she wants to hear the answer. 'I gave Antoine a copy of those files on your SIM card. I never looked at them until three days ago. I never told Gert about them. I trusted you, Daniel.'

The past tense does not pass unnoticed. Daniel remembers the feeling in the pit of his stomach as he walked away from Tiffany that morning in Whitby and the dozen letters he wrote and tore up before he settled on what he wanted to say. The finished letter sat for days by the sink in his bedsit.

> *... You are the best thing that ever happened to me ...
> No one wants to go out with a loser, I get that, but I
> swear I'm different ...*
>
> *... I want to understand more about Lupei and prove
> it is possible to use his powers for good things ... If I
> am wrong then I promise I will kill myself rather than
> become like him.*

He opens a bottle of water and pours them both a glass.

'I have been doing my best. So did Lupei, I suppose, in his own way. There are so many poor people here. Like the old lady. People who are old by the time they are forty. Orphaned children. And we help them. RJ, Karuna and I work with the

Dalit community, the untouchables. We find ...'

'Rich foreigners having liposuction or having their noses tweaked and butt cheeks lifted?' Tiffany says. 'And you living like a king while millions queue for fresh water in the slums.'

'It's not like that.'

'It looks like that. Gert were right.'

'Lupei lived in the past,' Daniel explains. 'When he started people didn't even know what their internal organs were or what they did. He saved lives in the dark ages but only saw one side of what his powers can do. We do deals with wealthy people to help poor people.'

'Lupei killed people. Do you kill people, Daniel?' She stares at him.

He stares at her.

She stares at him.

'Apart from the Rasta in the garage,' she says.

He still says nothing.

'I read some of the pages you took from Lupei. He were selling organs to rich people all over Europe. Putting people in his debt. That's why Eric at the Whitby Pavilion set you up; Lupei had saved his daughter. Same with the police inspector, Lupei had given his wife a kidney. He were killing people to order, weren't he? And he were making scravir. But you know all that, don't you?'

'Bad people, Tiffany,' Daniel tells her. 'He killed rapists and murderers, child abusers, people who prey on the vulnerable.'

'Is that what you do?'

Daniel shakes his head. 'You don't understand. I am helping people. Even the fat and the rich people who come here from Europe and America. It's only human and I help them. They want thinner waists or fuller lips, bigger breasts or wider hips. And the flesh they don't want helps the poor. Instead of the risks of complications, I can make the changes they want without using a scalpel. I help someone change the shape of their nose or move a little fat to hide the veins in their hands and they are happy. Then I can help a child with a cleft palate.'

Tiffany is uneasy. What happened to the youth who walked into her fish and chip shop? Is he still in there behind that flamboyant moustache?

'I'll show you everything. Everyone has bits they don't like about themselves; things they wish they could change to become the perfect version of themselves and ...'

Tiffany is remembering something she saw on television. A woman in America was having twenty operations to make herself perfect for her husband; her living body a meaty canvas for his fantasies. And the fifty-year-old man who had his skin scraped out from underneath to fill jars with orange fat while bags were stuffed in here, there and everywhere to give him pectoral muscles, biceps and 'proper' butt cheeks. She thinks of those fragile egos with frozen foreheads, so terrified of wrinkles that they would rather paralyse their faces than see the mark of time across their skin. The girls in Whitby pumping up their lips till they look like trawlers' catch offloaded on the quayside.

'.. I'll prove to you that it's OK and safe. What would you like to change about you? Just tell me and ...'

'No! NO, DANIEL!' Tiffany jumps to her feet. 'Shut up! I am the perfect me. I don't need changing. I don't want changing. I don't need bigger boobs or thinner bloody earlobes. I don't need all the fat sucking out of my body, or any of that shit. I know that one day I will look old and I know that everyone dies.' She cannot stop the tears from welling up.

'I don't want to look like a TikTok celebrity or satisfy your idea of what a perfect woman looks like. All of this ...' she sweeps her hands across her body, '... all this is me. No one is more me than me on this Earth and I am happy and proud of me just the way I am. So just get me a taxi to the airport and I'll bugger off back to Whitby. You're welcome to your superstar apartment, and your perfect Karuna and smart alec RJ, your white coat and hipster beard, and your sodding photos of happy clients and adoring fans. I shouldn't have come. It was a mistake. I'm sorry.'

Tiffany turns towards the window. Daniel gets up off the sofa, he approaches and stands silently beside her.

A flock of the tiny long-beaked birds she saw at breakfast (was it only yesterday morning?) are chattering in the branches of a semal tree, its big red flowers so waxy and bright that they look as unreal as a superstar's nose.

'Please. Can we just ...'

'No, get me a taxi.'

He fishes his phone out of his pocket and clicks the app.

'OK, I've booked it,' he says a minute later. 'It's pre-paid, you won't have to pay a penny.'

She hopes it arrives soon.

He hopes it will never come but knows it will and when his phone rings, he escorts her down, back through the clinic. In the lift he reaches out to touch her hand. She pulls away.

The taxi is waiting.

'I need to stop off at the Rainbow Lotus Hotel to collect my things.'

'No problem,' the driver says, opening a door for her.

Tiffany is climbing into the car as Daniel reaches again for her hand.

'You are as amazing as the first moment I saw you.'

She smiles sadly and sweetly. 'Can't give you free chips anymore. We've both moved on, haven't we?'

'Have we? You've not told me about your life now.'

'It's a long story.'

'I'm sorry, Tiffany.'

On an impulse, Tiffany hugs him and he hugs back like a sailor clinging to the mast of a sinking ship. Tiffany prises herself away.

'I've got to go.'

He nods. She gets into the taxi and it pulls away, the tyres crunching on the gravel. As the car turns onto the road she glances back.

Daniel is waving.

Tiffany is too upset to think about anything. She stares out of the window at the street sellers, the crowd emerging from a station, the jostling tuk-tuks, a couple of old men playing chess by the roadside. She fears for the young woman, about her own age, scrolling on her mobile phone as she sits on the back of a speeding motorbike. As the taxi becomes logjammed in a river of cars she recalls a similar traffic jam with Gert in a pointless journey through West London.

She watches a woman leaning out of a sixth-storey window, hanging out her washing. Pinks, yellows and whites bright against the grey concrete.

When the taxi reaches the hotel, she runs to the reception desk. Has Antoine collected his room key, she asks. No. She goes up to her room, changes into clean clothes, jeans and a fresh t-shirt, and gathers her luggage. Back down in reception they tell her a man just came in and left an envelope for her. It contains her smart phone, with almost zero charge.

Back to the waiting taxi, still numb with anger and disappointment. Still trying not to think about Daniel. More busy roads, more stop start. By a set of traffic lights a huge film poster shows a woman in sports clothes. In giant letters are the words:

PANGA

Saara sheher mujhe Mummy ke naam se jaanta hai

The strapline at the bottom of the poster reads:

'... an exhilarating ode to motherhood and chasing dreams'
The Times of India

It hits Tiffany like a thunderbolt. She has forgotten the one thing she promised herself she would do! The whole reason why she came to India.

'Please. Please.' She taps the driver on the shoulder. 'We have to go back to the clinic. The place where you picked me up.'

The driver turns to look at her as the traffic ahead starts to move. He shakes his head in disbelief.

'I can pay,' she tells him.

In the car behind the taxi, the driver thumps an impatient tattoo on his horn.

'What time is your flight?' the driver asks. 'It takes over an hour to go back.'

'Time isn't important.'

The klaxon cacophony is rising quickly as more drivers vent their frustrations.

'Please hurry.' Tiffany offers him twenty US dollars.

The driver shakes his head pityingly and sighs as he takes the money. He turns the car across the flow of the traffic as people shout and motorbikes screech to a halt. The car judders as it climbs the kerb over the central reservation, people shouting, brakes screaming.

They head off in the opposite direction away from the chaos. Tiffany finds the business card RJ gave her. She keys the number into her phone. No answer. She messages instead and awaits a response.

Half an hour and four unanswered messages later, the driver pulls up in front of the gates. Tiffany looks up at the pink apartment block and rehearses for the eleventh time what she is going to tell Daniel about his mother. Whatever has happened between them, he has a right to know. His mum never left him, she wasn't bored with him, she loved him. She died in an accident. And his dad loves him too. She can even play him the audio file that Gert sent her.

Then she can leave.

The driver sounds his horn again.

'Where is the bloody security guard?' Tiffany climbs out of the car. 'Hey! HEY!'

She rattles the gates.

'HEY!'

Finally the youth appears at the far end of the yard in his over-sized uniform.

'I have to go back inside,' Tiffany shouts, pointing at the building.

'Closed,' the youth shouts back. 'No one here, Madam.'

'The Aesthetic WonderSlim Clinic. They are expecting me. Please open the gate.'

The taxi driver is out of the car. He talks with the youth in Hindi.

'He says the white man, Doctor Jones, left twenty minutes ago. The red car picked him up. The building is empty.'

She is too late.

CHAPTER 45

11th March 2020

From his vantage point high up on the fire escape ladders of a nearby building, Antoine sees the action below through the trees. He sees the silver 4x4 screech to a halt at the back of the warehouse, loud rap music blaring through its open windows. Two guards emerge to greet the driver. They talk. A sudden eruption of anger and finger waving.

His escape has been discovered.

The guards and the new man race into the warehouse.

Antoine checks for the hundredth time that his hideaway is not overlooked. He has to get back to the hotel. Without his phone he cannot yet make contact with the outside world and he cannot risk being spotted out on the streets in daylight. He needs to ring his wife, contact the crime bureau in Delhi, and check in at Europol. Why did that idiot Varma get out of the car? It is hours since he saw Tiffany. Did their captors really take her to meet RJ or Daniel? Is she safe?

There is barely any shade on the ladders and Antoine has a splitting headache from dehydration and the pollution in the air. He passes the time dismantling and reassembling his favourite La Pavino lever espresso coffee machine in his mind. Removing each nut and screw. Gently tapping out the bolts and laying them out on a cloth. Descaling, fixing new sealing rings and gaskets. Polishing the wooden handle, resetting the pressure gauge.

Down below, the warehouse doors fly open. More shouting and finger pointing. The driver scrambles back into his 4 x 4, reverses wildly and speeds away in a thick cloud of dust.

Three hours later it is dark. Antoine, still on the fire escape, stretches his aching limbs. Carefully and quietly he makes his way back down the ladders to the ground. The birds have stopped chattering. The air is thick with the smell of cooking. Head throbbing, Antoine moves from shadow to shadow. He is approaching the open door at the back of a restaurant when a huge face looms at him in the lacklight. He jumps back.

A cow chewing slowly on a plastic carrier bag, oil-black eyes beneath heavy eyelashes. Sweet sulphurous breath, its bowels emptying, splashing and crackling on the carpet of plastic detritus around it.

A motorbike speeds by, carrying three youths, all shouts and laughter.

Antoine sneaks forward to steal a bottle of water through the open door. He drinks it greedily, toys with the idea of going back to grab some food then thinks better of it. He has to keep moving, to put distance between himself and the warehouse, find out where he is and make his way back to the hotel.

CHAPTER 46

12th March 2020

It is shortly after midnight and she has been sitting several hours in Departures, a space so vast that it looks empty even though there are several hundred people milling about. The in-bound flight from London arrived some 20 minutes ago and, across the hall, staff at the check-in desks scroll their screens for cancellations on the return flight.

Tiffany is numb. She has seen too much, heard too much, felt too much. The confrontation with Daniel and her disappointment at how he has changed have hurt her and she is furious with herself for not telling him about his mum. It isn't something you put in a text.

She has messaged her uncle Ted to tell him she will soon be on her way. The one-word reply - *Good* - suggests he will have more to say when she reaches home and it probably won't be polite.

Everything is a mess.

'Ms Harrek?'

She looks up to find a British Airways staff member at her side. The badge on his dark blue suit reads Bradley Bako - Customer Services Manager.

'I am delighted to report that we have found you a seat. There is just the paperwork to complete.' His smile is warm and reassuring. 'This way please.'

'Brilliant!' Tiffany gets to her feet. 'Thank you so much.'

She follows him towards the check-in desks.

'I can only apologise for the delay,' he says over his shoulder. 'I have remonstrated with the team.'

'I'm just happy you found me a seat. I were worried I'd be stuck here for days.'

To the left of the check-in desks is a door set into the towering marble wall. The manager holds the door open for her.

'A couple of forms to complete then the staff can tag your luggage and your journey can commence!' he tells her.

Tiffany steps through the doorway, the weight finally lifting from her shoulders.

A stairwell.

'It's upstairs?' she says, suddenly uncertain.

'That's right,' he answers right behind her. 'There is nowhere else to go, is there?'

The door is still closing as she feels fingers brush her neck. She spins round ...

The hair is cut short and is brown instead of white, he is somehow more bulked out than before and he must be wearing contact lenses.

But now she sees him.

She wants to shout but cannot even open her mouth.

'Oh Tiffany, Tiffany.' His face is a picture of disappointment. 'How easily we are deceived. You look every bit as pretty as you did in Whitby, by the way, but still a gullible chip shop girl at heart, aren't you? Is that why he loves you?'

As Tiffany loses conscious control of her own body, her vision shrinks into a tunnel until all she can see are his eyes, cold and hard as tombstones.

Thor Lupei.

Nobody thinks to intervene as the tall British Airways customer services manager escorts the young woman through the terminal even though she appears barely awake and is resting her head on his shoulder. He takes her through the exit doors into the warmth of the night. A couple of men approach to scam the foreigners with the most expensive taxi rides Delhi can offer but when they see the British Airways uniform they back off. Airline staff know all the scams.

As the car pulls away, the driver feels fingers on his neck.

Lupei is an opportunist.

It was the same after the Battle of Campaldino on the 11th of June in 1289.

By the time night fell, Arezzo had fallen. The Ghibelline army had fallen. The wounded had fallen, one by one, over life's edge down into death's dark depths. Their leader, Guglielmo Ubertini, had also fallen, stabbed in the throat and left floating with the fish in the river Arno.

The screams and clatter of swords and spears on the bloodied field were replaced by the sneaking steps of thieves, rats and scavengers. Lupei had been there, harvesting body parts from the dead and the dying, when a young Dante Alighieri stumbled over him in the darkness. Dante had fought with the Florentine army that day and Lupei's life might had ended there and then but for the good fortune that, when he was found, he was stealing organs from a Ghibelline and not a Guelph corpse.

Lupei's quick thinking and a shared love of language and philosophy ensured that in no time the two men were sharing bread and wine, and discussing the infernal condition of humanity. By dawn Dante was blind drunk and snoring at the foot of an oak tree while Lupei, having stolen the young poet's horse, was far away delivering an organ transplant to save the life of a merchant's son in Arezzo.

Six thousand kilometres and seven hundred and thirty-one years later, Lupei is again spotting an opportunity.

The taxi carrying him and Tiffany is passing an empty warehouse on the edge of the airfield. A rusty chain secures the perimeter gates. A battered *For Sale* sign droops against the railings. Beyond the gates, set back from the busy road, a decrepit two-storey building squats in a porridge of discarded packing crates, rubble and rusting containers.

It is exactly what Lupei is looking for.

The driver, who by now can do no more than obey instructions, turns the car, accelerates and ploughs through the gates, smashing one of the headlights in the process.

Tiffany is comatose on the back seat.

The taxi pulls up in front of a large roller door. The driver climbs out, walks to the office door beside it and smashes his fist through the window. If he feels pain he shows no sign of it. He disappears inside. A couple of minutes later, the roller door skreals and rises slowly in a cloud of rust flakes as the driver hauls the chains by hand. Emerging from the shadows, the man drives his taxi into the warehouse and cuts the engine. He carries Tiffany from the car into an office strewn with mildewed stationery, lays her on the desk then, after further instructions from Lupei, gets back into his vehicle and leaves.

Less than three hours later, shortly after 4am, the perimeter gates have been fitted with new chains and locks. The roller door has been lowered. A power generator, fuel, and enough food and drink to feed a dozen people for a week have been brought into the building. The driver, having served his primary purpose, is now in a basement room, his legs little more than skin and bone, his eyes as empty as his wallet.

In a supermarket car park four miles away, a nightwatchman lies bludgeoned and dying as feral dogs gather in the shadows.

The site secured, it is Lupei's turn to go hunting. In a city where hundreds of thousands are homeless, a few dozen will shortly slip unnoticed into the lacklight.

CHAPTER 47

Thursday 12th March 2020

Two hours earlier, a tall white man prises himself out of a shabby tuk-tuk outside the magnificent four-star Rose Garden Palace Hotel. He thrusts a handful of notes into the driver's palm and heads towards the hotel entrance. As soon as the tuk-tuk has vanished in an asthmatic puff of pollutants, Antoine turns away from the hotel entrance and heads back up the street towards the different hotel they passed a moment ago; no point in letting the driver know where he is really staying.

The doorbell of the Rainbow Lotus Hotel is hoarse with ringing by the time the young man behind the reception desk wakes up and opens the door.

Yes, Tiffany Harrek returned to the hotel towards the end of the afternoon, the young man tells him. She collected her luggage and her phone, that had been left at reception, and climbed into a taxi.

Antoine persuades the youth to find him something to eat. He heads up to his room, drinks both bottles of complimentary water, swallows a handful of painkillers, opens the room safe and retrieves his spare phone. Sprawled across the bed he fires off a series of messages, to Tiffany (where is she? Is she OK?), Floriane (to tell her where he is), the National Central Bureau in New Delhi (to complain), and to his wife (to apologise), then seeks the solace of a long shower.

On the twentieth knock Antoine finds the energy to roll off the bed and open the door. A plate of stale samosas has been left on the floor of the corridor. He eats two, the other two ending up crushed beneath him as he snores on the bed.

Antoine wakes up a little after eight o'clock. Another shower. Clean clothes and off he goes to knock on Tiffany's door before remembering she isn't there. Breakfast on the rooftop terrace. The coffee is passable. He wolfs four croissants while scrolling his phone messages.

The National Central Bureau's Deputy Inspector wishes to see him immediately.

Antoine's wife, Marijke, tells him that all museums, theatres and sports events, including the children's football at the weekend, are cancelled in the Netherlands. But she still expects him home on Friday.

'I understand my obligations to Interpol and foreign nationals perfectly, Mr Hoek,' the Deputy Inspector cuts Antoine off mid-sentence with a disdainful sweep of the hand. He takes a sip of tea and replaces the porcelain cup on its saucer on the vast mahogany desk between them. 'Varma paid for his stupidity with his life. His idiot driver is in the cells, having eaten my brain with his cocks and bulls stories. The rest of my team erstwhile are working arduously to apprehend the desperadoes involved in the recent riots and making preparations to protect 1.4 billion Indians from the imminent disaster of a global pandemic. And lastly, today is my good lady wife's happy birthday and it is my pious duty to organise the purchase of gifts suitable to her station.'

'Tiffany is in her early twenties and probably still in the hands of the group that kidnapped us,' Antoine reminds him. 'They were parading an elephant on the highway, carrying protest banners and the driver identified them so you must be capable of ...'

'No, Sir. She is no longer with the unscheduled caste miscreant riff-raff that attacked you on Holi. The last sighting of this young woman was at the airport yesterday evening where she approached check-in staff and asked to be put on the first flight back to London.'

A weight falls from Antoine's shoulders. 'So she is already back in Europe? That is a huge relief, thank you.'

'Incorrect. There was no spare seat on the flight but, by the time the British Airways team went to inform her, the young lady had vanished from the terminal.'

'Then look at the CCTV footage!' Antoine shouts, losing his temper. 'When did she leave? Did she meet someone? Was there ...'

'Do not teach me my job, Sir. The matter is in jolly good hands.' The Deputy Inspector has another sip of tea. 'Now, tell me about Rajesh Anvit Pandit.'

It is midday. Antoine is back at the hotel sitting on his bed and sending a message when the room phone rings.

'Mr Hoek?'

'Yes.'

'This is reception, Sir. A driver from the National Central Bureau has come to collect you. I will pass you over to him.'

'Hello?'

'Sorry to be disturbing you, Sir.' An older voice. 'The Inspector has sent me to pick you up. There has been important development.'

'What development? I have just seen the Deputy Inspector.'

'Sir. I am just the driver.'

'OK. Give me a couple of minutes.'

The car, another Mercedes, is waiting with its engine running. Antoine climbs aboard and the vehicle moves off. Unlike the previous car this one has a partition between driver and back seat, which suits Antoine; he is tired of small talk. The air-conditioning ensures the temperature inside the car is a perfect 22°C so he keeps his jacket on. No longer interested in the traffic - the driver must know where he is going - Antoine watches 24-hour news on his phone, a predictable parade of hysteria and doomsday conspiracies, interspersed with government ministers and experts projecting calmness and competence ... or ranting accusingly about their opponents. Combined with the drone of the traffic and lack of sleep, the cumulative impact is soporific. Antoine's chin drops on his chest.

He wakes with a start. The car has left the road and is passing over rough ground. The glass partition is no longer transparent but opaque. Antoine can see neither the driver nor through the windscreen. He pounds the glass with his fist.

'Where are we going?' he shouts. 'Hey! HEY!'

The doors are locked. Through a side window he sees they are heading towards a derelict building. A roller door is rising. The car enters the shadows. Behind them the door is already dropping back. The driver steps out of the car and walks away.

Antoine is caught in a metal box within a larger space topped by a metal roof upon which the sun is belting down. How long it will take for the cooled air within the car to fade? How long before he dies of heat stroke or asphyxiation?

Antoine is still shouting furiously and attempting to kick the car windows out as the driver disappears from view.

An hour later Antoine is in rolled up sleeves, his shirt unbuttoned to the waist, dripping with sweat and exhausted. He has left innumerable messages, tried ringing his wife, Hervé and even Winders. No one is answering. He curses the day people stopped using their phones to talk with each other.

Movement in his peripheral vision. At the far end of the warehouse a door has opened. Four men emerge, one is considerably taller than the other three. Two of the four carry sticks. By the time they surround the car Antoine is ready for them. As the car doors are unlocked he leaps out, kicks one man in the belly and charges off towards the open door. A fifth man appears in the doorway holding a knife. Antoine spins away looking for another exit.

There isn't one. He is cornered. He manages to lay a fist across the jaw of one of his assailants but he is outnumbered. A heavy stick smashes the back of his thigh, dead-legging him and crumpling him to the ground. The blows rain on his back. He adopts a foetal position.

'Stop!' commands the taller man in English. 'I want him alive.'

Antoine's hands are yanked behind him and he is handcuffed.

The taller man leans forward to peer into Antoine's eyes.

'All that time spent persuading your colleague to walk away and start a new life; a shame you ignore your own advice.' The deep baritone voice sounds amused. 'Carry him downstairs and lock him up.'

'They know where I am,' Antoine says. 'Geolocation. They'll be here soon.'

'Such an exaggerated faith in technology and in your own importance. The world is preoccupied. Why would anyone worry about a dripping tap when a typhoon is hammering the roof?'

It isn't the first time Thor Lupei has marched towards chaos. The escalating pandemic barely ruffles a man who has survived the Black Death, when half of the population of Europe perished. Now, while nations tremble, Lupei is busily creating a new army of dark angels. He will be the eye of the storm as he has been before, in wars, plagues, earthquakes, avalanches, and floods.

He is fury unleashed. Three years of pain have left Lupei thirsty to visit discomfort on humanity in general, and on one individual in particular.

It has been such a very long time since Thor Lupei experienced life as viscerally as others do. Over time the little lives of men and women had become as ephemeral as the mayfly's dusk dance over the warm whispering waters of midsummer. He has seen a thousand acquaintances and friends fastfall like flower petals; too brief for grief.

With no memories of parents, siblings, aunts, cousins, Lupei is a simulacrum of a man, isolated from any real attachment to anything. He shuffles people about like pieces on a chessboard; pawns, bishops, knights, kings and queens. He feigns concern, polishing some and scraping the lacquer off others to pass the time, while feeling nothing.

Except when playing or listening to music, Lupei has felt neither love nor hate, joy nor pain for longer than he can remember. And while privately, music still moves him to tears or brings joy to his heart, his virtuoso public performances have all too often been an callous exercise in manipulation, an opportunity to play his audiences like violins.

Watch the sheep, always watch the sheep.

But those two years teetering over the abyss, drowning in pain, his bed-bound flame-flayed body seeping, helpless and raw, have at least provided Lupei with time to reflect. *He* created Daniel Murray and taught him the arcane skills and secrets he now abuses. *He* provided Daniel with the opportunity to push him into an oubliette to burn among corpses. *He* enabled the apprentice to visit pain on his master.

And in a perverted way Lupei accepts the consequences. Does he not feel more than he did before? Is he not more alive and satisfied for having suffered? To suffer is to be. Isn't that what made Dante the poet he became after the Battle of Campaldino?

A scream rings out in the warehouse, pulling Lupei from his reverie; one of his new servants must be getting a little over-enthusiastic. Lupei heads downstairs to prepare for a very busy evening.

CATCH THEM

COPS HOPE TO NAB MONSTERS

By Special Correspondent
New Delhi Express MAR, 18, 2023

Another six emaciated bodies found overnight at the southern edge of Kusumpur Pahari slum.

The poorest of the poor are suffering again this morning, as a result of increasingly evil acts perpetrated by tantriks, ojhas and witchdoctors. According to local leaders.

The roaring business in dark rituals is symptomatic of ignorance and superstition. A witch is reported to be asking for onions. If a person is foolish enough to give one, the onion is cut and blood pours from it, killing the donor on the spot.

Fear of the looming pandemic grips the capital and some slum dwellers are taking desperate measures to protect their families, leaving them vulnerable to exploitation by rogues,

ragamuffins and drug-bitten
charlatans.

The bodies were all found at
dawn and reported to cops.
"It is a very curious thing that
two victims were only emaciated
from the waist down," said a
local man who refused to be
identified.

A middle-aged lady, who also
declined to give her good name,
alleged that the body of one of
two old men found at the scene
was in fact her neighbour's
nephew and she insisted that he
was only 19 years of age.

The police have confirmed that
feral dogs were found eating what
appeared to be human internal
organs deposited beside one of
the bodies. Police pathologists
are now investigating. The head
of police is confident that the evil
rogues will soon be apprehended.

'What are you reading?' Karuna asks Daniel.

'Nothing,' Daniel answers, folding the newspaper. 'Just some stuff about football.'

He should have listened to Tiffany. The only positive is that she is now back safely in the UK.

CHAPTER 48

23rd March 2020

'Do you need any help with that?' Daniel asks, stepping into the clinic's reception area.

'No, it's best if I do it,' Karuna answers, carrying boxes of medical supplies from the pallet to the shelves in the cupboard.

'Because I'm untidy?'

'Because you are not thinking straight.'

'Look, I'm sorry about ...'

'You are not sorry. You are thinking only about yourself and that girl. We have put so much time and effort into this.' Karuna won't even look at Daniel.

'That is not fair. We have all done nothing but work since Tiffany left. I haven't even slept in my bed for six days.'

RJ bounces into reception carrying several metal tiffins. 'Roll up, roll up for the best chicken and veg dishes in town! I promise that by the time you have finished this feast your stomachs will be as tight as tabla skins.' RJ pauses and registers the scene. 'Oh, come on! What's going down, guys? You both look like Delhi Capitals were all out for nine runs.'

'Ask her,' Daniel says.

'That's not fair,' Karuna says. 'I am just trying to protect ...'

'OK, stop right there.' RJ puts the tiffins down on the reception desk. 'We need to get our shit together, guys. The world is falling apart and we have to stay focused. They're now saying all foreign travel will be banned because of this virus. No more foreign clients. No more mash. No euros, pounds and dollars. We've got a stash put away but this could go on for months, capeesh?'

'We need to make new friends and find new patrons, but he won't listen to me. Why is that Halogen-Ji?' Karuna says.

'The more people we involve, the greater the risk of betrayal,' Daniel explains for the fifth time. 'Please tell her, RJ. You understand the Delhi police better than I ever will. It's better to help fewer people but remain safe.'

RJ sighs. 'This will all get a lot worse if there is curfew.'

'There will not be curfew,' Karuna insists. 'Can you imagine? How will those crazy rich Vasant Kunj princesses survive if all Dalit are forced to stay at home? Some of them have never blown their own noses or wiped their own behinds.'

'I hope you are right, but street sellers are being attacked and thousands are heading out of the city for their home states before they starve,' RJ tells her.

Daniel watches them argue and wonders what the future holds. 'Let's eat,' he suggests.

By the time they are clearing away the dishes they have decided to organise meetings in the slums to hear what the community wants to do. RJ agrees with Karuna that it is probably best if Daniel stays at the clinic; they are less likely to attract attention on the street and the elders are more likely to speak openly. Daniel watches them enter the lift and leave, then heads up to the apartment to watch the news.

He turns the sound up when the images stop showing pictures of the virus and panicking politicians. Live music concerts are banned, musicians across India are stuck at home recording new songs. Behram Siganporia, the singer with Best Kept Secret is working on a new album and hoping for better days ahead.

Suddenly the television is drowned out by the sound of running feet. RJ appears. He looks shaken.

'What's happened?'

'You're have to come downstairs, man,' RJ says, out of breath.

'Why?'

'Just come down and see for yourself.'

They use the stairs instead of the lift. Karuna is waiting in the entrance. The young security guard stands beside the closed gates. RJ's car is in the compound with its doors open. RJ instructs the guard to open the gates.

'Over here,' RJ steers Daniel towards the right of the entrance. 'The guard says he didn't see anything.'

The letters are large and sprayed on the wall in bright red paint.

Do you want to
see Tiffany alive?
85923 - 56741

CHAPTER 49

Hi Uncle Ted,

You won't be able to read this letter because I am not able to actually write it. I don't have a pen or any paper and it is actually pitch dark in my room.

But let's pretend.

It keeps me sane.

This foreign trip isn't exactly what I was hoping for. And, before you start, I don't need another *I told you so*. You were right and I'm a wazzock.

Let me describe my hotel. The rooms are small and the decor is what would be described as minimalist. You know those hotel rooms where you wonder why the curtains are so horrible or why there are fifteen cushions on the bed? Well, on the plus side there's no clutter here and no curtains to hate.

No furniture at all in fact.

Apart from the bucket I piss in.

The view from my window is rubbish. Not that I can see it, unless I stand on my tiptoes. There's a wasteland, a fence and fighting feral dogs.

And that's it.

The sun trudges across the sky like it does everywhere else.

But hotter.

At night things are a little more interesting. I think the airport is two miles away. I can see a string of white lights and the control tower; seven white lights stacked one over the other with a bright red light flashing at the top.

The planes land and take off every few minutes. I were close to being on one.

So bloody close.

There's no air-con, unless you count the air trickling in through the broken window. I dream of being on the flight home, the hostesses coming past to check my belt is secured, the ping of the intercom, the reassuring voices of the pilot and staff, the slight wobble as we rise through the clouds.

I do have room service though.

Which is nice.

They come round twice a day. Before they unlock the door they tell me to turn around, then they push the food into the room on a tray. They take my piss bucket and leave me a new one.

When I've finished I leave everything by the door for the next visit.

Not sure how many stars I'd give the place. The room stinks though, to be fair, it didn't smell this bad when I arrived. It's probably me. I've had the runs for three days. Don't know how long I'd last without food and water. I drink so much water.

You'll tell me it's just as bad on a fishing boat on the North Sea for a week, though you have beds, don't you? Here the mattress is what you'd call firm.

Concrete.

The important thing is to keep healthy. After I've eaten I wait twenty minutes then do an hour's exercise. I say an hour, but who knows really? My phone's long dead. Nobody bothered to take it, they didn't have to. All I really know is that I do my squats and jumps and press-ups and running on the spot until the sun through the window has passed the dead cockroach and reached the edge of the ugly black stain on the floor.

Haven't seen the hotel manager.

That's not strictly true, I did see him at the airport. When the bastard kidnapped me. God knows what he will do to me when he remembers I am here.

Since I can't go sightseeing and there's no television,

I lie on the floor after my exercises and imagine I am lying on the beach below the Pavilion. It is mid-May and evening is floating on gentle clouds. The sea whispers as it licks the beach. The Friendship Amateur Rowing Club crews are out on the water; I wonder should I go out with them. You know when the weather is getting warmer but the tourists haven't yet arrived? Those spring evenings when Whitby is quiet and the whole town belongs to us and you can run from one end of the beach to the other without tripping over anyone.

I lie on the floor, close my eyes and pretend I'm on those steps by the beach huts and the sinking sun is drying my feet.

And I feel OK.

The banging has started again.

And the shouting.

I have not slept much. There are bags in the bags under my eyes. There's no mirror but I can feel them.

One of the other *guests* keeps losing it. Every night after dark. It ends with a crash and some screaming. I try not to imagine what is happening but I can't help myself; there is nowt else to do. I guess people help him to shut up. My room is above ground at least, and there's a window and daylight. Most of the time I can't understand what he's shouting. But one night I heard shouting in English and then I thought could it be Antoine? Or even Daniel. It isn't, of course.

Why do we get frightened in the dark, Uncle Ted? Are blind people frightened or are they used to it? Bad things don't only happen in the dark. When the scravir attacked me on the ferry ...

... No, forget I mentioned that. You don't need to know.

Anyroad, he's banging again. Must be hitting a pipe with his shoe or something because the sound rings in the wall like a bell. I'll be honest, it is quite creepy.

Two days ago there were two of them shouting. But only one now ... Oh, hang on. I can hear footsteps. I'll stop for now and finish this letter later on.

Tiffany sits up. The room is a monochrome of shadows. Outside the moon is a fading slither. It will soon be invisible.

Footsteps echo in the corridor.

They don't come at night - food at dawn and before dusk - so why now?

She wants to hide ... not easy in an empty room. The footsteps stop on the other side of the door. Torchlight seeps beneath the door. Keys jangle. She flinches as a cockroach scurries across the back her hand. There are two locks, not in the door but on the door. Padlocks. She braces herself, muscles jangling. Metal scraping metal. Is that someone wheezing?

She's not made a noise or annoyed anyone. They were beating the shouting man, or rather she heard his shouting change to muffled thumps, gasps and groans. Then the cursing and laughter, the slamming of a door.

She is hyperventilating.

How far away is Daniel? Why didn't she tell him about his mum when she had the chance? Maybe she is wrong about him. Why did she lose her temper?

The door opens. Silhouetted behind the torch beam are two figures. Their clothes hang strangely, like curtains. Their movements lack fluidity. More staccato, more insect-like than human. One is holding a rope, the other a rusty knife. Now her eyes are adjusting, she sees their hands, the fingers thin and twisted like the talons of a bird of prey. She recognises them for what they are: scravir. Like the one under the van on the Rotterdam ferry; the one she kicked until his arm snapped.

Tiffany leaps up. She is taller than they are; determined to take the initiative. In one movement she grabs the metal piss bucket and swings it in an arc that connects against the jaw of the first scravir, cracking the bone with a sickening crunch. He howls. His head smacks the concrete and he is silent.

Tiffany lurches forward, slamming the second scravir back

against the wall. She leaps past him into the corridor and races off in the direction she thinks they came from, hoping she will find stairs or a lift. She is all but blind until the second scravir emerges from the room and waves a torch in her direction, lighting the corridor around her.

There is no lift. Just as well as she does not have the time to wait. The stairs spiral downwards into the gloom. Looking down the stairwell she thinks she can see the bottom. For now her limbs feel OK, all that exercise has been worth it. She runs down. Past a couple of doors. Almost at the bottom now. The light all comes from above; the scravir's torch is waving about, casting wild shadows on the walls. Tiffany keeps one hand on the rail to avoid going too quickly, she cannot afford to fall or twist her ankle.

By the time she realises she has come too far, she is in the basement. No time to go back up. There is a door. She twists the handle and the door opens with a soft click.

It can't be any worse than waiting here.

The room ahead is maybe thirty metres long and smells terrible. Crossing the threshold she prays that she can find another exit that will take her back up to ground floor level.

A faint red light at the far end illuminates a long row of twenty-five or more cages, each around a metre wide, down the length of one wall. The smell is rank, as if all the animals in a zoo had died here. The spaces between the bars at the front of the cages suggest they are designed to hold large animals: lion, bears, baby elephants or rhinos, or tigers or ...

Opposite them on the other side of the room is a tumbledown mess of smaller cages.

As she advances, Tiffany sees the source of light, a red bulb mounted on the wall ahead and, beside it, is a door!

The scravir has entered the basement behind her.

The air is suddenly full of chattering and agitation. The cells are not empty and the occupants of the cells are stirring. Hands reach out through the bars, pleading, groaning. The cages are stuffed with human beings!

Most are talking in what Tiffany assumes to be Hindi. Most but not all.

'Please, help us!' a youth pleads with her in English. 'The devils will kill us.'

She stops. In the lacklight the youth looks like the young men who kidnapped her and Antoine: jeans and t-shirt, thin metal-framed glasses, fade cut hair. A student perhaps.

'My parents have no one but me,' he tells her. 'We die here.'

Thirty or forty people are standing behind the bars, mainly men but also a few women in sari. An object is kicked and skids across the floor. Tiffany turns to see the scravir advancing towards her; she has to keep moving.

'Ah, there you are!' The deep baritone voice calls cheerfully, as if welcoming a late guest to a garden party.

Tiffany spins round. Someone is blocking her path to the exit. Someone tall. Silhouetted against the red light like a demon.

The muttering and pleading from the cells fades to silence. Only the smells remains: dank, fetid, sweat and urine and fear.

'Perfect timing, Tiffany. Well done. Sorry not to have made more of an effort to entertain you these past few days, I was otherwise engaged. Mustering my troops and the like. As you can see.' Lupei sweeps his hand to indicate the cells. 'It was most fortuitous to find a building so perfectly attuned to my requirements. One wonders what the previous occupants have been doing here. Human traffickers? Or animal smugglers perhaps? The acoustics are magnificent, don't you think? I wish I had time to record a few songs.'

Lupei howls *I need a doctor SO BAD!* in his big bluesy voice. The sound echoes and reverberates. He smiles.

'Maybe later. Anyway, back to business.' He looks beyond her and beckons the scravir forwards. 'Seize her but don't be rough, I want the merchandise in good condition.' Back to Tiffany. 'It is a shame we don't have time to freshen you up a little but, in the circumstances, you will have to do.'

Hands grab her from behind, pull her arms back and bind her wrists. Lupei advances and peers down at her, his head to one side; all legs and limbs like praying mantis. She shivers as his cool hand strokes the side of her face, caressing her hair, then descends to squeeze her breasts casually, as if evaluating the cushions on a sofa.

'What does he see in you?' he whispers.

His hand continues on its downward path. Tiffany stares back defiantly, refusing to cry or shout. She is not the first woman to be pawed by a powerful man while others look on in silence.

Her defiance both impresses and annoys Lupei. He grabs her chin and yanks it up. She fears he is about to kiss her. He is still in silhouette and the only light on his face is the faint red glow reflected off her own face. As he leans forwards his body blocks the light, plunging her face into darkness and, like an eclipsed moon, leaving his face no more than a black void against the ceiling.

A phone rings.

He pulls back, retrieves his phone from his jacket pocket.

'Yes?' Lupei says.

He listens.

'Really? No, I don't think so. ... Shh ... Do you have a pen, Master Murray? ... Excellent. You have an hour to find this address ... As of now she is in reasonable condition. And don't bring an army with you. Come alone. It wouldn't end pleasantly.'

CHAPTER 50

'I need weapons.' Daniel is sitting in the apartment with his head in his hands, his legs bobbing up and down. 'An axe, guns, grenades, body armour ...'

'Woah, hang on, action man,' RJ interjects. 'What's with the Armageddon vibe? We're partners, remember?'

'I have to go. Alone. She didn't make it. Never left Delhi. He's got her.'

'He?' Karuna says.

'Thor Lupei. She was right. I was wrong. He's alive and he's here in Delhi. And it explains the other shit.'

'The other shit?' RJ says.

'The bodies on the streets. Watch the news, read the bloody newspapers.' Daniel rubs his face and looks at the two of them. 'This is bad, really bad.'

'It cannot be worse than a global pandemic,' Karuna observes caustically. She's in jeans instead of a sari today and planning to go to the cinema with a friend.

'OK, you know more than me,' Daniel sneers. 'Well done. You're a fucking genius.'

'Hey, Dan. Dan! Cool it man. Deep breath. Rewind. OK. So Tiffany is still in Delhi?'

Daniel nods. 'You can have everything in my bank account, RJ. Just find me the stuff I need. You know people who know people.'

'I don't want your money. I'll help you but we also need you here helping us. More than ever.'

'You're wasting your time Raji. We're on our own.' Karuna's voice is flat. 'We cannot rely on outsiders. The Great White Hope has always been a fiction.'

Daniel stares at Karuna. Is that what she has thought from day one? He jumps up off the sofa.

'I've spent three years working with you! Saving lives in the slums. The people your bloody government ignores, and you think that ...'

'Guys, guys.' RJ steps between them. 'Come on, Dan. Give me the full run down on what the dude actually told you. The A-Team needs a plan! Right?'

'I have an hour to reach that address.' Daniel hands RJ the address he scribbled down.

'That's insane,' RJ passes the paper to Karuna. 'Mid-evening traffic in Delhi. An hour? Seriously?'

'I'll take him on the bike, it's faster,' Karuna says, relenting a little.

'OK, and I'll do the rest. Let's go.' RJ grabs his car keys. He slaps Daniel on the shoulder. 'Don't worry, mate. I'm on it. We'll be there.'

Riding pillion, holding on to Karuna, weaving through the late evening traffic, Daniel is thinking.

For three years, since he left London, he has felt safe. At first RJ protected him, using his uncle's smuggling operation to get them both out of the country. No one really expects people to use traffickers to escape out of the UK so a rigid inflatable boat from Kingsdown, north of Dover, across the Channel then overland across France all the way to Greece and beyond worked just fine.

By the time they reached Delhi they were friends. RJ had seen what Daniel could do, seen him fix people and deal with bastards, and Daniel had learned that RJ was more than a chess playing nerd in a homeless refuge. Obtaining new papers (voter ID, Aadhaar identity card, and PAN card) in a few hours, RJ changed his appearance, with Daniel's help, and became invisible to the law. Different earlobes, a shorter nose and a couple of other tweaks and it was done. For Daniel it was a little more complicated but within a few weeks he too had new papers, a hipster beard and certificates to practice cosmetic surgery. A friend of a friend introduced them to Karuna and they were in business.

Everything has been good. Challenging, heart-wrenching sometimes, but good.

Not anymore.

Karuna pulls up on the hard shoulder.

'You sure this is right?' Daniel asks, looking around. 'We're in the middle of nowhere.'

Beyond the perimeter gates the warehouse squats in derelict darkness. The *For Sale* sign has fallen and is now obscured by vegetation.

'This place was all over the news three years ago; just after you and RJ arrived. A gang were using it to trade in endangered wildlife: jackals, leopards, snakes, civets, pangolins, tortoises and even tigers. Live animals and body parts, like rhino horns. They used the airport to move animals in and out of the country. There was a siege that ended in multiple deaths and the place has been empty ever since.'

'OK.' Daniel hands her his helmet.

'Let's drive round to see if there is a back entrance then talk with RJ.'

Their argument is now forgotten.

'I'll use the front door,' he says. 'He's holding all the cards.'

'You sure you don't want to wait?'

Daniel shakes his head. 'You've seen what I can do, Karuna. Imagine someone ten times as powerful. Someone who uses his power to create monsters. The skills I have all came from him. He taught me and I repaid him by pushing him into a fire. It's me he's after, not Tiffany. Promise me that if she gets out of there alive, you'll take her to the airport.'

Karuna nods. She watches Daniel stride through the gate

and on towards the dark void of the warehouse. Her phone rings. She answers.

'Too late, he's already gone.'

Since he is expected, Daniel makes no effort conceal his approach. Lupei may have paid someone to shoot him before he even reaches the warehouse but Daniel guesses that Lupei wants a confrontation.

Is this what it feels like to climb out of a trench and run across no man's land towards the enemy? The road is now fifty metres behind him, the sound of the cars a background wash. To the rhythm of its wing-tip lights, a plane sinks out of the night sky towards the airport runway.

There are no lights in the warehouse. The roller door is partly raised, a gaping maw. Daniel folds at the waist, as if offering homage to a king, and steps into the lacklight. For the first half a dozen steps he can see his feet in the faint light entering the building from beneath the roller door. He kicks something, a can perhaps? It skates away in the darkness, the sound of its passage echoing off distant walls, revealing the size of the space around him. Was this once an aircraft hangar?

Daniel stops, hoping his eyes will acclimatise. Water is dripping somewhere. An animal scurries.

'OK, I'm here,' he announces.

Nothing.

Over there, an open door just visible in the gloom.

An electric motor hums. The roller door judders downward, cutting off his line of escape.

Daniel has no choice but to pull out his phone and use the torch to guide him towards the door. He is a magnet hovering over a box of nails, knowing he will be hit from all directions. He braces himself for impact but somehow reaches the door unharmed. Beyond the threshold is a corridor and offices, full of long discarded junk. Discarded takeaway boxes and plastic bottles strewn across the floor.

Where is he? Where is Tiffany? Is she even here?

A pile of shoes. Abandoned.

He leaves the office and continues along the corridor until he reaches a stairwell. Up or down? The air smells fetid. He wants to climb the stairs and search up there, where the air will be fresher, but he just knows he has to go down.

The smell increases as he descends. To prepare himself, Daniel tries to imagine what he will see. He thinks of the old buildings at London Zoo and the dozen Indian zoos that lost their licences to operate in 2019. The cramped cages, concrete floors. What is Lupei using them for? He thinks of the hay barn at Farview Farm where Emile Noir took him and Megan to confront the scravir.

That's not helping.

One hand cupping his phone's torch beam with his fingers, the other clamped around the handrail, Daniel misses the last step. He falls heavily, dropping his phone, and rolling his ankle. His phone has ended up under the steps, obliging him to wriggle into the restricted space, convinced he is about to be attacked from behind. All the power he has felt over the past three years evaporates; he's just another skinny Londoner who never went to college about to be beaten to death by a bunch of thugs in a piss-spattered stairwell.

The attack doesn't materialise. Retrieving his phone, Daniel reverses out and climbs to his feet. His ankle hurts like hell. He extinguishes his torch and pulls the door. The warm acrid smells of decay and latrines billow into the stairwell.

CHAPTER 51

Europol, Rotterdam

'Where is Antoine Hoek?' Hervé drums his finger on the desk. 'It's your team.'

Winders adjusts his skinny tie, says nothing. A bead of sweat slips down the side of his bald head. As if in sympathy, raindrops are sliding down the window; it is pouring with rain in Rotterdam. It is almost dark.

'And, while you are at it, what happened to Gert? You were keeping an eye on him, last I heard.'

'I've been stitched up.'

'How so?'

'You know where Hoek is.'

'This is what worries me, Winders. Whatever anyone does to try to make progress on the Lupei case, someone is always one step ahead.' Hervé says. 'Gert went to London. It made sense to send an ex-employee, gave us deniability with Scotland Yard. But as soon as he made a useful contact, that contact was killed. He takes himself off to Romania, without your knowledge, you claim, and promptly disappears. Antoine goes to India, following up a lead and he too disappears. Bit of a pattern, and you at the heart of it all.'

'Bastard. You think you can get away with this?' Winders sneers. 'Because you're going nowhere, like that obsessive, Muyskens, and his superannuated barista, Hoek. Three old men stuck in the slow lane. Drowning in pathetic stories about zombies and flesh-sucking monsters instead of ...'

'You digress,' Hervé interrupts Winders. 'Where is Antoine? He arrives in Delhi on 10th March along with Tiffany Harrek, sometime girlfriend of Daniel Murray. They meet Johar Varma, an assistant superintendent at the National Central Bureau. Hours later Varma is dead in an alley, his driver is in custody and Hoek and Harrek are missing. Has Antoine contacted you or anyone else at the bureau in the last 48 hours? Who was Gert messaging? Who intercepted, if anyone, those messages? I want answers on my desk before you leave.'

'I have a previous meeting arranged at 19.30.'

'I don't give a flying fuck what you have previously arranged, Winders, I want answers. Get out and do some work.'

If you cannot create a plausible narrative of who sent what to whom at Europol then where can you do it? It takes a little work and a conversation with a technician who has good reason to cooperate or find himself charged with illegal phone tapping for personal gain. In an hour Winders has assembled a report. Before handing everything over to Hervé there is a loose end to address.

'They left an hour ago, I'm afraid,' reception informs him.

That's OK, he has a home address. By the time Hervé Seznec catches up, Winders' report will be on the minister's desk.

The technician is decrypting the last messages when Winders uses a misdirection and sleight of hand to collect the man's pass card off his desk. Until the technician attempts, two hours later, to leave work and finds he cannot exit the building, being recorded as having already left in one of the pool cars, Winders is assumed to be in the building.

Winders parks outside an apartment block in Delft.

'Sorry to be rude but I am going out to visit my niece. Is it anything important?'

'Do you mind if I come in?' he says. 'It's cold out here.'

'It's Saturday night.'

'It will only take a minute.'

She presses the buzzer, lets him into the building and is waiting for him on the walkway outside her front door.

'Nice. Very nice view. You renting? How far are you from the canals?' he asks, stepping into her flat.

'Listen, Winders. This isn't a social call, is it?' she says, closing the door and taking him through to the lounge. 'Can you get to the point?'

'Yeah, sure.'

They face each other.

'You've been in contact with Antoine and Gert.'

'Of course. One is a work colleague and the other a friend of his.'

'Who else have you been talking with?'

'I'm sorry?'

'The information they're giving you, who do you pass it on to?'

Floriane shakes her head pityingly. 'You never give up. You've hated me from the day I arrived. What's your problem? A fragile male ego? A hatred of foreigners? The determination to convince everyone around you that you are a total dick?'

'I can find out. I just thought it was polite to come here and ask you face to face.' Winders smiles as he sits down, uninvited, on her large leather sofa and makes himself comfortable. 'Give you the opportunity to explain yourself.'

'Do you mind if I draw the curtains?' she asks. 'I would hate to think my neighbours might see me entertaining such a worthless racist misogynistic shit.'

'Be my guest,' Winders says as she passes behind him to reach the floor-to-ceiling window. 'Are you and Hoek doing it? Does his wife know? He's such a little rebel in his defeated going nowhere kind of way. Hervé is too chicken to deal with any of this but the minister understands the national security implications. With you being a foreign national. So I have a deal I would like to put to you.'

CHAPTER 52

New Delhi

He sees her immediately, at the far end of the long room. She is kneeling, slumped by the wall, beneath a red light, arms outstretched, head hanging down, chin on her chest, her hair obscuring her face.

Daniel counts to ten to steady himself; he needs his wits about him.

He notices the hands wrapped around the bars of the cells. Who are these people? Where has Lupei abducted them from? It won't have been difficult in a city where more than 2 million people live in slums. 60,000 street children in Delhi surviving from day to day, begging in stations, huddling under bridges. But why? What havoc and misery will Lupei create if no one stops him?

Where is he?

Daniel steps forwards.

He knows it is a trap but he has no choice.

Each cell has at least one occupant, several have two or three. Young faces and old peering cautiously as he passes. A few hands reach out in supplication. He is counting the number of cells, thirty-two in total along the left-hand wall. There must be forty people or more locked up here.

'Krpaya madad kare,' a voice whispers.

Please help.

'Sar krpaya,' says a second voice.

Please Sir.

He establishes eye contact with each face as he passes down the line.

He acknowledges each of them; he owes them that.

I see you.

About halfway down he passes a cell containing two youths. One is on the floor, sitting a metre back from the bars, head downcast. The other is lying on the bare concrete. Asleep? Dead?

'Hey,' Daniel whispers. 'Kya vah theek hai?

Is he OK?

The sitting youth looks up with dull eyes. He looks drugged or semi-conscious. He pokes his cellmate who turns over and mutters. The sitting youth pokes again and points towards Daniel. The other boy sits up and does a double-take.

'Ham use jaano! Halogen-Ji!' he whispers.

It's him!

Daniel nods and puts his finger to his lips, but as he continues on his way towards Tiffany he hears the muttering and whispering going up and down the line.

He is approaching the end of the long room now. Is Tiffany conscious? Is she is pain? What has Lupei done to her? Anger wells up inside Daniel, that righteous rage he focused on the jiggy-jiggy man, and those who abuse or exploit others. His body is as tense as a high-wire act. More cells, more tired faces. Two skinny men in rags.

Where is Lupei?

He doesn't call out to Tiffany, no sense in alarming her until he is there beside her and able to help. Her hands are secured against the wall with leather straps, leaving her unable to sit down.

A few more steps.

The attack comes from behind.

He hears metal scrape against metal at the same time as someone calls out.

'Dhyaan rahen!'

Look out!

Daniel spins round as the cell door he has just passed swings open. The two skinny men step out. As soon as he sees their mechanical movement and their vacant faces, Daniel understands.

Scravir.

Another cell door, at his back, also swings on rusty hinges and he is surrounded. Four scravir brandishing sharp blades, the skin on their faces thin as clingfilm.

A flashback.

He is with Megan and Emil Noir walking into the blackness of the barn at Farview Farm near Whitby. They are wearing infrared goggles and find a group of scravir piled up like corpses, writhing like snakes, in the darkest corner of the barn. He remembers how the scravir acted in self-defence, how they protected each other.

'Ah, at last!' Thor Lupei steps into view from behind the last cell. 'Daniel, Daniel, Daniel.'

If their paths crossed by chance on a crowded street it is uncertain that either of them would recognise the other. Daniel is maybe five kilos heavier, his skin is tanned from three years of sunshine, his face masked behind his hipster beard and handlebar moustache, his hair shoulder length. Thor Lupei's voice is almost the same, a little huskier perhaps but still the rich deep baritone that commands a room. The long white hair has gone; it is now short and dark. His eyes are different too, his jawline softer perhaps? It is hard to be sure in the weak red light but are his eyes now brown? He too has put on some weight.

'We have some bones to pick over, Daniel.'

'What have you done to Tiffany?'

'Oh, how selfless, worrying about her instead of yourself. Quite a saint.'

'Let her go. This is between you and me.'

'Forgive me, but you are really not in a position to give

instructions, Daniel.'

The hum of voices in Hindi rises and falls around them. Daniel doesn't follow every word but he understands plenty. He hears the desperation, the anger, and the fear. He hears the word Halogen-Ji passing up and down the line. He sees the hesitation in the eyes of one of the scravir.

'You visited unspeakable pain upon me, Daniel,' Lupei says as he advances towards him. 'I will return the gift. To you and to the fragrant Tiffany. An eye for an eye, tooth for a tooth.' He smiles maliciously. 'We haven't lived until we have suffered, isn't that so?'

Daniel stakes a step back towards the cells. The scravir keep their distance, awaiting instructions from their master.

'Come, take my hand and allow me to share my memories of thirteen months spent lying on a flayed back with plasma oozing from every ounce of burned flesh. What Dante would have paid for this!'

Lupei is almost on him.

Daniel cries out in Hindi. 'Join hands! All of you! Make a chain and trust me no matter what!'

His voice echoes off the walls. Beyond Lupei, Tiffany stirs and tries to lift her head.

'Halogen-Ji Haan,' a woman's voice calls out. Hands appear through the bars along the line.

Lupei thrusts his hand towards Daniel, oblivious of the commotion around them.

'Aap bhee! App sabhee!' Daniel tells the scravir.

You too! All of you!

Over three years Daniel, working with RJ, Karuna and a number of community leaders, has built a reputation among the Dalit or untouchables in the slums of Delhi. News of the strange foreigner who works with RJ and the scheduled caste protest movement, the young man who heals the sick, has spread far and wide. Now in this moment of crisis, trapped like dogs in cages in the basement of a warehouse, people lock hands. But Daniel cannot reach the nearest hand reaching out towards him between the bars. He cannot link with the chain!

Then, as Daniel is believing his plan is lost before it even starts, the unexpected happens. The face of one of the four scravir becomes contorted in visible torment. He wrestles against the power of Lupei's will, his soul, his buried humanity, defying the master's control. As if trying to walk upstream in a raging torrent, he drops the knife he is holding and pushes and strains the muscles of his arms to extend one shaking hand towards Daniel and the other towards the chain of hands formed by the prisoners in the cells.

Lupei seems oblivious to the danger. As the scravir locks hands with the nearest of the prisoners, Daniel takes the scravir's other hand in his right and grabs Lupei's hand with his left.

The surge of energy from both sides almost tears Daniel apart. From Lupei he experiences an overwhelming arc of pain, scythe as a lightning strike. The skin of his left arm blisters and smokes.

Awaken the creierul anticilor that lies within you.

The scravir in the barn in Whitby pooled their energy; they shared it to give one of the number the strength to fight. Has Lupei ever known they could do that? Daniel used that experience to reach his tormentors while strapped to a gurney in the house in Thurloe Square, jumping through one body to reach another. Now he uses that same power to draw on the collective strength of the forty people trapped in the basement, channelling their life force, their anger, and their bodies through himself as a conduit.

It is like half his body is being immersed in the frozen waters of the Arctic while the other half is sprayed with boiling water from an erupting geyser.

Daniel throws his head back and howls but he doesn't let

go of either hand. The combined energy of those imprisoned beneath the warehouse flows through him like a storm raging sea throwing itself at the harbour jaws in Whitby. Lupei, who has only ever acted alone, is stunned at the collective force Daniel is marshalling against him. By himself Daniel is no match for Lupei but this is something else. Lupei reels. Daniel refuses to let go. If he is to die then so be it. Tiffany's life and the lives of everyone else in the basement depend on him. With the reckless courage of youth he uses the skills he has learned in the clinic to flood Lupei's face with flesh drawn from the forty souls he is connected to. Lupei has no answer as his face swells up like a football. He can no longer open his eyes. His nose disappears from view. His cheeks balloon outward. His neck thickens and bloats until it resembles the treble-chinned thickness of a walrus, his lips so engorged he is struggling to draw breath.

Finally he lets go of Daniel's hand and falls to the ground clawing at his face, gasping for air. And then lies still.

The scravir who came to Daniel's aid also collapses, an empty husk, drained of muscle. The other three scravir stare vacantly into the void, no longer receiving any input from their master. Daniel takes the knives from their hands and hurls them towards the other end of the room.

He drops to his knees beside the fallen scravir.

'Chaambiyaan? Chaambiyan Kahaan Hain?' Daniel asks.

The keys? Where are the keys?

The scravir opens his eyes. Daniel repeats the question.

A skeletally thin finger points at Lupei. 'Pantaloon kee jeben.'

Trouser pockets.

Daniel turns and fumbles Lupei's pockets and finds a thick bunch of keys. He crosses to the first cell and tries one key after another until he finds the one that tumbles the lock. He hauls open the door and two youths step out. With their help, Daniel drags Lupei into the cell and locks him in. Daniel unlocks the next cell and hands over the keys to the youths. Nothing needs to be said. With the cell doors being unlocked, one by one, Daniel races over to Tiffany.

She is conscious but groggy. Daniel leans against her to hold her weight and prevent her from falling as he loosens the leather straps holding her to the wall.

'You're OK, Tiffany. Nearly there ...'

First one hand, and then the other. Daniel lowers her gently to the floor. He brushes the hair from her eyes. She looks utterly broken.

'Wait here. I'll be back in a minute,' he says, turning to see whether everyone has yet been liberated from the cells.

She grabs his ankle. 'Don't leave me! He's a monster!'

'I'm not leaving you. He's locked up. Give me a minute to help the others and I'm carrying you out of here.'

He prises her hand away.

'I promise, Tiffany.'

The three scravir still on their feet are immobile, like a group of shop dummies. He pushes past them to check on the one who helped him.

No pulse, the man is dead, the strain of being a conduit for forty other people was too much for his already compromised body.

All the doors are now open and the prisoners are gathering outside the cells, hugging each other and talking quietly. They have each lost a little weight; the flesh on Lupei's bloated face has come from the bodies of forty prisoners. They all appear groggy but OK.

One man has gone to the far end of the room and opened the door that leads to the stairwell and up away from the horror.

Daniel calls at him to wait; they will all leave together. The man shakes his head and disappears through the door. The rest stay put.

As he speaks, a youth shouts, 'DHYAAN RAHEN!'
WATCH OUT!

Behind Daniel the three scravir are reanimating. A guttural moan from within the cells suggests that Lupei is regaining consciousness.

Tiffany gasps as she sees the scravir turn slowly towards her. Daniel races the length of the room, grabbing the knife that fell from the first scravir's hand, and leaps past the other three scravir, to stand in front of Tiffany. In his wake two youths and a young woman collect the other knives that Daniel threw across the room and advance on the scravir.

All three scravir are young Indian men; Lupei must have snatched them off the streets and created them in the past few days. Daniel hopes that they have not understood or learned how to pool their strength.

He sweeps his knife in an arc in front of him. The ghouls step back only to find themselves confronted by the young men and woman behind them.

'Let's push them towards the cells,' says one of the young men.

As the scravir retreat, one becomes agitated, snarling and clenching his fists. The red light on the wall above Tiffany starts to flicker. Daniel guesses that the electricity comes from a generator; when the fuel runs out, the room will be plunged into darkness. With little time left he steps forward and slashes the closest scravir with his blade. Clutching his arm, the scravir backs off.

Daniel wants to save these men but he still has no idea how Lupei creates them. He remembers Emile Noir, transformed into a shadow of a human being, staggering on emptied legs, willing, when opportunity presented, to sacrifice himself to kill Lupei. He remembers waking up in the castle with thighs as thin as broom handles, dragging his body hand over hand across a cold castle floor. But this is about the mind. What are the scravir? Can they be unmade?

The lights are spluttering, more off than on now. There no time left. The survivors at the other end of the room are pouring out, desperate to escape.

Waving the knives, the youths, the girl and Daniel finally drive the three scravir into a cell and slam the door.

'Chaambiyaan! Keys!' shouts one of the youths running forward.

The scravir, now aware of their fate, reach through the bars, lashing out, trying to grab the keys from the youth as the girl slashes her knife back and forth, stabbing at the flailing arms.

It is done.

The scravir locked up, the youths and the girl race towards the exit, kicking the keys to a distant corner of the room.

Daniel returns to Tiffany's side and picks her up. She drapes her arms around his neck.

'OK,' he calls out, walking as fast as his legs will carry him. 'Let's go. Let's get out of here!'

He is almost at the door when the electricity dies, plunging the basement into a void darker than the grave. From the other side a youth pushes the door open and, in the faintest glow from a window high up in the stairwell, Daniel staggers out and up the steps holding Tiffany as she clings to him.

In the main warehouse space, four people are heaving on the chain that lifts the rusty roller door.

'We must set fire to this place and kill these devils!' a man shouts.

'There are people coming with weapons,' Daniel reassures the crowd. 'They will deal with Thor Lupei when they arrive.'

The bedraggled survivors pour out of the building and across the waste ground towards the main road, hauling open the perimeter gates and filing out onto the main road. One by one they negotiate the traffic. Safely on the other side of the road they head towards some houses some 500 metres away.

'I need my papers,' Tiffany says as Daniel releases her. 'My passport, everything. It's all in the building. They'll not let me leave!'

Daniel takes her across the road, helps her hide in a thicket of bushes and trees.

'Stay here. I'll run back. Where exactly ...'

'I'm sorry and stupid.'

'You're not stupid and you did nothing wrong,' he says. 'Wait here.'

She kisses him and tells him where she has been held and he runs back towards the gates before she can stop him.

The building is silent as he re-enters and finds his way to the stairs. He has his phone but is wary of using his torch and giving away his location. Where is RJ? Are there other scravir in the building?

Climbing the steps two at a time he reaches the second floor, following Tiffany's instructions. Down the corridor. The third door on the right is ajar. He pushes it open, enters and switches on his torch. A scravir lies where he fell, his broken jaw hanging strangely, the metal slop bucket and a length of rope beside him. Daniel approaches cautiously, kicks the scravir for signs of life. He's dead.

He jumps over the body and grabs Tiffany's backpack.

Something dry snaps out in the corridor.

Tiffany squats in the bushes, just three metres from the road but invisible to the speeding traffic. She crosses her fingers and tries to think about long showers and shampoo, airports and boring in-flight meals.

Daniel must have reached the room by now.

My passport is in the front pocket of my backpack. Just bring my bag.

A few more minutes and he'll be back.

Then she hears rustling in the dead leaves.

CHAPTER 53

As the scravir crosses the threshold, rusted blade in hand, Daniel swings the slop bucket catching him smack in the face. The blow pops one of the creature's cheekbones and blood pours from his nose. Daniel steps behind him and wraps the rope around his neck.

Daniel is stunned by the scravir's strength. How can a human being who has lost two thirds of his body weight be so strong? Where has he come from? What has Lupei done? Daniel grips the rope with all his strength as the scravir tries to shake him off, slamming him against the door, lashing out with thrashing legs and sharp elbows. Daniel cannot attempt to use his own powers to control the situation, he is under attack and anyway weakened by the earlier confrontation with Lupei; all he can do is cling on and hope.

The bruising frenzy continues until finally the creature tires and the fight fades, and the confrontation is done. Daniel leans forward and feels for a pulse. There isn't one.

How many more scravir are there?

How long was Tiffany imprisoned here? How can bad things happen to people you love without you knowing? For days he has assumed Tiffany is safe and 3,000 miles away when in reality she has been festering in this shithole.

Back in the corridor, he toys briefly with searching the rest of the rooms and thinks better of it; he must get back outside. The rest can wait.

He has almost reached the perimeter gate when half a dozen motorbikes arrive. Karuna, RJ, and six others. They are armed with sticks, machetes, and guns. It is 21:45. There is an aura of excitement and adrenalin.

'Halogen-Ji, Hey!' RJ shouts. 'The A-Team has arrived! Where do we go?'

'We don't have everything you wanted but we have enough,' Karuna tells Daniel, showing him her machete.

'You look shattered, man. Are you ready to go in?'

'I have already been in.'

Daniel explains the state of play. 'So what we really need to do is to set the building alight, while they are still trapped in the basement,' he concludes.

'OK, we can do that,' RJ says, taking his phone from his pocket. He takes the call. 'You sure? How many? Yeah, thanks.' He turns to the others. 'Bad news, the police are heading ...' Before he can even finish his sentence, they see the flashing blue and red lights a kilometre away up the road.

'Shit! The survivors must have called them.'

'It's OK, Halogen-Ji. Let the police deal with this,' RJ says. 'Tactical withdrawal.'

'We're armed,' says one of the bikers. 'We can take on the cops.'

'Are you mad?' Karuna shouts.

'I need to find Tiffany.' Daniel heads for the road.

'The last flight out of India leaves tonight,' Karuna shouts after him. 'It was on the news. Get her to the airport.'

'Let's go,' RJ revs his bike.

The squad cars are now visible, approaching at speed, as the motorbikes scream away down the road.

The front car drives straight at the gates, bursting them open. One after the other the police vehicles stream in and screech to a halt, bathing the warehouse in strobing blue and red light. Police officers pour out of their cars. The lead officer is on his phone, directing the team and liaising with the Parakram SWAT team who arrive less than a minute later. The capital's first all-woman commando team pile out of the vans in full body armour and carrying automatic weapons. They advance in formation as the regular police spread out to form a ring around the whole building.

Across the road in the bushes, Daniel is at the spot where he left Tiffany. No sign of her. He spins round desperately seeking a clue of what has happened, his face flashing red then blue in the lights from across the road.

'Tiffany! Tiffany!'

Fuck, fuck, fuck.

Less than fifteen minutes have passed. What has happened to her? His foot catches on detritus hidden beneath the leaves, almost sending him flying.

Across the road the SWAT team, all in black and wearing night vision googles, are entering the warehouse in formation, two by two, under the roller door.

Daniel tries to identify the object at his feet. Long, thin, sinewy. Suddenly it moves.

A head rears up.

A king cobra.

A huge one, its hood expanding rapidly. Daniel is no longer thinking about the warehouse or the police. He stands still as the snake moves its head from side to side, judging the distance for a strike. The cobra's head is over a metre off the ground, the snake must be three or four metres long.

Daniel steadies his breathing, resists the urge to run. Where is Tiffany? Has the snake bitten her? If so, she needs antivenom. With a cobra bite you can have as little as fifteen minutes to reach a hospital. Incrementally he takes a short step back and freezes. The snake's jaw opens to reveal its fangs.

Pause. Another step. Pause. The cobra is focused on movement. No movement, no threat. Play it super cool.

Time drips slowly.

Once he is a couple of metres away, Daniel chances calling out again.

'Tiffany?'

Another backward step, hoping he won't tumble backwards over her body.

The cobra's head is swaying, its skin catching the faint glow from the flashing police lights across the road. It growls and further expands its hood.

Another step back. Over three metres apart now.

'Tiffany?'

A noise above his head. Another snake? Daniel lifts his head slowly to gaze up into the trees. A shadow of something moving. Something large.

'Daniel?'

'Yes. Are you OK?'

'There was a snake or something.'

'There still is. We're eyeballing each other right now. No sudden movements. Can you get down?'

'I think so but ...'

'Very slowly. It can't see us if we don't move.'

'How can I come down without moving?'

'We have to get out of here.'

'I get that. Trust me, I get that.'

'I am going to take you to the airport.'

'Great. I'd like that. Very much.'

'So get down from the tree.'

'I'm trying.'

'With respect, try a little fucking harder.'

The sound of rustling and creaking branches.

'Tiffany?'

'Yes.'

'I am moving to the side to draw the snake away. When you hit the ground, get out onto the road and shout. OK?'

'That's the plan?'

'That's the plan.'

Daniel steps to his left then waves his arms, calculating he is now far enough away from the cobra to avoid instant death.

The snake turns and follows him. And another step.

To his left he hears shaking leaves, a cracking branch followed by a heavy thud.

'Over here,' he calls to the snake, doing a dance.

'Shit!'

'You OK?' he says.

'Ripped my jeans.'

'Oh dear,' Daniel says, not entirely sympathetically. 'Now get onto the road and hope the police don't see you.'

Daniel waits for the sounds of Tiffany trampling in the undergrowth to conclude then crouches down carefully to collect a large stick, his eyes fixed on the cobra.

Do snakes chase sticks?

There's always a first time.

He throws the stick one way and runs the other. Branches snatching at his face he pushes through the vegetation and emerges on the road. No sign of the snake.

She runs to him. 'Are you OK?'

'I'm scathed.'

She looks confused then gets it. There's blood on his face.

'I'm sorry, I saw the snake and panicked.' She leans forward and kisses his cheek.

'Let's go.' He smiles, and winces with pain.

No one notices the couple walking along the road; the police at the warehouse are otherwise engaged. Five minutes later they reach a service station where Daniel buys chocolate and two of the new and obligatory face masks, then flags down a passing tuk-tuk.

The SWAT team fan out, securing one zone after another. They move with guns raised in rehearsed staccato movements, securing each position as they pass from hangar to office and through to the corridor where one group descends the stairwell towards the basement. Walkie-talkies crackle as they communicate with the team leader outside.

With torches in the fist-up grip that enables them to keep the light source close to their eyes the team sweep the space for signs of threat. They move rapidly down the line of empty cages. Two bodies lie outside the cages, three quarters of the way down the long room.

So emaciated that they barely fill their shabby clothes, the corpses have lain there for months; or that is the assumption until someone reaches down to touch them and find them warm and as yet unaffected by rigor mortis. One of the men, missing both ears, is clinging to a bunch of keys.

'Over here!'

Only one of the cages is locked. It contains two malformed bodies with grotesquely large heads and chests.

'Are you seeing this?' The SWAT team member, Kiran, ensures her body camera points in the right direction.

'Yes,' comes the reply on her radio. 'Are they alive?'

'We're about to find out,' Kiran answers as a colleague hands her the bunch of keys recovered from the first body.

Two other members of the team have reached the far end of the room, checked out the straps hanging on the wall, and are passing through the door they have just opened. Having found the right key, the cage door is open and Kiran enters.

The bodies are pressed up against the side of the cage, their faces contorted in extreme pain, their arms reaching out into the adjoining cage. The raw lumpy masses on their heads and chests look as if someone has injected them with flesh or fluids. Aside from these brutal swellings, the corpses are as emaciated as the body found clutching the keys.

'Both dead,' Kiran confirms.

'Any sign of the foreigners?' replies the voice on the radio. 'Tall Caucasian, brown hair, very light skin. The others are ...'

'Not yet. Securing back exit then we move upstairs.'

As she steps out of the cage, Kiran notices blood on two of

the bars of the door. She positions her torch and makes sure her bodycam is recording what she is seeing, then she returns to the first corpse. The man has no ears. Instead, on both sides of his head, the skull is visible in the deep wounds gouged into the skin and scalp. Was this individual also in the cage? Did he remove his own ears in order to squeeze between the bars in a bid to escape? Did someone else mutilate him?

Either way, it's horrific.

'Forensics will have their work cut out making sense of this,' she mutters.

'Arriving any minute,' says the radio.

The team moves upstairs.

On the first floor they find two storerooms. One is a food store packed with food, camping gas stoves, water, cooking utensils. The other is a hardware store: jerry cans of fuel, two generators, power tools, padlocks and chains, ironmongery, blankets, buckets, knives and other weapons. Someone has been living in the next room along. It contains a table and chair, a camp-bed, kerosene lamp and a tray bearing the remains of a meal and half a bottle of Clos Fourtet St Emilion Grand Cru beside an elegant crystal glass. A copy of *Deep Blues - a musical and cultural history of the Mississippi Delta* lies on the camp-bed.

The team continue to the end of the corridor; the other rooms are all empty. On the second floor they find the room Tiffany was held in, and two more bodies.

'Blunt force trauma to the head,' Kiran describes what she is seeing for the radio. 'The second victim has been strangled. Both emaciated like the bodies down in the basement.'

As she steps back into the corridor another member of the team beckons her. Further along they have broken down a door and found another prisoner, lying in his own excrement, naked, bound hand and foot. Kiran crouches down beside him and feels for a pulse. He is alive.

His eyelids flutter.

'Sir. Sir. Can you hear me?' Kiran asks in English.

The eyes open, red and bloodshot.

'White male, forties, brown hair. Birth mark on shoulder. Ambulance needed,' she says for the radio. 'Indian police, you are safe now.'

The man flinches, his body is covered in bruises.

'Please. What is your good name?' she asks.

His mouth opens but he has neither the saliva nor the strength to speak.

'Water.' Kiran orders.

Another woman steps forward and passes Kiran a flask. She lifts the man's head and gently pours water into his mouth. He splutters, gags, swallows, grimaces.

'Hoek,' he whispers finally. 'Antoine Hoek. Europol. Danger. You must ...'

'It's OK, Sir. We have a large team, you can relax. We will get you out of here shortly.'

'Antoine Hoek,' she says for the radio.

'Yes, can confirm identity from database,' comes the reply. 'Well done, guys.'

The other rooms are empty.

In the last room the SWAT team makes its only mistake.

No one looks up.

In the ceiling is a trapdoor. Lying on the roof is Thor Lupei, his eye pressed to the keyhole in the trapdoor. Beside him is the long pole he took up with him after he had used it to open the door and release the rope ladder.

Lupei's face aches and hangs loose in the wake of Daniel's attack. He quickly disgorged the unwanted flesh into the bodies of the scravir caged beside him, saving himself and punishing them for failing to protect him. He will soon abuse other victims to complete his recovery.

Every lacklit fibre of his being screams for revenge.

CHAPTER 54

The airport is in chaos. All the check-ins are surrounded by huge queues, raised voices in more than a dozen languages, frazzled staff, and mountains of luggage.

Daniel and Tiffany, in their new face masks, join the queue to begin the process of registration. Announcements over the tannoy urge people to stay calm and not to shout at staff. The announcer reassures everyone that efforts are being made to ensure that all foreign nationals will be able to leave.

'Once we reach the check-in desk it should be easy,' Daniel tells her. 'You've got all your papers and your backpack counts as hand luggage so you will ...'

'Why don't you come with me?'

'I don't have my passport and besides ...'

'You can tell them to contact the British Embassy.'

'It's not that simple. There's no record of me leaving the UK. I was smuggled out.' He changes the subject. 'Do you want something to eat?'

'Coffee would be nice.'

Daniel wanders off to find her a coffee. Ten minutes later when he returns, the queue has hardly moved.

Everywhere tempers are rising.

'I really stink,' Tiffany declares.

'Nobody is thinking about body odours right now.' He brushes hair out of her face. 'Look, I got you a book to read, a thriller set in Delhi. In case all the in-flight films are rubbish.'

Tiffany takes it, reads the title and smiles. '*The Price you Pay.* Is there a message?'

'Not really.' He wants to explain but cannot find the words.

The queue is moving again.

'Do we stay here once I've checked in or do I get whisked away?' she asks anxiously.

Daniel shrugs. 'We'll see.'

She takes his hands. 'I need to talk with you about something important. But not here in front of everyone. Promise me that ...'

She is interrupted by shouting at the back of the queue.

'I have to get through! I am not pushing in. I want to talk with my friend. Let me go!' A woman's voice. 'LET ME GO!'

Everyone is looking around with that weird mixture of embarrassment and extreme interest. Who is shouting? What does she look like?

'Bloody Indians. Always making a scene,' declares a large English woman standing just behind Tiffany. 'It's all me, me, me. Never think about anyone else. Brian, tell that man to turn the air conditioning down in the hall; it's perishing.'

'Racist shit,' Daniel mutters.

'Let me go!' the woman at the back of the queue is shouting again and jumping up and down to try to see into the crowd while two members of staff try to restrain her.

'Halogen! HALOGEN-JI!'

Suddenly Daniel recognises the voice. 'I'll be back,' he tells Tiffany as he pushes past the ranting xenophobe.

He reaches the edge of the crowd as the staff are frogmarching the woman away. 'Wait!' he calls.

Flanked by airport staff the woman turns.

On seeing Daniel she smiles.

He hurries forward.

'Hey, Karuna,' he says. 'Everything OK?'

Karuna nods, glancing over his shoulder and spotting someone else she recognises.

Tiffany has followed Daniel out of the crowd. She is looking visibly disappointed while putting on a brave face.

Daniel hasn't seen Tiffany emerge behind him.

'Everyone OK? The police didn't ...' Daniel starts.

'Forget the police. Everyone is safe. I brought you something. Hi Tiffany,' Karuna adds as Tiffany joins them. The airport staff look impatient.

Karuna can't see Tiffany's attempt at a smile because of the face mask but the rest of her face is frowning furiously.

'This will only take a minute, OK?' Karuna tells the airport staff. She turns towards Daniel and reaches into the pocket of her jeans. 'Here, take it.'

It is his passport.

Daniel and Tiffany look gobsmacked.

'Go with her. She needs you.'

'But what about ...' he starts.

'We're good. Everything will work out. This is your chance, Halogen-Ji. You belong with Tiffany and if you don't go now, who knows how long it will be?' Karuna smiles at them both. 'This bloody lockdown could go on for years. They say curfew starts tomorrow. Nobody will be going anywhere.'

Daniel glances at Tiffany. Sees the hope in her eyes. He smiles at Karuna and goes to hug her but she backs away. 'You are something special,' he tells her.

'Perhaps,' Karuna replies. 'See you later, OK?' She nods to the airport staff. 'We can go.'

Daniel and Tiffany watch Karuna and the staff walk away. Suddenly Karuna turns. 'Oh, I almost forgot. RJ says hi and you still owe him that game of chess!'

Tiffany and Daniel are now stuck at the back of the queue. Not that this worries Tiffany who now looks radiantly happy.

'When we get on the plane, I'll tell you what I have been trying to tell you,' she tells him excitedly, holding his arm. 'Do you think they will be feeding us? We shouldn't get fussy, we're just lucky to get places, aren't we? They did say everyone would get on board. That's really sweet of Karuna to come to the airport. I'm feeling bad now for ... What's the matter?'

Daniel looks thoughtful.

'What? Is something wrong?' Tiffany persists.

He sighs, opens his passport and passes it to her.

'What?' she says.

'Turn the pages,' he tells her quietly.

She starts flicking the pages. He leans in close so as not to be overheard by the family just ahead of them. 'It's a fake. A counterfeit. Look at the name.'

The passport is in the name of Halogen Jones.

'They'll never let me through with that. I'll be lucky not to get arrested and thrown in jail. It works everywhere else in India but not here at passport control.' His voice is flat. 'I'm sorry, Tiffany.'

Tiffany is looking at the photo. It must have been taken shortly after he arrived in India.

'No, Daniel,' she says. 'Look around. It's total chaos. They just want to get everyone out. You're British. Everyone can tell the minute you open your bloody mouth! Trust me, Daniel, you're going to make it onto the plane.'

He is still not convinced.

'There is one thing you should do though.' She whispers in his ear.

He doesn't understand at first, so she shows him his passport.

'Don't be long,' she tells him. 'I'll keep your place.'

He nods and wanders off towards the shops.

Fifteen minutes later Daniel reappears at her side in the queue. She does a double-take. Ten years younger. In fact, he looks like the man she thought she would be meeting when the plane landed in India two weeks ago.

'Wow!' she kisses his cheek.

'Feels weird,' he says. 'It'll take ages to grow back. I

thought it looked cool.'

'It did. You looked very ...' she wrestles to find something reassuring. '... very two Hairy Bikers meets Mario. But if we're trying to get you through passport control, removing the beard and that massive moustache so you look something like your photo won't hurt, will it?'

From his position on the roof, he watches the planes taking off a mile away, thick as bees leaving a hive. The warehouse is still crawling with police, the building surrounded, and the forensic team bringing bodies out to the tent they have set up in front of the roller door. They may not leave before dawn.

At the edge of the wasteland half a dozen feral dogs are pacing back and forth.

He saw Daniel and Tiffany walking away along the road, and wished he had a sniper's rifle.

They took Hoek away in an ambulance. Lupei had been keeping him as a bargaining chip. A mistake; he would have done better feeding him to the dogs.

You live and learn.

PART 5

March 2020

Whitby

CHAPTER 55

Tuesday 24th March 2020

It shouldn't come as a shock but it does.

After the chaos in the airport in Delhi, the long flight where passengers and crew alike teetered on the edge of hysteria like tired children, the subdued journey into London on the tube with everyone two seats apart and wearing masks, Kings Cross station crawling with transport police and all the food shops closed, the train stopping at Leeds and the passengers ordered off the train, the half hour walking about until Daniel found a motorbike to steal (hot-wiring it like he had been shown in New Delhi), and the three hours it took to cover the 90 miles from Leeds to the coast on back roads, without helmets ...

... after all that, it shouldn't be a shock.

But it is.

It is mid-afternoon.

The sun is strutting boldly across the sky. The sea is purring, and

> Whitby's
>> streets
>>> are
>>>> empty.

No locals ...
No tourists ...
No one. Nobody. Nothing.

Tiffany is visibly shaken. They scuttle the motorbike between the bins in Dark Entry Yard and hurry past hushed hostelries and silent shops, up Golden Lion Bank and Flowergate to Tiffany's flat on Cliff Street.

Tiffany shoves her key in the lock and twists.

'Bugger. She must have double-locked it. The other key's here somewhere.' Tiffany rummages in her backpack. 'Got it!'

The door stays shut. She bangs on it.

'She's bolted it. Daft cow.'

Daniel looks up and down the street. A curtain flinches two doors down.

'Who is it?' Tina's voice on the other side of the door.

'It's me.'

'Tiffany?'

'Of course.'

A pause. 'Sorry, love, you can't come in.'

'What!'

'Lockdown.'

'I *live* here.'

'Where have you been?'

'What do you mean?'

'You've been away two weeks.'

'What's that got to do with anything?'

'Bumped into your uncle Ted. He said you were abroad. In India.'

'Can we come in and talk about this, Tina, instead of shouting through a door?'

'We?'

'Daniel's with me.'

Tina is talking with someone else behind the closed door. A male voice.

'It's not Ben's flat, Tina,' Tiffany says through the letterbox. 'It's ours, yours and mine.'

'We have to think about Ethan,' Tina's voice is brittle, defensive, tearful. 'Babies' immune systems are weaker than ours. I'd never forgive myself if ...'

'So you're leaving me out on the street, Tina? Is that it?' Tiffany shouts.

'Can't you go to your parents?'

'Oh, it's OK if I kill them as long as you're all right?'

Daniel takes Tiffany's hand. 'We'll find something else.'

'It's my flat too, Daniel. Not just hers.'

'I know.' The calmness in his voice steadies her. 'Leave her to it. Is it always so bloody cold in Whitby?'

'It's not cold.'

Twenty minutes later they have walked the length of Church Street, past the boat yard and up the hill to her parents' house on Abbots Road.

Different street, same result. She leans on the doorbell but her parents aren't in. A neighbour across the street opens a window, screams about lockdown. Leave or he'll call the police.

Uncle Ted now lives in Staithes, ten miles up the coast. Tiffany rings and he explains her parents went to see her mum's aunt in Pickering. Her mum's refusing to come back until the pandemic is officially over. Said she'd changed the locks. He advises against Tiffany going into the house.

'Don't try to get in. She'll throw a fit, love. It's not personal, you know what she's like.'

'Not personal?' Tiffany shouts at her phone. 'I'm her bloody daughter! What am I meant to do?'

Riskaverse is Tiffany's mum's middle name. Her dad's is *Gowithflow*. David *Gowithflow* Harrek.

Daniel steers Tiffany gently away, back down Spital Bridge towards the harbour; the last thing they need is attention from the police.

In the old town most of the houses are as empty as the streets. No one there to shout murder; it's all holiday cottages. One discretely smashed window later, in Blackburn's Yard, and they are out of the elements. Neither is particularly happy with breaking and entering but they are dog-tired and cold, everything's shut and they cannot face the prospect of a night on the streets.

The front door opens directly into the front room, with sofas, coffee table, television and the stairs to the upper floors. While Daniel replaces the broken pane with another one from higher up in the building, Tiffany goes to the back room which serves as a kitchen diner, finds the spare front door key on a hook in a cupboard and forages for food. The electricity and gas are on, and the water. There's a cupboard containing *Welcome to your Cottage* stuff: pasta, tomato sauce, tinned mackerel, teabags.

They have travelled, found shelter, showered, had food and drink and are side by side on a sofa. On the television is part three of a landmark series on how to boil an egg.

Tiffany makes the first move, leaning in, resting her head on his shoulder.

'Do you recognise where we are?'

'Henrietta Street is that way. Right?' He points.

'It's nearly three and a half years ago.'

'I always knew I was coming back. You do good chips in Whitby.'

She looks up at him and smiles. 'Not anymore, I don't.' A pause. 'I need to tell you something. About your mum. Been meaning to for days.' She sits up. 'In fact, now my phone's charged, you can hear it yourself. Gert sent it me.'

She put her AirPods in his ears and presses play.

Sound of knocking three times.

Gert: 12th April 2017, 9am. I'm outside the home of Wayne Murray. He was out when we visited in January. Hoping for better luck today.

Sound of knocking.

Gert: Here we go.

Latch turns, door opens.

Voice: Yeah?

Gert: Good Morning. Mr Wayne Murray?

Voice: Why?

Gert: I'm a friend of your son, Daniel. Can I come in?

Voice: What's the little bastard done now?

Daniel stops the playback.

'Let it play. Honestly, you need to hear this. I'll put the kettle on.'

She waits in the kitchen. Gives him time. By the time she returns to the front room, mugs in hand, Daniel is curled up in a ball. She sits down beside him.

'She loved you, Daniel. And so does your dad,' she speaks quietly, a hand on his shoulder. 'She didn't find you boring. And he were trying to protect you, but it all went wrong.'

When eventually he uncurls, his eyes are red.

'I never said goodbye.' His voice is flat.

'Gert were like a little terrier,' Tiffany tells him. 'He knew something weren't right and kept going back until he got an answer.'

She takes Daniel in her arms. His body shakes, aftershocks of sixteen years of shame and hurt. Three quarters of his life.

'I could use a drink.'

'And a hankie. Good job we don't have any booze.'

'I can't forgive him.'

'You have to.'

'I've always been rejected, been boring and ...'

Tiffany let's go of him. 'You haven't always been rejected. That's crap and you know it. Self-pity's not a great look. Why did I fly to India to find you so that ...'

'OK,' he interjects. 'OK. Just getting my head round it.'

'Fancy a walk?' she changes the subject.

'Let's wait until it's dark. Less chance of bumping into anyone. Maybe we should get some shut-eye.'

'We haven't even looked upstairs.' Tiffany realises.

'Shall I use the sofa?'

'What? No, you wazzock. You and I are getting down to business!'

'What?'

'You'll see.' She winks. 'Come on, lover. We've waited bloody long enough.'

It is almost midnight when the two lovers tumble out of bed, throw on some clothes, stagger the steep stairs down and out into the night air. Daniel claims he is neither cold nor jet-lagged as they saunter, hand in hand up an empty Church Street, but he is visibly shivering.

They barely feel the cobbles beneath their feet, passing the cottage that stores the memories of a Goth weekend in November 2016. At the end of Henrietta Street they descend the path towards the east pier.

Today is the new moon so there is no pale round face rushing between the clouds to catch a glimpse of Whitby below as sea-sucked stones scumble, flying foam froths frack and bo, and a wayworn wind winds the lighthouses round like a cow's long tongue wraplicking a block of salt.

At the end of the pier they kiss, fingers fumbling in each other's hair as the waves wash white and whisper.

They are alone. Together.

No. Not alone.

From the graveyard high up on the cliff they are observed.

A storm is brewing.

CHAPTER 56

Shop Hill, Raw, Whitby

25th March 2023

She gets up at four forty-five, same as every morning. The animals have to be fed. Since last autumn there's only the six sheep, a goose, the horse, and four cats, all of them as retired as she is. Smurthwaites Farm down the road deliver straw along with food for the animals once a week, and she catches the bus into Whitby for the rest. She wonders sometimes what the Smurthwaites think of her, playing at farming, but nothing gained from worrying what others think so it's quickly forgotten and if they don't like it, they can jolly well lump it.

It was her retirement dream to move from the town and set up a smallholding with a menagerie of her own. Like the one she and her sister would visit as children when they were staying at the caravan park between Hawsker and Whitby in the 1950s. Somewhere safe. Somewhere away from the troubles of the world. And it was just a dream until an uncle she'd not seen in forty years died and suddenly she had a pot of money and bought the last cottage on Shop Hill.

Her sister's long gone and she's no family, and no mirror in the cottage either so she doesn't even see herself. She sees no one from one day to the next, except on the bus and at the shops once a fortnight. There's no telephone, only nasty people trying to sell you things you don't need. She couldn't give a fig about anything aside from her routine and the company of her animals.

She has her green dressing gown on as she fills the kettle

at the kitchen sink. The yard outside is tunnel black. The devil makes work for idle hands so she'll keep busy till the day she drops, not that she's ever done anything devilish in her life unless you count handing a discount coupon she found at a bus stop over to the cashier at the Co-op and pretending it was hers. All it got her was twenty percent off some washing powder and a month worrying that she would end up in prison.

The kettle whistles on the stove and she fills the pot, she'll drink one cup now and the rest when she's back from feeding the animals. The tea will be strong enough to stand a spoon in by then.

She finds a headscarf and boots and steps outside, leaving the door on the latch. It'll be gone six when the sun rises, if the clouds let it. The night wraps her like a shroud and her feet find their own way across the gravel to the first shed. A miaow curls round and through her legs as she creaks open the door and breathes the smell of dry straw and chitting potatoes. If she hurries, she'll be tucked in bed with *Thought for the Day* on the radio before the first blackbird sings.

She crosses the threshold. There is just enough light coming through the window to see the pitchfork and the wheelbarrow already laden with straw; no need to flick the switch. So focused is she on her chores that she fails to notice the shadow that passes across the yard behind her.

She reverses out of the shed, pitchfork resting on the barrow. Is that little mouse still hiding in her old wellingtons? Cheeky thing!

The sheep first, then Edgar. Does he even remember the last time he was saddled up? Probably not, the big softie.

It is muddy by the field gate. Still too dark for now but in half an hour the moors will be visible from this spot. She leans her shoulder against the wooden bars and pushes the wheelbarrow through the gap.

The juddering of the gate masks the footsteps at her back.

She really must ask Mr Smurthwaite to send someone round to fix the gate; it is getting harder and harder to open. Whether or not anyone will come is anyone's guess with this dreadful Covid that she hopes will all be over by the weekend, when she next has to go shopping.

She slips about in the mud but reaches the stables in one piece. It seems mean keeping them inside but she is taking no chances. If this wretched pandemic is real - they do talk such rubbish on the radio; she's been up half the night worrying about what she can do - then all the God's creatures must be protected. They've done nothing wrong, have they?

The bolt slides back and she pulls open the top door and goes up on her tiptoes to peer inside. Six white furry faces look up at her.

'There you are!' she coos. 'You do look snug. I've brought you some straw. Yes!'

A sheep bleats.

'I know. Mummy is naughty, isn't she? I should have cleaned you out yesterday. You're a little bit stinky and ...'

She interrupted by the goose who is suddenly kicking up the most dreadful racket.

'Esmeralda, please. Wait your turn, dear.'

The squawking gets louder, accompanied by a frenzy of flapping. So much better than a guard dog. How many dogs lay eggs? And the way she runs at intruders, brave as bazookas that one. But she must wait her turn.

She pitchforks the straw in over the lower door. The girls can sort it out for now; she'll give them a proper clean out at lunch time.

The squawking stops quite suddenly. But now Edgar is stomping about, goodness only knows the noise he'd be making if he was wearing shoes. And he sets off the sheep. It's like being on the Ark, she smiles to herself!

The straw all tossed in, she returns to the shed to fetch the hay; they can have the mangels for lunch.

Didn't she close the door earlier? Why is it open?

'Will you all shut up?' she tells the animals. 'I can't hear myself think.'

She peers into the lacklit shed. It must be the wretched cat. She steps inside. Muddy footprints on the floor, wet shiny against the dry dust. Not cat feet.

Human feet. Bare feet.

How dare they? This is her shed. Someone is in for a rude awakening. There was a young chap last summer, doing his Duke of Edinburgh award. Wandered in bold as you please, said he was looking for a drink of water. She sent him packing with a thick ear for his troubles.

Pitchfork in hand, she follows the footprints towards the gloom at the back of the shed and almost steps on the cat as it backs into her, hissing like a snake, its ears flat and its tail tucked under its body. With a yelp, it bolts out of the door.

'Who's there?' she says firmly, stepping forward between the hay bales, pitchfork at the ready.

The attack comes from the side. The wall of hay bales falls on to her, knocking her off her feet. Before she can pick herself up, a shadow leaps out, pinning her to the floor, its hands wrapping round her neck. A face looms into view.

Scrawny, with black sunken eyes.

She tries to scream and kick out with her feet but she is simply not strong enough and can only gaze at her murderer as life ebbs out of her.

Minutes later, reflected in the goose's dead unblinking eye, a figure passes by in a stolen green dressing gown, dragging something heavy. The first raindrops tap a tattoo on the dead bird's beak and soft nestle among its cooling feathers.

CHAPTER 57

Whitby

Kissing Daniel's forehead, Tiffany leaves him sleeping. He was tossing and turning half the night and needs to rest.

A quick shower then downstairs to make herself a cup of coffee and plan the day. An email apology to the university is in order for missing two weeks of lectures. There's food to sort out. Obviously a home delivery is out of the question when you are squatting illegally in a holiday cottage.

She's glad of the portable radio in the kitchen, with Yorkshire Coast Radio chuntering in the background. A tetchy call-in with locals complaining about outsiders coming into town to walk on the beach and putting everyone's lives at risk. 420 confirmed cases of coronavirus in Yorkshire. Residents in a street in Scarborough have put their Christmas decorations back up to "spread a little hope in dark times". Everyone in Whitby knows they're nuts in Scarborough.

The presenter reminds listeners of the rules; people should stay at least two metres apart when they're outside.

Good luck with that on Church Street.

Tiffany scribbles a note for Daniel, empties her backpack, slings it over her shoulder and lets herself out.

If you pretend it is seven o'clock on a Sunday morning then everything is fine, but it is half past ten on a Wednesday. No cars, no delivery vans, no tourists, no locals. She's through Sandgate and over the swing bridge before she sees a soul; an old man coming out of Baxtergate who stops and stares, his head turning slowly like a CCTV camera as she passes.

Tide is out and the boats moored along New Quay Road

have all sunk from view.

No taxis queuing outside the station.

A sea fret is coming into town and everything is fading into the mist.

She's not the only one out shopping. Outside the Co-op there's a line, socially distanced, stretching back from the front door and down the side of the building. Tiffany joins the back of the queue. Half an hour later she has been inside, done her shopping and is heading back over the swing bridge. She's bought Daniel a fresh set of clothes and a woolly hat, and for each of them a thick jumper. After three years in India, Daniel is going to struggle with the cold. The fret is racing up the Esk now, so thick that, from the middle of the swing bridge, the lifeboat station and St Ann's Staith have both disappeared from view.

Suddenly overwhelmed by the thought that someone is following her, Tiffany stops and turns. Not a soul to be seen. Only the fog, thick as thugs, stalking up Bridge Street, strangely ignoring the narrow entrance into Sandgate.

Two days ago she was shackled to a wall four thousand miles away in New Delhi. Now she is home but her body still shakes to the echoes of those skeletal hands that pawed her.

The fear subsides and she continues, out of Sandgate and across the square past the old town hall. On Church Street she walks straight past the entrance to the yard, even though there is no one else in sight, and carries on to the 199 Steps and climbs them to the top. If anything is following her, they will have nowhere to hide on the steps.

At the top she turns to look back. Nothing to see except a lamp post and the steps leading down. The town is lost in the fog. The loud klaxon shriek of a pheasant disturbed among the tombstones startles her.

Remembering the item that she has kept close for over three years, Tiffany removes her backpack and rummages through her shopping. There it is, small, hard, round as a pebble and slightly cool to the touch.

The compass Daniel gave her. She lifts the lid and releases the catch that holds the tiny black crow needle in place. The bird turns to face north. Tiffany finds the black spot on the base of the brass case and presses it. The crow turns slowly turns this way and that, not settling anywhere, not pointing at anything. Her heartbeat slows.

There are no scravir.

With the global lockdown, no one can come to the UK. Not even Lupei.

They are safe.

She is still smiling at this thought when her eye is drawn back to her hand. The crow needle has stopped spinning and is now trembling back and forth, pointing in the direction of the graves along the cliff top!

Tiffany shoulders her backpack, shoves the compass in her pocket and races back down the steps. At the bottom the fog is so thick she can barely see the entrance to Henrietta Street.

Not a soul on Church Street, except the ginger cat that lives in Arguments Yard. Footsteps clattering on the cobbles, Tiffany stops to catch her breath only once she is back in the cottage with the door locked and bolted.

'Yo,' Daniel says appearing from the kitchen, in t-shirt and pants, his hair tousled and messy. 'Saw your note. Weird thing, I woke up with this tune going round and round. *Nani nani puisor, nani nani dormi usor*. Don't even know what language it's in! Don't think it's Hindi but ... Hey ...' he finally notices the look on Tiffany's face. 'What's the matter? Are you OK?'

'They're here.'

The compass lies on the table between them while they have a late breakfast, the crow needle facing north. Tiffany picks at her food. Daniel is eating greedily. Sausages, bacon, scrambled egg, tomatoes, mushrooms and baked beans. And he looks good in the new jumper.

'Maybe the gravestones are north of where you were standing,' he suggests. 'Maybe you just got mixed up.'

Tiffany changes the subject. 'Is it weird eating curry all day every day? Antoine said I would get bored pretty quickly.'

'Delhi is a big city,' Daniel talks with his mouth full. 'Like London. All sorts of different food. Nothing like this though. This is great!'

Tiffany is pleased to see him looking happy. 'I've found your song,' she holds up her phone. 'Look. Nani nani puisor. It's Romanian.'

'Romanian?'

'It's a lullaby. Maybe your mum sang it to you.'

'My mum?'

'She was from Romania, wasn't she?'

'Middlesbrough.'

'You know what I mean.'

Daniel stuffs his face with bacon. 'By the way, have you heard from Jordan. I tried ...'

He sees the look on her face. 'Did something happen?'

'Not sure you want to hear this,' she says.

'Sounds like I need to.'

Tiffany explains. Daniel listens, scratches his head.

'I'm sorry.'

'It's not your fault.'

'I thought he stopped drinking. When he became a Rasta.'

'He cut his locks. Works for London Underground now.'

'Shit. Should I speak with him?'

'Like I'm your property?'

'No, not like that. Like you are both my friends and ...'

'He sent a pretty grovelling apology.'

'OK. OK. Sounds like I butt out and let time do its ...'

'Yeah.'

'So what are we going to do today?'

'Let's explore the house. We need to know all the exits in case ...'

'Good idea. What's in there for a start?'

There is a low door, about one and a half metres high, beside the sink. Daniel pulls it open to find various bits of cleaning equipment: a pan and brush, mop, vacuum cleaner. He is about to close the door when he notices the floor is painted white wood and has a brass handle. They pull the clutter out of the cupboard to reveal a trapdoor, which he lifts.

Steps going down.

'I'm not going down there unless the outside doors are locked,' Tiffany says, the memories of incarceration in New Delhi still too vivid.

Moments later they are climbing steep wood steps down into the basement.

No larger than a couple of garden sheds, with whitewashed brick walls, there is barely room for an old bicycle (front wheel separated), a dismantled pool table, and a tall thin bookcase that contains games, old magazines, maps, books, spare crockery and a large old metal box. A single naked light bulb hangs from the ceiling. Tiffany is already back in the kitchen when Daniel hauls the old box into the middle of the room and unbuckles the leather strap securing the lid. It contains a pile of yellowing papers and two cash boxes. He replaces the lid and carries the whole thing up the steps. Tiffany is unimpressed.

'It'll give us something to do,' he tells Tiffany. 'Apart from ...' He jiggles his eyebrows. 'Full of old newspapers and stuff,' he explains, taking the box through to the front room and putting it down beside the coffee table.

'How exciting,' she flatlines.

'We might learn something about your home town.'

'We might catch something, more likely. Fret's in the yards now.'

'Frets?'

He follows her line of sight. Through the window the yard has disappeared in a blanket of fog.

Tiffany's phone ringtone bursts into life. *I'm Gonna Be* by the Proclaimers. She wanders out to the kitchen while Daniel rummages in the box.

The newspapers go way back. Daniel, who has never really paid much notice to history, is intrigued. The Whitby Gazette dated 1859. He turns the pages idly. Adverts for hair pomades made from *the very finest lards and local lavenders*, and Holloway's Astonishing Ointment that allegedly cures: *scrofula, cancers, sore throats, piles, bad breasts, scurvy, chilblains* and pretty much everything else. Then the local news stories. No pictures, just a wall of text with short stories all jumbled up. A man loses an eye on a boat as the result of a prank. His crewmates packed his pipe with gunpowder. Ladies are complaining about a new hat, the shape of which is judged "*deformed*", and a Rosie Seeker has died at her home in a yard off Church Street. Rosie took over the general store established in 1823 by her mother, Rebecca Anne Johnson. Rosie was the first woman from the yards admitted into the Whitby Philosophical Society. "*For an uneducated woman of a humble fishing background, she showed a remarkable understanding of fossils and contributed beyond expectations*" said David Draper, acting president of the society.

Beneath the newspaper are two rusty keys and various other documents, including a set of deeds and, as he reads, Daniel realises these relate to the cottage. Owned by Rosie Seeker. The papers list seventeen occupants, from four families. Four households crammed into these small rooms.

'Well that's me buggered,' Tiffany says, returning from the kitchen. 'I've to go back to Middlesbrough for my training tomorrow and, in two days' time, they're sending us off to Scarborough. They need all student nurses on the wards. I've closed that trapdoor and shoved stuff back in the cupboard, by the way. Gives me the creeps.'

'Is this a good moment to talk about *business?*

'How about a new enterprise zone in the second bedroom?' she winks. 'While we still can.'

He races upstairs after her.

A couple of hours later they are lying in the second bedroom, tired and shagged out, when Daniel groans beside her.

Tiffany turns to find Daniel clutching his temples.

'Are you alright?'

'Yeah. Migraine. My head's thumping. You know when you see like fuzzy lines? I've had them from time to time over the past few months. Dehydration, I think.'

He staggers out of the room. Tiffany lies back and smiles. They have some serious talking to do but she is feeling so happy about finally being together. Doesn't want to use the word *love*. Not yet. Comfortable, easy, perfect, magical. But not the other word.

Give it a few days.

She finds him downstairs wrapped in a towel, on the sofa.

Tiffany finds a blanket from upstairs and tucks him up. 'You'll catch your death.'

'Better warm me up then.'

'I can make you a cup of coffee.'

'Migraine.'

'Hot water?'

'Whatever.'

She boils the kettle, makes them both a drink.

'We really need to talk. About everything. I'm worried about you.'

'Yes, Nurse.'

'I'm serious.'

'Do they give you masks and hazmat suits, or whatever they call them? In the hospital. If they're sending you into the wards?'

She shrugs. 'I suppose so. They have to look after us.'

'I hope so.' Daniel opens his eyes, then grimaces at the bright light.

'Get some sleep. I'll make us something to eat in a while.'

He closes his eyes. From the other end of the sofa, Tiffany watches him quietly. When she is satisfied he is asleep, she picks the scravir compass up off the dining table and opens it. The small black crow judders very slowly back and fro, frack and bo ...

Searching.

CHAPTER 58

Kori Creek, India

The journey is interminable. A whole day to get from Delhi to Kori Creek via Ajmer, Radhanpur, Bhuj, Dayapar, and an infinity of one-street towns and villages sandwiched between biscuit-coloured earth below and sun-smacked sky above. The lorry rattles, bumps and grinds like a tired belly dancer on a sea of sand dunes. Sweat smears every surface. He and his fellow passengers smell ripe as collapsing bananas.

At Narayan they drop him off outside the tourism hotel where he meets his guide, a man of dark complexion and a long thin face, all chin, nose and brow like an Easter Island statue, who books him a room and then drives off in a cloud of dust to organise the next phase of the journey. The hotel window looks on the desert. It is 35°C.

Two minutes to decide his guide is a crook.

Twenty minutes to shower away the dirt.

Three hours for the guide to return.

At dusk he is taken to a remote beach where three local fishermen are waiting beside a rigid inflatable with a sail, oars, and outboard motor. Lupei scrambles aboard, backpack slung over his shoulder.

The contested India Pakistan border is some 30 kilometres to the west through a labyrinth of waterways, islands, marshes and wetlands. Hundreds of fishermen from both countries have been caught and arrested over the years for crossing the border illegally. Hardly surprising, the perpetrators are usually illiterate and possess neither maps nor geolocation devices. Anxious wives profess to never having heard of Pakistan.

Fishermen on both sides of the border languish in jails for years.

The boat makes rapid progress, covering the twenty-five kilometres in three hours then, around midnight, the outboard engine is cut and the sail is lifted. There is land up ahead.

When the boat beaches, the fishermen get out and instruct the guide and Thor Lupei to do likewise. They haul the vessel up out of the water, remove the outboard motor then, gripping the strategically placed handles, carry the craft inland.

'Where are we going?' Lupei asks his guide.

'We must cross this strip of land. One kilometre then back into the sea.'

'Aren't we in Pakistan?'

'No, not yet. But close. Maybe three kilometres.'

As they hurry across the rough ground, Lupei recognises the good sense in leaving the outboard motor behind; the land is flat but it is still an effort to carry a boat from one finger of the creek to another. Yesterday was the new moon and there is little light to guide them. The night sky is freckled thick with stars as they navigate between clumps of brush. Since there are four men to carry the boat, and since he is paying them all handsomely, Lupei makes no effort to help.

Eventually they reach the shore of Sir Creek, the last stretch of water before Pakistan. The boat is lowered with a gentle splash and they climb aboard. Oars supplement the thin breeze that flaps the sail.

Lupei sits quietly at the back of the vessel, planning the next stage of his journey. He cannot waste weeks making his way through some of the world's most difficult countries: Pakistan, Afghanistan, Turkmenistan, Iran, Azerbaijan, and Russia. It is too dangerous. International flights are cancelled around the world, but on minor airfields in this empty quarter he will surely find smugglers, opportunists, and entrepreneurs more than happy to fly him home if the price is right.

In the middle of the creek, in no man's land and bang on cue, his guide turns and explains that circumstances have changed, that the fishermen are reluctant to go any further, that he has had to negotiate, that they insist they be paid more. The men have stopped rowing.

'How much more?' Lupei asks almost disinterestedly. He has been expecting this moment since he met the guide, in fact ever since he negotiated the trip back in Delhi.

'One million Indian Rupees,' the guide answers, without looking Lupei in the eye. 'Eleven thousand US dollars. The situation is very difficult. The men will need to pay their contact an inflated fee on the Pakistan side. I am very sorry. The men have families and a very difficult ...'

'Spare me the stories,' Lupei raises his hand. 'Yes, OK for the money. Just get on with it.'

'Thank you for your understanding, Sir.'

God, he sounds like a bloody air steward apologising for running out of ice cubes.

Eleven thousand dollars, ten thousand euros.

The guide speaks with the men who take up their oars again and the boat continues heading west.

Less than ten minutes later they reach Pakistan. They are still twenty metres from the shore when two of the men jump out, the water up to their thighs as they pull the boat forwards. They are whispering now and clearly nervous.

The guide turns to Lupei and smiles. 'We have arrived. Can you hand money over, please?'

'Eleven thousand dollars?'

'Plus the six thousand remaining on the ...'

'I paid you your cut up front,' Lupei snarls.

'No, Sir. Respectfully, you made down payment. Ten thousand dollars but there is also ...'

Enough is enough. Lupei was willing to swallow the extra eleven thousand, even though it is chicanery; he is in a hurry and the fishermen have provided a service. The guide, however, is a shyster and there is no guarantee even now that this is the end of it. In a few seconds, a machete will probably appear, or an ancient revolver, along with a fresh demand. The man will not stop now until he has taken every last dollar.

Only the very obvious agitation of the crew, and the torch signalling in the bushes about fifty metres ahead, convinces Lupei they have actually reached Pakistan.

He removes his backpack, leans forward and beckons the guide to come closer. The man grins, the grin of a player who holds all the cards. He is enjoying taking this stuck-up European for everything he has. It will buy him a new car. It is payback; for colonialism and for that sense of entitlement and superiority that has swaggered across India for hundreds of years. They could simply kill him and split whatever monies the European is carrying in his bag but there is also pleasure to be had in the humiliation.

The guide leans forwards, eyes dancing with pleasure. As soon he is within touching distance, Lupei grabs his neck and, through his fingertips, draws the life out of him so quickly that the guide doesn't even have time to cry out.

He is dead before his Easter Island face hits the deck. The third fisherman, busily directing his colleagues from the front of the boat, is facing forward. He has seen nothing. Lupei clambers over the seats and is all over him before the vessel hits the shore, collapsing the arteries in his neck.

By the time the two who are hauling the boat ashore stop and turn, it is just two against one and the odds of survival for Lupei have increased significantly.

A minute later two bodies are floating face down in the water. Lupei reaches into the boat to retrieve his backpack then saunters up the beach towards the flashing light.

CHAPTER 59

Whitby

Tiffany has made soup, that's what her mum would do if she was here and not hiding twenty miles away in Pickering. Uncle Ted was right. She's checked. They are indeed both in the bungalow on Mill Lane with Auntie Claire. Her dad says that if the pandemic isn't over by the end of next week Tiffany should go to the house and water the houseplants, particularly the geraniums.

'I can't, she's changed the locks.'

'The plants are all in the shed. We moved them.'

'You care more about plants than you do about me.'

'Mum is terrified of being infected, Tiff. It'll be a bugger to get her home,' he tells her. 'And she doesn't want any trouble with number 17. If you do go water them, promise you'll wear the mask and the pair of Marigolds I've left by the compost bag. And wipe the outside tap down with 5% alcohol-based solution or she'll have palpitations and ...'

'Have to go, Dad. Catch you later.' She hangs up.

Sod the plants, David *Gowithflow* Harrek.

Tina finally replied to her messages so Tiffany has collected her course books, medical kit, clothes and toiletries from the flat. Everything dumped in a couple of black bin liners outside the front door.

And sod you too, Tina.

Daniel is asleep on the sofa, tossing and turning and muttering in what she assumes is Hindi.

The sea fret still divides the town east from west along the Esk, smothering and vanishing the muffled streets. No sound from the roofs and chimney pots; the gulls have flown inland, there being no chips to steal or boats to follow.

She closes the curtains, double-checks the doors are locked and gently shakes Daniel.

'There's soup, love.'

He blinks, disorientated.

'You need to eat.'

'I feel sick.'

'Probably temperature shock. It must be twenty degrees colder here than in Delhi.'

He sits up. Winces.

'Do you want toast?'

He shrugs.

Tiffany returns with a bowl of soup on a tray and watches him eat.

'I've had mine,' she explains. 'Change of plan. They're picking us up tomorrow morning at six and taking us straight to Scarborough Hospital. So many nurses self-isolating they need student nurses. I feel bad leaving you and ...'

'I'll be fine, Nurse Tiffany.'

They start a Scandi noir series then stop when the bloodied bodies start showing up. Just forty seconds in.

It is all too real.

A comedy game show is safer ground. They binge watch eight episodes, giggling mindlessly until late evening. Time for some fresh air. The fret makes halos round the streetlights. Cold clings to coats.

'It's like a film set,' Tiffany says when she catches up with him on Henrietta Street by the snicket that leads down to Tate Hill Sands.

They've walked separately to avoid attracting attention. You can't see the harbour in the fog but you can smell the sea. Hand in hand, they step over fragments of seaweed, bits of wood, a barnacled boot, a plastic bottle. Suddenly Daniel remembers standing exactly where he is now, nearly three and a half years ago, beside the huge rocks that protect the cliff.

'Are you all right?'

'This is where I found Dr Nigella Shaveling,' he tells her. 'He must have pushed her at the top of the cliff then run down the steps. She died in front of me.'

Don't let him touch you skin to skin. He moves slowly when he is full. Those were her last words.

'Will he find us?'

'He can't. No flights, no ferries. While the pandemic lasts we are safe. Besides why would he think we were here? We could be anywhere on the planet.'

'Safe in a pandemic. That's ironic.'

At the other end of the beach a figure emerges from the fog, tall and thin. They are both thinking the same thing and are gearing up to run when a dog runs out to join its owner.

'What? You thought that was Lupei?' Daniel teases Tiffany.

'And you didn't?' she pushes him playfully.

'Let's go back, it's freezing.'

They head back up the beach.

'I've been doing martial arts training,' Tiffany tells Daniel as they climb the steps back up to Henrietta Street. 'At university. Have you heard of Krav Maga?'

'Is he the teacher?'

'Stupid. It's a form of self-defence.'

'Is that how you kicked a scravir's arse in Delhi?'

'Sort of.'

Without warning, Daniel crumples on the steps. For an instant Tiffany wonders if he has been shot.

In the fog? Get real, girl.

A groan at her feet. He is alive. No sign of blood.

'Daniel. Can you hear me?'

He looks confused, nods slowly and holds out a hand. Tiffany grabs it and pulls him up into a sitting position.

'Sorry.'

'We need to get you inside, where it's safe.'

He nods again.

She hauls him to his feet, puts an arm round him and steers him up the steps.

'Good job you're skinny.'

Daniel focuses on lifting his feet. Back up on Henrietta Street they make faster progress. Past the 199 Steps and down onto Church Street. Daniel allows himself to be directed back towards the yard. Tiffany doesn't relax her grip until they are in the cottage.

He smiles softly as she hands him a cup of tea and Tiffany remembers the state Daniel's friend Alex was in when they found him skulking the shadows on Farview Farm all that time ago. He too had been acquiescent, subdued, little boy lost; before going full out psycho.

As if reading her thoughts, Daniel, makes an effort, and sits up on the sofa.

'It's OK, Tiffany. I feel sick, that's all. The basement of that warehouse was full of people, I must have caught something. I promise I am not turning into a scravir,' he smiles encouragingly.

'OK.'

With all her heart she wants to believe he is an ordinary guy who has been through a tough time.

But it's not really that simple, is it?

'Maybe I should get to a hospital and have tests. I'll do that. The last thing I want is to hurt you or give you some illness that ...'

'I've got an idea.'

CHAPTER 60

It is daylight as I leave the house, posting the key back through the letterbox, so he isn't stuck inside all day. Radio says rain but not all day. I walk to the station where the minibus is waiting to take us to Scarborough Hospital. The sea fret has cleared and it's back to grey skies. No taxis, no bins out for collection, no one waiting for the early buses up or down the coast. It is 6am on a weekday morning and everything is closed.

Lauren is already on board, wearing her mask, dressed up to the nines. Her foundation and eye makeup must have taken her an hour to organise. I don't get it. It's not like we're going clubbing, we're going to a bloody hospital. To work. I don't say anything; no point getting into a fight, we've enough to worry about. Daniel were fast asleep when I left, which has to be good.

'Mask and gloves before you get on. Two rows apart and leave the windows open. There's bottles of hand gel on the seats. You listening?'

The driver seems nervous. So am I.

Rubber gloves make my hands sweat. God knows how I'm keeping those on all day. The mask isn't too tight, which is something. Chloe arrives. Last. Which is weird because she is usually first at everything.

The driver takes the Swing Bridge route up past empty carparks and parking bays to the empty Scarborough road. We're glued to our phones, can't really talk two rows apart with masks on and the noise of the bus. I look out at the countryside from time to time. The fields are so green, after India. The daffodils are out.

There's a personal message from Tina telling me it's nothing personal. Right. She wants forgiveness and understanding. She can bloody wait.

I play a mindless game on my phone until we arrive at the hospital.

An overweight manager arrives and barks out orders as we get off the bus and walk in single file, two metres apart, along a line that has been painted on the ground, like convicts in a chain gang. We're led to a prefab where we strip off and shower then climb into the uniforms they've laid out for us, along with an apron, visor, clean mask and gloves.

Lauren is instructed to go back and start again, removing her makeup this time, including her camel eyelashes. She'd give Tina a run for her money, that one.

When the manager is satisfied, we are marched into the hospital. Lauren mutters about fascists and official complaints.

It's a war zone. People rushing round in all directions, alarms going off, machines dragged from one bed to another.

Because we are students, we aren't administering drugs or anything like that, we are there to offer *emotional and social support* to patients who are in a bad way and terrified about what is happening to them. Not sure what I were expecting. It is scary but I cope. Perhaps it is because I have seen all this before, small scale, when my brother were dying. And what I saw just days ago in the Delhi slum with the old lady and the little girl. Love and compassion, solidarity and kindness. All of us pass through these portals of life and death and we have only each other to help us through. And God, I suppose, but today I am not thinking much about God, I am thinking only of Mike, the middle-aged man gasping for breath in the bed in front of me, his eyes wide with fear. He is realising that the world he enjoyed without thinking less than 48 hours ago - his friends and family, his plans and dreams - are all about to be taken away forever. And there's nothing anyone of us can do.

The nurses, the real nurses, around me are incredible. A

furiously focused zen-like calm packs each second with an intensity that is overwhelming.

After a while I am sent to another bed at the other end of the ward. I reassure Mike that I will be back soon and that he is in good hands. I promise I will speak with his wife and tell her he loves her. Beneath his mask he nods ever so slightly. His eyes close and I rush to where an elderly lady is propped up in a semi-sitting position, intubated with a flexible tube down her windpipe. She is unconscious, her stick-thin arms lie beside her on the yellow sheet like damselflies pausing momentarily on a water lily.

'I need you here while I fetch Sister,' the nurse tells me. 'Linda is drifting in and out of consciousness and I don't want her to wake up and find no one here.'

'Is there a phone number for Mike's wife? I promised ...'

'I'll find it.'

I smile, not that the nurse can see my smile, except in my eyes. He has the tired eyes of someone who has seen too much. He hurries away. Even if he and I never hear her speak, the patient in front of us is a person and her name is Linda.

And so it goes, through to half past one when the ward sister tells me it is time for me to have a twenty-minute break. There are sandwiches for us students in the prefab. In a daze I walk down the long corridor, everyone two metres apart, all masked and visored.

'Tiffany?'

I stop, causing everyone behind me to stop. Across the corridor is a woman in blue scrubs with straight blond hair.

'Tiffany! It is Tiffany, isn't it?' She has a foreign accent. 'Dr Ivanna Albu. Remember?'

She beckons me forwards so that the people waiting behind me can move on. Behind her is a door to a small courtyard. She opens it and I follow her out.

'I don't believe! Look at you! You are nurse now?' Ivanna

sounds so happy, I can't help but break into a smile.

Three years have passed. She was the first person who took us seriously when we arrived at the hospital with Hannah. The only person who was prepared to believe that Hannah had been turned from a healthy young woman to an emaciated living corpse in less than an hour because of Thor Lupei. Ivanna Albu believed us because she is Romanian and she knows things others dismiss out of hand.

'Yes, I know. Why am I still in Scarborough you are thinking,' Albu says, 'I think this too! How are you? Did you hear from your friend? Is she recovered? And Daniel? Do you hear from him?'

It is all too much. After a morning on the ward, and everything else that has happened, I well up with tears. Albu steps forward to comfort me then stops and keeps her distance, as we must.

'I bring difficult memories, Tiffany. Forgive me.'

'It's OK.'

And then it hits me.

'Actually, Ivanna, you are the most perfect person I could hope to meet. I hadn't even thought that you might be here. I have something for you. I were going to hand it in at reception, which would probably have been a waste of time with everyone so busy. It's in my bag in the prefab out in the car park. They haven't told us when our shift finishes and you might be gone. Where can I find you?'

'Let us do it now,' Ivanna says.

She doesn't ask what it is I want to give her, she trusts me. We head down the corridor through reception and out to the car park. Eight other student nurses are in the prefab sitting at individual tables eating their sandwiches. I go to my locker and a minute later I am back outside handing the envelope to Ivanna Albu.

'Can you run a full diagnostic check? I can't tell you exactly what to look for but he is ill. Dizzy spells and migraines. Yesterday he collapsed near the beach and I am worried. I remember you did one before and it changed everything.'

'What are you giving me?'

'We've had the kit at home as part of our training. A blood sample. It's Daniel's.'

It is nearly nine pm when they drop us off back at Whitby Station. No one has spoken on the bus, we are all shattered. Lauren is crying.

'See you tomorrow,' I shout at the pair of them as they walk off towards Bagdale.

Only Chloe turns. She waves.

I walk to the yard and knock. Daniel opens the door. The smell of cooking is in the air and I feel hungry, but first things first.

'Turn around and don't look,' I tell him.

I strip off, leaving all my uniform in a pile on the door mat.

'Can you open the washing machine door?' I ask.

He wanders off to the kitchen, looks me up and down as I come in.

'Don't even think about it. I have to shower. To decontaminate.'

'I can help you with that.'

'No. You can't.'

'Food's ready in ten,' he calls as I run up the stairs, careful not to touch anything.

I feel better after a shower. Daniel has made shepherd's pie.

'Have you been out?' I ask, drying my hair with a towel.

'Only to the shops.'

'Where's the scravir compass?'

He shrugs.

'It was on the table,' I say.

'I haven't moved anything.'

For some reason I don't believe him.

'Just tell me, Daniel. If they're out there, I'd rather know.'

'How was the hospital?'

'Intense. Scary. Everyone in special suits, masks and visors, like one of those Netflix dystopia series. They're saying there will be tens of thousands of deaths. It will be worse tomorrow.'

'Tomorrow?'

'They've told us three days on then four days off. But on the days off we have to do our training on-line.'

'No weekends?'

'One day off at weekends. Sundays. I handed your blood sample in, by the way. You won't believe who I met at the hospital.'

'Dr Albu.'

I obviously look surprised and irritated.

'Just a guess,' he admits, 'but, to be honest, there's no one else I could possibly know at Scarborough Hospital.'

'Smart alec.'

He smiles back. 'So you're one of our national heroes!'

'I don't feel heroic.'

'I'll be your in-house staff. Catering to your every need.' He bows.

'Sounds nice. Dubious, dodgy, but nice.'

'I learned about the house,' he says. 'Found another exit door.'

'Where?'

'No big deal. Hidden behind that bookcase in the basement. I think the cottages are all connected. It was in the old papers in that box. Rosie Seeker the woman who lived here. She was born here. Her mum was a tenant, way back in 1820 then, somehow, they made enough money to buy the whole property but there were still three families crammed into this house. She wrote some insane stuff about smugglers, fossils, and time travel.' He grins. 'Anyway, the bottom line is that there are tunnels connecting places in the old town to enable people to escape tax collectors and press gangs.'

'You made that mistake before.'

'What?'

'Dismissing the supernatural.'

'So now we're going to believe in time travel?'

'Not saying that. Glad you're feeling better. Does this door have a lock?'

'And two heavy duty sliding bolts.'

'Have you spoken with RJ or Karuna? What's happening in India?'

'Lockdown, same as here. RJ says there's been nothing on the news about the warehouse, but word on the street is that six bodies were found.'

'Including Lupei and Antoine Hoek?'

He shakes his head. 'One tall European was taken away in an ambulance but no one knows any more than that. Or if they do then they are not saying. How tall is your man Antoine?'

'Tall. So we don't know who they rescued.'

Daniel shrugs.

'The pie is really good,' I tell him. 'Maybe you can be my caterer. I need to get to bed, I'm shattered. Oh, no kissing or anything, I mustn't take the virus into the hospital. Or give you anything. Sorry.'

'Can't they test you?'

'Ward sister said it will be weeks before we all get regular tests. Have you been OK today, by the way?'

Maybe it's all those hours I spent watching Gert at work; I notice that Daniel says he's fine but takes just a little too long before answering. And the way he looks at me doesn't add up. And then he says he doesn't think a walk is a good idea.

'How long are they going to ask you to work in the hospital?'

'I don't know. No one knows anything or, if they do, they're not saying.'

I do get it; he's travelled halfway round the world to be with me and within like a day of finally getting our stuff together we are being pulled apart. I get it. I am as annoyed off as he is but what can we do?

At eleven I say I need to sleep and he watches me go.

'I love you.' he says.

I nod and walk upstairs alone. Those three little words ...

Six and a half hours later I see him again as I leave the house. He has emptied the washing machine and put my clothes out to dry and is asleep on the sofa. He wakes up as I open the front door.

'I'll message you at lunchtime,' I say and blow him a kiss.

'I'll get a second key cut,' he says, climbing off the sofa to lock the door behind me.

Why is there a kitchen knife on the floor beside his shoes?

Day Two at the hospital is Day One on steroids. More chaos and pain. People's lives being crushed like a ball of paper. 168 deaths yesterday across the UK. 2,885 more positive tests for Covid-19. Spiralling out of control.

I am in awe of the ward sister. In the frenetic foaming tide of fear that threatens to engulf us all, she is as strong as the keystone on a bridge, steadying the whole team.

'Leave it, Tiffany. I need you over here. Well done with Linda, she is at peace now. I'll do that, Kate. You go and have your break. Ten minutes, love.'

It's raining. Only six of us eating our sandwiches in the prefab at one o'clock. Today we are less defensive. Everyone looks everyone in the eye. Lauren didn't show up at the station this morning. As the bus set off I was sneering, then I grew up. We are tiny cogs but we are part of a team and she's at home feeling rubbish.

My phone goes off. A message from Antoine on his dark

web email account. He is in a hospital in Rotterdam. It is such a relief. I tell him Daniel and I are safe in Whitby. Bare bones, nothing more, I imagine he will want to be in touch when he is out of hospital.

It is late afternoon when Ivanna finds me. Dog tired. I probably look the same.

'Sample went off. Should hear tomorrow,' she tells me. 'I haven't forgotten. We double-check.'

'Double-check?'

'Strange result. But no conclusion jumping, please. Everyone works so hard and mistakes are made. How are you feeling, Tiffany? It is hard on wards?'

'I'm OK. We have ...'

'Dr Albu, could I borrow you for a moment?'

Ward sister is already steering Ivanna away towards Jason in bed seven, the overweight young man with asthma. Another one losing the battle.

CHAPTER 61

Daniel is lying in the dark. Around him are tiny noises. Like someone scratching. He cannot move. He knows that. He cannot be comfortable. It is too late.

The sounds resonate like he is lying inside a large acoustic guitar. The rough surface snags beneath his fingerprints as he inhales and exhales.

Trapped.

'Please, help me.'

Did I say that?

No.

He cannot speak. So who is calling?

The moment overwhelms him. Tears slipslide the curve of his cheeks, water flowing over a rock towards a precipice where plants cling to the rockface, trembling in the spray.

No, that's wrong. The trembling is inside him. His frozen limbs are crawling with activity just below the skin, like dozens of little children wriggling under a quilt.

Not children.

Leeches.

Nothing good.

Detritus. Leftovers. But why?

You know why.

Do I?

Not done to you, done by you.

He is a thief. Why has he done these unspeakable things?

I am helping people.

Helping people? You are grotesque.

Organs glistening in mucus. A still life festival of flesh in browns and pinks and sulphurous yellows, heaving blindly over each other like maggots in a tin.

There is Tiffany, running for dear life while he struggles to break free, knee-deep in letters, words, and formulas. What rules? What jumbled languages are pawing him?

Creierul anticilor. Go with the flow.

Oh I get it! This is a dream.

But he doesn't get to wake up.

He is in a tuk-tuk. The driver is huge, long white hair tumbling halfway down his back. He bends his head to stop it piercing the roof as the rusting three-wheeler thunders along the kerb, throwing dust into the faces of poor children gathered by the roadside, playing chess.

Now he is running on Henrietta Street, his feet sinking into the cobbles.

A tuk-tuk packed with scravir is drawing closer. He needs a barricade. A force field. But it is too late.

He is falling.

Daniel wakes up on the floor in the cottage, having fallen off the sofa in his sleep. A sharp pain in his shoulder. He rolls over and finds the handle of the bread knife beneath him. He put it there in the paranoid small hours, to defend himself from an imagined imminent attack.

Frightened, he sits up, lifts his t-shirt. Looks at his belly.

Nothing.

Normal.

No, not normal.

Nothing visible on the surface but very far from normal.

He is wracked with guilt. If Tiffany is going to be working all day every day and sleeping alone at night, if she is now safe from harm, then why is he here? He can only bring her danger. Might as well leave.

You're just pissed off because you can't sleep with her.

No, that's not it.

Well, it is a little, but that's not her fault or his.

He is happy, the girl he has loved from afar, the one person he has ever wanted to impress, has accepted him as he is.

That's not the whole truth, is it?

He parks that thought. It is immediately replaced by another; the memory of wishing, wishing, wishing his mum was there for all those years at school; wishing he might impress her and somehow persuade her not to find him boring. And not leave home. That endless dream where he wakes up and finds her there, smiling conspiratorially as they plan a silly prank on dad, like hiding a pickled onion in his breakfast cereal.

They did do that, he remembers now.

He sees his mother's face, beautiful as the moon as she sings *Nani nani puisor, nani nani puisor*. Slow and gentle. Water lapping a lakeside. He must be three or four years old. That moment makes him feel whole and safe. The whole world is wonderful and pure and true, and love stretches from one end of the universe to the other.

But she is gone.

She died.

He knows that now.

So why was the Dutch policeman, Gert Muyskens, bringing up Mum being Romanian?

Winding Dad up, backing him into a corner.

What had any of it got to do with him?

Thor Lupei.

Gert said he was looking for me; it was Lupei he was after.

Now Gert has vanished, according to Tiffany, and Lupei is still out there. Daniel saw Lupei fall into the burning pit onto the piles of burning bodies. And yet there he was in Delhi. Is Lupei immortal?

Daniel climbs to his feet, feels dizzy and sits down again. Brain fog. Jet lag? Is he coming down with something? Has he caught the virus? He switches on the TV and allows a silly cartoon to wash over him. Half an hour later, he tries standing up again, feels better, decides to go for a walk.

It is raining. He found an anorak hanging in a wardrobe in one of the bedrooms. With the hood up he is anonymous to the curtain twitchers. He climbs the 199 steps and heads out past the Abbey and onto the road that leads towards Hawsker, the rain pattering on his hood. He has no plan. To his right, over the low hedges, open fields stretch on for ever. At the top of the hill the fields are cram packed with row upon row of empty static caravans, end on, perched on tiny wheels, blank windows facing the road like big eyes, like abandoned fledglings awaiting rescue.

The walk and fresh air clear his head. Two gulls drift overhead. Wind rattles the hood of his anorak. When he reaches the turning on the left, he takes it without thinking and retraces his steps until he is ... forty months ago ...

... on Farview Farm.

The place has hardly changed. Paint is flaking on the door of the farmhouse where a wife kept a husband's body for weeks. The chimneys have collapsed to leave leprous stumps in the roofline. The tents in the field, where two campers died, are gone. The caravan beside which a policeman died has been moved to the side of the barn, where it decomposes slowly, its once white walls now green with lichen and moss.

Here, in a place he never expected to see again, Daniel is nineteen again, standing in the damp lacklit middle of nowhere, his belly full of chips bought from the girl in the shop by the harbour. The girl who tried to dissuade him from coming here.

He crosses the yard, over the cattle grid. At the far corner of the field he finds the spot between an outhouse and a hedge where he pitched his pop-up tent. Dead grass fills the hole in the hedge where he crawled through to get a better phone signal and almost fell over the cliff edge to his death.

Back in the farmyard he remembers the black double

decker bus that brought him here and that first conversation with the driver, a certain Thor Lupei. In his mind, Daniel hears the fire in the yard, sees the skulls gleaming in the flames. The outhouse with the mangy dog. The echoing rooms of the farmhouse. The large barn in which a jumbled mass of half a dozen naked and painfully emaciated figures, the scravir, crawled over each other in the lacklight like crabs scuttling around a deep-sea vent.

It is daylight now but he will not enter any of the buildings. Daniel senses that Farview is not dead. The farm is sleeping. Waiting for a sucker to cross a threshold.

What happened to the syringe gun that the scravir hunter Emile Noir gave him? He gave it to Tiffany. Does she still have it? Daniel takes the compass he stole from Lupei's office out of his pocket.

Tiffany was right, he did hide the compass.

To stop her worrying.

He lifts the lid and releases the catch to set the crow needle free. It points north. Daniel walks towards the large barn and, once inside, presses the black spot. The crow turns, searching ... never settling. Which is a relief. The barn is empty.

Then he has a dangerous idea.

He leaves the barn, puts the compass on the ground, presses the spot again and takes three steps back. The crow turns randomly for a moment then swings purposefully and decisively ...

... and stops.

It's pointing straight at him.

Daniel looks over his shoulder ... but he knows ...

There is nothing behind him.

He lunges, grabs the compass and sinks it in his pocket.

Hiding what he has just seen.

As he walks away between the rusting gates, Farview sighs.

Some time later, back in the cottage via a detour to the supermarket, Daniel cooks a meal. Dhal and coconut rice; she'll like that. He also bought himself some new clothes, warm stuff suited to the frozen north. His wet clothes drip onto the shower tray upstairs.

His phone beeps.

15:06 Message from RioJman
Dan my man! How's it hanging?
Shutdown Shangri-la here in Del. Only
27 deaths in country of 1.3 billion but
we are having full lockdown. 1000s of
migrant workers waiting in bus stations
or walking for days to get home.

Since we can't work and no one will play
chess with me ... I've been looking again
at your old manuscript (still have snaps)
Dig this. Those pages with weird letters.
It's GOTHIC. I swear!!! Didn't know
Gothic is being an actual language until
now :-) Did you?

I am guessing it's a cipher. My university
buddy, Gopal, a prof of linguistics and
thick thack boffin is promising to help.
How amazing is that?!! Love and
blessings. Karuna says hi.

JPG

𐍃𐌰𐌹𐌷𐌲𐌹𐍈𐍈𐌰𐌽𐍃𐌷𐌿𐌽𐌰𐌰𐌽𐍃𐌹𐍈
𐌹𐌽𐌽𐌰𐍈𐍂𐌴𐍃𐌹𐌽𐌰𐌲𐌽𐌰𐍆𐌴𐍃𐌲𐌹𐌰
𐌲𐌰𐌽𐌰𐌰𐌽𐍃�²𐌰𐌷𐌸𐌰𐍂𐍈𐍃𐌸𐌴𐌷𐌰

It takes Daniel a moment to process what RJ is talking about.

The pages he stole from the castle. The pages from Thor Lupei's book. Daniel hasn't thought about them since showing them to RJ two years ago. Since then they've sat in the back pocket of his backpack, in a sealed plastic envelope. If RJ hadn't been probing for some backstory one drunken evening, having won the right to ask a personal question after thrashing Daniel at a game of chess, the vellum pages would have stayed hidden, unseen and unremarked. RJ asked what was in Daniel's bag. Why did he keep it either close to him or locked in a safe ever since they first met in the homeless refuge in Camden? That was his question. So Daniel had shown him.

The lists of names and addresses meant even less to RJ than to Daniel, but the pages of weird letters had fascinated him. RJ loves puzzles. Blind drunk, he declared it must be a code and bragged he could crack the cipher and change the course of history.

As you do.

Roll on two years ... RJ is busy and Daniel is conflicted. He senses that Lupei wants the pages back and won't stop until he has them. They are a magnet. Daniel thought of destroying them, burning them as Jonah Tallman, the Rasta, would have done in the garage. That he has not done so owes a great deal to a nagging suspicion that the pages have a mystical power. After all, they came from a room where carved wooden animals and a table came to life and tried to kill him and, deep down, Daniel suspects he will not be free until Lupei's book is reassembled and whole.

He retrieves the black bin liner he has hidden in the freezer, extracts the sealed plastic envelope, opens it and spreads the vellum pages across the coffee table. His head is throbbing again so, with the food ready, he downs a couple of paracetamol and sits down to peruse Lupei's book.

He ignores the lists of addresses and focuses on the blocks of strange letters, page after page without any form of break. He searches *Gothic language letters* on his phone. RJ is right, the markings are the same! A language invented in the 4th century by a real Goth, a geezer called Wulfila; the name means Little Wolf. Wulfila created the alphabet from a mixture of Greek letters and ones he invented in order to translate the Bible from Greek into Gothic so that he could evangelise among the Goths in the lands north of the River Danube. Apparently the language died at some point in the sixth century and disappeared from human consciousness until the seventeenth century when a partial copy of a Gothic bible turned up in Sweden.

Why would Lupei's books contain Gothic? Surely he was never a priest?

So you're assuming he was alive in the sixth century?

No, I'm not

Yes, you are.

Daniel parks the issue of how old Thor Lupei is; nothing good comes from dwelling on stuff that is beyond rational understanding. He concentrates instead on the letters of the text in front of him, the letters in the jpeg RJ sent him.

$$\text{sᴧIhɣI𝜓𝜓ᴧNShUNᴧᴧNSI𝜓}$$
$$\text{INNᴧ𝜓ᴚ℺SINᴧɣNᴧϝ℺SɣIᴧ}$$
$$\text{ɣᴧNᴧᴧNSGᴧhΘᴧᴚ𝜓SΘЄhᴧ}$$

Is that one long word or random letters? Is RJ right? Could it be a cipher?

It is raining again, the room now so dark he needs the light on. Daniel carefully copies the text onto a piece of paper and stares at it, hoping something will leap out at him.

He think he sees 'h', 'i', 'N', 'S' and 'E'.

And that's it. The rest of it might as well be ...

Maybe there is a Gothic dictionary online.

As it happens, there are several. But either they don't work or he doesn't know how to use them. Or both.

Daniel is scratching his head and feeling he should have worked harder at school when another message arrives.

> 16:54 Message from RioJman
> OH YEAH. Bow before masters of
> Cipherverse ... Gopal and I are storming
> brains and cracked 1st sentence! (see jpg)
>
> We spun a parallel text of the Codex
> Argenteus (only known book written in
> Gothic) through an AI prog. Cute.
>
> Translation: "Beware of dogs, inwardly
> they are ravenous wolves".
>
> So first base! but after that we think that
> your pages may just be letter soup. It's
> eating my brain! Thoughts?
> RJ
>
> JPG
> **𐍃𐌰𐌹𐌷𐍅𐌹𐌸 𐍅𐌰𐌽𐍃 𐌷𐌿𐌽𐌳𐌰𐌽𐍃**
> **𐌹𐌸 𐌹𐌽𐌽𐌰𐍅𐌸𐌴𐍉 𐍃𐌹𐌽𐌳**
> **𐍅𐌿𐌻𐌵𐍉𐍃 𐍅𐌹𐌻𐍅𐌰𐌽𐌳𐌰𐌽𐍃**

Daniel replies:

> 17.01 You replied
> You are King of the Blues! What can
> I say? There are wolves near Lupei's

castle. Maybe it's a poem or old Viking
saga. Don't know. Leave it to you
eggheads :-)

Tiffany worried Lupei escaped
warehouse and coming to kill us. Better
for you (but not for us) if he does. Delhi
slums needs scravir like a smack in the
head. Hi to Karuna. 8C here. Freezing!
No fish & chips bcz of lockdown. Covid
sucks.

Staring at the letters, even when reorganised by RJ, doesn't help. It's just not Daniel's skill set. His mind wanders. He searches *guitars* online. While he hasn't used his time in India to get rich, he has put money by and can easily afford a good guitar. A Gibson ES-335 perhaps. Then he can be cutting his chops in the day while she is working. Who knows, one day, when Covid has burned itself out, he may even get to do a few gigs, join a band ... Trouble is where to have it delivered without giving everything away? Maybe Tiffany can come up with a plan.

He needs to buy her something too.

Avoid beauty stuff.

He still feels terrible. He wasn't telling her she wasn't perfect. In a world where millions of people fiddle about with changing how they look, Tiffany amazes him. He has never seen her wear makeup. She is beautiful as she is.

The trouble is that he has spent three years catering to the vulnerable, the insecure, and people who believe that changing the shape of your nose, inflating your lips, lasering your armpit hair or turning your belly button from an outie to an innie, is the secret to happiness.

To be fair, for every individual who paid for cosmetic

tweaking by Daniel the clinic were able to treat half a dozen people with real needs. Children with harelips, facial tumours, acid attacks. And the reconstructive work was not always by Daniel, sometimes the clinic would sponsor a team in another city. He never had a chance to tell her that because he had already put his foot in it.

Anyway, the bottom line is that he needs to make the effort to know Tiffany better, to listen, to understand what makes her tick. Maybe it isn't a thing she wants but an experience.

And maybe he should try talking with his dad.

Tomorrow.

On a whim, Daniel finds the compass, opens it, presses the black spot. Without hesitation the crow needle points at him.

He slams down the lid and thinks where to hide it; he definitely does not want Tiffany scared out of her wits. It has to be broken, after all he is not a scravir, but why should she believe him?

At seven forty-five there is a knock on the door.

'It's blowing a bloody gale. Rain's horizontal over the bridge. Why haven't you closed the curtains?'

The smell of fresh sea air enters the room with her.

'You're early.'

'Please close the curtains, open the washing machine door and face the wall.'

'It's already open.'

'The *other* wall, wazzock.'

'OK,' he sighs.

'They took pity on us. But we have to go in tomorrow,' Tiffany strips off on the door mat.

'I got you a door key,' he tells her. 'There's a place on Baxtergate ...'

She walks through to the kitchen, shoves her clothes in the machine and runs upstairs.

'What are you cooking? Smells good.'

'You're beautiful.'

'Oh! You noticed?' she laughs.

'Are you hungry?'

'Having a shower,' she shouts. 'I'll be down.'

Tiffany loves the curry and she is happy Daniel wants to buy a guitar. It can be delivered to the bin store by her flat on Cliff Street; she'll warn Tina. And she'll think about an experience she'd like to have, though the only experience advertised in Whitby is the Dracula thing and she saw that when she was twelve.

'Maybe we can create our own experience,' he says suggestively.

'As long as we wear masks.'

'O ... K. You mean like Zorro and Touka Kirishima?'

'What?'

'They're characters who wear masks. Just trying to make your suggestion less weird.'

'*Less* weird?'

His eyes drift up towards the bedrooms.

'Hold your horses, Zorro.'

'That's the Lone Ranger, not Zorro, and it's 50 years before we were even born.

She yawns. 'Whatever.'

'Oh, I thought of a joke while I was walking about. What do you call a gazelle with a Dracula complex?'

'Go on.'

'Vlad the Impala.'

She winces playfully and throws a cushion at him, then yawns again.

'I'm jiggered, love, and I'm up at five. Sorry.'

'Don't be sorry. I am proud of you. I wish I could be useful.'

'I'm not sure they could handle your talents in a hospital. We need to have a proper talk about all that, by the way, and I'm not talking about your comedy routine.'

'No worries.'

'Tomorrow evening?'

'Masks on or off?'

She shakes her head pityingly. 'Did that compass turn up?'

He shakes his head. 'Do you still have that syringe gun? The one that Emile Noir gave me?'

'I'd forgotten about that.'

'Was it empty?'

'No. There were three bullets left. Well not bullets really, were they? More like little glass vials.'

'So do you have it?'

'It's somewhere in my room. In the flat.'

'Would Tina let you have it?'

'It's mine.'

'I mean would she let you in to find it?'

'I don't think so. Why?'

'Just in case.'

Tiffany doesn't pursue it; she doesn't have to.

'Can you hear that wind?' she changes the subject. 'Sea'll be rough. You won't go to the pier tonight, will you?'

She goes up to bed. Daniel hopes she hasn't noticed the waves of pain engulfing him; he doesn't want to worry her. He needs something stronger than paracetamol; he's nauseous and feels his head might explode. When he is confident she must be asleep, he moves the coffee table, lies down on the floor and closes his eyes.

Meditation, concentration, relaxation.

I awaken creierul anticilor, the brain of the ancients. That which we understand we can control.

Daniel has now done this thousands of times. As he enters the trance, the centre of his brain lights up from within like a lighthouse shining over a dark storm-swept sea, as it did, under instruction, in the cave beneath Lupei's castle. It is no longer Lupei who steers proceedings as Daniel calms his body, balancing each and every muscle against its counterpart. The one that opens and the one that closes. The pairs of muscles in his forearms that open and close each of his fingers, the intercostal muscles, those servants that accompany his each and every breath. He feels his tongue, and the tight twisted ropes that hold his head. The opposing muscles that power his thumbs, his eyelids and cheeks and lips. And he puts all of these into balance to quieten them.

He inhabits his skin, the frontier between him and the rest of the universe. He feels the size of himself, his place in space and time.

Such things any ordinary mortal may do with practice but now Daniel moves on and feels his bones, his vital organs, his spleen, liver, stomach, bronchioles, inner ear and on until, in a state of meditation, he knows and experiences the totality of his physical self.

He feels the residue of all the material he has absorbed from others prior to disposing of them or relocating them in a third party. Fragments scattered through him like space dust. Fragments he must dispose of.

Since the brain cannot physically feel itself, Daniel focuses not on his grey matter but rather on the waves of energy that ripple back and forth within its structure like the light and colour that pulse through a cuttlefish.

Finally Daniel separates himself from everything that is not him and he lies there on the floor of a cottage in a yard in a small town beside a sea on a spinning sphere, no longer feeling the floor beneath his back, no longer hearing the wind and rain at the window, no longer feeling warmth or cold, nor light or dark, nor the passage of time.

And in that moment he finds what he has feared.

Hidden within him is something that is not him. Something that he has not chosen or put there.

He remembers another sentence that Lupei uttered in the

cave beneath his castle.

Mi ritrovai per una silva oscura, chè la diritta era smaritta.

Not Lupei's words but Dante's, from the Inferno, written hundreds of years ago.

I found myself in a shadowed forest for I had lost the path.

Daniel is that shadowed forest; confronting black corners within him that he cannot penetrate. As if he is inhabiting a house that contains a room without a door; something is squatting within him ... loitering, festering, ticking ...

Is that why the tiny crow compass needle turns and points accusingly? What does it see?

Unable to make further progress, Daniel slowly abandons his trance and returns to normality. The heating has switched off and the cottage is cooling. Rain slaps the windows. The wind swings a rusty sign back and forth. Daniel nestles down on the sofa beneath a blanket and drifts off to fitful sleep.

He awakens to the sound of a closing door and immediately feels a crushing sense of foreboding.

Is something about to happen to Tiffany?

The opening curtains reveal a pale monochrome dawn. Flagstones slick with last night's rain. Has she already left? He runs upstairs calling her name.

The bedrooms are empty.

Daniel jumps into his clothes, his trainers, and leaves the house. A pain in his chest as he races down Church Street, Market Square, Sandgate.

No sign of her.

Over the swing bridge, smacked from the side by the gusting wind off the sea. Along New Quay Road towards the station. As he passes the lobster pots stacked on the quayside, he spots the minibus pulling away from the station forecourt and off up Bagdale. Daniel is too far away to attract the driver's attention or see how many people are on board. Hands on knees, he catches his breath. Towards the sea the light is a sick yellow grey.

An old man, tugging a reluctant terrier scowls from across the road as Daniel coughs.

'Get back inside,' the old man snarls. 'You'll kill us all.'

Daniel gives him the finger and heads back towards the swing bridge. Reaching it, he continues straight ahead, along St Ann's Staith. He wants to see the waves and, at this time of day, the chances of being stopped by the police must be zero.

The tide is loitering. Neither the Esk emptying itself into the sea, nor the sea flooding back up the river; the water hangs in the harbour with no particular place to go. Daniel reaches the amusement arcades on Pier Road and the gap between the whelk stalls.

Four people are standing in a row on the quayside staring across towards Henrietta Street and Tate Hill Sands.

At the top of the steps at the end of Tate Hill Pier are two police vehicles, light bars on their roofs flashing blue & red. But the spectators aren't looking at the police vans or the pier ... they are looking towards the beach.

YORKSHIRE COAST RADIO - REPORTS ARCHIVE

Interview Transcript: 28 MARCH 2020
DAVID LAMPHORNE Interviewer
SERGEANT JANE GRAYFORD North Yorkshire Police

LAMPHORNE
It's 7.05 on a grim slapcrashy drizzling grizzling mizzling Saturday
morning. Chucking it down so hard the rain's cracking flagstones in
Market Square. I kid you not. If you're warm in bed, stay there. After
the news we ask why are chips our favourite food. Don't pretend
you prefer bulgar wheat! But now, more on this morning's story
about the yacht that broke up on Tate Hill Sands during last night's
storm. Sergeant Jane Grayford, Hello. I believe police have sealed
off the beach?

GRAYFORD
Yes. We're not anticipating any inconvenience to the public since
the lockdown means that Tate Hills Sands is closed, but we are
keen to hear from anyone who heard or saw anything out of the
ordinary between 2am and 4am this morning.

LAMPHORNE
Where was the boat from? Was it leaving the marina?

GRAYFORD
No. The swing bridge and marina are closed, because of lockdown.

LAMPHORNE
So this vessel came in from the sea?

GRAYFORD
Er, yes, that does seem the obvious conclusion.

LAMPHORNE

Sorry, stupid question! So what happened?

GRAYFORD

We aim to give a fuller statement later but it is likely the boat was badly damaged as it attempted to enter the harbour. Last night saw rough seas with a very heavy swell. Strong northerly winds were creating five metre waves at the harbour entrance, which is not that unusual here in Whitby. Local skippers can negotiate safe passage if they have to but for an inexperienced crew these conditions are treacherous.

LAMPHORNE

There was a similar tragedy about fifteen years back, I recall.

GRAYFORD

That's right, in 2007. Though that was in broad daylight. It appears that last night the vessel drifted into the seaward side of the east breakwater extension and suffered extensive damage. There are also signs of a vessel smashing against the breakwaters within the harbour entrance, possibly damaging her below the waterline. Our teams are working to establish a causal link with the wrecked yacht.

LAMPHORNE

So you believe that she limped in from the sea as far as Tate Hill Sands where she was abandoned.

GRAYFORD

We are not in the speculation business, I'm afraid.

LAMPHORNE

Understood. Any sign of the crew? Any survivors? Is there a risk of the coronavirus having been brought ashore?

GRAYFORD

I'm sorry, there is very little more I can say. No bodies have been recovered from the sea as yet so whoever was on board will probably have made it safely to shore.

LAMPHORNE

This is not a small vessel. Twenty metres long. There could have been have a dozen people on board. A party that drifted off-course perhaps? How far can a boat like that travel?

GRAYFORD

No comment. But people can rest assured that we are working as quickly as we can to identify the owners and establish the circumstances that led to this boat ending up on Tate Hill Sands. As I said, the beach is closed. We are putting measures in place to keep the public away from the vessel.

LAMPHORNE

Lastly, someone on Henrietta Street has reported to the news team here that shortly after the vessel broke up on the sands in the small hours, they saw an individual handcuffed or shackled to the wheel of the vessel. He was, and I quote 'shouting for help at the top of his voice before suddenly going silent'. Can you confirm or deny whether a body was discovered shackled in this way?

GRAYFORD

I suggest that someone may need to cut back on late night overconsumption of alcohol and Gothic literature, Mr Lamphorne. We are not in the nineteenth century and this is a serious incident.

Lamphorne

(Laughing) Touché. And on that note, over to Kathy for the traffic news. Sergeant Grayford, thank you.

CHAPTER 62

Daniel kills the radio and slumps on a chair. The police may not know why or how the boat has arrived in Whitby, or who was on board, but he knows.

> 7.13 To Tiffany Harrek You said:
> Hi, call me ASAP. Smth has happnd.

Where is Lupei? In a house on Church Street? Hiding in one of the closed shops? In one of the yards? How many are with him? Are there scravir?

Daniel checks his phone. Nothing.

Answer your bloody phone, Tiffany!

What if he has already caught her? Maybe she never reached the minibus. Maybe scravir are out there scouting the streets. Who were those four people on the quayside?

Daniel runs to the front room and looks out into the yard.

Empty.

He draws the curtains shut.

We are so stuffed.

I should have killed him at the warehouse.

Yeah, you can kill Thor Lupei? Dream on.

I had him.

Like you had him when you pushed him into a pit full of burning corpses? That went well, didn't it?

How has Daniel imagined anywhere is safe? He has dragged Tiffany into a nightmare. He is as dumb as the sorcerer's apprentice stumbling blindly about in his master's magic cape. Daniel runs upstairs, presses himself against the wall, peers down into the yard. Empty.

The confidence of three years in India has evaporated.

Come on, Tiffany, check your bloody phone.

What if the boat has nothing to do with Lupei?

Don't be dumb.

He surprised Lupei when he threw the energy of forty people at him but Lupei won't make the same mistake twice and, in any event, how do you assemble forty people in a town under lockdown? How can he protect Tiffany? As soon as Lupei has killed him he will do what he likes with Tiffany. Who will stop him? The police?

Daniel finds the number for Whitby police station. After pressing a succession of buttons and being repeatedly assured that his call is important, he gets through to the duty officer.

'I'd like to report some weird-looking men walking down Church Street early this morning,' Daniel says. 'Really skinny. Three of them, walking together. They were holding knives. Do you have CCTV cameras?'

'Can I take a few details first please?'

'What for?'

'I need to know where you are. Are you in danger? What is your name, Sir?'

'I'm not important,' Daniel insists. 'They may be from that boat that broke up on the beach last night.'

'I understand, just need some personal details, if that's OK.'

Daniel cuts the call and curses.

Immediately, his phone vibrates in his hand. He drops it.

07.43 Message from RioJman

DAN MY MAN! omg. Been up 30hrs without
a break with my house genius Gopal.
Prepare for mindmash!!

Turns out your Gothic manuscript contains
a text in Latin hidden with a transposition

cipher. How funky is that? Gopal studied
Gudhapada and Gudhavarna and the
kamasutra ciphers for his maths degree. (he
has 5 degrees!)

Attached pdf. As you see, this is a fragment
from a longer text. Some pages are burned
at one end. When did that happen? Anyway,
done our best. (If Lupei wrote this it would
make him at least 720 years old!)
Hope it is useful, bro.
Attachment: gothtrans.pdf

Daniel downloads the attachment but isn't sure he wants
to look at it. He paces back and forth. When he and Tiffany
are captured, as they surely will be, there will be no passers-
by to intervene, no witnesses, no police.

Will the police check their CCTV?

Daniel curses himself again for coming to Whitby with
Tiffany. He should have left her by the swing bridge and
driven away. Left her safe. If he hadn't been here she would
have found a friend to stay with somewhere, instead of
breaking into a cottage.

It has taken Lupei literally just a couple of days to find
them and to enter the UK, despite a global lockdown. Lupei
has already used Tiffany to get to him and won't hesitate to
do the same again. How has he found them so quickly?

Overwhelmed by questions he cannot answer, Daniel sits
down and opens the file RJ has sent, looking for inspiration.

... must remain hidden. Powers temporal and spiritual
condemn the knowledge herein and ... cursed by the
fallacious belief that all which can be known is already
known, the world swims in ignorance. Who shall know

the body's fabric and how defects may be treated to prolong life?

History has thus far understood nothing. The Leechbooks of Bald prescribe a posset of ale with saxifrage and parsley, or a supper of roast starling for those suffering a failing kidney ...

... prescribes shaking a dung beetle while shouting "Remedium fac ... ventris dolorem". Ancient Egyptian scholars believed kidneys to be advisors, the right giving good advice and the left bad advice; such advice deciding the fate of their owner's soul in the afterlife.

Galen claimed the liver surrounds the stomach to keep it warm and ... icenna declared the liver made of blood and not solid at all. Still others believe it the source of melancholia and sadness.

I have discovered all these theorems to be false. Both ... and liver are vital to a functioning and healthy body. And I have proved these members may be replanted from one body to another.

... this I taught Mondino de Luzzi years ago at his dissections at the University of Bologna in 1315 though for obvious reasons, we did not speak openly of such things .... fear of torture and death.

The replanting of body parts is not new. The Egyptians took elements from one body and ... and details were shown to me, transcribed on a papyrus stored in the library at Serapeum in Alexandria, prior to the great fire of AD391.

> ... the explanations here detail my modus operandi and
> how I replant members, natural, spiritual and generative,
> from one body to another, and ...
> ... with that vital force I employ for such undertakings,
> that others may one day learn and lift this world out of
> the dark ages. A veil of secrets is ...

Daniel is barely registering what he is reading; the dangers out on the streets of Whitby feel far more pressing than Lupei's 600-year-old anatomy lesson. At the same time he knows that the arcane skills he has himself been practising in Delhi are the result of Thor Lupei's experiments in a distant past where people thought stars to be lights painted on a ceiling, and where even educated people had no idea what the heart or the brain were or how they worked.

The contradictions of transplanting organs and flesh from one body to another without tissue rejection still makes no sense to Daniel even though that is exactly what he has been doing in the slums of Delhi. Hidden within Lupei's account must be the explanations for acts that are as incomprehensible in the present as they were unintelligible a thousand years ago.

His head fuzzy, he lies down and tries to sleep. It is nearly midday when he awakens, dehydrated and nauseous.

He grabs his phone, still no reply from Tiffany.

Having grabbed a glass of water from the kitchen, he forces himself to carry on reading the cipher translation.

> ... and I was helping the man who had been stabbed in
> the head on the battlefield when I learned more of the
> brain's mysteries.

> Aristotle wrongly believed the ...brain a device for
> cooling the blood but as I replanted matter from the head
> of a nearby cadaver into the head of the injured man his

behaviour changed. He stopped shouting and crying and became quiet. By further work I saw the man compliant and receptive to instruction, and was even able to make him play music of my bidding on a lute abandoned close by on the field. This I achieved by imagining myself playing the instrument and transmitting same to his compliant brain.

... though unable to speak, he became my guard and defended me from attack twice in subsequent days before being ...

... many years I have since learned to shape servants to my choosing, at first by wielding a knife but now by the power of my mind. Moving matter within the skull proved clumsy. Entering the mind by that process I have described elsewhere as creierul anticilor, that I use to move matter from one body to another, is more effective and enables me to tame the spirit and create slaves that offer their obedience to my will. I shall now set out how ...

A crash in the yard. Daniel leaps to his feet and races upstairs to peer down from a first-floor window. A wheelie bin is on its side, it contents splayed about like intestines.

But the yard is empty.

Daniel snaps. He cannot remain cooped up, a quivering victim waiting for the front door to be smashed down. He has to fight back and it will be easier in daylight.

Sending Tiffany yet another message, he grabs a knife from the kitchen, tucks it in the pocket of his anorak and heads outside.

Church Street is dead. In a bookshop window a sign reads:

CLOSED SORRY

See you on the other side
one day soon we hope
Stay safe everyone :-)

No sign of the police, the squad cars have left Tate Hill. He takes the long way round, up Henrietta Street and down the ginnel between the houses to reach the beach.

It's an expensive-looking yacht some twenty metres long and lying on its port side. There's a gaping hole in the starboard bow. Deep scratches, as if gouged by the talons of a giant predator, run the length of the hull. The vessel is cordoned off with police tape, stapled to posts sunk in the sand.

POLICE - INCIDENT SCENE - KEEP OUT

DANGER - DO NOT ENTER

The yacht's name written across the stern is a little weird: *Deter Me*. But then boats do have weird names.

He is not deterred.

Having glanced round to check he is alone, Daniel ducks under the tape, clambers over the broken gunwale and climbs aboard. The helm is a mess, tables and chairs overturned, the broken remains of an electric guitar, two navigation screens smashed and bent. Through the window he sees an open hatch on the foredeck. He makes his way along the outside of the vessel to peer inside.

A jumble of long boxes, like flight cases. Four of them. Three are empty, the lids floating in the seawater gathered on one side of the hold. The fourth box is damaged but the catches are still locked. Daniel drops down into the hold and crosses the steeply angled floor. He releases the catches, lifts the lid and lurches back.

The gaunt face of a drowned scravir stares up at him. Little more than skin and bones in a black t-shirt and trousers, the creature's hands are reaching up for help that never came.

Why have the police not removed this box? Did they assume it was empty?

Tempting as it is to continuing searching below deck, it's not necessary. Daniel has the confirmation he needs; Lupei is in Whitby. He clambers up out of the hold. There is movement across the harbour; two people on the quayside have seen him and are gesticulating in his direction. Jumping down onto the sand, Daniel hurries towards the steps that lead back up to Henrietta Street. He feels sicker than ever.

CHAPTER 63

Scarborough Hospital

'Are you OK?'

'It's just ... ' Tiffany is struggling. 'I were hoping ...'

'I understand. We all hope for best and we are all tired.' Ivanna's eyes smile sympathetically. 'Come downstairs, we sit outside.'

'I'm needed on the ward and ...'

'I have spoken with ward sister. They are letting all students go home early. You finish at two o'clock. Come.'

The two women sit at opposite ends of a bench in the garden area between outpatients and A&E. Ivanna slides the envelope containing the test results along the bench towards Tiffany. The sky is dark as a shroud and the air smells of rain.

'It sound crazy but you remember sample from Thor Lupei?'

Tiffany is shattered, physically and emotionally. 'It could be a mistake, couldn't it? Maybe they jumbled up a bunch of ...'

'No. I am sorry. Not mistake. I met you in café with Dutch policeman, Muyskens, with results of tests on Lupei blood. In Whitby. Remember?'

Tiffany nods dejectedly.

'Specialists calculate contributor DNA in blood sample from crime scene. How many people. They separate Y-chromosomal haplotypes and count ...'

'This says more than 200 different ...' Tiffany clutches the report.

'Yes, even worse than Lupei. Though all human. No wild animals or dogs in Daniel sample.'

Tiffany buries her face in her hands. 'Can he be cured?'

'There is something else,' Ivanna continues. 'Did Daniel meet Lupei recently?'

'Why?'

'Has Lupei attacked Daniel? Did Daniel tell you what happened to him in 2016? Have they met again?'

Tiffany drops her hands and stares despairingly at the Romanian doctor.

'There is Lupei DNA in Daniel, Tiffany. Lupei transplants organs. Could he have injected Daniel with something? Now or in past?'

Tiffany does not know where to begin. She is too far from the shore in water so deep her feet no longer reach the bottom. Who knows what Lupei did to Daniel when he kidnapped him during Whitby Goth Weekend? What just happened in India? What if Gert was right? What if Daniel is as bad or worse than Lupei? If she says the wrong thing will Daniel be arrested? Or hunted down like a mad dog?

'Yes, perhaps,' she says vaguely. 'How can I help him?'

'Talk with policeman. Talk with Gert Muyskens. He will find Europol files for Thor Lupei and ...' Seeing the expression on Tiffany's face, Ivanna stops.

'Gert were sacked from Europol years back,' Tiffany mumbles. 'And from the Rotterdam harbour police because he wouldn't give up about Thor Lupei. A few weeks back he went to Romania to catch or kill Lupei and now he's disappeared.'

A door opens and the ward sister sticks her head out.

'Now then, Tiffany. Minibus is waiting in the car park. Don't miss it and have a quiet day off. You've earned it. Thanks for all your hard work, love. See you Monday.'

Fifteen minutes later, Ivanna is alone in the garden, lost in thought, as the rain starts.

Tiffany scowls at the moors through the minibus window, a Krav Maga podcast on self-defence playing in her AirPods as they head northwards into the intensifying rain. Her heels are bobbing up and down. She's only just seen Daniel's message from this morning. And he hasn't responded to her reply.

On the podcast an American is talking excitedly about smashing your foot down on someone's knee to disable them while you bring the heel of your hand up hard under their chin. There's a link to a '*really cool video.*'

Maybe Lupei will never make it to Whitby. Maybe she is worrying over nothing.

But dealing with Daniel isn't going away. Was not telling Ivanna everything as stupid as not telling Gert everything?

She checks out the 'cool video' but halfway through her phone runs out of juice.

Tiffany is still mulling stuff over when the minibus pulls up in front of Whitby station. She and Chloe head off in opposite directions without a word, too shattered for pleasantries. It's just gone three o'clock.

The climb to Cliff Street is harder than usual; she is tired and soaked to the skin by the time she reaches Flowergate so she changes her mind, sod going to the flat. She'll collect the syringe gun later on. Back down the narrow ginnel towards Pier Road. Someone said a couple of chip shops have re-opened, with socially distanced queueing outside. She'll get fish and chips to cheer Daniel up.

'You're in luck, Tiff. I can give you a couple of shifts,' says the voice behind the fryers.

'Haven't come for a job, Dave. Just buying tea.'

'Shame. Half the team are pulling sickies. Someone told me they took all you students down Scarborough to work on the wards. You'll be safer here, love. We're getting perspex screens tomorrow.'

'Two large cod and chips, with curry sauce. I've a guest to feed.'

'Oh yes, who's that?'

'None of your business. And, in case you've forgotten, you're the one who told me to spread my wings and get a better job instead of pissing my life away in your chippy. *You only get one shot, love*, wasn't that it?'

'Ouch! Should have kept my big gob shut. Anyroad, can't blame me for trying. You want scraps?'

'Go on then.'

'That boat wrecked on Tate Hill Sands. It's like bloody Dracula all over again.'

'When?'

'Last night. In the storm. Don't they have news in bloody Scarborough?'

Dave even gives her a staff discount *for old times' sake*. He's all heart ... when he wants something.

The rain is easing off as Tiffany crosses the swing bridge.

There's an overturned wheelie bin in the yard; they'd best tidy up before rats come.

'I'm back! New key works, by the way. They let us out early. Brought you a surprise.' Tiffany puts her bags down by the door, closes the curtains, and starts stripping out of her uniform. 'Is the washing machine ready? Daniel? Are you there? You're not hiding somewhere to catch me in the buff, are you? Hey!'

There's a pile of papers on the coffee table. She wants to look at them but holds back. Shower first.

'This isn't fair!' she calls out.

Maybe he has gone out, in which case he won't be leaping out, laughing his head off. Tiffany sighs, and steps out of her underwear, double checks the front door and heads to the kitchen, her clothes in her arms.

The washing machine door is open, which is something. She shoves her laundry inside, squirts antiseptic gel on her hands and sets the machine running. Water starts to gurgle.

It's so dark outside. Tiffany plugs her phone in to charge

and is turning towards the light switch when she notices the vacuum cleaner by the fridge. The mop leaning against a chair. The pan and brush on the pedal bin.

The cupboard door is closed but a slither of light is escaping beneath it. Tiffany feels vulnerable. First things first, she must find some clothes. But then she is leaving the problem in front of her unresolved.

Whatever is or isn't happening in the basement she will not face it stark naked. She turns tail and runs out of the kitchen and up the stairs.

Maybe Daniel is asleep on one of the beds.

He isn't.

She forces herself to have a shower before finding clean clothes.

Back downstairs in the kitchen her phone is at 8%. No message from Daniel.

There is a muffled knocking sound coming from somewhere.

Probably the washing machine.

She presses her ear to the washing machine. Nothing but gentle gurgling.

A kitchen knife from the drawer.

She approaches cautiously, worried the cupboard door will fly open and ...

And what?

The cupboard is empty. The light is coming from beneath the trapdoor. Her phone now has 10% charge; it will have to do. She lifts the trapdoor quickly in one movement. Light pours up from below. The thump thump thump is louder now.

Leaning forward she can see down into part of the room below. Stuff strewn across the floor: books, crockery, boxes.

'Daniel?'

The space echoes back at her.

With the low ceiling, you have to go feet first into a space you cannot properly see. She imagines her feet being ripped off the steps as someone drags her down into the basement.

'Wait for Daniel,' she tells herself out loud.

No, waiting is dumb. He could be anywhere. In a few hours it will be night and ... She climbs down the steps, her heart in her throat.

He said he found a door behind the bookcase. The stuff scattered all over the floor has come from the now empty bookcase that has been pulled to one side. The banging is coming from the dank darkness beyond the open doorway. Her phone torch reveals a curtain of broken cobwebs.

Knife in one hand, torch in the other, Tiffany crosses the threshold.

CHAPTER 64

Rotterdam
3pm, 28th March 2020

'Please stay in bed, Mr Hoek. Your body needs time to recover.' The nurse looks despairingly at Antoine Hoek's wife, Marijke. 'We have a global health emergency, the hospital is very busy. I need your husband to do as I ask. He may only have bumps and bruises but until all the tests are completed we cannot release him.'

Hoek looks at Marijke and shakes his head. She and the nurse are wearing full PPE: gowns, gloves, goggles, hair covering, and type IIR surgical masks.

'It is like being in a science fiction movie,' Antoine says through his face mask. 'I am tired and aching but otherwise good. I don't need 24-hour care and I don't want to catch Coronavirus virus sitting in hospital.'

The nurse's pager bleeps. 'I am wanted on the ward. I can accompany you to the lift, Mrs Hoek. I will call you if further visits are allowed, the rules change every few hours at the moment.'

Antoine waves goodbye to Marijke and watches the two women leave. He counts to ten and jumps out of bed. His clothes are in the cupboard. In a minute he is dressed.

It is his lucky day. In the corridor, just metres from his room, is a trolley laden with PPE kit. With a full face mask, gown and hair cover, he is unrecognisable as he makes his way through the hospital to the entrance. Through the revolving doors and out into the fresh air where he dumps the gown and hair cover in a flower bed and hops on a tram going towards the Europol headquarters. At the entrance he remembers that he doesn't have his pass card. He rings the buzzer. The security guard glances at his CCTV screen and turns away. Antoine rips off his face mask and tries again.

'Lucas, hi, it's me. I've been an idiot,' he says to the video screen on the intercom. 'No pass. Open the door please.'

'Sorry, sir. I didn't recognise you. I cannot let you without a ...'

'Contact Hervé.' Struggling to stay calm.

'Monsieur Seznec isn't in today.'

'Then call him on his mobile and tell him it is a code black request. Do it now,' he barks.

The screen goes blank. Antoine drums his left shoe up and down as he waits.

'Antoine, I thought you were in hospital.' Hervé's voice is tinny on the intercom. He sounds like he has had a few drinks.

'I was.'

'Are you sure that ...'

'Absolutely sure. I'll ring you from my desk.'

'Good. That gives me time to finish my lunch. Lucas, let Mr Hoek into the building.'

Antoine takes the lift instead of the stairs. From his office he calls Hervé who cannot understand a word he is saying because of the full face mask Lucas has instructed him to wear while in the building. Antoine dumps the mask in the paper bin beside the desk and briefs Hervé on what he is about to do. His second call is to Marijke to let her know where he is. And the third is to Winders.

No answer.

Next stop the armoury, mask back on and with the new pass card collected from reception, then back outside and onto another tram. He would have loved a coffee but it will have to wait.

Fifteen minutes later he is in Zoetermeer in front of Winders' modern villa. No car on the drive but Antoine doesn't know if Winders owns one. He leans on the doorbell then leans again. Has Winders guessed that the game is up and fled? Antoine walks round the back. No sign of anyone inside. He smashes a window and lets himself in.

The rooms have the look of showrooms copied out of an IKEA warehouse. Antoine half-expects to turn a corner and find several rows of shopping trolleys and a tall stack of catalogues. Winders lives alone and clearly doesn't rely on his salary to feed his expensive tastes. In the master bedroom a fitted wardrobe is packed with expensive suits, and orgy of silk ties, and several dozen pairs of expensive leather shoes.

One of the bedrooms has been converted into an office. Shelves stacked with ring binders, arranged by colour, run along one wall. A floor-to-ceiling window looks out on a park and cycle path. On the desk is a large iMac. Antoine jogs the mouse and the screen comes to life.

Password.

Winders is not a creative thinker.

Antoine types *iMac* and he is in.

Google maps is zoomed in on an apartment block in Delft.

'Shit!'

Antoine races out of the house and back to the road where he hops on a different tram, heading to Delft. He glances at his watch and wishes for once that he was in a car. Thirty-five minutes shuffle by. The canals loom into view. As soon as the tram doors open he is running towards the apartment block.

With luck on his side, someone is leaving the building as he arrives, he is able to slip inside without waiting for a response from the intercom. He takes the stairs rather than waiting for the lift, and is out of breath long before he reaches the front door of the apartment.

The curtains on the window that looks out onto the walkway are closed. No sign of any lights on inside. It will be dark soon.

He hammers on the door. Waits. Hammers again. Should he call for backup?

Too late now.

Antoine throws himself at the door. At the third attempt the door frame splinters and he falls into the apartment.

He advances gun in hand.

Kitchen. Empty.

There is a through lounge-cum-dining room. Also empty but there are signs of an altercation. Overturned chairs, a broken vase. Is that blood on the floor?

Antoine is cursing himself. He should have paid more attention. Winders, a racist with a chip on his shoulder had made no secret of his dislike of Floriane. She must have found something incriminating, evidence that he knew would blow him out of the water. Maybe he has taken her hostage.

Upstairs.

The first bedroom is tidy. And the second.

He pushes open the door to the bathroom.

The smell is a smack across the face. A thick trail of blood across the floor to the bath. The shower curtain has been pulled shut, blurring the view of what lies beyond. Handkerchief over his nose, treading carefully to avoid disturbing the crime scene as best he can, he pulls back the curtain. His jaw drops. He pulls his phone from his pocket. Takes a dozen photos, steps out onto the landing, rings Hervé.

'We need crime scene investigators here right now ... In her apartment ... Floriane? ... No, not her. It's Winders. In the bath. Dead. Yes, I'll be waiting outside.'

Less than two minutes later, a squad car screeches to a halt at the entrance to the apartment block and Antoine jumps inside. They drive away as the scene of crime investigators are arriving, lights strobing in the gloom. From the car he messages Tiffany. Is she OK? Where is she? Has she found Daniel? Does she need anything?

Back at Europol, he clears his weapon with security to get back into Europol headquarters. Lucas hands Antoine another surgical mask along with a lecture about public health.

Halfway up the stairs, his tired body gives him a second lecture. Head spinning, Antoine is obliged to stop to catch his breath. He smashes his fist against the wall in frustration.

The open plan office is largely empty, it being late on a Saturday afternoon, but it is already clear that the worldwide lockdown won't reduce criminal activity, just shift it about. Cybercrime is rising as people sit at home relying on the internet for everything: information, news, human contact, shopping, etc. Sub-standard healthcare products are already flooding the market. Antoine waves at the counterfeit team meeting as he passes.

He finds her in his office, using his terminal. Her back is to the door and the drawers of his desk have been emptied.

'OK, that's enough,' he says.

She doesn't even turn around. 'You're too late. For an experienced investigator you really took your eye off the ball. Winders is right, you are ...'

'Winders isn't anything. You killed him. Move away from my desk and do it slowly. I have a gun pointing at your back.'

Floriane turns. She is holding a paperweight.

'Don't even think about it,' Antoine advises. 'Put it down.'

'What really annoys you is the thought that while Winders' was a misogynist racist careerist little dick, he was smarter than you. Apart from good coffee ...'

She is fast but not fast enough. Her hand is barely off the desk when Antoine shoots her in the shoulder.

He has her pinned to the floor before the first member of cybercrime team reaches the door.

'Call security and Hervé,' Antoine orders.

By the time Hervé arrives, Floriane Onyemachi is in a cell. Antoine has brewed a pot of coffee and has established that Floriane has been intercepting all his communications, including the last message he sent Tiffany, and her reply.

Thor Lupei knows everything.

'We'll use my office, if you don't mind,' Hervé says from the doorway. 'And make sure you don't bring bloody footprints with you.'

CCTV - Officer Report

OFFICER:	PCSO G.Pannet
File No.s:	23/8 & 9
START:	2020.03.28 05.03.33
END:	2020.03.28 05.04.30
FILE TYPE:	Regular
BIT STREAM TYPE:	Mainstream
CHANNEL:	1, Church Street.
FILE SIZE:	15368KB

(NB: No activity recorded during period 00.00.00 and 05.03.37)
All data on discs backed up 16.32 28 March 2023.

05.03.37	Two pers in dark clothing walk from N, down Church St towards Bridge St. Bth tall and male.
05:03.39	Three further pers appear. Also male. One pers tall, other two much shorter. All five pers wear jackets or anoraks with hoods obscuring their faces. One pers is limping. They stop outside jet jewellery shop. Interaction suggests that one of the first two pers is in charge, others displaying submissive body language.
05.03.56	Sixth pers arrives from White Horse Yd. Female, in dressing gown or poss. coat. Short, thinning hair.
05.03.59	Female throws herself at the feet of 'leader' and buries her face in his shoes. He pushes her away. The woman repeats her actions with second taller male who reaches out and touches her head with hand. He looks up towards the sky and, as he does so, his hood slips to reveal his face. Video quality poor but male 2 appears balding and v. thin. Nose appears damaged.
05.04.14	'Leader' walks away northwards on Church St. towards 199 Steps. Others continue south to Bridge St and turn R towards swing bridge.

CHAPTER 65

Whitby

Tiffany pushes her way through the cobwebs and along the passage. After a few metres there is a side passage to her left with a short set of steps to a door, leading presumably to the next cottage. She continues straight ahead towards the knocking, her fingers thick around the kitchen knife. Her fear is subsumed in anger. She wants done with it.

A corner to the left. Two steps up. A turn to the right. More steps. The banging is louder. The sound of splashing water. She advances cautiously. Suddenly she stumbles, loses her footing and starts to tumble forwards. It takes all her strength to somehow drop back onto her weight-bearing leg and fall backwards, winding herself and hurting her hip and shoulder in the process. After a few seconds she rolls over and gets to her feet.

In front of her is a hole. Splintered rotten floorboards above a dark void. She shines her torch down.

'Daniel!'

He is a metre down and up to his armpits in greasy-looking water and floating detritus.

'What are you doing?'

'What do you mean, what am I doing?'

'How long have you been there?'

'Can you see a clock?'

Tiffany lies on her front and reaches down. At the second attempt Daniel catches her hands.

'Slowly. I don't want to fall in with you.'

He tries climbing up her arms but his hands keep slipping.

'I'll be back.'

'I'll tell the dead rats. They've been here longer than me.'

Tiffany returns a few minutes later with a length of washing line and a candle. Her phone has died again. She folds the line in half and ties a series of knots then drops one end down to Daniel while she leans back and braces herself. This time he is able to pull himself up. He is frozen to the core and shaking violently.

'What kind of bastard puts a death trap in a passage?' she says. 'I thought only pharaohs did that kind of thing.'

'It is probably just where they hid contraband 150 years ago,' Daniel tells her. 'Before it got flooded and the boards rotted away. There has to be an exit up ahead. I'm sure of it. Into the next yard or something.'

'I don't care. Let's get you dried off.'

They make their way back to the cottage and climb the cellar steps to the kitchen. He stands there shaking while she helps him out of his wet clothes.

'Upstairs. You need a shower. Not too hot. Funny you being the one running upstairs starkers. Your eyes are really red by the way.'

'He's here, Tiffany.'

She stops fussing.

'Lupei,' he says. 'Did you hear about the boat?'

She nods. 'Dave told me.'

Daniel looks confused.

'The manager at the chippy. My old boss. I bought us fish and chips.'

'You should have fetched that syringe gun. Not chips.'

She ignores the jibe. 'How do you know it's Lupei?'

'I'm trying to keep us safe.'

'Yeah, OK. Have your shower while I warm the food then tell me what you know.'

She escorts him upstairs, sets the shower going and comes

back down. Down in the cellar she closes the door and sets the bolts then back upstairs to check Daniel is OK. He is lying on one of the beds asleep. They can eat when he wakes up.

Looking down into the yard she spots the overturned wheelie bin. A minute later she is outside, pulling the bin upright and shoving everything back in. She wonders who put it out, there's been no sign of any of the other cottages being occupied.

The rain has almost stopped. Tiffany decides to seize the opportunity to go up to the flat to collect the syringe gun. She leaves Daniel a note on the kitchen table. Her phone is back up to a ten percent charge; it will have to do.

She hurries across town, takes the ginnel up from Pier Road and emerges on Cliff Street, almost opposite the flat. There are lights on in most of the houses. Knocking on the front door ... it moves. The door isn't properly shut. She pushes it open. It is dark inside.

'Tina. Tina?'

No answer. Could they have gone for a walk? Is that within the rules, two adults and a baby? Along West Cliff, perhaps.

'Tina, are you there?'

The coats are all hanging up by the door. The toddler, Ethan, normally shouts when he hears Tiffany coming in. She hesitates but she cannot stay out on the street. Putting on the mask and gloves she has in her coat pocket from work, she steps inside, switching on the hall light and pushing the door shut behind her. There is a strange smell in the air, damp, metallic, cloying. The internal doors are all shut. Self-closing fire doors.

First things first.

The door to her room swings shut behind her, obliging her to turn on the light. She fishes the red cashbox out from beneath her bed. The syringe gun is in there; all three remaining vials seem fine. Nothing broken. Does she need anything else?

At least this way, with them all out, there won't be a confrontation; she'll be away in a couple of minutes. She fetches her travel case down from above the wardrobe, opens it on the quilt, collects all the stuff she wants to take with her and sits on the bed to fill the case. A couple of books, extra underwear, her turquoise fleece, slippers ...

A sound in the hall.

They're back!

She rehearses what she is going to say.

Look, sorry, the door was open, Tina. Anyone could come in. You're lucky it's only me.

Footsteps outside her door. Still no noise from Ethan. He's usually burbling non-stop. The door is opening. Tiffany turns.

The scream catches in her throat.

The woman is of medium height with patches of hair on her head. Her face is filthy and covered in flaking scabs. She is so skinny that it is a surprise she is able to stand. Wearing a green dressing gown over what look like rags, and a crumbling pair of trainers. Her hands and mouth are red, her eyes black as Whitby jet. Her head moves like a predator, turning from side to side to scan the room.

Blood trickles down her chin.

Tiffany knows.

Scravir.

Her right hand reaches blindly across the bed, finds the cash box, fumbles inside, retrieves the syringe gun. Slowly she lifts it out of the box and swings it round.

The scravir notices the movement and tenses up, like a cat about to pounce, a guttural grunt in her throat. She throws herself across the room, throwing Tiffany back on the bed, her long nails swiping three deep scratches in Tiffany's check.

But Tiffany is ready for her. The self-defence classes have given her strength she did not have on the ferry the last time a scravir attacked. She has the syringe gun pointing straight ahead and the scravir impales herself on the end of it. Tiffany pulls the trigger with the index fingers of both hands. The vial cracks and the burning liquid enters her attacker who howls and spasms.

Tiffany pushes with all her strength, keeping the scravir's claws and teeth away from her face. The creature tumbles backward to the floor, writhing in agony, hissing, limbs flailing.

The best form of defence is attack, Tiffany has learned her lesson. She kicks the scravir's kneecaps, hears one of them crack and pop. The scravir's skin is a rippling carpet of bumps and lumps as what there is of muscle in her face and neck dissolves away. The fight fades. Now in a foetal position and whimpering, the last flicker of life leaves the scravir's eyes and she is still.

Tiffany closes the cashbox and tosses it and the rest of her stuff into the travel case.

Zips it.

Syringe gun tucked into her waistband, travel case in hand, Tiffany opens the door and steps out into the hall.

At the front door she turns, sees her face in the hall mirror and flinches. One side of her face is a curtain of blood, dripping from her jaw down onto her coat.

Just get out.

But if someone on the street sees you ...

She opens the bathroom door. It will only take a minute to wash her face then at least ...

... They are all there.

All three of them.

Dead.

Including the baby.

Tiffany grabs the door frame to steady herself. She gasps for breath. The room is spinning.

No. Keep it together. Breathe. Breathe.

Tina is slumped by the toilet, her hand reaching out to touch

Ethan's tiny dead fingers. Ben's legs are sticking out of the bath.

The scravir has taken a bite out of his calf.

Tiffany leans over the sink and runs the cold tap to wash the blood from her face and coat. The scratch marks sting like hell, God knows what infections she might get. In the bathroom cabinet above the sink is a tube of antiseptic. She rubs it in, wincing in pain.

You're leaving your DNA all over the flat.

No, I'm not, I'm wearing gloves!

In a fog, Tiffany wipes and rinses the taps and around the sink. The water runs red. She carries on until everything appears clean. One last look at her friend, and the baby, and boyfriend Ben. She mutters a prayer and leaves.

Back on the street, Tiffany hurries across the road and into the ginnel.

Were there anyone at windows as I left?

You didn't do anything, Tiff.

I just killed someone.

Not someone. Something. A scravir.

That is still someone.

The bitch killed Tina, Ethan and Ben.

She stops in her tracks, leans her head against the wall. It's not enough. Whipping off her mask she throws up, helplessly, over and over, until her throat is burning. She walks unsteadily away and, halfway down the ginnel, slumps down on the wet cobbles, exhausted.

It's the rain, soothing, tender and cleansing, that prevents her from curling into a ball and drifting off to sleep. Her head clearing, she picks up her face mask and puts it on, messages Daniel "On my way back!" and scrambles to her feet.

Back down on Pier Road she is tempted to walk to the amusement arcades, to look across the harbour at the wreck on Tate Hill Sands but there isn't time. Church Street is empty.

The streetlights are coming on. She slips into the yard, now thick with shadows. Her shoes clatter on the flagstones as she hurries to the cottage, lets herself in and closes the curtains.

'Daniel!' she shouts, then catches herself.

She runs upstairs.

Both bedrooms are empty.

The fish and chips are still on the kitchen table, untouched. The cupboard door and the trapdoor within are open.

'Not again! Daniel, you bloody idiot!'

Beyond the unbolted door in the basement the passage yawns black and dank. Tiffany hurries, furious, promising herself that if he is back in the water-filled hole, he can fucking well stay there.

He isn't.

She takes five steps back, runs and jumps the rotten planks and lands heavily on the flagstones beyond. Another corner, a dozen steps up.

A second door.

The bolts have been drawn back and the door pushed open. The signs of a scuffle are clear: two broken teeth on the ground, flecks of blood on the door frame and, in the shadows by a drainpipe, a small round and broken brass box.

The scravir compass.

CHAPTER 66

The night is hungry and keen to get started.

I am in an old building. High on a wall, and fitted with security bars that bulge into the room like a belly, is a small window through which drip the drab dregs of daylight.

The air is fat with the aroma of decaying vegetables and rotten fruit. The floor is bare drusty earth, uneven, rough to the touch. A small pile of hessian sacks. The ceiling is a geometry of beams and joists. Two light bulbs but no switch.

The door opens inwards. I know that because I have felt around the frame, very carefully. As carefully as I could with my hands tied behind my back.

I have also given the door a good kicking.

Someone has scraped round the inside of my skull with a scouring brush.

It feels that way.

I am concussed.

This is bad.

A vague memory of being jumped on. I am coming out of somewhere, up some steps. I push open the door, step out and there they are. Three of them. A thickset bloke with a moustache who punches me. I fight back as best I can but it's no contest. And this other bloke, tall with a flaking scalp and bad teeth, he grabs my arms and pins me down.

I have seen him before ...

In a castle. Sod knows what I've been doing in a castle ...

Why am I here?

Footsteps on the floor above. Tiny clouds of dust drop down and dance in the weak light from the window.

Someone is coming!

The door opens and the room floods with light. As my eyes adjust, I see a tall figure holding the torch. He points the beam down at the floor and I see he is the tall one with the missing nostril and the smile like a bent coat hanger and ... I realise I know his name.

Pepene.

He pushed my wheelchair.

My wheelchair?

Memories come cascumbling back.

Scravir.

A hall with a huge fireplace.

Back in the here and now, Pepene indicates the open doorway. I don't want him at my back but I have no choice. A second scravir, a shorter one with pitiful sunken eyes and an absurd tuft of dark hair on his otherwise bald head is waiting in the passage. Did I damage his face earlier?

The passage.

Now I remember the cottage.

WHERE IS TIFFANY?

I went back down to the cellar. She was out and I wanted to find out where the passage led. I jumped over the broken planks and climbed the steps and ...

A thump on my back. I could probably knock the smaller scravir over but not Pepene. Despite his emaciated condition he is strong, I guess he was once a thug or a murderer that Lupei ...

Thor Lupei!

We climb the steps and emerge in a corridor that leads to a large room containing a tatty sofa, and a large dining table surrounded by half a dozen chairs, and I think I know where I am.

The old farmhouse at Farview.

The room is lit by three chains of festoon lights hanging from nails hammered into the walls.

'Daniel, Daniel, Daniel,' his rich baritone voice drops in pitch with each repetition of my name.

He is standing at one of the windows, staring out into the gloom.

'Aren't they marvellous? Battery powered lighting. What humanity would have paid for these in the 15th century. Human progress. Do take a seat.'

The sofa is too low to the ground. I pick one of the chairs, pull it away from the table and sit down.

'We got off on the wrong foot in Delhi, did we not? But in truth you have proved such a difficult fellow to pin down.'

He wears a full-length black leather trench coat, as he wore at the concert in the Pavilion nearly three and a half years ago. I am confused by the long white hair. Is it a wig? Was the short hair in Delhi a wig?

'Something satisfying about cold northern nights. Scuttling clouds and the tang of a cruel sea. I walked along the clifftop earlier looking down at the wreck in the harbour. Breathing it all in. Cost me an excellent guitar and ...' The sentence hangs unfinished. Lupei turns and studies me for a moment.

'Can you imagine the pain you visited upon me, Daniel? No one could help me until I could help myself. A year without a face, my whole body leaking fluids, unable to speak. It was ... it was ... medieval.'

He crosses the room and takes my chin in his hand, forces me to look up at him.

'And the pain of betrayal.'

He releases my face, fingers bunching into a fist. I brace myself for a flood of pain.

'Leave us,' he orders two scravir. 'And send Felini.'

My body bristles, shivers with fear. Anticipation.

'And ripping pages from my diaries. You, barely out of swaddling. Daring to enter *my* sanctuary,' his voice rising with fury.

His anger rough-rags me like those deep bass notes that rattle ribs at a gig. What has he put inside me?

'Rifling through *MY* possessions, ferreting *MY* history with your grubby pubescent fingers and DARING TO ...'

He stops mid-flow, visibly wrestling to control his rage. He forces himself away, withdraws across the room to a plateau of ice calm from which he observes me like a raptor perusing livestock in a valley below. Watch the sheep, always watch the sheep.

'No one has ever entered my room and emerged alive,' he says, so softly that I almost miss it. 'The claws, beaks and fangs of my savage forest have hitherto torn every trespasser to shreds. Mi ritrovai per una silva oscura ...

'...ché la diritta era smaritta,' I finish the line for him.

Lupei's face betrays surprise.

'Ahi, quantoa dir qual era è cosa dura esta selve selvaggia e aspira e forte ...' he whispers, waiting for me to complete the sentence.

'I only know that one line you taught me,' I tell him. 'Sorry.'

'Oh. What a pity. Udirai le disperate strida vedrai li antichi spiriti dolenti. You will hear howls of desperation and see the ancient spirits in their pain.'

Lupei takes one of the other dining chairs, spins it round and straddles it in front of me with the back of his chair between us.

There is a knock at the door.

'Come.'

I recognise the man from Lupei's castle. Short, stocky, grey hair and thick moustache. 'Sir.'

'Ah. Very good.'

The man stands awaiting instructions.

Lupei looks to the doorway, then at me, then back at the doorway. 'Have we found her?'

'She is in the cottage.'

Lupei takes a long deep breath.

'Fetch her. Take the policeman with you.'

'DON'T TOUCH HER!' I shout.

Thor Lupei dismisses the man with the flick of a finger. He smiles at me, stands away from the chair and paces the room.

'If you touch Tiffany, I'll kill you.'

Lupei chuckles. 'You've tried more than once and failed at each attempt, my young pup.'

He stares at the windows where night has now spread its ink, and studies me in the reflection.

'Let's change the subject,' he says, adopting a brighter tone. 'Tell me about yourself; what have you learned these past three years? How have things been?'

I stare at him. One second he is enslaving people, threatening Tiffany, imprisoning the destitute, raining mayhem on the world, and the next he want to be *mates*?!

'And *you* are a paragon of virtue?' he says, second-guessing my thoughts. 'Climb from your sanctimonious little pony and see yourself as your pretty Tiffany sees you. The girl is doing her best to see only the clumsy young man in the cowboy suit who breezed into her godforsaken little town to attend a festival with his friends. But she doesn't only see that, does she? To her, you are as unreadable and frightening as I. Your only asset is the dream she clings to; that naive girlish hope that she can change you. When she loses that ...'

He comes to stand behind me.

'Face it, Daniel, she is a trifle.' His voice intimate in my ear. 'You will know hundreds of such trifles in the years ahead. Thousands. Each as pretty and as fleeting as a vase of roses beside a nuptial bed. *The moving finger writes and having writ moves on* as that drunken rogue Omar Khayyám wrote in his rubaiyat.'

'No idea who that is, or when it was, but if you need to name drop ... Suppose you shared a beer, back in the day.'

'Wine. Omar was a wine connoisseur. Caused him a few problems. In Persia.' Lupei comes round in front of me, sits back down, chin on his hand. He smiles. 'Back in the day.'

For what feels like minutes we sit in silence, staring each other out until Lupei walks to the door. Opens it.

'Pepene!'

The scravir appears.

'Our guest wishes to have some solo time. Would you escort him to his room?' Lupei turns to me. 'We can chat again later, perhaps?'

I snap.

'WHAT IS THE POINT? You want to kill me? DO IT. KILL ME. I caused you a shitload of pain, my bad, but you will not ...'

'Pulling the energy from all those beggars in Delhi, in order to resist me ...' he says, ignoring my rant. 'Quite unexpected.'

He is impressed?

'And the clinic, what have you been doing there with the powers I gave you? Here is the main riff; I created you in order to refresh my work, to conjure pastures new. If you, my little pup, make amends and offer your fealty, then I will forget your misdemeanours and together we will fashion a new world of opportunities. But, if you say no, then this experiment is done. I will wipe away the memory of it and move on. The choice is yours and you have until midnight to decide.'

Lupei turns to Pepene. 'Take him away.'

'I want to scratch my nose.' I shake my tied wrists. 'And use a toilet.'

'My servants will assist you, I am sure.'

Pepene smiles lopsidedly.

CHAPTER 67

In Scarborough, at the end of another long shift, Dr Ivanna Albu suddenly understands. She messages Tiffany,

> 17.45 Message from IvAlba24
> Must talk. I understand Daniel's test results.

A couple of minutes later she tries to call. No answer. She cannot, will not, put her thoughts in a message; she wants to speak with Tiffany face to face. Grabbing her things, Ivanna rushes to her car and fires off another message.

> 17.53 Message from IvAlba24
> On my way to Whitby. What is address?

She throws the car into gear, races out of the car park and heads north towards the moors and Whitby.

Over in Whitby, Tiffany recognises where the underground passage has emerged; she is in the next yard along, towards Henrietta Street. She collects the scravir compass and shoves it in a trouser pocket; maybe it can be repaired.

The bolts on the heavy oak door dragged back into place, and with her phone battery flashing red on 2%, Tiffany shines her torch down the steps. As long as she can see her way safely over the rotten planks, she can fumble her way along the passage.

When the torch does die, the jump having been negotiated, she curses Daniel for being such a twat, and waits for her eyes to adjust. Sure enough a faint breath of light spills along the passage from the basement room ahead. One hand brushing along the wall, Tiffany inches forwards in the lacklight until she reaches the cottage cellar where she slams the door, locks it and applies herself to erecting a barricade.

The bookcase is dragged into place, refilled with books, games, kitchenware, crockery. She wedges the pool table between the bookcase and the wall opposite. Lastly, for good measure, she piles the frame of the old bicycle on top of the pool table.

Satisfied, she climbs the steep steps to the kitchen. Trapdoor slammed down, everything thrown back into the cupboard.

She plugs her phone in to charge and sits down at the kitchen table.

She eats a cold chip, wrinkles her nose and puts the oven on; she has to eat and maybe Daniel will show up.

Who are you kidding?

Her phone vibrates on the worktop. Messages from Ivanna Alba. Almost twenty minutes ago. Damn it!

Tiffany replies with the name of the yard but does not identify the cottage.

Call it superstition. Or paranoia.

She will keep an eye out.

Outside night gatecrashes the remains of the day.

Tiffany eats in the front room. The comforting smell of fried food hangs in the air. She is wracked with guilt; she should not have left Daniel alone.

I had to fetch the syringe gun.

Where is the gun?

Right beside her on the sofa.

A flashback to the bodies in the bathroom on Cliff Street. Her body recoils and flinches.

It's not my fault. Daniel is not my fault.

A noise in the yard. Maybe that's him!

She leaps up, pulls the curtain back a fraction and peers out. Barely believing her eyes, she cannot suppress a gasp of joy.

It's not Daniel. Even in the cold glow of a single streetlight, she'd recognise that face and huge frame anywhere!

At last, a knight in shining armour!

She flings open the door, steps out into the yard and runs towards him.

'Bloody heck! How did you find us? I thought you were gone! You won't believe what ... Look, I'm so sorry about what I said. I played Daniel your recording and he knows about his mum.'

Gert Muyskens is standing in the middle of the yard, staring back at her, hands at his sides as she reaches up and hugs him.

'We've all been worried,' she tells him, burying her face in his coat. 'Your friend Antoine. I met him in London. He told me you had gone to Romania then we found Daniel and ...'

She suddenly realises Gert hasn't said a word or moved a muscle. She stops, takes two steps back and looks up at him.

His face is blank. He isn't even looking at her.

Tiffany's joy evaporates. What has happened to him? Why is he here? How has he got here during a global lockdown?

The bright sound of heels taps the flagstones in the entrance to the yard from Church Street.

Ivanna emerges from the shadows of the passage, in her white medical coat and face mask, clutching a briefcase. She waves happily.

'Thank God, Tiffany, I thought I miss you,' Ivanna calls out. 'No traffic so I drive quickly and ...' She registers the figure beside Tiffany. 'Oh my God! Is that really you? Gert? How perfect!'

Ivanna hurries forward. 'Look, I understand now! All makes sense. Where is Daniel? Gert can ...'

Mid-sentence Ivanna is attacked from the side. A short thickset man hurls himself at her from the shadows, slamming her hard against the frontage of one of the houses. So hard that bones crack audibly. Ivanna crumples at the foot of the wall, twitches a couple of times and is still.

'NO!' Tiffany screams, turning towards Ivanna's assassin.

Felini grips a long, serrated blade.

Gert is slowly turning toward Felini.

'Grab her!' Felini orders.

Gert's arms slowly lift, blocking Tiffany's passage.

'No!' Tiffany yells. 'Gert! It's me. Wake up!'

Is that regret in his eyes?

Tiffany is obliged to acknowledge the truth.

There is no regret.

Gert Muyskens is scravir.

Tiffany spins on her heels, races back to the cottage, slamming the door behind her. In the kitchen, with the sound of a heavy body throwing itself at the front door, she realises her mistake. The kitchen window leads nowhere.

The front door splinters.

The kitchen cupboard is closed, the trapdoor covered in junk. In her fear she has blocked off her only avenue of escape.

No contest.

Faced with a choice of a serrated hunting knife or a set of handcuffs, she accepts the latter. She holds her hands out in front of her and Felini slips the cuffs on her wrists.

In the doorway Gert stares impassively, his eyes dead to the world. Tiffany wonders if he is conscious. Felini pushes him aside as he frogmarches Tiffany out of the kitchen. Crossing the front room towards the door she spots the syringe gun on the sofa where it has fallen between two cushions. For a fleeting moment she considers throwing herself towards the sofa but realises that with her hands cuffed there is no way she will be able to reach it and, besides, who will she kill with it? Gert?

They head down the passage to Church Street, with Gert

trudging behind. He has served his purpose, winkling Tiffany out of the cottage without a fight. Ivanna Albu's body lies where she fell, a trail of blood trickling from the back of her head. Tiffany's eyes flood with tears.

What was she going to tell me?

'Move,' Felini growls, kicking Tiffany's shins. He has no idea who the woman was, only that she arrived at the wrong time and appeared to recognise Gert.

They turn right on Church Street, heading towards Henrietta Street. Tiffany wonders if Lupei is in one of the cottages. Given that the boat ended up on Tate Hill Sands, that would make sense. She knows the alleys, yards and ginnels better than the short man, who is plainly not a local. Maybe she can run off and lose them. Is the tide coming in or going out? Felini moves to her left and draws close, effectively blocking off the ginnels towards the harbour.

'Up,' he says when they reach the foot of the 199 steps.

About forty steps up Tiffany stops to look back at the town. The lights of the houses shimmer on the harbour waters. Black clouds are sweeping inland. Felini, four steps behind, barks at her to move. Gert is four steps further back. She could run for it; she must be fitter than either of them. But where would she go? There is nothing up there.

Race round the church then come back down the steps.

The chances of slipping on wet grass are too high and with her hands cuffed she would struggle to break her fall.

Get to the top and turn back down onto the Donkey Path.

Same problem. The Donkey Path, below her to her right, is way too steep, the raised strips of cobbles so irregular and so slippery that she can guarantee stumbling and knocking herself out.

Abandoning the idea of running away, Tiffany decides instead to buy time to think by walking as slowly as she can.

'Faster.'

'I'm asthmatic,' she says, stopping and turning to face the short man. 'I can't breathe.'

She gasps for breath and clings to the railing for effect.

Felini crosses over to stand a step below her, uncertain what to do. No one told him she was asthmatic. He is itching to beat her, punish her, force her to move, but the boss wants the girl in one piece.

As Felini wrestles with the conundrum, Gert is slowly catching up.

'I need to sit down,' Tiffany says.

'No, you move.' Felini produces the hunting knife to focus her mind. He leans forwards and pokes her belly with it. 'You move or I cut.'

Tiffany makes a show of taking several deep breaths. 'OK, I'll try but not too fast, please.'

Gert's head has appeared behind Felini's as the tall Dutchman closes the gap. It is bewildering watching a man she knew as fit and able reduced to this ponderous shuffling gait, barely controlling his limbs, unable to speak. What has Lupei done to him? How is Felini controlling him?

Gert is on the step immediately behind Felini, still staring blankly ahead. He lifts his right foot and places it on the step beside Felini, shifts his weight and lifts his left. As he does so he blinks furiously several times and his eyes drift to his right as he takes a huge breath. His face contorts in concentration. His right leg collapses under him and he falls heavily against Felini.

Gert is a big man, he must weigh well over a hundred and twenty kilos. Whatever Lupei has done, it hasn't yet included transforming Gert into a living skeleton. The narrow black iron handrail is too low to save Felini who falls sideways over it, knife in hand. Gert tumbles after him.

It is a four-metre drop down onto the Donkey Path below.

A brief scream from Felini followed by two sickening

thuds. Shaking uncontrollably, clutching the railing, Tiffany forces herself to look down. Her first impression is that both men are dead. Then one man flinches.

There is no easy way to reach them.

Tiffany hurries up the remaining steps and follows the path along the edge of the graveyard until she reaches the gap in the wall where she is able to cross over onto the top of the Donkey Path and head back down. The damp stones are treacherous. It takes forever to reach the spot where the men fell.

Felini is dead, combination of the impact of hitting the stones with Gert's weight landing on top of him, and the hunting knife he was holding, that has stabbed him in the heart. His blood flows downhill, glistening in the light from the lamp post up on the 199 steps.

Beside Felini lies the broken body of Gert Muyskens. Crouching beside him, Tiffany realises she was wrong. While his upper body is still strong, the fall has ripped his trousers to reveal legs that are painfully thin. His skull is cracked, blood and cerebral fluid gathering on the stones beneath his head.

'I'm calling an ambulance,' she tells him, not expecting an answer.

She doesn't have her phone.

It's too late.

She kneels beside Gert and takes his hand in her own. She thinks of the hospital, where humans are separated from each other by masks, gloves, visors, goggles, hazmat suits ... none of that here, but she could not care less.

'I don't know if you can hear me but, you have just saved my life again. Thank you. You're a good man, Gert. And thank you for never giving up. I'm so sorry for not being honest with you. You knew I were hiding stuff. Lying to protect him. For what it's worth, I still don't think Daniel is evil, but you are right, he is a bloody mess.'

Tiffany looks down the Donkey Path towards the harbour,

her vision blurred with tears.

'Remember when we found you by the river? I were terrified we'd lost you. Then you sat up inside that pile of leaves and I almost died of shock.' She squeezes his hand gently. 'You'll be OK.'

She knows that like the people she has supported in the Covid wards in the hospital, Linda and Jason and the others, Gert will not be OK but she will offer him comfort. She can do that.

One of his legs is at an impossible angle. His breathing is more and more laboured. Tiffany wonders if his leg is causing him pain, if she should move it.

'I guess that when you've recovered you'll be wanting to get back to your turtles. I'd love to visit,' she struggles to keep her voice steady. 'Maybe I can bring Daniel with me and ...'

She thinks she has imagined it.

Then it happens a second time and she knows. The faintest pressure; his fingers gently squeezing back.

Gert is there.

He hears her voice from far away in that dark place on the edge of death. His eyelids flicker and open and he is staring up at her. Somehow, he has travelled back to the threshold. He sees her face and is overwhelmed at the miracle and mystery of life. He feels the breeze on his cheeks, sees light and shade, smells her perfume, smells the sea, sees the clouds shifting above him, hears the tenderness in her voice, the light pressure of her fingers on his hand. Every moment of his existence that was ever good and beautiful and enriching suffuses his being, replacing pain with joy and peace.

He tries to speak, to thank her. He feels the muscles of his mouth begin to move. She is seeing it. Can he do this?

No.

A step too far.

Gert slips away, his senses shrinking, closing, fading ... life rushing away from him ...

For several minutes Tiffany holds Gert's dead hand, oblivious to the rest of the universe. Slowly she returns. Lupei is still out there and he has kidnapped Daniel, and she must do everything in her power to avenge Gert and all the others he has killed, and somehow rescue Daniel.

They were walking up the steps towards the Abbey. Tiffany understands instinctively where the short man was taking her; she knows what lies across the lacklit fields east of Whitby.

Before she leaves, she closes Gert's eyes and rifles the short man's pockets to find the key to the handcuffs. His passport identifies him as Radu Felini, Romanian. He has the keys to a BMW.

CHAPTER 68

Farview

An hour has passed, maybe two, sitting here on the floor, shivering in the cellar beneath the farmhouse. At least the handcuffs have been removed and I have been given a bucket.

I have wrapped several of the hessian sacks around myself and, as they warm up, I stink of ancient vegetables, collapsed potatoes and bin juice.

The waves of pain and nausea that I have been feeling since arriving in Whitby are intensifying. What did Lupei do to me in Delhi? Or am I actually ill with a tropical disease or the coronavirus? Where is Tiffany?

I feel Lupei's presence inside me, rummaging about inside my head. I focus all my energy to block him out but he is too powerful. His attack overwhelms me and I fall unconscious.

'Ah, there you are.'

That rich baritone voice just behind my head. I am strapped down face up in the room with the festoons of hanging lights. On a table perhaps.

Hanging in front of me is a man, suspended from the ceiling by wires that pass beneath his skin, arms, legs and collar bones. A ragged tuft of hair on the top of his head, I recognise the shorter scravir from earlier. He appears unconscious.

My body is experiencing extreme stress.

'We have much to discuss,' Lupei says, close by but out of view. 'We have, I hope, a long journey ahead of us. First, I will help you recover a sense of who is the master and who the apprentice.'

Steam emanates from the man above me. A fine blue filigree of flames lacelicks the surface of his skin. A thousand tiny hairs frizzle away to nothing. I sense what is coming and open my mouth to shout NO, to tell Lupei he is obscene, no one has the right to do this to a fellow human being, but I no longer have control of my vocal chords.

The scravir's eyes are closed. What does he feel?

I feel everything. We are burning together.

Pain devours me in a lacerating nightmare of brutality. Patches of skin balloon in coalescing blisters that bloom, split and peel back to reveal red raw flesh beneath.

An incremental roar gathers. A million nerve endings hurl chemistry at my brain, overwhelming my spinal cord, bombarding my thalamus, drowning my cortex, burying me deep in an orgy of suffering.

Plumes of black smoke billow as what little fat the scravir has starts to smoulder and flameburst.

The sweet smell of burning fat.

The scravir's eyes open as the flames spread. His eyelashes crisp and curl.

He is conscious!

His eyes poach in their sockets.

I cannot turn away or close my eyes.

My lips bloat and blister, my nostrils buckle and burn. The smell repels me. An ear peels away.

The searing heat swirls my abdomen, legs and arms.

My fingers and toes swell and split like sausages in a pan.

My arms lift into the air and I see my hands flayed, burning flesh and bone, tendons popping like over-tightened guitar strings.

My lungs claw the air but find only choking smoke. My chest heaves to cough, ripping the skin on my chest. I would weep if there were any water left in my head as I tumble helplessly into the abyss.

Then,

abruptly,

the pain stops.

I glance up at the body on the wire and see that all the skin has burned away and with it all the nerves that fed the pain. Flames dance brightly on an insensate body. The air is thick with the aroma of roasting meat.

And in that instant, the pain abating, my eyes close and I understand. I look inside myself, awaken creierul antecilor, deep dive ... and find my nerves ... intact.

And there he is waiting for me, inside my ancient brain, in his long black leather coat and top hat, leaning casually against my medulla oblongata, strumming my neurones like he's playing the blues.

You Bastard!

I open my eyes and Lupei is beside me, looking down.

There is nothing on the ceiling.

I try to move but nothing moves, I am still strapped to the table.

'All that and more you did to me, Daniel. You cannot imagine how many bodies it took to piece me together again once I was sufficiently recovered.'

I say nothing.

'Would you say I had the right to retribution?'

'What do you care what I think?'

Lupei flinches as if in pain. Rubbing his left temple, he strides away towards the door.

'Pepene!'

The scravir appears in the doorway.

'Has Felini returned with our guest yet?'

Pepene shakes his head.

'Wait here.' Lupei leaves the room.

Strapped down as I am, the instruction seems unnecessary.

CHAPTER 69

Having taken the short man's hunting knife, collected the syringe gun, retrieved the old bike from the basement and reattached the front wheel, Tiffany has cycled out along Church Street then left onto the steep Green Lane. She manages to cycle most of the way up; all that exercise is paying off.

At the top of the lane her gut says turn right, but could she be making a mistake? She turns left, cycling into the salt wind, towards the Abbey's looming serrated silhouette.

There is no sign of life either in the church or the Abbey visitor centre or any of the other buildings. But there is a large grey BMW with fat tyres parked in the turning point at the end of Abbey Lane. On the back seat are a lady's coat and headscarf alongside a couple of shopping bags and a jemmy. The front passenger window is missing and, on the seat beside it, shattered glass and dark drops of what might be blood. She clicks the car keys she took from Radu Felini. The doors unlock, answering the question of why they were climbing the 199 steps. She imagines the car owner, left for dead in a car park somewhere.

She touches nothing, leaves the car where she found it and heads back up the lane, cycling past the Abbey and on towards the darkness and Hawsker with the wind at her back.

A sickle moon snatches between the speeding clouds.

Tiffany is in the zone; efficient, fluid, focused, firing. The deaths in the hospital, the violence and brutality on the 199 steps and in the yard, have cauterised her senses. Whatever happens in the coming hours she will do her best; for Daniel, Gert, Ivanna, Antoine, and all the other victims.

Leaving Hawsker Lane, she reduces her speed, alert to

potholes on the rough road. She passes the spot where she and Jordan waited in the car for Daniel and Megan to re-emerge from the farm.

A lifetime ago.

Overgrown hedges thick with dead brambles crowd the roadside.

Dismounting, she leans the bike in the shadow of the trees. As she treads a path through the mud at the farm entrance, she almost slips on a sheet of paper. She stoops to remove it from her shoe. The faded words, in Comic Sans, are barely legible:

Welcome to Farview!

Loose cladding panels slap back and forth on a barn. An owl screeches. Shadows crouch and cower bereft beneath cold surfaces. The place is dead. As inviting as an abandoned ghost train at Chernobyl.

Maybe she was wrong.

Damn.

She heads back to the entrance, shining her torch on the ground, wishing for the fortieth time that it was an actual torch and not just a power-draining extra on her partially charged phone.

At her feet are a set of fat tyre tracks that run in through the main gates and into the barn.

She isn't wrong.

CHAPTER 70

Lupei re-enters the room and stands beside the table.

'Time is short. Let's get down to business. Where are the pages you stole?'

'If I return them will you promise to leave Tiffany alone?'

'Don't try to strike a deal, impudent pup.'

What's the point? After all, every page has been photographed and RJ is busy right now decoding the cipher. If I survive I may yet learn the book's secrets.

'OK. They're in the cottage, hidden in a tin among other papers down in the cellar, but promise me that ...'

'Excellent. I shall assume that you are telling the truth. The matter is now closed. Now tell me what you have done with the faculties I gave you.'

'What's my motivation? The only thing I have that you cannot take from me are my memories and experiences. Or can you take those too? In which case why are you even bothering to ask?'

For the second time in a few hours, Lupei seems almost impressed. Surrounded by servility, as he is, maybe he finds being challenged entertaining.

'A life, however long, is an incremental voyage from a single point, experiences stacked one upon the other like tiles, each held in place by its predecessor like the steps in a ziggurat.'

It seems rude to ask him what a ziggurat is.

'For all your coarse edges, your naivety and youthful bravado, you offer a fresh perspective on what those skills I have lent you might achieve,' Lupei continues. 'The lyre players of ancient Mesopotamia could not imagine the Delta blues artists that would one day strum guitars and holler so magnificently. Change requires input from multiple origins and you, Daniel, are my second origin. My chance to learn new tricks. *I* am your ticket to eternity. You castigated me once for my actions and choices so, pray, tell me what you have learned. Let us grow together.'

'You want me to make you a better person?' I say, incredulously.

'If that is how you wish to express it.'

'What makes you think you can change?'

'Indulge me. Start with Thurloe Square.'

Lupei releases the straps, takes my hand and helps me into a sitting position. I climb down from the table and walk unsteadily to the sofa.

I suppose I am flattered. It's like Albert Einstein asking the cleaner for tips on quantum theory. Besides, over the past three years there has not been anyone I have been able to speak with about anything. No one who could understand me. Not like he can.

So I talk.

And he listens.

He is a good listener; offering occasional comments or suggestions, asking questions, challenging my assumptions.

Lupei has never considered using his powers to carry out cosmetic surgery. He struggles to believe a person might part with their life savings simply to change the shape of their backside or their nose. He honed his skills in a different world.

Lupei has a photographic memory. He remembers Finch-Porter of Thurloe Square. *That pampered powdered over-ripe hedonist with more money than sense.* I do not tell Lupei that it was Finch-Porter's shyster butler Adam Allen, AKA Dorothy Makepeace, who spotted the market opportunity for painless, scarless cosmetic surgery. Nor do I tell him that Allen imprisoned me to deliver it; he probably knows.

When the tall scravir appears at the door Lupei sends him away to bring us nourishment.

Lupei switches to India. What was I doing there? Who were my clients? Where did they come from? How did I have such a great idea to set up a clinic there? I start to explain the steady trail of people flying to Delhi, from Europe, Canada, the US, and Australia, to have me reshape their overfed bodies,

He primps my plumage, seduces me, inveigles me, encourages me to boast and brag.

I cannot stop myself. I explain how I become a conduit, shifting fat, muscle and organs from rich to poor, holding two people one in each hand, removing one person's legacy of excess and self-indulgence to replenish another person's failing body in a single fluid process.

He nods thoughtfully, a smile passing his lips. He is proud of me!

But that little voice is whispering in my head.

When I have told him everything then what is left? What is to stop him killing me and heading back there to wreak havoc on Delhi? Or somewhere else.

Can he really become a changed man? Does any of us really change?

Noticing that I am becoming more circumspect and sketchy in my explanations, Lupei compliments me on my concern for the poor, my charitable deeds. How does the caste system work? Why are RJ and Karuna committed to the noble cause?

Pepene returns with bread, cheese and wine. Lupei instructs the scravir to send Felini in the moment he arrives then turns to me.

'You look exhausted, dear Daniel. Let us pause a moment to fill our bellies.'

CHAPTER 71

Tiffany enters the large barn and follows the car tracks. They stop behind a stack of hay bales. Fragments of shattered glass lie on the ground.

The arctic wind blustering off the sea causes loose cladding panels to slap and echo in the barn. The air smells of straw and motor oil. The place feels knee-deep in malevolence and Tiffany is keen to get back outside. The breeze whistling in her ears and tousling her hair, she crosses the farmyard towards the house. Clumps of dead grass hang from the gutters like wax dripping from a burning candle. The empty windows stare bleak blank black.

She passes the corner of the farmhouse, revealing the alley that runs between it and an old brick cow barn.

Is that the faintest fog of light on the path ahead?

She hesitates.

Tiffany has been here before when she helped Ivanna gather evidence about Thor Lupei three years ago. Ahead of her, at the far end of the alley, is the back of the farmhouse on the right and a collection of sheds and a lean-to greenhouse on the left. Are there lights on somewhere? Could the patch on the ground be a reflection of light from a window she cannot see, or simply lighter coloured gravel?

Fearful that she is already too late to help Daniel, Tiffany grips the hunting knife and steps into the alley. Twenty steps and she will reach the back of the house. It is starting to rain.

Halfway down is a door that leads into the house.

The handle squeaks. The door is locked.

Above her head, out of Tiffany's line of sight, a face appears briefly in an upstairs window.

She presses herself against the wall, walks in the weeds that have grown where water has dripped from the roof.

Three steps.

Two.

One.

Electric light is coming from the back of the farmhouse. Angling the blade to act as a mirror, she advances the knife to see what lies beyond the edge of the house.

The reflection of a bright window.

A chaos of movement behind her.

Too slow to react, Tiffany's hand is smacked heavily from above. She drops the knife. Her wrist is grabbed and yanked forwards, spinning her round and pulling her into the light.

A huge scravir.

Pepene picks her up by the lapels and tosses her across the alley. Before she can get to her feet he is all over her, kicking her thighs and ribs. She rolls away and kicks back, hitting the scravir hard in the kneecap. He staggers back. Tiffany scrambles to her feet and races away down the alley with the scravir in pursuit.

Only to find her exit blocked by a second scravir.

Pepene catches up, lifts her and throws her a second time. This time as she falls, she feels something crack underneath her.

The syringe gun!

She rolls to the side and pulls the gun from her jacket pocket. It is leaking fluid onto her hand. One vial has broken but the other is intact. In one movement she spins the chamber to line up the remaining vial and swings round to face Pepene as she reaches to grab her. With all her strength she lunges forwards, plunging the syringe into his chest and pulling the trigger with both hands.

He is stunned. And furious.

He growls then roars as the liquid eviscerates him,

devouring him alive from within, dissolving his muscles. No longer able to control his movement, he slams into the wall, a thrashing writhing cacophony of limbs.

Sensing movement, Tiffany turns to find the second scravir rushing down the alley towards her, a gap in his mouth where Daniel kicked out his teeth in the yard earlier. The kitchen knife is too far away and she is still on her knees.

She raises the syringe gun and points it at her attacker.

'Do you want some of this?' she shouts. 'Do you want what he got?' She nods in the direction of the flailing Pepene. 'Come on then!'

She prays the scravir is too stupid to see that she is out of ammunition.

CHAPTER 72

'You were explaining your network of volunteers in the slums. Is that how you have become known and trusted?' Lupei asks, placing his empty wine glass on the table.

I want to resist, to refuse him, but I am drowning. The headache that has gripped me for days is in full spate. Only when I please Lupei does the pressure seem to drop a little. What is he doing to me?

This is the man who locked forty people in cells beneath the warehouse. Men and women, young and old. The man who creates scravir. The man who shackled Tiffany to a wall. What does he really care about volunteers and trust?

And still he shamcharms me. My magnificent work. Together we will achieve great things. We will do blah and blah.

But it isn't about us; it is about others. I know how easy it is to stray from the narrow. In my nightmares I see the smirking pot-bellied man leading me into the slums to find a young girl for some jiggy-jiggy, the man I killed in a shadow-pocked alley to protect the vulnerable and to source a kidney for a poor woman struggling to support her children.

Daniel Murray, judge and jury.

'Are you tired, Daniel? Shall we have another short break?' His voice a sweet posy of tenderness and forget-me-nots.

I shake my head defiantly, find my voice.

'Why should I trust you? I've seen your diary. It's all about money and power to you. Taking poor people's organs and selling them to the rich. I am not like you, and you will never be like me.'

Thor Lupei looks as if he is going to contradict me then he

decides against it and lets me ramble on.

'People are trifles to you, as fleeting as flowers in a vase. That's what you said. I get it; everyone you have ever known is dead. decades or centuries ago. Every friendship turned to dust. Every love decayed. And when you become bored with me, you'll dispose of me like all the others. I'm only alive, for now, because you are lonely.'

Lupei chuckles. 'Daniel. Why do you imagine that a life of a thousand years must be lonely? Because others, desperate to rationalise their brief lives, say so? What do they know? No one wants to die but, since everyone does, people persuade each other that they don't want to live forever. Without evidence, they assert eternity must be lonely, and you tell me that *I* must be lonely. It's nonsense. Do you mourn the absence of all the nursery school classmates you no longer see? Or the teacher who bored you to death with algebra? Even short lives are packed with loves lost, friendships furloughed, acquaintances extinguished. Life moves on and there are always new things to experience and enjoy. Abandon the herd and fulfil your destiny, Daniel. You have real talent and the energy of youth. Together we will learn from each other and shape the world.' He pauses for a second. 'By the way, aren't you curious about your mother?'

'What?'

He smiles. 'Your mother. Do you know where in Romania she came from?'

'What's that got to do with anything?'

'They let you down, didn't they? How did she survive even six years with that woeful oaf?'

I hear dad's voice on Gert's recording, talking about mum, in tears about the accident, about her dying in hospital, about how he tried to protect me and how it all went wrong. I hear mum's voice singing that lullaby. Out of nowhere I think to myself, was Lupei driving the car that hit her?

He's messing with me, trying to break me. What can he know of how my life has been?

'Leave my parents out of it!' I shout. 'You know sod all about either of them.'

A starburst of pain explodes in my head as a reward.

Lupei sighs. 'Why are the young so sanctimonious, self-assured and stupid? Your mother was pregnant when she arrived in England, did you know that? It happens a lot in those small mountain villages.'

I fight the waves of agony.

'So what? Maybe she had an abortion, maybe the baby was adopted. Why should I give a monkey's? Didn't you have a family? Oh, right, you were adopted a million years ago and you're jealous. Is *that* what this is all about? I can't keep up, mate. One minute we're collaborators on an adventure, the enlightened ones, best of friends, the next you're slagging off my parents and rubbishing me. Bloody psychopath!'

'For the love of God, Daniel, STOP! Have you heard of the cuckoo? You were left to grow up in someone else's nest. That weak, indolent homunculus who can barely tie his own bootlaces is not your father.' He waits until he has my full undivided attention then whispers. '*I* am.'

At that precise moment, as the bombshell smacks the ground, as my sense of self implodes, we hear the scream.

A woman's voice.

I know instinctively, immediately, that it is Tiffany.

Lupei rushes from the room shouting for Felini.

I take advantage of being forgotten. There is little point in following Lupei. Pepene must be out in the corridor waiting to tear me limb from limb.

I leap up off the sofa, grab a chair and hurl it at a window. Clambering over the broken glass, I drop down into the garden. It's pelting down. In seconds I am soaked to the skin.

Brambles rip my clothes as I push my way through the

overgrown garden to the path, my head in a numbcloud.

What did he just say?

Who am I?

I reach the alley, my feet skating about in the mud, rain blurring my vision.

Where is she?

There. A body in the shadows by the house. I race forward to reach her before Lupei.

It's not Tiffany, it's Pepene, leaning against the wall, eyes vacant, mouth hanging open, his deflated body little more than bones in his rough brown peasant clothes.

Has Tiffany collected the syringe gun? Did she kill him?

Where is she?

It is too dark to make sense of the chaos of footprints on the ground. I stagger forwards towards the farmyard.

Movement in the darkness by the main gate. Is that Tiffany disappearing into the large barn? It was too fast for scravir.

I think it was her. I pray it was her.

Three metres to my left, the farmhouse door is opening.

Thor Lupei steps into the yard.

Distract him, draw him away, give her a chance to escape.

An idea bounds into view. It is insane but I have no alternative. Desperate times, desperate measures. As Lupei turns to look at me, I stare away towards the field pressing an imaginary phone to my ear.

'Pepene's dead. Yes, you killed him. Stay where you are, Tiffany, I'm coming. We're getting out of here!' I shout into my hand then, without checking to see whether Lupei has seen or heard me, I make a show of shoving my imaginary phone into my pocket and race off towards the field gate.

Scrambling over the gate I allow myself a glance over my shoulder. Lupei is still standing by the farmhouse door.

Follow me you bastard! We're getting away!

I wave at a corner of the field beyond the farm buildings,

out of his eyeline, as if she is waiting for me there, then drop to the ground and run.

In my peripheral vision I see him finally start to move.

The thick vegetation snags my legs, slowing me down. I faceplant in the wet grass, pick myself up. Lupei has pushed the field gate open and is giving chase. I head for that first spot, the place where I pitched my tent in the corner by the outbuildings and, as I run, the idea blooms, becomes a plan!

He is twenty metres behind me and will soon see that Tiffany is not waiting for me.

Unless ...

The field ends in a corner, the outbuildings on one side and the tall hedge on the other.

The ghost of a gap is still visible in the thick hawthorn hedge. He is ten metres behind me now, running quickly for a man in his second millennium. I drop to my hands and knees and scramble forwards.

'I'm coming through,' I shout to my imaginary girlfriend.

The branches claw at me, thorns scraping my head, tearing a gash in my forehead, snagging my jacket. Lupei catches up. He grabs at one of my ankles. I pull my foot away and kick out and lurch forwards and come out the other side.

It is terrifying, vertiginous. A sensory overload of wind and rain and crashing sea. My hand slips from under me and I almost tumble forwards. I twist my body and shift my weight sufficiently to fall to the side.

Behind me Lupei is breathing heavily and struggling with the vegetation. Desperately, I wriggle away across the narrow ledge pulling my legs out of reach. Grabbing hold of the larger branches, ignoring the pain as thorns bite deep into my hands, I pull myself up onto my knees, twist my body round and climb to my feet to be ready for him. My legs are shaking with fear. I cling for dear life to the branches, blood pouring from my hands, as Lupei emerges on his hands and knees from the maw of the hedge and out onto the narrow ledge.

He doesn't even have time to register his surroundings. I kick his arm away from under him and he tumbles forwards out into the void and down, down onto the jagged rocks fifty metres below. I hear the sickening crunch. Glancing over the lip of the cliff I see his body. Spreadeagled. A broken four-pointed star. Waves lick and roar the rocks.

I bury my face in the hedge, ignoring the pain, gasping for breath.

The pressure in my head has vanished.

It's over.

I turn to face the sea. The horizon to the north is a shadow shift of greys and blacks. The wind whistling my face has swept Svalbard, jostled icebergs, whittled waves, gouged furrows across the tundra.

It's *not* over.

I am *his son*.

I am not the result of a short training programme beneath the castle. The ancient powers have been inside me from the start. They are in my DNA. Thor Lupei simply taught me how to access it. There was no random set of events; he made me.

The evil that infested him is here within me. In every cell of my body. If he is condemned, then so am I.

Who was I fooling; believing I could tame the beast? No wonder he laughed at my impudence. The only way to rid the world of Lupei is for me to join him on the rocks.

Free at last from the self-deception, the lies and half-truths, I feel I can fly. I spread my arms.

I can choose.

I can end this.

I slowly let go of the branches.

'Daniel.'

I prepare to launch myself over the edge.

'DANIEL!'

EPILOGUE - Whitby

'They were all self-isolating, Ma'am. The only officer on duty was a PCSO. After producing his report, he transferred all the data and backed up the disc. Only he didn't back up anything. He hit the wrong button and wiped the entire hard drive. In an ideal world we would ...'

'Everything?'

'Church Street, Bridge Street, New Quay Road. The lot. We've his written report and that's it. No video evidence from the 23rd to the 30th.'

'Jesus wept.'

YORKSHIRE COAST RADIO - REPORTS ARCHIVE

Interview Transcript: 2 APRIL 2020
DAVID LAMPHORNE Interviewer
SERGEANT JANE GRAYFORD North Yorkshire Police

LAMPHORNE
It's not been a good week, has it, Sergeant? A young family murdered up on Cliff Street, two bodies on the Donkey Path, a doctor killed in Blackburn's Yard, and now a body floating in the harbour. What on earth is going on? Why aren't the police keeping us safe?

GRAYFORD
First of all, let me reassure your listeners that ...

LAMPHORNE

I'm not sure they want reassurance, they want answers. There are a lot of frightened ...

GRAYFORD

If you'll let me answer ...

LAMPHORNE

Sorry, go ahead.

GRAYFORD

So, first the body recovered from the harbour earlier today. An adult male, possibly in his fifties or sixties. Long white hair, possibly albino. We believe the gentleman may have fallen from the east cliff three or four days ago, his body brought into the harbour with the tides. Maybe he was going for a walk and strayed too close to the edge. We would very much welcome information from the public. Has someone seen something ...

LAMPHORNE

We're all stuck indoors, Sergeant. No one is going anywhere. It is unlikely that ...

GRAYFORD

I am simply saying if someone has seen anything untoward, please report it. And the same goes for the other deaths.

LAMPHORNE

Do you not have CCTV footage? Surely, with everyone at home, it would be easy to ...

GRAYFORD

I am not sure that the public wants investigations of this gravity to be run by radio presenters, Mr Lamphorne.

LAMPHORNE

If someone does have information, do they run the risk of being arrested themselves for being ...

GRAYFORD

Oh, for goodness sake, stop it. Let me talk directly to the public. Are you a Whitby resident? Have you seen something that caused you concern between the 27th and the 29th of March? Have you witnessed a crime? If so, please contact us by calling Whitby Police station or by reporting the crime online on the North Yorkshire Police website. Thank you. Goodbye, Mr Lamphorne.

LAMPHORNE

Thank you. That was Sergeant Jane Grayford of North Yorkshire Police. They're struggling, aren't they? And now our special reporter, Max Chinless, continues his nostalgic dive into the amazing history of Whitby's fish and chip shops. This week it's the famous, or should that be the infamous, Nuclear Fishun Chips shop that opened its doors on Pier Road in 1956. Over to you Max.

The tide is out; the day's story typed in footfont bold across the sand.

Tiffany's and Daniel's footprints cross the length of West Cliff Beach from the pier, past the beach huts and on, three metres apart, as the last rays of the setting sun kiss their faces.

From up by Whitby Pavilion, the words 'HELLO WORLD!' can be seen down below, etched in huge letters beside a smiley face, where someone has dragged a heel close to the whispering waves.

Dusk now. Not a soul in sight.

In a few minutes the beach will bear witness to a Covid crime.

Two sets of footprints approach each other and make a tangled mess before running side by side to the edge of the waves where they weave in and out playfully.

By the time a woman hurries down the ramp from Upgang Ravine, dragging a reluctant terrier behind her, the conniving sea will have washed away the evidence of two people lying hand in hand, side by side just beyond the shifting water's edge.

Tiffany and Daniel pause at the Whalebone Arch to look over to Tate Hills Sands. The wreck of the boat has been removed. Lights are coming on in the houses on Henrietta Street.

'Is he going to report us?'

'Don't think so. He mumbled some crap about young people murdering the elderly. I told him I were watering my mum's plants for her and invited him to sod off. He's just an old tosser with time on his hands. As long as my mum doesn't get to ...'

'Maybe you were right. Maybe we should have stopped at your parents' and changed the locks instead of breaking into that cottage.'

'Spilled milk, Daniel. Forget it. It's done.'

The gulls are back, grumbling loudly about the lack of tourists and easy food as they settle down by the chimney stacks.

'RJ organised the bank transfer so I'm good for a few months.'

'We're sorted then.'

'As long as the police don't pin Tina's murder on you, and you don't get Covid.'

'It's not only in hospitals. You do know that?' Tiffany says. 'Oh, did I tell you that Antoine messaged me? It were this woman Floriane, the woman who took Gert to meet you in Briançon, only it weren't you, it were someone called Kevin who had stolen your Oyster Card ... anyroad, she were the one who were passing everything on to Thor Lupei. They think she were hoping for, or had been promised, a liver transplant for her niece who had contracted Hepatitis C as the result of a back street tattoo she had done on holiday. And that cost Gert his life. I'm so angry.'

'People do mad things when they can't see a way out. We'd best go, it's almost dark.'

'Promise me that ...'

'I've told you. It's over.'

Emotions tumble over each other on Tiffany's face, like the shimmering waves of light on a cuttlefish: love, fear, sadness, longing, resignation, hope.

'If I hadn't stopped you, would you have jumped?' she says.

He takes a deep breath but cannot answer.

'Oh, Daniel.' She grabs his hand and squeezes hard.

Donning their face masks, they head down the steps towards the bandstand.

Coming up in the other direction is an obese man who is visibly distressed and clinging to the railing. His wife is following five steps behind. As they approach, pressing against the cliff to maximise social distancing, the man sinks to his knees in front of them.

Daniel immediately takes two steps forward, ready to intervene.

Then stops.

And steps back.

'My girlfriend is a nurse,' he tells the woman. 'Is it alright for her to help your husband?'

The woman nods. Daniel makes space for Tiffany to get past him. Tiffany kneels beside the man, checks for tags, diabetes, epilepsy, checks for bleeding.

'Does he have pre-existing conditions?' she asks the wife.
'Aside from diabetes? Daniel, can you ring 999?'

'Asthma,' says the woman.

'He's breathing. Are you alright?' Tiffany asks the man.
'Can you hear me?'

He nods weakly.

'Have you broken anything?'

An almost imperceptible shake of the head.

'They're on their way,' Daniel says.

'Do you think we can sit you up?' Tiffany asks the man,
having decided that the recovery position will not be possible
on the steps.

No response; the man is focusing on his breathing.

Tiffany co-ordinates Daniel and the wife to help her
manoeuvre the man across the step. By the time he is sitting
with his back against the cliff, the sound of a siren is audible.

Daniel walks down the steps and watches as Tiffany and the
paramedics get the man down the steps and into the ambulance.

The ambulance pulls away and Tiffany crosses the road
towards Daniel. The face mask cannot hide her smile as she
steps up onto the pavement.

'Thank you!'

'Thank you?'

'For showing you can change.'

'I love you, Tiffany. I don't want to lose you. Ever.'

'Me too.'

She reaches out and hugs him then suddenly looks anxious
and steps back. 'Bloody social distancing.'

They walk to the bandstand. Two metres apart. On the hill
opposite the streetlights are lighting the 199 steps. The abbey
ruins hide behind St Mary's church.

'What did you and Lupei talk about?' she asks him. 'At
Farview.'

'He wanted me to feel his pain.'

'He didn't come all this way just to make you feel pain. He could have done that in Delhi.'

Daniel does not know what to say. 'He bad-mouthed my parents, told me I was his protégé, his best apprentice, pretended he wanted to learn from me, promised we would rule the world together and achieve greatness if I learned obedience and fealty. You know; evil megalomaniac bullshit.'

'Ivanna thought he had injected you with something. All that DNA and ...'

'I don't want to talk about it. We're starting over. OK?'

'Yeah, OK. Let's get you home. I love you too.' The words slip out before she can stop herself.

They are crossing the swing bridge when Daniel's phone vibrates.

> 13.43 Message from RioJman
> DAN MY MAN! How's it hanging? You won't believe this. Gopal and I have only cracked a full page of the manuscript. All about skraphir or skravir. Is that what you were hoping for? It has a recipe vibe.
>
> All pretty freakshop and dark, if I'm honest. Medieval magic bullshit. At this rate prob. have all five pages deciphered in a couple of weeks. I'll let you know.
>
> Missing you, man. Stay cool and Hi to Tiffany.

'Who's that?'
'Nothing important. Just a message from RJ. He says hi.'

ACKNOWLEDGEMENTS

*Thanks to my partner Mary, as ever, for reading the draft
and offering her comments and suggestions; to Peter for
proofreading, insightful comments, and his encyclopedic
knowledge of Whitby; and to Chris, Fiona, Angela, and
Jenna and all the other wonderful independent bookshops for
their support; to Dominique for her artwork; to Injini Press;
and to you and all our readers for joining us on this journey!*

*Thanks also to Whitby's old town for its lacklit corners, its
narrow ginnels what whisper the echoes of old footsteps,
and those streetlights on the 199 Steps that look out over the
harbour as if awaiting the return of family members lost in a
raging sea.*

From such jewels are stories born.

If you have loved this book you can learn more about it
and about C.M.Vassie's other Whitby books, and about
Whitby itself on our website.

www.injinipress.co.uk

... and we would relish your review ...

www.injinipress.co.uk/product/scravir-lacklight

SCRAVIR

While Whitby Sleeps

Discover where it all started with this best-selling contemporary gothic horror story.

The famous Whitby Goth Weekend is in full swing. But while a mysterious guest star's music rocks the Pavilion, emaciated corpses are appearing in the streets. Dark forces are mingling with the thrill seekers.

Outsider Daniel Murray has never believed in the supernatural. Local girl Tiffany Harrek is not so sure. If they are to survive the next 48 hours they must wise up. Fast.

"Intelligent, intense and genuinely original."
"A dark brain-itching blend of gothic and contemporary"

A FEW REVIEWS OF SCRAVIR
"Brilliant. I was hooked & stay in bed all day reading it."
C. Somkowicz

"Wow! The only reason I put this book down was to go to work. Decided to take the bus home so I could read uninerrupted for 50 minutes on the journey. Loved it ❤"
S. Shelton

"An eerie brew of supernatural energy, antiquity and intrigue, Scravir is a real page-turner."
S. Buckton

"Love this book ... absolutely fantastic, cannot wait for the next installment."
L. Crowcroft

"Well the plan was to read this on holiday this week but silly me started it and finished it before we'd set off. Great read, loved that it was set in Whitby. Can honestly say it's my favourite book."
R. Martin

"Wow, read this in 3 sittings. Great use of character viewpoints between chapters and flows well. Story turned out not how I thought but still scary in the end. It actually answered questions and tied everything off in the end which I truly enjoyed about the book. Hate when the ending is flat but this was great. Perfectly executed."
L. Hall

"Being a fan of gothic horror, urban fantasy and of the beautiful, enchanting town of Whitby, this book appealed to me from the outset ... From the perfect descriptions of the town to the complex characters it's a book I was hooked on from start to finish ..."
J. Dunning

"This fast-paced supernatural thriller is a cracking read. Full of surprising twists and turns. Evidence of a monstrous crime accumulates as we follow first-hand the sequence of events, the blur between fiction and a documented moment in the hidden history of Whitby adding to the excitement."
ESK VALLEY NEWS

"The central characters are very engaging and the novel is told from different viewpoints which helps with the exciting plot twists and also creates the suspense and tension that keeps the reader on the edge of their seat."
WHITBY ADVERTISER

Ordered, received and read! Loved it!
S. Birkby

The
WHITBY
TRAP

The time travelling adventure from C.M.Vassie, best-selling author of the Scravir books.

"Exciting, thought-provoking, weird and intense in all the best ways."

It is 2022. Derek is drowning in the dreary routine of his job, his love life, his friends, everything ... a weekend break in a Whitby cottage is just another excuse to get drunk but waking up on a whaling ship in a snowstorm, with a hangover the size of Yorkshire, is a bit of a jolt.

While Derek is lost on the Jurassic Coast, his friends – Amy and Sarah - are desperately seeking him in the early 19th century. Even the simplest things are a struggle in a town where people work twenty hours a day to survive.

With betrayals, double-dealing, wild experiments, piracy, love and loss ... the strange duckfoot pistol in the hands of the eccentric snuff-snorting sleuth who breaks into their lodgings is the least of the women's problems.

What exactly is happening beneath the old town hall. Is there any way back? Why would you go back?

"Time-hopping pirates in the Jurassic. Insane. I love it!"

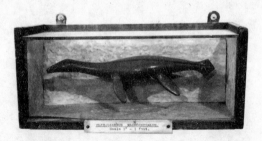

Reviews of The Whitby Trap

Great read really enjoyed this book, history and imagination combined. Well worth a look
C Mcnamara

Highly imaginative and well written. An interesting take on the concept of time travel. The Whitby setting is an added bonus!
S Buckton

Yet another gripping read from C.M.Vassie. a great page Turner from being to end
E Lancaster

Readers who enjoyed Vassie's previous novel Scravir will be in for a treat with The Whitby Trap. This all-action adventure thriller set in the present-day slips through cracks in the timeline, taking us back to two hundred years ago, and then millions of years to the Jurassic Coast. An epic time-travelling page-turner from Vassie which captures the sounds and sights of Whitby now and in the past.
Esk Valley News

Fabulous book. Well written – you are hooked after just reading the first few pages
P Cooper

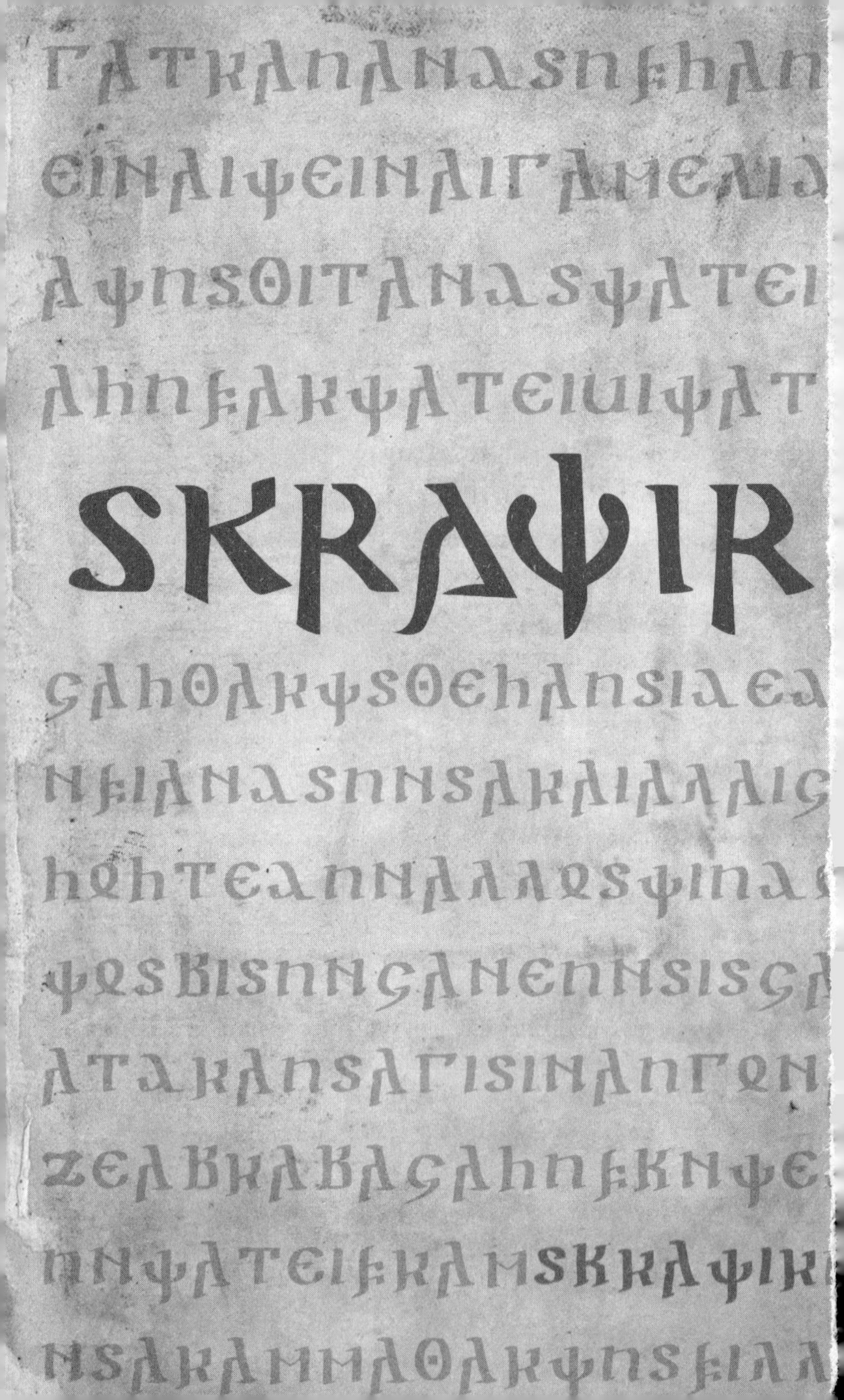
𐍃𐌺𐍂𐌰𐌸𐌹𐍂